Not Meant for Human Ears...

The sound shattered the still morning air, ripping through him like a physical blow. The Grus, now awake and aware of the invading Aquila, threw back their beautiful dark heads on their long white necks and called loud and long. Again and again the warning cry rang out.

The frequency and volume of the call struck the humans' unshielded ears, doubling them over with pain. The delicate headpieces went flying from Meg's hands as she fell forward. Both humans' eardrums burst and the pain of those alien voices drove Scott to his knees in agony.

◆　　◆　　◆

StarBridge
Book Two: Silent Dances
Don't miss Book One of this exciting new series—*StarBridge*

"A space adventure series patterned strongly after much of [Andre] Norton's early work . . . Crispin's aliens are a diverse and fascinating lot . . . She'll be the leading candidate for the title of 'the Norton of the 1990s!'"
　　　　　　　　　　　　　　　　　　—*Dragon*

The STARBRIDGE Series

STARBRIDGE by A.C. Crispin
STARBRIDGE 2: SILENT DANCES by A.C. Crispin
and Kathleen O'Malley

STARBRIDGE 3: SHADOW WORLD
by A.C. Crispin and Jannean Elliott
(coming in January)

Also by A.C. Crispin

V
YESTERDAY'S SON
TIME FOR YESTERDAY
GRYPHON'S EYRIE *(with Andre Norton)*

StarBridge
★★★★★★★★★★★★★★★★★ *Book Two*
SILENT DANCES

A. C. CRISPIN and
KATHLEEN O'MALLEY

ACE BOOKS, NEW YORK

This book is an Ace original edition,
and has never been previously published.

SILENT DANCES

An Ace Book / published by arrangement with
the authors

PRINTING HISTORY
Ace edition / July 1990

ISBN: 0-441-78330-9

Ace Books are published by The Berkley Publishing Group,
200 Madison Avenue, New York, New York 10016.
The name "ACE" and the "A" logo
are trademarks belonging to Charter Communications, Inc.

PRINTED IN THE UNITED STATES OF AMERICA

10 9 8 7 6 5 4 3 2 1

Acknowledgments

Silent Dances had many midwives attending its parturition and delivery, all of whom deserve thanks. This is only a partial list:

My collaborator, A.C. Crispin—our long-standing friendship was only enhanced by our partnership in writing this book, Ann. Thanks for believing in me and keeping me on course.

My friend, cowriter, editor, proofreader, partner, and computer consultant Anne Moroz—who became, during the final stages of this book, chief cook, bottle-washer, landscaper, and animal caretaker. Now, you can finish your *own* book!

For their continuing support and encouragement through the years and especially with this project, I'd like to thank my mother, Evelyn Benecke, my father, Al Benecke, my brother, Alfred Benecke, and Teresa Bigbee and her family, who've been more than a family to me.

My friend Holley Stepp made significant contributions to *Silent Dances*, as did the many Deaf students and sign language teachers and interpreters at Gallaudet University, and elsewhere. You introduced me to the fascinating world of Deaf culture and helped shape the characters and events of this book. I hope you will be as happy with it as I am.

I want to thank my readers and critics Debby Marshall, Martha Midgett, and J. M. Dillard. Your insights and encouragement were invaluable. A big hug and lots of thanks to *golubchik* Jeanne Dillard, for extra help with foreign names and phrases and long-distance pep talks.

For help with the scientific and technical aspects of this book I have to thank Drs. Josh Dein, Glenn Olsen, George Gee, and Mr. Roddy Gabel of the Patuxent Wildlife Research Center for their continuing interest, advice, and support. Special thanks go to Dr. David Ellis of the PWRC, for his invaluable information on raptor behavior and prehistoric avians; to Dr. Hodos of the University of Maryland for his help in avian opthalmology; and Dr. Yoji Kondo of NASA for his ability to set the universe right. Special thanks must also go to Dr. James W. Carpenter whose interest in this project never wavered and whose constant nudging pushed this project along in its earliest days. (It's finished, Dr. C., it's really finished!)

To the many characters at the Patuxent Wildlife Research Center—animal caretakers, wildlife technicians, veterinary technicians, and biologists—with whom I've had the pleasure to work with over these past years and who helped fill these pages with insight, humor, and personality—you know who you are. Thanks, guys, and I'll be in on time on Monday!

To Harlan Ellison, for all his kindness through the years. I did what you said, Harlan. I wrote what I know.

And, most important, though they will never read this, or even know of it, I must thank the whooping cranes of the Patuxent Wildlife Research Center—especially the individuals that have meant the most to me: Canus, Lazarus, Faith, Jack, and Blue 52. Without their beauty, their strong personalities, and the haunting power of their call, this world would be an empty place.

Anyone interested in learning more about cranes, one of the most endangered families of birds in the world, can write to the U. S. Fish and Wildlife Service, Washington, D. C., or to the International Crane Foundation, E-11376 Shady Lane Road, Baraboo, Wisconsin, 53913.

—Kathleen O'Malley,
December 1989

This book is lovingly dedicated to
the person who inspired me to write
by entertaining me for hours with her own tales—
my mother, Evelyn Benecke.
You bought me my first typewriter, Mom,
and my first word processor.
I only hope that someday
I'll be as good a storyteller as you.

—K. O'Malley

SILENT DANCES

Prologue

Scott Hedford opened his eyes and checked the time. Fifteen minutes to daybreak. He called to his partner and grabbed for his clothes. He couldn't miss sunrise!

A yellow sun stood at the heart of this crowded solar system that included a monstrous gas giant planet four times the size of Jupiter, plus a red dwarf star in its outermost reaches. From the surface of the living world the humans called Trinity, the giant planet and the red dwarf shone so brilliantly they were visible even in full daylight. The astronomical configurations of what appeared to be three suns had, for centuries, shaped the beliefs of the planet's people and, Scott knew, today was of special importance. The three "suns" would rise in a triangle. Scott couldn't miss sunrise today.

His partner, Margaritka Tretiak, scrambled around just as eagerly. The gray-haired xenobiologist was almost seventy, but could outrun him, outclimb him, and, in the rush to see sunrise, outdress him. She was already out of their shelter while he was still hopping around on one foot pulling on his other boot.

Silently they left their spacious shelter and walked the

hundred meters to the end of the overhanging bluff. There was little evidence of last night's fierce electrical storm. Camped on this small hill, they had an excellent view of the freshwater wetlands extending to the horizon.

At the cliff edge, the biologists viewed the expansive marsh. The vegetation was a collage of brilliant Earth-autumn hues, colors Trinity kept year-round. The wildlife and native people were all still sleeping. Usually, none of them woke until all the suns were well up.

The red dwarf peeped over the western horizon, since Trinity rotated opposite to the direction that Earth did. The huge, white, cranelike people the humans called the Grus could be seen sleeping in scattered groups either in the water or on the small islands they built out of rushes and grass, their black-beaked heads tucked beneath their winglike arms. The Grus were beautiful to watch, especially when they danced.

The second sun, the yellow star the Grus called the "Father Sun," rose to the right of the apex star. The sky faded from dark blue-black to a startling lavender. Soon it would be an intense blue. Scott stared, not with the cool detachment of a biologist, but with the unabashed wonder of a tourist.

The man started as a rousette whistled in shrill warning. *What's* **he** *scared of at this hour?* Scott wondered, glancing uneasily around. The red, fox-sized flying mammal should be sleeping in its burrow.

The call came again, piercing, terrified. The third "sun," the gas giant planet that appeared as a small, brilliant star, was now visible, but Scott barely noticed.

Something's wrong, Scott thought, just as a monstrous winged shadow sailed over the humans—a shadow that was bound to wake the sensitive Grus at any moment. And when they woke . . .

"My God!" Meg gasped.

It's an Aquila! Scott realized. *What's it doing here, why is it flying* **now**?

The biologist fumbled at his belt where his sound nullifier should have been, but it wasn't there. *Meg doesn't have hers, either,* he remembered with a stab of dismay. *I was working on them last night—I left them on the workbench!*

With a muttered curse he grabbed Meg's arm. "Never mind the Aquila! The nullifiers are in the shelter on the workbench. We've got to have them! *Run!*"

They began sprinting toward the shelter, Meg quickly out-distancing the younger man. The Aquila circled closer to the Grus' village. Then Scott saw another, and another, high in the atmosphere, winging in from their dark forests to the west. With their bronze-colored bodies and contrasting gold heads and tails, the Aquila bore an uncanny resemblance to the eagles that had once been the symbol of an OldAm nation.

The big predators' sudden, unusual behavior made Scott wonder again whether they might be intelligent. The Grus claimed that the Aquila were nothing more than savage predators, their enemies. But why would the Aquila use the extra energy for flap-flying when they could wait until later in the day and glide on the thermals as they usually did? Were they just flying by on their way to distant hunting grounds, or were they deliberately trying to surprise the Grus before they woke? And why were these normally solitary hunters suddenly massing in such numbers?

Hoping he was wrong, that the Aquila wouldn't breach the invisible boundary that would cause the Grus sentries to sound an alarm, Scott wished now that he'd had more time to study the films from his hidden cameras.

Ten strides ahead of him, Meg dived into the shelter.

He'd just reached the door when she burst back out, the nullifiers in her hands. "Put it on! Cover your ears!" he yelled—then the preliminary humming shook his entire body. *Oh, God, no!* He clapped his palms over his ears.

The sound shattered the still morning air, ripping through him like a physical blow. Again and again the cry rang out as the sentries sent their warning to the flock.

The frequency and volume of that call struck the humans' unshielded ears, doubling them over with pain. The tiny, delicate headpieces went flying from Meg's hands as she fell forward. Both humans' eardrums burst and the pain of those alien voices drove Scott to his knees in agony.

Lucky Meg, he thought, seeing that his friend lay unconscious. Retching, hands shaking, he scrabbled frantically through the dense rust-colored ground cover that had swallowed the dropped nullifiers. He grabbed one headpiece, but it was cracked—*useless*, he thought despairingly. *Where's the other? Oh, God, the pain* . . . He was crawling now, facing the end of the bluff and the still beautiful sunrise, now forgotten. Despite his suffering, he forced himself to search.

As his fingers fumbled over the precious instrument, the gigantic, terrifying shape of an Aquila came winging up over the bluff. The enormous bird loomed before him, its ruby-red eyes staring straight at Scott, its great wings straining for altitude—its talons gripping a struggling young Grus.

The white avian met the biologist's eyes. Recognition stabbed through Scott, almost eclipsing his physical pain. *NO!* his mind screamed. *Not my friend—not Water Dancer!* The golden eyes of the avian were dimming, and in desperation, he threw back his head, voicing a dying call to his people.

The sound tore through Scott's body, making him jerk like a puppet whose strings had been yanked. He fell across the ground, arms askew, the nullifier pinned beneath him. Rivulets of blood flowed from his ears.

"What is man without the beasts?
If all the beasts were gone, men would die
from a great loneliness of the spirit.
For whatever happens to the beasts
soon happens to man."

Chief Seattle
1854

CHAPTER I

◆

The Choice

Rob Gable looked up from the clutter on his desk, startled yet relieved. A tall, dark woman was storming into his office, fuming, her anger and frustration barely held in check.

Boy, she's pissed! Rob thought as she came around the desk toward him, barking her shin in the process. That stopped her, and blinking from the pain, she rubbed her abused leg.

"Tesa, where've you been?" he began tentatively in her language. "I looked for you everywhere." The slightly built, dark-haired psychologist moved around his desk to diminish the height advantage she had over him. "I wanted to find you before the ceremony, but I was in meetings up to the last minute. When I finally got to the Arena, there was too much of a mob."

"What happened, Dr. Rob? Why wasn't I tapped?" Her hands moved almost too quickly for him to follow the subtleties of her complex language, American Sign Language. ASL had its own grammar structure, but Rob couldn't help translating it into English, the language he'd grown up with. "The other students were tapped on schedule. Why didn't you tell me mine was canceled?"

Rob looked at her startling, pale hazel eyes—large, almond-shaped eyes that seemed almost golden. Staring at them, you could almost miss her high cheekbones, strong jaw, and brilliant white teeth set against smooth brown skin. The young Native American woman towered over Rob at 1.85 meters. (*Six foot one*, Tesa insisted, since Old NorthAm had never fully accepted metric.) At nineteen, Tesa's broad face and hawkish nose couldn't be considered beautiful, but once you saw those eyes you'd never think about that. Having watched her grow from a gangly fourteen-year-old, Rob was sorry he wouldn't be around to see her figure out what she could do with those eyes.

Holding up his hands placatingly, the doctor motioned for her to take a seat. She drew herself up, declining the offer.

Clothed in the dress version of StarBridge Academy's uniform, Tesa had offset its classic pants and jacket with a quill-worked leather pouch on her waist and three white-tipped eagle feathers tied into her long, wavy black hair. Richly hued turquoise brought out the warm highlights of her skin. The effect of the new and old lent her an aura of wildness.

Should I have paged her? Rob wondered. *Made an announcement that everyone but she could hear?* He still felt self-conscious about her deafness. "I sent a message to your voder," he told her, his signs much slower than hers. "Didn't you see it?"

She seemed to deflate as she dug around in her pouch for the small translator most human students kept on their wrists. When she finally retrieved it, its tiny red telltale was shining.

Tesa looked ruefully at its message. "Well, I should've been wearing it." She looked at Rob, disgusted, and settled into a chair. "But that still doesn't explain why I wasn't tapped."

Explain, he thought, wanting to groan. *Where do I start?*

Tesa was one of StarBridge's older human students. Bicultural and multilingual, she'd grown up on the plains of Old NorthAm in the multitribal "living museum" that sprawled across millions of acres of parkland and wildlife preserve. Before she'd been recruited for StarBridge, Tesa had vacillated between becoming a Native American historian or a linguist, an interest she'd discovered when she went east to study at Gallaudet.

This well-known educational center for the deaf and hearing-impaired had expanded over the centuries until it had become a small town, a cultural cornerstone for people who did not consider themselves deaf, but Deaf. It was at Gallaudet that Tesa had discovered her natural aptitude for languages, a talent that had brought her to the Academy at StarBridge.

"What about my pair project with the Ashu Mizari?" Tesa signed, looking more dejected now than angry. "Don't tell me all my work's been for nothing."

The tapping and the pair project were the culmination of a StarBridge student's training. Each student would learn his or her alien partner's language and culture, and in turn teach the other theirs, while completing a special project that required each partner's cooperative abilities. Tesa had been trained to be teamed with one of the reptilian, multitentacled Mizari, eldest and founding members of the Cooperative League of Systems.

Rob plopped wearily into his chair. "The Ashu are very disappointed, Tesa, believe me."

The Ashu, a sea-dwelling race of Mizari, who lived off an island continent on Shassiszss, their homeworld, had only vestigial auditory organs, and communicated with an elaborate sign language. Tesa was to have been paired with one of them and travel to Shassiszss. Now all those careful plans were shot.

Rob sighed. "I've got lots to tell you, so be patient."

Bast, Rob's small black cat, chose that minute to leap into Tesa's lap, and the young woman gave her a friendly embrace.

"Okay." Now that the moment had come, Rob could barely suppress his excitement. "A doctor on Earth has perfected an electronic nerve relay. She says she can give you hearing."

"*That's* why you canceled my tapping and my pair project on Shassiszss?" Tesa was plainly surprised—and irritated.

She wasn't the only one. Rob's eyes widened as he signed, "You don't think that's important?"

"No!" She shook her head angrily. "I've spent two months preparing for this project. *That's* what *I* was looking forward to. Not a one-way ticket back to Earth to become hearing. How's that supposed to help me with the Ashu?"

Tesa had been born with only partially formed ears, due to "improper fetal development," a favorite catch-phrase of baffled physicians. She had no eardrums, and her semicircular canals were imperfect, giving her occasional balance problems. Both ear canals were sealed, and her ears were unusually small.

"I've got a film that will explain the technical aspects," Rob signed. "The doctor came to our attention because someone on a planet called Trinity had an accident that involved nerve damage. She was deafened but now her hearing has been restored."

"Well, that's different than . . ."

"I know," Rob interrupted her, "but I've talked to Dr. Volski. She says she can do it!" He felt frustrated in the face of Tesa's indifference. "Well, *I'm* excited about it!"

Tesa's mouth twitched up on one side. "Sure, *you* are."

As much as Tesa respected Rob's struggle to learn ASL, she felt that he would always define her by her deafness. She'd told him that he could only see her as someone who was *missing* something, instead of as someone with different abilities. He couldn't help it, Rob told himself. He was an M.D. as well as a psychologist. He believed in repairing things that didn't work.

"Tesa," Rob signed, "you'll be able *to hear*. Can't you imagine what that will mean to you?"

The young woman looked at the small cat curled in her lap, purring. Tesa touched Bast, then signed, "Can you hear that?"

Startled, he nodded.

"Well, I can, too, with my body, my eyes. Not *less*, Rob. Just *different*."

"Come on, Tesa, that's semantics. You can't hear Mozart."

She looked impatient. "Mozart! Hearing people are always throwing him up to us. Well, I have so *heard* Mozart, at Gallaudet, in a special auditorium. I heard him through the seats, the floors—I heard Mozart in my *bones*."

"Okay. But you've never heard birds, or wolf calls . . ."

"True"—one corner of her mouth turned up—"but there are other ways to hear spirit songs. Ask Doctor Blanket."

Technically, "Doctor Blanket"—an alien who was a powerful telepath that looked like nothing more than a plush baby's blanket—couldn't hear either. But Tesa wasn't an Avernian, she was a human. "Aren't you even curious?" Rob asked, baffled by her attitude. "I can't believe you're this disinterested."

She shrugged. "Would *you* become a telepath if you could?"

"That's not the same issue. Besides, I can experience telepathy with Doctor Blanket. And I don't find being a non-telepath any less desirable than being a telepath."

"*Same* issue," she insisted. "I can experience hearing through vibrations, and *I* don't find being Deaf any less desirable than being hearing. If I had this surgery, I'd have to completely *redefine* myself. Who would I be, with hearing?" She stroked the cat gently. "Dr. Rob, the elders of my tribe believe. I've been marked by the Wakan Tanka—the Great Mystery—for a special task. I was given a significant name."

Tesa's full name was Ptesa' Wakandagi. *Ptesa'* meant "White Buffalo," but implied more, since the white buffalo was not only rare, but sacred. And *Wakandagi* indicated someone unique.

"Growing up with *that* hanging over you," she continued, "is hard. When I was selected to come to StarBridge, everyone felt it was a sign for my *nagi*—my soul—to follow its path. It's not a good idea to fool around with your *nagi*." She looked tired. "And what would my friends at Gallaudet say?"

The mention of the school reminded Rob of the conversation he'd had with Tesa's former adviser just the night before. "To you," the woman had signed, "deafness is a physical condition. Tesa sees it as a cultural one."

"Tesa," he argued, "you're light-years away from Gallaudet. You might never see those people again."

She looked at him curiously. "The same could be said of my family. I wouldn't stop being Indian. Of course, you'd never suggest that. But being Indian is part of what makes me who I am . . . my culture, my identity. Well, so is being Deaf."

"That stubborn streak is going to get you in trouble someday," he signed grudgingly. He wondered if he was giving in too easily, since he had a hidden agenda. "If that's the way you really feel, I'll push my hearing prejudices aside. But I'm glad you mentioned your family, because this talk with me is just a warm-up. Your parents will be calling in less than an hour."

"My parents!" Tesa stood abruptly, dumping the cat off her lap. "You called my parents! Oh, *shit*!" In signing the expletive, she accidentally swept a disorderly pile of flimsies off the edge of Rob's desk.

"I had to, Tesa . . ." Rob gave up signing while they grabbed at the drifting forms slowly fluttering to the floor.

"I'm over eighteen, Dr. Rob," she signed abruptly, before snatching a wafting sheet in midair. "You should've asked me first. If I can't explain this to you, how can I make *them* understand? They think it's *their* fault I'm deaf."

Tesa's parents, both hearing, worked in space, building stations. When Tesa and her brother and sister were little, her parents had commuted from the living museum to Australia and worked Earthside. As the children grew, their grandparents, aunts, and uncles had filled in as the two engineers took on short jobs around Earth and the Moon. Now they were working on a station only two weeks' metaspace journey away from StarBridge, close enough to afford monthly calls.

Even though doctors had tried to reassure them, Tesa's parents felt as though they must have been exposed to something. Her younger brother and sister were both hearing, and genetic screening had ruled out damaged chromosomes, but, Rob mused, it was the lot of parents to find themselves lacking. He thought of his own eleven-year-old daughter, Claire, the problems he had relating to her during their infrequent visits, and sighed.

"I *had* to call them," Rob insisted, sitting on his heels on the floor, a sloppy mound of flimsies before him. "There's more going on than just the surgery, and your parents had to know."

Tesa sat tailor fashion across from him. "What, *more*?"

Rob nodded. "Have you heard of Trinity?"

Tesa's eyes widened. She hadn't really paid attention the first time he'd spelled it, but every Terran at StarBridge had heard of it. "What about Trinity?" she asked, her eyes bright.

"It was discovered by a Terran colonizing company—Jamestown Founders," Rob told her as they resumed their seats. "It's at an evolutionary stage similar to Terra's Pleistocene—virgin wilderness, giant animals, mammoth trees, rich mineral deposits, and even fossil fuels. A planet to make an investor's dreams come true. But there's a snag. This world is inhabited by a species of intelligent avians we're calling the Grus."

His intercom called his attention. "Excuse me, Tesa."

"Rob," said Kkintha ch'aait, the school's Chhhh-kk-tu administrator. "Meg Tretiak is on line in my office."

"Uh, Tesa's here."

"Sorry, but this can't wait. Meg's got to catch a shuttle."

"Be right there." He turned back to Tesa. "Wait here, please. We haven't finished our talk."

"But what about Trinity?" Tesa complained.

"I've got films you can watch," Rob signed, going to his closet. Pushing a door aside, he rummaged through a box, finally pulling out two cassettes. "You know how to operate the viewer. It's raw footage, no *Intergalactic Geographic* stuff. I'll be back shortly," he promised, and jogged out of the office.

Tesa turned the unlabeled cassettes over in her hands as she entered the sequence to activate Rob's big wall holo. Could he be thinking of sending *her* to Trinity? Or was she jumping to conclusions because of her eagle dream last night? She always had eagle dreams before some big event—it was just her subconscious playing games with her.

Movement near the open office door caught her eye. Her roommate, Jib, was waving to get her attention. Two years her junior and no taller than Rob, the brown-skinned Maori had become Tesa's surrogate sibling.

"Come on in," she signed, "it's okay." She should've known he'd be lurking around, dying to find out the news. He'd looked more upset than she had when she hadn't been tapped.

"Tesa, what happened?" he signed, his doe-eyed, good-looking face full of concern. "Why weren't you tapped?"

"Dr. Rob canceled it because of some medical breakthrough," she explained. She set the hologram for captioning and inserted a cassette. "Some doctor wants to give me hearing."

Jib's big brown eyes opened wide. "Really? You'll *hear*? Wow!" He grabbed her in a jubilant hug. "You must be thrilled!"

She pushed him away, feeling as betrayed as if he'd slapped her. *Dammit, I thought at least* **Jib** *would understand!*

"You're *not* glad," Jib stated, finally realizing. "I'm sorry, Tesa, I should've realized how you'd feel, but . . ." he hesitated. "Are you sure about this?"

"Yes . . ." she signed, but without her earlier strength of conviction. Jib was her brother, and even he didn't understand. *Maybe I need to think this through more,* Tesa thought, feeling her resolve wavering. What had been so clear to her just moments ago now seemed muddy and gray. She wished fiercely that she were back at Gallaudet where people understood her.

Frowning, she popped one of the cassettes into the machine.

The holo-vid came to life, presenting a title, "A New Technique for Nerve Relay Reconstruction in Auditory Repair."

"Damn!" she yelled, ripping the cassette from the slot and flinging it against the wall. It bounced off wildly, hitting her sharply on the forehead before Jib caught it. "Damn!" She rubbed her head, feeling choked with anger and confusion.

"Hey, come on, Tesa, it's okay," Jib tried to soothe her.

She scowled. He was probably afraid she would start hollering expletives, since cussing was the only thing Tesa had gotten out of speech therapy that she liked.

"Don't do it if you don't want to," he continued hastily. "It doesn't matter what *anybody* thinks. It's your decision . . ."

Her eyes flashed, filling against her will. "Rob told my parents. They'll be calling here any moment."

Jib sagged. "Oh, shit," he signed, making Tesa giggle in spite of herself. That helped her get a grip on her feelings.

When Jib handed the cassette to her she waved it away. "I don't want that. Rob said there were films of Trinity . . ."

"That new planet they've discovered? How come?"

"He got called away before he could tell me." She slipped in the second unmarked cassette. "But I've got a hunch. I think they want to send me there."

"Before your pair project?" He looked skeptical.

The holo flickered to life again. There were no preliminary titles, just an open panorama of undisturbed wetlands, hills, and virgin forest awash in the brilliance of autumn shades.

A small caption appeared. "No narrative," it read.

Jib leaned over and raised the volume. "No sound, yet."

Now, why should that be? Tesa wondered.

Suddenly a group of white birds soared into view, flying in a slow, effortless manner. *Are those the Grus?* Tesa wondered.

One by one they backwinged and, stretching their thin, black legs earthward, landed gently. Their long, white wings ended in black primary feathers, and they had elegant black head and facial markings. A small, brilliant red crown capped their skulls with a stunning shock of color. Round, golden eyes made them seem ever alert, and when, as a group, they threw back their heads and arched those graceful necks to call to the sky, goose bumps raced up and down Tesa's arms.

"What does that sound like?" she asked Jib.

He shrugged. "There's still no sound."

Another scene shift showed a group gathered on a raised

platform of dried grass and reeds, white bodies against a jumble of reds and yellows and blazing orange. Sitting on their hocks like any Terran wading bird, they were making grooming motions with their long, black bills, while their wings, drawn in front of them, fluttered over something.

There was an abrupt close-up of the wingtips, showing that the black primaries were not feathers at all, but elegant, tapered fingers moving in rhythm with their wings and bills.

"They're weaving," Tesa signed. "They're plucking their down and feathers and weaving them with grass fibers into cloth."

She reversed the film, then played it back, slower and enlarged. "Look"—Tesa pointed—"they're using sign language!" She looked for repetitive handshapes, the position of the hands to the body, and the use of the body itself. She had no idea what they were saying, but while weaving, they chatted.

Abruptly the image dissolved into static. "Internal cassette error," the holographic caption read.

"But that would mean these creatures are *intelligent*," Jib realized. "It'd mean that Earth's made a First Contact . . ." His signs trailed off as Tesa smiled at him, her eyes glittering.

"Is that why you think they want you?" he asked, skeptical. " 'Cause you *think* these creatures use sign language?"

"Oh, they're using it all right," Tesa assured him. "Dr. Rob said he had *two* films—maybe he pulled out that medical cassette by accident. I'm going to look for another one."

Jib nodded, then ran the weaving scene again.

Rob Gable's antique films were meticulously organized, but educational material was often casually tossed in an open box in his closet. Tesa rummaged through it for anything unlabeled.

She found one, buried at the bottom. *This has got to be it,* she thought, and tossed it to Jib, bumping into the other closet door and causing it to open partially. As she reached to pull it shut, a glimmer of whiteness caught her eye. Among an assortment of Rob's classy suits, something shimmered. Just then Jib waved at her, and she turned her eyes back to the holovid. Another weaving scene began to unfold, this time with an elderly human woman kneeling beside the weavers.

"Is she a midget?" Jib signed in surprise.

No more than your people were to the Moa, Tesa thought. It was the first chance she'd had to see the avians in scale. The

Grus were huge, dwarfing the human woman. Suddenly the entire group, human included, stood, and one of the avians handed the old woman the result of their weaving. "They're at least ten feet tall!" she signed to Jib. What must their wing-span be like to get those bodies off the ground?

"Can you give me that in meters?" the New Zealander asked.

"See? They're using sign language!" Tesa looked smug.

Jib nodded. "Why do you keep looking at that closet?" he finally asked. "Did Dr. Rob buy *another* old movie poster?"

Tesa pushed the door open and let the light hit the white material that had been sparkling at her from the dark. As she'd suspected, it was a Grus weaving, identical to the one in the film. Gleaming with tiny shimmering rainbows as the light played over it, it seemed woven of gems. *Feathers and grass,* Tesa thought. *This is made from feathers and grass?* Tentatively she touched it, then examined the reverse.

Jib joined her. "There's two of them," he signed, reaching into the closet. As soon as he touched it, he stiffened. "Oh, God, Tesa—tell me that's not what I think it is."

Slowly the young man turned the fabric wrong side out, and Tesa ran her fingers lightly over it. The softly tanned leather of the Grus *skin* slid beneath her hand.

They dropped the skin, and Jib hurriedly shut the door as they edged away from the ugly artifact. Staring again at the marsh people who continued to chat and weave and fly, Tesa wondered, *Which of you lost your life to make that skin?*

"You must be wrong, Tesa," Jib signed. "Dr. Rob would never have the skin of an intelligent being in his closet!" But as the friends glanced back at the holo, the graceful beings interacting with each other put the lie to Jib's words.

"I'm *not* wrong!" Tesa insisted. "They're signing!"

Just then Rob touched them on their shoulders, making them both jump and gasp.

"Didn't you hear him come in?" Tesa asked Jib peevishly.

"He was *quiet!*" the boy retorted, clutching his chest.

"I figured you'd be here," Rob signed to Jib, then looked at the holo. "So, Tesa, what do you think of Trinity?"

Tesa smiled weakly, watching the scene. An impossibly tall avian walked beside a small human woman and Tesa ached to walk in her place. Tonight, instead of eagles, she'd dream of beautiful white-winged people and feel herself run across rust-colored grass to lift off into the sky with them. She wanted to learn their signs, as she had learned the signs of the Ashu, and live with a people who could share with her a common language.

But . . . what about that . . . that *thing* in Rob's closet?

Jib was gaping, waiting for her to ask Rob about it.

Her mind suddenly envisioned the edge of a bronze wingtip, a background of blue sky, as though she were the Wakinyan, the mystic thunderbird, gliding the thermals and looking past her own outstretched wing. *Part of last night's eagle dream coming back,* she realized. Tesa's fingers tingled with the memory of a feathered cloth and a silken skin.

All Tesa could think to ask Rob was, "Are the Grus deaf?"

Jib looked dumbfounded and started to sign something, but she gave him a look that stopped him.

Rob laughed, shaking his head. "No, they're hearing. I'd like to tell you more, but . . . your parents are on hold. I'm sorry everything's happening so fast, Tesa. That woman in the holo is Meg Tretiak. She's coming to StarBridge. She may ask you to go to Trinity with her, but that's not definite."

"I'd be a good translator for the Grus, Dr. Rob, I would! Meg could teach me the language on the way." She'd signed too fast, and Rob looked confused. Jib translated quickly.

"First," Rob signed, "you've got to decide whether or not you want that surgery. You just can't toss the chance to hear over your shoulder, I won't let you. Besides, we don't need a translator at Trinity, we need an Interrelator."

At StarBridge, students were exposed to studies that would prepare them to be translators, telepaths, or interrelators. Translators worked for the CLS as interpreters. While telepaths had to be born into their ability, their schooling would eventually prepare them for the search for intelligent life. When interrelators graduated, they were ready to live on an alien world as diplomatic liaisons or even ambassadors.

Before she could manage to ask about the skin (What did it have to do with the Terrans on Trinity? What impact would it have on the First Contact?), Rob removed the cassette.

Trinity disappeared as though it had been encased in a bubble that popped. With growing dread, she watched Rob patch in the call from her parents. *Why did they have to call now?* she wondered. She didn't know enough about Trinity—yet—and she no longer felt she knew enough about herself to talk to them.

Rob signed to Jib, "Let's give Tesa some privacy."

The young Indian woman stared after her friends as though they were abandoning her. Jib looked back at her, but Rob closed the door behind them. Tesa took a deep breath. What was wrong with her anyway? These were her *parents*—they *loved* her. She hadn't seen them in a whole year and hologram calls were only tantalizing cheats. You could see, but not hug.

Shutting her eyes, she touched her eagle feathers, feeling a shock of static electricity. The image from her dream came back unbidden. The edge of a bronze wingtip, a background of blue sky. Only now beneath her flew a Grus, neck extended, black-tipped white wings stretched for gliding, stick-thin legs trailing behind. With a splash of blood across its back.

Jerking her eyes open, Tesa blinked the image away. Tapping the controls, she repressed her conflicting emotions as the "Call Holding" caption dissolved to be replaced by the coalescing image of her parents.

CHAPTER 2

◆

The Dream

Tesa's parents stood eerily in the hologram field, like spirits beckoning her.

Her mother, AnadaAki Lewis, of Chippewa-Blackfoot ancestry, was tall and trim in her company's uniform, with dark, short-cropped hair and bright brown eyes. Her name meant "Pretty Woman," and she was.

Tesa's father, Dan Bigbee, had to stand behind Ana to fit the hologram's parameters. He was a Lakota Sioux traditionalist, and his braids swept past his shoulders. Like Tesa, he was a dancer and kept his hair long for summer powwows on Earth. His eyes were jet-black beneath heavy brows and he was taller than Ana by a head. He had given his strong face to his daughter.

Ana reached out a hand as her daughter extended hers, but their fingers met only empty air where warm flesh should've been.

"Your image is so real," Ana signed in Plains Indian Sign Language. It had been Tesa's first language.

Tesa smiled. "Mom, Dad, how are you?"

"We're fine!" her father signed. "We miss you. Our work

has gone very well—this station's almost finished.''

Tesa nodded, hesitant to add much to the conversation.

"We'll get good bonuses, too," AnadaAki added. "And we'll be coming home soon . . . to be with you."

"That is, *if* you're coming home," Dan amended hastily.

Tesa's jaw clenched. It was on their faces, that expression she hadn't seen since childhood. The expression they'd worn every time they'd checked out any specialist they'd thought might be able to "do something for Tesa."

"It's been a week of good news," her mother signed. "Your brother Nato has been accepted to Dartmouth. And Sissy's been approached by StarBridge."

That was a happy surprise. SikskiAki wrote diligently, wanting to know every detail about StarBridge and the aliens her older sister encountered.

"She'll begin attending the Earth-based satellite school in six months. She's very excited." AnadaAki hesitated for a moment. "And then there's this new surgery that can help you." Her mother was trembling slightly. "You'll finally be able to *hear*! It's so wonderful, Tesa . . ."

Dan squeezed Ana's shoulders, halting her. "You've said almost nothing," he signed. "How do *you* feel, Tesa?"

"Well," his daughter began tentatively, "I haven't had much time to get used to the idea . . ."

Her mother's face lit up. "I know it's not easy facing a big change, honey, but we'll be with you. Then you can go back to speech therapy and improve your voice."

Tesa had always been self-conscious about her voice. Aliens expected you to mangle their languages, but Terrans were less forgiving. She'd gotten tired of people's reaction to her speech, so Tesa rarely spoke aloud.

"Just think, baby," Dan signed, "by this summer, you'll be able to *hear* the drums, instead of just feeling the beat."

When Tesa danced, the drummers intensified their rhythms so she could feel the vibrations that helped her keep time, while she watched the synchronized pounding. The drumming represented the heartbeat of the planet, and feeling it made Tesa a part of the drum, made her one with Mother Earth. She didn't think that hearing it would improve that for her.

"Honey," Ana signed, "I'm afraid we've done all the talking . . . and you don't look very excited."

"It's just . . . well, there's more going on than just this surgery, Mom. Didn't they tell you?"

Her parents both nodded. "Dr. Gable said you have a chance to work on a new project," her father signed, "but he didn't give us any details."

"This project could be critical to Earth—it could mean Earth receiving full credit for a First Contact! That's im—"

"Couldn't you do that after the surgery?" her mother interrupted.

Tesa paused, trying to find the right thing to say. Her eyes settled on a mini-holo hovering over Dr. Rob's desk. In it, a smiling Mahree Burroughs and her eleven-year-old daughter, Claire—Dr. Rob's own little girl—perpetually rode an antique carnival ride. It had been Mahree's book, *First Contacts*, that had convinced Tesa to leave Earth, to go to StarBridge, to follow the *harder* path. Fifteen years ago, Mahree and Dr. Rob had followed their own hard path, when they abandoned the *Désirée* and, with their Simiu friend, Dhurrrkk', headed for Shassiszss.

Tesa lowered her head to escape the distraction of the holo, and as she did her eagle feathers brushed her face. *Tell them how you truly feel*, she ordered herself.

But, despite her resolve, when she met their eyes, she signed, "I'm not sure this surgery is right for me."

"Sure," AnadaAki agreed, "it must seem scary . . ."

Tesa forced her gaze to remain steady. "It's not that, Mom . . . I just don't know if I want to be . . . hearing."

Her mother swallowed, and Dan seemed to grow taller. Ana signed, "Don't you want to hear my voice?"

With a smile, Tesa answered, "Don't you think I have?" She remembered herself as a child in Pretty Woman's lap, her mother's strong arms around her, a tune humming through her body.

The clarity of the hologram showed AnadaAki's eyes slowly filling with tears, shattering Tesa's resolve.

"Mom, don't cry. I haven't made any decisions." *Maybe I'm being selfish*, she thought. She really hadn't examined the issue; she'd just responded emotionally. *Don't I owe them that much?* "I need to find out more—about the surgery, *and* the project," she signed. "And I needed to know how you felt. Have you told the grandparents?"

Ana brushed away tears and tried to smile. "My mother told me not to cry in front of you."

"Grandfather Bigbee said," Dan signed, "listen to your heart before making a decision that could pull you from your path."

"That sounds like him," Tesa signed. The old man was fond of saying he looked at things the "Indian way" when what he meant was the harder way. He said it was because he'd been a *heyoka*—a contrary—when he was young. He'd gotten the name Laughing Bear in those days. Tesa had trouble visualizing him as a sacred clown. They'd always scared her as a child.

Her mother looked rueful. "The grandparents also said they love you just the way you are. I don't know why I didn't think of that until now. We do, too, Tesa."

"And I couldn't love *you* any more than I do right now."

"Dr. Gable warned us you might not be ready to make a decision," her father signed. "Find out more about that project and about the surgery. We'll wait."

You've been waiting nineteen years now, Tesa thought sadly.

The smell of fragrant smoke and the hot breath of the rocks surrounded Tesa like holy garments, even though she was outside the sweat lodge, not in it. She flitted over its roof, wondering who was inside burning sweet grass. She danced on the air like a gnat, but not a gnat—a little flying thing with shiny wings.

Caught in a waft of escaping steam, she drifted higher, until the tiny lodge seemed only a hump of autumn-hued grass against rust-colored ground. The sky was a more vivid blue than she'd ever seen, even over the endless plains of home.

Suddenly the air was rent with jagged streaks of white-hot lightning. It was the Wakinyan, throwing their power around. The terrified gnat couldn't see the Thunder Beings, but then, no one ever saw the fierce giants clearly, even in dreams.

The Wakinyan opened their mouths and thunder rolled out, but of course, Tesa couldn't hear it. This angered the spirits, and lightning zigzagged from their huge red orbs, arcing through the sky to strike the ground near the sweat lodge.

"She'll hear this!" boomed the great red thunderbird. His taunts were not words, but feelings directed to her.

"And this," cried the blue, his beak opening wide enough to swallow the World. The yellow spirit did likewise.

The little gnat was tossed about, terrified, but she still could not hear the thunder.

"Enough!" bellowed the largest Wakinyan, a great black being covered in mist and clouds. A drifting column of sweetgrass smoke wafting up from the lodge enveloped the black thunderbird, mingling with the clouds that made his body. "In the loudest sound, she hears silence. When she should speak, she says nothing. What a backward-forward way to be!"

Those words struck more terror into the gnat than the lightning had. She froze in horror, just as the black Wakinyan opened his great red eye and threw his biggest bolt.

The searing hotness hurled her down, blasting a hole through the lodge's orange and red roof. The vision-seeker looked up and took the gnat into herself, and was filled with the gnat's fear. Lifting a dipper of water to throw on the hot rocks, the occupant peered into the cool liquid. The face she saw was not her own, but the face of a laughing bear.

The Wakinyans flew above the lodge, their wings blocking the sun, so that its light flashed on and off in her face.

Light and dark.

Light and dark.

Tesa burrowed under her old star quilt to escape the light that was flashing light and dark, hot and cold. She awoke with a jerk, sitting bolt upright, then looked around, not knowing where she was. Her bedside lamp flashed on and off.

The dream fragmented and she scrambled after its memory, but nothing was left except a nameless dread, the warmth of the old quilt, and the flashing bedside lamp. *Just a bad dream ended by the door signal,* Tesa chided herself, climbing out of bed.

It was Jib, and with him came the tantalizing smell of coffee. "Hurry and get decent, Tesa. Dr. Rob's coming by."

"Talk to the servo about breakfast," she signed one-handed. "I'll be out in five. Does the place look like hell?"

"Merely heck. He gave me a ten-minute warning."

Now I'll find out about Trinity, Tesa thought with a stirring of excitement. Jib had told her last night that he'd pumped Rob for details, but the psychologist had been closemouthed. Tesa had been tempted to call him herself, but she'd been exhausted after the conversation with her parents, following yesterday's confusing events, and she'd fallen asleep.

She stumbled to the shower, passing her wall holo, currently showing the Black Hills. There was a lone eagle gliding through the scene. The holos had many random variations, but for some reason, this image made her shudder. "Mirror," she signed. *Oh, that's worse,* she decided.

"Good morning," Tesa signed to Rob. Clean hair gave her a different outlook—refreshed, cheerful. "Where's Jib?"

"I tossed him out," the psychologist told her. He sat on the neutral-colored sofa in Jib and Tesa's shared living room. On a table sat a pile of doughnuts and a pot of steaming coffee. "We've got lots to discuss. Come, plant yourself."

She did, then helped herself to a plain old-fashioned.

"So, how'd your parents take it?" Rob asked kindly.

Tesa stared at him, confused.

"When you told them you didn't want your hearing fixed?"

"Well . . ." she hesitated, "I said . . . I hadn't decided."

Rob was surprised. "But you were so sure when I left you!"

Exasperated, she scowled. "I thought you *wanted* me to reconsider! I thought you wanted me to have it done."

He looked annoyed in turn. "*Only* if the surgery is what you really want. What did your parents say to change your mind?"

"Nothing . . . I just said I'd think about it," she signed.

"Tesa, I didn't call them to complicate things, but because I knew you'd have to talk to them about it." Rob ran a hand through his dark, curly hair distractedly.

"When I told you about that new surgery," he signed, "I expected you to jump at the chance. However, when you *didn't*, it set something else in motion. Now you tell me you're not sure."

"I can't make any decision without more facts," she signed.

He nodded, took a cassette from his pocket, and plugged it into the holo-vid. "Sorry this had an error on it yesterday," Rob signed. The living-room scene—seven sacred Maori canoes cresting the waves—dissolved, re-forming as Trinity. "I had it patched. I'm sure you recognized the Grus, even without narrative. These shots were taken by the colonizing company's scientists. They'd been making observations for months when one of the biologists, Scott Hedford, was approached by the Grus." Rob fast-forwarded the footage. "Here's that scene."

A sophisticated hologramic blind blended invisibly into the reeds as an avian walked up to it and patiently waited. After a moment, the occupant of the blind turned it off. It disappeared, and the human and Grus stood a few feet apart, face-to-face.

The ruddy-skinned, sandy-haired man with a moustache watched as the improbably tall Grus held out a folded cloth. Tesa instantly liked Scott for his open delight in receiving a gift that would change his life forever.

"Scott was a good researcher," Rob signed. "He believed that the Grus were truly intelligent. His partner, Meg Tretiak, agreed. Voder translations backed them up. However, this decision did not please their employers, Jamestown Founders."

I bet, thought Tesa.

It had only been fifteen years since the *Désirée* had met the Simiu, the powerful, four-legged baboonlike aliens, the first extraterrestrials the humans had found. That First Contact had nearly ended disastrously when a young Simiu, Khrekk', had violated the complicated Simiu honor code by committing suicide, shaming himself and his family. But then, humans had also shamed themselves by using weapons—the Simiu's most serious taboo. As the conflict escalated, Mahree Burroughs, Rob Gable, and their Simiu friend, Dhurrrkk', stole away to plead for help from the Cooperative League of Systems—a union of the Known Worlds.

The CLS intervened and the situation *almost* ended perfectly. Because of the travelers' accidental discovery of the telepathic Avernians, the Terrans and the Simiu were each granted half membership in the CLS. For the humans, this was an unexpected reward. But for the Simiu, who had lost their bid for full membership because of their mishandling of their attempt at First Contact with the humans, this was a shameful disappointment. Even now, many Simiu held the humans responsible for their perceived dishonor in the entire affair.

As for the humans, they had to get used to the idea that the universe wasn't theirs alone. At that time, Earth had already profitably colonized three planets. Columbus was still venerated on Terra, and colonizing was big business. However, Terra's new half membership made some politicians realize that there might be other profitable things to do in space. The oldest and founding members of the CLS, the snakelike, many-tentacled Mizari, were much more advanced scientifically than the Terrans. Mutual trade could be very beneficial. Many humans felt that full membership in the CLS would help Earth immeasurably.

One of the most crucial requirements to be granted full membership in the Cooperative League of Systems—something the Simiu still coveted—was to meet and establish nonexploitative, peaceful relations with another intelligent species. But, what might happen if the Simiu were to gain full membership first? Full membership had become the pennant in a race, similar to when one Earth country had raced another to be the first to orbit the planet, or the first to land on Terra's Moon. Only now, the Terrans were racing the Simiu.

"Scott and Meg notified the CLS about the Grus," Rob continued, "*over* the objections of their superiors. They requested that the CLS regard this as a genuine First Contact, so a board was established to review the progression of the relationship. That was about three years ago."

Tesa knew that the giant corporations in the colonizing business had a different view of CLS membership—they were against it. A year after the *Désirée* encountered the Simiu, Rob Gable had sponsored a law on Earth that *required* all colonizing expeditions to search for intelligent life on the habitable planets they discovered. The corporations had managed to water down the law's language—what, after all, was *intelligence*?

Similar situations had inspired the Mizari to begin plans for StarBridge fifteen years ago—a school where diplomacy, the diversity of cultural values, and, above all, the waging of intergalactic peace would be taught. It had taken Rob Gable and the Mizari Mediator, the Esteemed Ssoriszs, almost ten years to finalize those plans and construct and staff the asteroid school they were now on. But StarBridge—located in an area of space that had long been used as a transition point for spacefarers—*was* now a reality—and things would begin to change.

"Jamestown Founders didn't want to sink a lot of money into a planet they couldn't colonize," Rob told Tesa, "but they didn't want to lose their claim if the First Contact was denied, either. So the core of their scientific team stayed at Trinity, including Scott and Meg, but as independent researchers. We suspect the others stayed to cover themselves—there'll be recognition if this *is* a verified First Contact, and they can keep an eye on their claim if it isn't. Earth sent in a few more staff members to assist the core team."

The holo scenes shifted, and Rob pointed to a group of avian weavers. "The fabric they make is incredibly beautiful. The weave is very complicated, and the patterns are illusory, shifting with the play of light.'' He lifted a case from the floor, removed a mound of whiteness, then tossed it over Tesa's lap. Rob smiled at her reaction.

"The Grus," he signed, "line their nests with the cloaks. They may also use them in their religion, but we're not sure."

Tesa touched it tentatively, then checked the other side. The tight, even weaving reassured her, and she stroked the iridescent feathers.

"Like a lot of beautiful things, these cloaks have turned out to be both a blessing *and* a curse. The Grus enjoy giving them away, so we began to trade."

Tesa felt a sense of foreboding. "So what does a space-age planet trade for this 'incredibly beautiful' fabric?" she asked.

Rob grimaced. "Don't look at me like that, Tesa. Scott and Meg could only find one thing the Grus wanted that their world didn't supply them."

It couldn't possibly be **alcohol**, she thought. "What?"

"Wind chimes."

Tesa looked at Rob blankly, not understanding.

"*Crystal* wind chimes, specifically," he elaborated. "Meg had a little cheap one and the Grus became enamored of it. They said that the refracted rainbows it threw reminded them of an insect that omens good luck, so crystal wind chimes have become official trade items." He shrugged.

Tesa rolled her eyes. "Have we bought Manhattan yet?"

"*If* you go to Trinity, maybe *you* can come up with a better solution!" Rob finished his coffee, then continued, "That first cloak was sent to Earth, where it generated a lot of excitement. As the Grus gave us more, museums, governments, the wealthy and powerful, all lined up for them. Demand far outstripped the supply. Then, two years ago, one of *these* was found in a routine customs search by special agents—biologists working as law-enforcement agents who'd been trained to recognize illegally obtained wildlife artifacts."

He opened the case again. In it was the feathered skin. Tesa was drawn by its beauty, but repelled by its brutal origin. Rob gestured for her to take it.

Reverently she spread it between them on the couch, marveling at its size. Here was the long white neck, with tiny black feathers where the head had been joined, and bits of the knubby red skin that made the crown, now an ashy plum color. There were the impossibly huge wings. Tesa shuddered as her hand touched the black primaries and she felt the delicate bones that made the three-fingered, almost palmless hand.

How could **anyone** *do this?* There were ragged tear holes by the spine.

"When this was confiscated," Rob signed, "it had a data-card identifying it as a genetic reconstruction. The card was an incredibly sophisticated counterfeit that got the skin past a lot of spaceport checkpoints. We traced it as far back as we could, but the trail died when it entered Sorozssow Sector."

Tesa started in surprise. Rob had spelled the Mizari word that most Terrans translated to Sorrow or Outlaw Sector. Literally, the Mizari word meant "place outside the law," or "place with no ethics," since, to the Mizari, law and personal ethics were one and the same. It was all the more astounding that the notorious criminal underworld operating out of a mysterious, distant cluster of systems was supposedly run by a very old Mizari—a Mizari without ethics. To Tesa's knowledge, the ancient renegade had never actually been seen, but then, no law officer or journalist who'd entered Sorrow undercover had ever emerged to confirm or deny his existence.

Sorrow Sector was home to anyone needing refuge from the law and willing to support the operations of its network, which included the best in illegal technology. In Sorrow Sector, *everything* was available—for the right price.

"When Scott and Meg found out about the skins," Rob signed, "they were stunned. Because of the connection to Sorozssow, no one can find out who's obtaining the skins, how they're getting off-planet, or who's fencing them. Those marks on the hide are from a predator attack, so it was presumed at first that privateers had found the planet, and were stealing dead Grus from predators and salvaging the skins." He paused for a moment.

"However," Rob signed, "things are getting worse. Lately, *flawless* skins have been impounded—hides that could've only come from Grus killed with modern weapons. Of course, our staff isn't permitted to have weapons, so they're exonerated."

"Aren't the League Irenics doing anything?" Tesa asked. The CLS peacekeepers were charged with protecting intelligent life.

Rob nodded. "Meg and Scott petitioned the CLS board for protective status for the Grus until the First Contact could be resolved. However, a Terran on the board vetoed that request."

Tesa's eyes widened indignantly. "What the hell for?"

Rob smiled ruefully. "Because, of the two Terrans on the board, one is a past president of Jamestown Founders. She, and others like her, believe that membership will severely limit Earth's ability to colonize newly discovered planets. If the CLS intervenes on Trinity, it could set a precedent, giving the CLS a say in all Earth's colonizing expeditions. If the Grus aren't intelligent, Trinity *belongs* to Earth—and Jamestown Founders. If the CLS steps in now, Trinity might never belong to anyone."

Tesa felt as though she'd traveled back in time and was hearing Columbus tell Queen Isabella how he had "discovered" an inhabited continent, and how all its resources were now hers.

"The corporations' opponents," Rob continued, "insist the companies would be happy to thumb their noses at CLS membership and all it represents in long-term achievements just so they can have unfettered opportunities to pursue short-term profits."

Tesa sagged back on the couch. "I shouldn't be surprised."

"Those of us who are convinced of the Grus' intelligence are hampered in other ways as well. There are many different species of Grus . . . and not all of them want us on Trinity."

Rob leaned forward. "Fortunately, the most respected of all the Grus leaders—the avian named Taller who had so boldly met Scott—has befriended the humans. However, he's old and his power is waning. His people are edgy about his alliance with aliens, making our situation there very sensitive.

"As a result, Taller has insisted on limiting the number of humans permitted at Trinity. If we believe in the Grus' intelligence, then we have to respect his wishes. So, only six people were posted there, with only Scott and Meg living planetside. It makes it impossible for them to do much about the invaders, but, really, even if we had six *hundred* people there, they couldn't police a planet."

Rob touched the skin gently. "Trinity is too far removed from the hub of CLS activity to get quick assistance in an emergency. After the skins started showing up, Meg and Scott asked Taller to allow more staff, but his people objected. I'm not even sure I can blame them. Somewhere on their planet there are privateers—possibly human—who are killing Grus . . . should they believe *we're* harmless just because *we* say so?'' Rob frowned. "We've got to prove the Grus are intelligent. Then, anyone possessing those skins will be accomplice to murder."

"Haven't the voder translations proved that?'' Tesa asked.

"They might have, if the Founders had had Mizari voders, but the company used old-style Terran voders."

"Those voders were good enough for you aboard the *Désirée*,'' Tesa signed impatiently, "and they've been upgraded since then."

"And a study of recent voder upgrades,'' Rob signed, "found a glitch in one program that would allow some voders to translate *any* communication—even an interaction with domestic animals—into meaningful conversation. Jamestown Founders presented the study results to the board. Of course, it was the same program they use, and it cast doubt on the Grus' intelligence. The Founders insist the Grus are very intelligent animals, perhaps on the level of apes or dolphins, but not *intelligent enough* for a First Contact. And certainly not intelligent enough to avoid having their planet colonized."

Rob shook his head at Tesa's expression. "In spite of that, the other Terran board member''—he smiled faintly—"Mahree, voted for the Grus' protection, essentially neutralizing the corporation's vote. However, the Simiu saw this as the perfect opportunity to prevent us from getting full membership. They voted against protection and those three votes encouraged the Heeyoon to side with them. They're colonizers themselves. The board had to table the request."

"That's ridiculous!'' Tesa signed. Irritated, she crammed a powdery doughnut into her mouth, carefully avoiding the Grus skin.

Rob shrugged. "*That's* politics. When Meg and Scott found out, they were crushed. They appealed to the board for Mizari voders, and they've just gotten clearance. Meg's going to pick them up when she comes."

Tesa stuffed the last of the pastry into her mouth, brushed her hands off, and signed, "So, how do *I* fit in?"

"I told you,'' Rob reminded her, "that Meg had lost her hearing on Trinity."

"I remember,'' Tesa signed.

"There was a terrible accident, and it's changed everything. Taller's son, Water Dancer, was being trained to become the leader so Taller could 'retire.' Taller's almost seventy Terran

years old. Water Dancer had become good friends with Scott.''
Rob glanced at the peaceful holo-vid view of Grus lazily walking along, probing the ground with their bills.

"There was an early-morning predator attack," Rob signed flatly. "Water Dancer was killed. And so was Scott Hedford."

Tesa felt as though she'd been slapped. She recalled Scott's delight and awe as he touched the gift of another being. After seeing him on the holo-vid and calmly discussing his work, she felt as if she'd come to know him. "No!" she signed. "He was killed by animals on Trinity?"

Rob shook his head. "I feel like I've told you this backward. He was killed, accidentally, by the Grus."

She was completely bewildered now.

"The Grus sign, but they use their voices, too."

Tesa nodded numbly.

"However," Rob continued, "their voices are so loud, the vibrations so powerful, it can be fatal to humans. We had to send special filming equipment that wouldn't be affected by it. The films are all soundless. Meg and Scott had to begin wearing industrial sound nullifiers when they arrived."

Rob paused, glancing at the holo where Scott still walked, vibrant and alive. "Over the years, they got careless. They wouldn't wear the nullifiers in the evening when it was usually safe. The night before the attack, Scott had dismantled them to recharge the batteries, something they did once a month. The next morning they were watching the sunrise without the devices. The Grus called out a warning. Meg was deafened and knocked unconscious, but Scott had a weak blood vessel in his brain. It burst, killing him."

"How terrible!" Tesa signed.

Rob sighed visibly. "Water Dancer was also killed, as was his mate, and their egg with its unborn male chick. This brought new politics into play. With no heir, Taller is now in real danger of being deposed." Rob paused to sip his cooling coffee.

"From the very beginning," he told her, "Taller has instinctively grasped that our presence has changed the lives of his people in ways he can't yet comprehend. Many of them would prefer to either ignore the humans or drive them from Trinity."

"Either scenario," Tesa signed, "would be perfect for the Terran colonialists or the privateers marketing those skins."

"Exactly. Right now things are bleak." Rob smiled ruefully. "But there's one ray of hope."

Tesa looked at him curiously.

"Taller's mate, Weaver, laid an egg after Meg left. That in itself wasn't any big deal, she lays one every year. However, for the last ten years they've been infertile."

Rob fixed Tesa with a look. "Three days before your tapping, the crew called Meg at Shassiszss where she was hospitalized. *This* egg is fertile. Taller says it's a male."

Is this where I come in? Tesa wondered.

"Before the accident, Scott was going to be 'adopted' by Water Dancer and help rear Dancer's chick. This was Taller's idea, and it's very radical, since chicks are usually raised in strict isolation until they can fly."

So, that's why they need an interrelator, Tesa thought.

"Taller wanted to wed Scott to the Grus through family ties, but Scott would have had to wear his nullifiers twenty-four hours a day. He wouldn't have been able to take them off even for an hour. Meg would have had to shuttle recharged units to him . . . but then Scott died, and Meg had to leave."

"And that's when you learned about the surgery?"

Rob nodded. "While recuperating, Meg looked for someone to take Scott's place. She had decided, impulsively, to ask Gallaudet to recommend some deaf candidates, when the crew told her about the egg. That lent real urgency to the search. Then Meg found out about you, she called Kkintha, and here we are."

"Was it your idea to throw me a curve about that surgery?"

"It wasn't a curve," he responded defensively. "I couldn't ask you to do this while withholding information that could mean a lot to you, personally. Meg had her work done on Shassiszss, but yours would be much more extensive. You'd have to go to Earth and spend more than a year in surgery and therapy. You couldn't do that *and* raise this chick, so I told you about the surgery first. My first obligation is to *you*. True, part of me was relieved when you didn't want it. If you have doubts . . ."

"I can have the surgery *anytime*," she signed firmly. "I need to go to Trinity now."

Rob looked at Tesa skeptically. "You're hedging. You think you've found an excuse your parents will accept."

"Is that so terrible?" Tesa asked, annoyed. "This will lessen their disappointment. It's not that I'll *never* have it done . . . just not now.'' So why did she feel like she was lying?

"Well, when Meg comes she'll interview you. The final decision is hers. If she agrees, you'll leave immediately. You've got to get to Trinity before that egg hatches.''

Tesa looked over at Trinity, imagining herself there.

The scene shifted to a massive forest full of monstrous multicolored trees, larger than Earth's redwoods. Tesa thought this was how the Earth might have looked when her people kept their own ways. But that was hundreds, even thousands of years ago, and those old buffalo days were only stories now.

She recalled her last night on Earth, hugging Grandmother and crying, fearful she'd never see her again. The old woman had brushed Tesa's tears away and told her, "Somewhere there's a world where the way of life we loved, the old ways, are not just interesting relics of the past. You could find that world, *takoja*, but you can't find it sitting here.''

Suddenly a huge, dark form swooped across the holo's scene, skimming the treetops, snapping Tesa from her memories.

The image grabbed her by the heart, startling her so much that she stood up and bumped into the table with the doughnuts. Tesa stepped closer to the hologram. The creature alighted on a monstrous nest built on a limb of that gigantic tree.

"What is that?'' Tesa asked Rob, pointing.

"We call them the Aquila,'' he signed.

The bird was clutching prey in its talons, tearing it apart with its hooked beak, feeding it to a chick huddled in the nest.

"It's intelligent,'' she signed.

Rob frowned. "No, the data hasn't indicated that.''

Tesa couldn't explain why, but she *knew* she was seeing an intelligent being.

The Aquila had a bronze body with a golden head and tail. unlight made the bird seem as though it were made from molten metal. The creature raised its head and its fierce red eyes stared straight through the young woman. She gasped and stumbled back onto the couch.

Rob was alarmed. "What's wrong? Tesa, you okay?''

"It's the Thunderbird,'' she signed, pointing to the Aquila. She was shaking all over, not knowing why, the feeling of dread she'd waked with now smothering her. The baleful red eyes of the Aquila continued to bore into her.

"*That*," Rob informed her, "is one of the most formidable predators on Trinity. They kill and eat Grus."

Enemy to the Grus? Tesa thought numbly, the terrible sense of déjà vu almost suffocating her.

He nodded. "Those big babies pose a king-size problem for the First Contact team." She looked at him dazedly as Rob continued, smiling. "But, you've got experience with raptors. You might be able to find a deterrent to keep them away from the camp. You might even be able to tame one like the old falconers did."

Tesa smiled wanly. The Wakinyan was not a creature to be *tamed*. She turned to meet the gaze of the red-eyed Aquila, its wings stretched against the wind, its beak open in a scream. Tesa still could not hear the thunder.

CHAPTER 3

◆

Blanket Advice

"Tesa! Pick your feet *up*!"

Giving her Simiu instructor a sour look, Tesa pulled one stilt laboriously out of the marsh muck, set it down, then struggled to lift the other. She didn't care if the gravity *was* less than Earth's, this was hard work. Her calves and thighs ached and she was covered with a gray goo from numerous falls.

Awkwardly, she trudged behind the baboonlike alien she had long ago nicknamed, in sign, "Dr. Noisy." They slogged through a mock-up of a freshwater marsh, balanced on four-foot-high, lightweight, black, mechanized stilts, while the Simiu's rapid-fire commands flashed from her voder.

The stilts had been invented by a Simiu and, Dr. Noisy had proudly informed her, were "intelligent."

The word is "possessed," Tesa had thought, the first time she'd flexed her foot to give the "walk" command only to have both stilts collapse beneath her. They folded almost flat for storage, and that seemed to be their favorite command. The stilts made her feel like an awkward giantess, but they would allow her to walk the marsh while she lived with the Grus.

It didn't help that Meg Tretiak was sitting on a dry hummock,

33

her clear blue eyes closely observing Tesa's progress.

The constant flash of the Simiu's commands on the voder screen made Tesa question her decision to take this assignment. *You can still back out,* she thought. *A ship leaves for Earth tomorrow.* Gritting her teeth, she plopped around grimly.

Tesa not only had to torture her body, but there were hours of lessons to master the Grus' signs. The Ashu language had been difficult enough, but the Grus language sometimes required a four-foot neck, the ability to turn one's head 360 degrees while standing on one leg, and *feathers!*

Glancing at Dr. Noisy, she realized that the P.E. teacher was shrieking. She'd gotten so used to the flashing voder she'd stopped paying attention to it.

"I said, pick your legs *up! Up, UP, UP!* You'll be spending the next year on these things, so get used to them!"

Enough was enough. Meg or no Meg, Tesa turned the voder off and made sure the Simiu saw her do it. She was lucky not to have to *hear* his maniacal screaming; she didn't see any reason to aggravate herself further by *reading* his shouted instructions.

The infuriated teacher leaped up and down, waving to get her attention. His salmon-colored crest, marked with darker red mottling, flared erect, and his violet eyes were blazing.

Talk about earning your name! Tesa thought. "Don't you know it's silly to shout at a Deaf person?" she signed. Carefully, she turned her back on him. *Now he can scream away.*

A ball of mud landed square in the middle of her back, throwing her wildly off balance. Desperately she windmilled her arms and tried to slow her inevitable fall by weaving back and forth. This activated the "collapse" command, and Tesa fell flat on her face in the shallow water. Pulling herself out of the mud hand over hand on the mock weeds, she turned to see the alien hugging himself with mirth while Meg covered her own mouth.

Balancing precariously on the collapsed stilts, Tesa moved her toe to activate the "rise" command. If she'd ever considered giving up, that thought was gone now. She advanced on the Simiu.

She was almost on top of him when he stopped laughing long enough to catch his breath. Opening his mouth with what must've been a tremendous shriek, he scooted out from under her threatening advance and began scampering all around the mock-up.

Tesa chased him, walking faster and faster. Finally, he doubled back, dodging in and around her stilted legs to throw her off balance. She lifted one leg, then the other high out of the water, determined to stay upright. When he finally latched onto her leg, she was forced to spin around like a caricature of a ballet dancer, arms outstretched for balance. But when she fell, she had the pleasure of taking the alien with her in a tangle of furred and bare arms, legs, and mechanical stilts.

When Dr. Noisy pulled himself out of the water, he extended a long arm to help Tesa up, but by that time she was laughing too hard to move. Finally, they sat together, trying to catch their breath as they unstrapped their muck-covered, *intelligent* stilts. The Simiu sat on his haunches, gray goo and water plastering his mane flat, but wearing that unmistakable Simiu twinkle of amusement. He pointed to Tesa's voder, and she turned it back on.

"I knew you could master those stilts," the voder read.

"After a while the only hard part will be remembering how to use your legs *without* them." That was from Meg, smiling at the two mud-puppies from a safe distance. Tesa smiled back a little shyly, still not sure of what Meg thought of her or how the older woman felt about having her on this project.

Dr. Noisy picked up his own stilts. "I know you will earn much honor on this assignment," the Simiu said formally. "And as you humans say, I wish you luck, as do many of my people."

Tesa looked at him with a little surprise.

"I wanted you to know, Tesa," the Simiu continued, "that while some of my people have bitter feelings about the past, many more respect your people's differences and do not judge you by our code. As your teacher, and your friend, I wanted wish you well. I'll miss you."

"Your friendship has always been a great honor to me. Dr. Noisy," Tesa signed, clouding up. "I'll miss you, too."

"You're scheduled to meet with Dr. Xto in an hour," the Simiu reminded her abruptly. The wasplike Apis was scheduled to teach Tesa how to handle the diamond-shaped portable flying sleds. "Now, flying an air scooter is my idea of *real* fun!" Without another word, the Simiu turned and left the mock-up in a typical Simiu wordless departure.

Tesa realized he was trying to give her something else to

think about, instead of dwelling on their farewell. Glancing at Meg, she saw the older woman reading the Simiu's words on her own voder. Tesa would be glad when she and Meg had enough of a language base to dispense with the damned things.

At least that was one area where Tesa knew she'd impressed the biologist. Her almost-instinctive grasp of the Grus language had allowed Tesa to meet Meg with the appropriate Grus greeting when she'd arrived. That'd been a great icebreaker and, the younger woman hoped, had shown Meg just how much the chance to go to Trinity meant to her.

"Don't look so forlorn," Meg said in Russian, while signing in Grus. Tesa's voder showed the literal translation—"Your feathers are needlessly fluffed"—plus the English equivalent. The humans on Trinity also found it necessary to use the English manual alphabet to spell words like "Mizari" that had no literal translation—at least until the Grus would create new signs for them.

"This is a good mock-up," Meg continued, "but the gravity's not right. Maybe it's psychological, but when you're on Trinity you feel . . . well, *buoyant*. Like you could fly away with the Grus." She brushed wispy, silver-gray curls from her face. "Rob said you used to work with birds, doing rehabilitation work."

Tesa nodded. "On the plains when I was a kid. There's a big rehab place near our summer tipi camp—where the powwows are held. We had raptors, songbirds, and sandhill cranes. One year I helped with some peregrine falcon studies in the Grand Canyon and got to do some old-fashioned rappeling." She'd earned one of her eagle feathers there when she'd saved a peregrine chick from becoming a mountain lion snack.

"That experience will certainly help you on Trinity." She gave Tesa a long, appraising look. "I think you're going to do just fine with Taller's chick."

With that casual statement, Meg confirmed that Tesa was indeed going. There would be no formal tapping ceremony, but she didn't care—the thought of Trinity's untamed land filled her with a deep yearning.

"I checked on our transport," Meg signed. "We're leaving tomorrow."

Those words hit Tesa hard, and she felt her emotions go to war, thrill and regret all at once. *"Tomorrow?"*

Meg nodded. "You'll have time for that flying lesson, then you'll have to pack. We'll have two months on the ship . . ." The older woman looked drawn. "Two months to cram three years of research into you. I bargained, but we'll have to spend the last month in hibernation. It's the best I could do. We'll arrive about five days before the hatching."

"Meg," Tesa asked curiously, "why didn't you want to raise Taller's chick yourself?"

"A couple of reasons. For one, I'm too old."

Tesa looked shocked. It was the first time Meg had ever referred to her age as a restrictive handicap.

"Don't look like that, it's true. I love living outdoors, but these days I'm only good for a week on the ground and then it starts affecting my mobility.

"Besides, I raised my own kids a long time ago and found out I wasn't great parent material even then. Every time I go home and one of my 'darling' descendants calls me babushka, I want to slug the little beast. I've got most of them trained to call me by my first name, even though the in-laws disapprove." Her expression clearly said, "too bad about them," and Tesa had to laugh. Meg returned it good-naturedly.

"Scott used to tell people I was 'nobody's grandma,'" she continued. A shadow crossed her face at the mention of his name. "And, besides, the person who raises the chick should be more of a sibling than an elder."

Meg looked at the young woman solemnly. "I want to tell you how much I admire your willingness to postpone your ear surgery for this project. There aren't that many people who would make that kind of a sacrifice. I couldn't wait to get to Shassiszss. It's hard enough to have to wear sound nullifiers, but when I thought I'd lost my hearing forever . . ." Meg shook her head as she trailed off into her own thoughts.

Tesa kept her expression under control with an effort. She wished Meg hadn't brought that subject up.

"And your parents were so supportive when you explained why you wanted to delay the operation! They must be wonderful people. They'll be very proud of you, Tesa, and don't worry— the time will go by fast. Grus chicks are fully grown in six months, and by then he'll be flying. I'm confident that even before that we'll convince the board of the Grus' intelligence. Before a year's over, you'll be free to go. Just think, when you're hearing, we can have a *real* talk. I'll bet you have a lovely voice. Your laughter is almost musical.''

Tesa knew Meg would interpret the flushed look on her face for a modest blush when in fact she was fighting anger and frustration. Hearing people were always so smugly *convinced* that their language was better than hers, that speaking was superior to signing, that sound was critical to the enjoyment of life—that theirs was such a better way to live! Gritting her teeth, she forced a smile. Meg couldn't understand how she felt, any more than other hearing people could. *Tell them how you really feel,* prompted something inside her.

What for? she responded bitterly. It wouldn't do a damned bit of good.

''The transport will be leaving StarBridge Station tomorrow afternoon,'' Meg said, pulling Tesa's attention back. ''I hope that'll give you enough time to say good-bye to your friends.''

Say good-bye? Tesa thought inanely.

Meg patted her shoulder comfortingly. ''I know how hard it is to leave people you love.'' She brushed herself off, preparing to leave. She was small, and Tesa tried not to loom over her.

The Indian woman picked up the stilts, feeling overwhelmed. In twenty-four hours she'd be leaving StarBridge! She'd always hated good-byes. Wrenching her mind from the thought of saying farewell to so many people that she'd come to love, she quickly changed the subject. ''When the First Contact's completed, would it be possible for me to get involved in another project on Trinity, so I could stay two years instead of one?''

Meg looked thoughtful, then shrugged. ''Well, it's a big planet, there's a lot to learn.''

''I was thinking . . . with all my work with raptors . . . maybe, when there was time, I could study the Aquila, their . . .''

Meg's blue eyes suddenly blazed with fury, surprising Tesa so much she stumbled, slipping on the mud.

''Aquila!'' Meg's rapid mouth movements and the way her head moved told Tesa she'd spit the word out. ''Those filthy carrion-eaters! Tesa, you have to understand that those creatures are *taboo* on Trinity. The Grus don't even have a sign for them—they use the sign for death and move their heads as though they were throwing up a casting. Didn't Rob tell you about them? About what they *did*?''

"He said they were . . . predators . . . He said Trinity had *lots* of predators . . ." Tesa's signs trailed off.

Meg visibly tried to calm herself, but her anger was still so palpable, Tesa could feel it. "I shouldn't blame Rob . . . I've gotten so used to avoiding the subject, I don't think I ever told him." She took a deep breath.

"It was the Aquila that killed Water Dancer and his entire family, Tesa. They carried the Grus' future leader away like a chicken and *ate* him. They lifted him . . . so close to us, so close to Scott . . ." Meg trailed off, lost in bitter memories.

"The cameras filmed the whole thing. Later, I made myself watch it . . . I had to know. That *sukin sin* hauled Water Dancer up over the rise as if he knew that . . . Dancer would have to call out to his people, to warn them . . . he *had* to, even though he knew his call would hurt Scott . . ." Meg swallowed. "They were friends, Tesa. Good friends. Alien to each other, but still . . . Scott watched Water Dancer be carried off for lunch and Dancer watched his warning to his people kill his friend."

Tesa gaped at her, stunned.

"You must *never* bring the Aquila up! Don't even mention their name to the Grus. It's their worst taboo." Meg looked exhausted, as though all her youthful vitality had drained away. "Dancer couldn't help what he did. He would never have deliberately hurt Scott. As far as I'm concerned, the *Aquila* killed Scott Hedford." Turning abruptly, the older woman splashed out of the mock-up.

Tesa's mind reeled from Meg's revelation. Suddenly her mind's eye filled with the glint of sun on a bronze wingtip and the bluest sky she'd ever seen. And talons grasping a tanned skin with ragged holes across its back.

Late that night, Tesa still couldn't close her eyes. After finding out the bitter reality of the Aquila, she was afraid to sleep, afraid to dream. She'd almost called Rob, but what she really wanted was an elder, a shaman who could interpret dreams.

After tossing for hours, she'd felt the gentle touch of Doctor Blanket's telepathy, bidding her to come. Eager to talk to the Avernian, Tesa had left her room, wearing nothing but her oldest StarBridge nightshirt, its logo of a glittering rainbow bridge connecting two planets faded from too many cleanings. Using her quilt as a robe, she'd gone to the Avernian's dark quarters and, as she had many times in the past, draped the whisper-light alien on her shoulders like a cape. Protecting the Avernian with a Mizari light damper, since visible light could actually burn the alien's delicate cilia, Tesa went to the observation dome.

Doctor Blanket liked the dome and its panorama of brilliant stars. Tesa enjoyed it, too. StarBridge Academy was built on an asteroid in a part of space with no nearby sun. With nothing to hide their brilliance, the stars arched overhead in a stunning profusion of color. Blue, red, yellow—even mauve and indigo. In Tesa's loneliest moments, when she didn't think she could bear being away from Earth any longer, she'd come here to send her spirit through her eyes to dance among those colorful stars.

Tesa carried Doctor Blanket to the middle of the observation dome and sat on the floor, tailor fashion. The Avernian was featureless, about the size of a baby blanket, almost flat, and covered with short cilia on one side and small pseudopodlike appendages on the other. The being slid off her shoulders, as the cilia undulated like a miniature grainfield in a stiff breeze. Tesa sat in the darkness, with the alien's phosphorescent form opposite her, and stared up at the heavens, knowing the eyeless alien could "see" them through her eyes.

The first time Tesa had met Doctor Blanket, she'd been struck with the sense of the creature's incredible age. When she'd felt the being's telepathic touch, she'd discovered that this person had a depth of wisdom no human could plumb. She realized this was someone who could understand her spiritually as well as mentally. Tesa had come to love the Avernian, who seemed more like a spirit being than an alien.

Doctor Blanket was, in reality, an intelligent fungus, incredibly old, who, someday, would reproduce through spores. But no one who'd ever experienced the alien's gentle wisdom and humor could ever refer to the Avernian as an "it." Instead, everyone used the Mizari neuter pronoun "seloz."

Finally, Tesa opened the parfleche she'd brought and removed a small, red stone and a bundle of sweet grass. Placing the stone between them, she pulled a pinch of sweet grass from the bundle, crumbling it onto the stone. She used the parfleche as a screen, so the fire she needed to ignite the sweet grass would not harm the Avernian with its brightness. Slim curls of smoke wafted around them, climbing to the ceiling.

Speaking telepathically, Doctor Blanket told her how much seloz enjoyed the scent of the burning sweet grass.

"I do, too," Tesa signed in Plains Indian Sign Language. Doctor Blanket encouraged students to use their own languages when communicating with seloz. "There are so many memories in that smoke, so many ghosts . . ." She stopped. "You know I'm leaving."

The Blanket knew.

"It's so hard to say good-bye . . ."

Even with Doctor Blanket she avoided the subjects that had kept her tossing in bed—her confusion, her dreams. The dreams, especially, were a subject she feared to touch. If she discussed them, she might remember them.

Besides, she argued with herself, *how serious is a dream dreamt on this asteroid, that had to be towed to where it is, and can't even support life, left to its own devices?*

Doctor Blanket drew up on end and stood erect. The pearllike sheen of seloz' cilia reminded Tesa of the Grus' woven cloak.

<Human beings have such a love/hate relationship with their dreams.> The Blanket's thoughts tickled Tesa's mind with gentle amusement. She didn't experience seloz' thoughts as words, but as ideas—she thought of them as *feelings* directed to her.

<What you call "dreams" seem like fantastic mental inventions to me,> the Avernian "said," <a vivid literature of the mind full of smells, textures, colors. These dreams are like the "stories" my people invent for entertainment. Yet most humans either ignore their dreams or turn them into ominous warnings from the dark sides of their natures. Few humans ever see the beauty of their dreams or look on them as a visionary side of their minds.>

They'd talked of this on other nights, but then it had just been philosophy.

<I suppose it was my curiosity,> the Blanket continued, <my "dreams"—that caused me to be the first of my people to leave our homeworld. The others couldn't understand my interest in seeing new worlds, or communicating with different beings. No doubt they attributed my interest in adventure to my youth.>

The idea of Doctor Blanket being young startled Tesa so much she couldn't respond.

<Among my people I'm just a youngster, even though by

your standards I'm incredibly old,> the being replied, amused.

"Are you saying you have no answers for me?" Tesa asked.

<Your mind is in such turmoil, I wouldn't know where to begin. Tell me first why you are trying to change your own feelings about your hearing. That confuses me.>

Too weary to put into signs all her conflicting feelings, Tesa opened her mind. She thought of her choices and the bitterness she felt at having to make them at all. When she finally began to wind down, she felt emptied of anger and sorrow. But the terrible indecision was still there.

<Hearing is so valued among humans?> the Avernian asked.

"Maybe not *hearing* itself as much as the perception of being normal. I want to be Deaf, but that makes me feel *selfish*, as though I'm depriving my parents of the one thing they've always wanted. Or I feel scared—afraid I haven't got what it takes to function in the hearing world as a hearing person."

<I don't feel that in you,> the Avernian replied. <I sense only a reluctance to change something you are not unhappy with, and a desire for the people you love to understand that. There's nothing wrong with that, Tesa.>

"You make it sound so simple, Doctor Blanket." Tesa looked down, feeling heavyhearted.

<I thought the people of your culture prided themselves on their individuality?>

Tesa nodded. "But it's hard to maintain culture in an homogenized world. Even in the living museum we have the same media, the same obligations and opportunities as the rest of the world. In our most remote lands, you can't watch a sunset without seeing contrails overhead. Culture becomes something you save for vacation."

<You feel good about leaving for Trinity?>

She looked up at the flickering stars. "Yes, I want to go . . . but what if I screw up?"

<Tesa, this is not like you, this conflict and doubt. You're hiding something from yourself.>

She faced the Avernian squarely. "Doctor Blanket, it's my dreams. Even mentioning them makes me nervous. My people believe dreams carry messages . . . sometimes warnings. Dreams shouldn't be ignored. When they are, harm can come to the dreamer . . . or those close to her. We believe that spirits send their power to Earth through dreams, that the dreamer must use this power by acting out the dream.''

<And with power comes responsibility.>

Tesa nodded. ''Before every big event, I've always dreamt about eagles . . . but I could never remember enough of the dreams to find out what I was supposed to do. My grandfather told me that if the Wakinyan wanted something of me, he would let me know. But, whoever dreams of the Wakinyan . . .''

< . . . becomes a contrary, a sacred clown.>

The Blanket's thought was like a blast of cold air over an exposed nerve. Suddenly she saw clearly the old *heyoka* that came to summer camp. He was decrepit with age but as spry as a boy, since he had been touched by the Thunder Beings when he was young. Everywhere he went, he walked on his hands. In summer he wore furs, and in winter, everyone said, he sweated like a race horse and wore nothing but a breechclout. He was the finest rider in the camp—he had to be, since he always rode backward. He said no when he meant yes, bathed in dust to get clean, and jumped in water to dry off. Wherever he went, he made the people laugh and as her grandfather often told her, laughter was very sacred, very powerful. In the years when the people had suffered from disease, starvation, and persecution, the ability to laugh was sometimes all they had to keep them going. The *heyoka*'s medicine was always powerful.

But Tesa had never laughed at the old man. Instead, she always felt an ominous dread whenever he came near. Anyone could become a *heyoka* just by having the right dream. When Tesa was young and believed in magic, she was terrified that someday the Thunder Beings would touch her and turn her life upside down forever, as they had that sacred old man.

''No one *wants* to dream of the Thunder Beings,'' she signed.

<Tell me about the dream.>

Tesa looked at the Avernian for a long moment. ''I can't *remember*. I see a wingtip, as though I'm the Wakinyan looking over my own shoulder. I see the sky. I see lighting. And I feel afraid. Then, when I saw the Aquila . . .''

<Sometimes human beings experience feelings that they have been somewhere before . . . >

Tesa nodded. ''Déjà vu. I wish that's all it was. Everyone talks about the *heyoka*'s power, but no one wants to walk his path. Lately, I've *been* nothing but a contrary. People make me angry, and I act pleasant. I don't want to have ear surgery, but I say I'll have it done in a year. I see the Aquila and feel . . . no, I *know* that they are intelligent, when they are among the most hated, savage creatures on the whole planet. If that's not contrary, I don't know what is.''

<I could show you your dreams,> the alien offered. <If that is what you wish.>

Tesa had suspected that Doctor Blanket could release her subconscious memories, but it wasn't something she had actually expected seloz to offer. She shook her head. "You're the elder. I'm supposed to tell *you* the dream and you're supposed to interpret it for me. If these eagle dreams are significant, I should remember them myself.''

<Your troubled dreams are a warning that you're facing your life's path. Of course you're afraid to make the wrong move.>

Even before her scheduled tapping with the Ashu, Tesa had felt a vague apprehension, a sense of impending *something*. If she'd been at home she would've prayed for a vision.

She closed her eyes and thought of Trinity. There was the marshland, becoming savannah, then forest, and before she knew what had happened, she was seeing again the glint of sun on a bronze wingtip. Gliding beside her was another Aquila, its red eyes staring into her own. The image was so powerful, she could feel the rush of air against her arms/wings, against her face/beak. She opened her eyes to find she was standing, arms outstretched, poised as though performing the Eagle Dance. She looked at the Avernian, lowering her arms.

"Couldn't the Aquila be intelligent?" she asked. "If they are, couldn't they change, couldn't they stop killing the Grus?"

<Your answers lie on Trinity,> Doctor Blanket replied. <There, perhaps, you will even learn what to say to your parents.>

On Trinity, she could live the way a human was meant to live, with sky overhead, on land teeming with life.

<Trinity is full of *nagi*,> Doctor Blanket "said" cryptically.

In spite of the fact that her problems still loomed ahead unresolved, she felt better. Impulsively, Tesa snatched up the light form of Doctor Blanket and tried to hug seloz.

Undulating rapidly, the alien managed to convey that fierce hugging was not good for a being with seloz' anatomy. Apologizing, Tesa made it easy for the creature to again drape about her shoulders. Gently she touched her cheek to the waving cilia. *Good-bye, Doctor Blanket,* she thought. *And . . . thank you.*

It was almost time to board the shuttle that would take Tesa and Meg to StarBridge Station, where they'd board the S.V. transport *Norton.* Jib was double-checking her luggage.

He glanced at the pile. "What a mess of stuff!"

"That's all StarBridge issue," Tesa complained. "Stuff they think you can't live without. This is all I wanted to bring." She showed him her bow and arrows, a lariat, a piece of flint, the Clovis point she'd made herself, and a small hatchet.

"Yeah, but you're still missing something," Jib told her, then tossed her a small box.

Surprised, Tesa opened it. It was a Swiss Army knife.

Jib had one, a deluxe model. It had been his mother's, and was his pride and joy. Whenever anyone needed an obscure tool, Jib always seemed to have it on his knife.

Tesa had coveted that knife, that perfect all-tools-in-one. She looked at her friend, dumbfounded, and turned the knife over in her hands. On the other side, engraved in the red plastron, were the initials of Jib's mother.

Tesa looked shocked. "Jib, this is *yours*!"

He shrugged. "I couldn't let you go to this wild world without the right knife. I changed some of the tools." He eagerly unfolded the new items. "Here's a micro cell analyzer, and I'll bet you can't guess what this is!" He pulled out a short tubular thing with a telltale on the end.

She shook her head, still stunned.

"It's a bioscanner," Jib signed. "If someone comes within twelve meters of you, this light will flash. That's in *any* direction, land, sea, or air!"

"Jib," she signed, "I can't take your mother's knife . . ." She ran her fingers over its stiff leather case, decorated with curling, intricate Maori designs.

"You told me that you're supposed to give away the stuff that means the most to you," Jib protested.

Impulsively, Tesa reached into her inside jacket pocket, removing a piece of quill-worked leather. Smiling, she unwrapped her eagle feathers and handed one to him. It was his turn to look surprised.

"Tesa, you *can't* give me this. You *earned* it," he signed, half in delight, half in protest.

She gave him a quick kiss and a Maori nose-rub. "Soon you'll finish your courses and do your pair project, and before you know it, you'll be on another planet, working. Who knows, maybe you'll end up at Trinity with me. But you'll earn that feather. In the meantime it'll inspire you to great things. And when you look at it you'll think of me."

He held the white-tipped tail feather of a golden eagle respectfully. Its quill was wrapped in leather, decorated with beadwork. Leather thongs with large, colorful pony beads dangled from it. "Do you really think I need this to think of you?"

Tesa touched his hand that held the feather. "We'll write?"

He nodded, then they began loading the baggage onto a null-grav transport before they dissolved into a mess of blubbering good-byes. But, as Jib led the unit out the door on his way to the loading dock, Tesa turned back for a last look at their suite. Jib had turned the living room's holo to the Black Hills. There were two eagles flying there now. For once, the sight of them made her smile. Clutching her new knife, Tesa followed Jib out, closing the door behind her.

CHAPTER 4

◆

The *Singing Crane*

Margaritka Tretiak handed Tesa a cold glass of fruit juice. "Tesa," she signed in Grus, "wake up. Drink this."

"It's been barely an hour since we started the wake-up," Dr. Li Szu-yi reminded Meg. The health specialist of the *Singing Crane*, the Terran space station orbiting Trinity, was a plain, brown-skinned woman in her forties. Reed-thin, she had short, dark hair, almond eyes, and a cool businesslike manner. She peered into the young woman's eyes. "Besides, she probably doesn't know a thing about the missing voders."

Meg felt disoriented herself. An early arrival meant both women were still in hiber-sleep when the *Norton* had docked with the *Crane*.

"Neither of you have had enough time to get the hibernation drug out of your systems," the doctor continued. Meg noticed that Szu-yi never looked directly at Tesa when she spoke.

Tesa drank the juice down, holding the glass in both hands.

Meg wanted nothing more than to get off the station. The one-gee gravity made her feel old when she wanted to feel buoyant. What she wouldn't admit was that everything about the *Crane* reminded her of Scott. But before they could leave,

47

she had to find out what in hell had happened to their voders.

Tesa combed fingers through her hair, rearranging two feathers she'd tied there.

The crew were beginning to straggle in, stealing sideways glances at Meg, acting like strangers. She should've expected that. When she'd left she was in pain and grieving for Scott. She would have to reassure them that she was okay and, most important, that this young woman was just the person they needed.

"I've talked to Captain Stepp, Meg," Lauren Nichols said. The crew's primary computer tech and data analyst was round, Anglo, and thirty-five. Meg always thought of her as "pert," with tight, brown curls framing a pretty face. "The Captain's shipping invoice," Lauren continued, "ordered that container down-loaded onto the S.V. *Holly* during a regular cargo transfer at space station *Orion*, while you and Tesa were hibernating."

"That's ridiculous," Meg grumbled. "I logged the datacard onto the lading bill myself. What made them think those voders were supposed to be delivered to the *Holly*?"

"Ask 'em to give us a copy of the bill, will you, honey?" Bruce Carpenter's soft drawl startled Meg. What surprised her more was how much she'd missed him. He had loved Scott, too, even though they'd never agreed on anything. Lanky, of medium height, Bruce's thinning red hair seemed to have become sparser. She couldn't remember it being so gray, either.

He hugged her, kissing her forehead. "I really missed you, ol' girl," he whispered.

"Who the hell you calling old?" She laughed. "Lot more snow on *your* head than when I left."

Moving to a chair, Bruce sat with arms crossed, stretching his legs out. "If we had that bill," he said to Lauren, "we might be able to find the error."

The technician turned to the infirmary's comm unit.

Bruce, Lauren, Meg, and Scott had been the core of the colonizing team that had first discovered Trinity. The four of them had elected to stay when their company ship had left— Meg and Scott because they believed that the Grus were intelligent, and Bruce and Lauren in spite of their doubts. The four had always worked as a team, and after fifteen years of space-hopping they were practically family.

"Lauren, call Peter in here, please," Bruce requested. "Maybe he can get to the bottom of this."

"Right," Lauren answered, and turned back to the comm.

"Does she know anything about it?" Bruce asked in a low voice, indicating Tesa.

"I'll ask her," Meg said. She could see the young woman's confused expression. *Poor kid,* she thought, *I'd planned an organized briefing session, not this. She looks so lost.* Meg remembered suddenly that Tesa's birthday had passed while they were in deep-sleep. She was twenty now, and had left her teens while asleep with no one but a stranger to even think of it.

"Tesa," Meg signed in Grus, "we can't find those new Mizari voders. Is there any chance they're in your luggage?" It was a long shot, but Meg was desperate.

Meg could see Tesa thinking it through, fuzzily.

"Ask her again," the doctor said. "She didn't understand."

"She understands just fine, give her a chance," Meg answered curtly.

"The Mizari voders?" Tesa signed, finally. "They went in with our cargo. Did you check——"

Meg turned away from Tesa at the sound of a new voice. "I've got that lading data from Captain Stepp, Meg," a black man said from the doorway. "Want to give me your data-card so I can compare? By the way, it's sure good to have you home again."

Peter Woedrango, the *Crane*'s chief engineer, software specialist, and ecologist, gave Meg one of his expansive smiles as he took her card. The tall Senegalese man had his computer link in his ear and a pocket crowded with computer pens. He was good-looking, with a shaggy mane of hair and laughing eyes.

Tesa tapped Meg. "Can we go to Trinity now?"

Meg felt a stab of guilt. *This is terrible. I turned away while she was in the middle of a sentence. I haven't introduced her to a soul. This voder thing has me too rattled to think.*

"Captain Stepp," Meg signed, "can't leave till we know what happened to the voders, and you and I can't go planetside until this is solved."

Tesa nodded, glancing self-consciously at the strangers.

"She'll feel a lot better after dinner and a night's sleep," Dr. Li announced to the room.

"Szu-yi, please stop talking about Tesa in third person," Meg said quietly. The doctor pressed her lips together.

"Sleep!" Tesa signed abruptly. "I've been doing nothing but sleep for the past month! Can't we go? Please?"

Meg was surprised. "You understood her?"

Tesa smiled wryly. "How hard is it to understand a 'no-go' when you see one?"

"What was all that about?" Bruce asked, interested.

Before Meg could answer, Peter interrupted. "Meg, both your data-card and the lading bill tell Captain Stepp to transfer our voders to the *Holly*."

"Those things are halfway to Novaya Rossiya by now," said Lauren, ruefully. "Maybe your brother can send them back, Meg."

"How could that *happen*?" Meg demanded. "It's impossible!"

Peter shook his head. "You could've picked up an error while that card was accruing its approvals. Government cards are used over and over. After you transferred the data onto the lading bill, something happened, the data hiccuped or eroded somehow and old orders came through instead." He shook his head. "You know the government. Penny-wise, pound foolish."

"What are we supposed to do without those new voders?" Meg fumed. "It took *months* to get them."

"We'll contact StarBridge," Lauren assured her. "We'll get new ones, don't worry. I'll tell Captain Stepp she can go."

Meg wanted to scream.

Tesa tapped her lightly again, distracting her. "The voders are gone?" she asked.

"Yes," Meg signed, and explained what had happened.

Tesa frowned, then began rummaging around in her belt pouch.

"Forget the voders," Bruce suggested. "Let's start this meeting over. This young lady's gonna think she got dumped into a crowd of rude techno-types. Nobody's even said hello."

The gray-haired man stepped forward, holding out his hand. Tesa hesitated, then took it as he said softly, "How do you do, l'il darling? I'm Bruce Carpenter, resident meteorologist and xenoichthyologist. Hope you'll enjoy working with us."

"*Bruce*," Lauren complained, rolling her eyes. "She's *deaf*! How much of that do you expect her to understand?"

"I'll bet she's a champeen lip-reader," Bruce said. He gave the Indian woman a conspiratorial smile, which Tesa returned.

"Got a nice firm handshake, too. You're gonna be all right."

"I'd like to see anyone lip-read 'xenoichthyologist'! Honestly, Bruce!"

Tesa returned Bruce's greeting in Grus, but then her face clouded. "I said, 'Hello, good flight,'" she asked Meg, "should it have been, 'Hello, good fishing'?"

Meg nodded reassuringly as Bruce said, "Peter, come greet our new partner."

The tall black man stuck out his hand, smiling. "HOW ARE YOU, TESA?" Peter shouted.

Embarrassed for him, Meg had a vivid memory of the hospital on Shassiszss and the human attendant who kept hollering at her, though she could hear nothing. Bruce murmured to the programmer.

Peter lowered his voice, but still overenunciated every syllable. "I am Pe-ter Woe-drang-o. How are you?"

Tesa turned to Meg. "Please, tell them I've studied with you, that I sign Grus well. I'd rather they sign than speak."

Meg realized with a start how little she'd told Tesa about the crew. She'd been so busy briefing her on the project, the Grus, the planet, she'd hardly mentioned the crew. *Tell the truth, Margaritka. It made you think of Scott, so you avoided the subject.* Meg hesitated before admitting, "They don't know how to sign Grus . . . Rob told me that you read lips, and that you spoke English and Mizari. We all know English."

Peter asked Meg, "Can she read lips?"

"I read that even expert lip-readers can understand only twenty percent of what's said," Lauren told him, pushing back a stray curl. "You guys are just confusing her. You might as well give up." Bruce gave her an offhanded glance.

The doctor shook her head. "Meg, what were you thinking of? This place won't be ready for a StarBridge student for ten years! *If* then. We don't have time to baby-sit."

Meg started to respond hotly but Tesa began signing. "I'm not comfortable speaking. After all the time they've been here, I thought they'd *all* sign Grus."

"What'd she say?" Bruce asked.

Meg translated and the crew glanced uneasily at one another, except for Bruce. "Looks like you caught us on that one," he said, his brown, friendly eyes never leaving Tesa's face.

"Learn *Grus*?" the doctor snorted, glancing at Lauren. "That's what voders are for." Lauren nodded quick agreement.

"Tesa," Meg said, signing at the same time, "they can get their Terran voders, or I can translate."

The younger woman was clearly unhappy. "Can't we just go to Trinity?" she signed. Meg translated her signs to the crew. "It's been *years* since I've seen woods, or running water, or clouds. And I want to see the Grus. *Please*."

"Ms. Sacajawea's in quite a rush, isn't she?" Lauren said cynically. "Wonder how she'll feel when she's plastered with mud and feather dander and reeks of fish. Those Grus won't seem so glamorous then, I'll bet."

"Lauren!" Bruce snapped. "Be quiet!"

"Oh, Meg," Dr. Li said quickly, "don't translate that!"

"Why should I be quiet?" Lauren asked Bruce, her fair cheeks flushing at his reprimand. "She's not a telepath!"

Tesa's face clouded with sudden anger. Meg felt confused, unsure of what was happening, as Tesa stood tall and approached the short technician, showing her something cupped in her hand. Lauren blushed furiously. Then Tesa showed it to the others.

It was a Mizari voder, the one Tesa had had on StarBridge. She'd stopped using it early in the voyage when she'd developed a good base in Grus vocabulary. Meg had totally forgotten that she'd had it. It must have been in her pouch. Meg remembered how effective the "save and recall" feature was.

Tesa was showing everyone the "Sacajawea" speech, preserved for posterity. Lauren squirmed uncomfortably.

"Do you know who this was?" Tesa signed to the computer tech. She indicated Sacajawea's name, trusting Meg to translate.

Lauren shook her head.

"She was a Shoshone," Bruce said. "She helped guide the Lewis and Clark Exploration in the 1800s. She was their translator, right?"

Tesa read his words, nodding. "Yes, but because she was, herself, one of the *people*, she was more than a translator. She was an *interrelator*." The Grus signs Tesa used actually meant "the one who teaches us to fish together"—an elegant choice, Meg thought. "Did you know that 'Sacajawea' means 'bird woman'?"

"I didn't know that," Bruce admitted.

"But later," Tesa continued, "she was called 'the woman who brought barbarians to our country.'" She turned back to

Lauren. "Let's shake hands, before mine smell like fish, and be friends. I'm Tesa." She held out her hand to the tech, giving her a tight smile. Lauren took the proffered hand gingerly.

"Be a sport, Lauren, she caught you fair," Peter said.

Tesa gave Bruce a warmer smile, "You'd be surprised at what a 'champion' lip-reader can pick up." Tesa turned to the doctor, "I'm *deaf*. I'm not a baby, and I'm not stupid. I won't fill the void Scott Hedford left behind, but I'll work hard."

Dr. Li looked at Tesa with that tight, enigmatic expression that exasperated Meg so much.

Meg examined Tesa's voder. "You don't know how happy I am to see that thing."

Just then, Dr. Li said in a low tone, "Meg, you should take this young woman planetside before . . . her enthusiasm for landfall gives us cabin fever. Besides, you don't want to miss sunset your first day back."

Tesa grabbed Meg in a hug, nearly knocking her over.

"We'll bring the new equipment tomorrow, Meg," Peter said.

"I'll call up a flight pattern," Lauren offered.

"I'd better go check the weather," Bruce said. He waved at Tesa and got a smile in return. "See you tomorrow."

Meg and Tesa moved to leave the infirmary. As they passed Lauren, the tech smiled and said plainly, "Have fun, Tesa."

"Our stuff's in the hall," Meg signed to her companion. "You'll meet Thom planetside." She watched as Tesa sorted through unloaded equipment for her belongings. *Hope that meeting goes better than this one did!* Meg thought.

Thom Albaugh watched the shuttle, the *Patuxent*, soft-land silently on the hillock's small pad. He touched the sound nullifiers nestled in his ears. They neutralized all noise on Trinity, en the landing of a space shuttle. *Well, Meg,* he thought, *you still pilot better than anyone except . . . Scott.*

Thom had just talked with the *Crane*, and Bruce had given him an earful about their new "interrelator." The weatherman had sounded totally smitten with the new crew member and had even made some remark regarding Thom's height, or lack of it. At five feet six, as they still measured it in rural Wisconsin, Thom was a bit shorter than Bruce. With blond, curly hair, a trim, dark beard, and blue eyes surrounded by laugh lines, Thom thought of himself as a man who was comfortable in his surroundings, wherever they might be. He supposed that an attractive young woman could have a powerful effect on an older man like Bruce, but at twenty-eight, Thom didn't expect to be easily impressed.

As he reached the pad, the *Patuxent*'s door unsealed. A stiff breeze blew up as Meg emerged. Thom was pleased by her appearance—she looked good, even vibrant, but that was Trinity, Thom knew. She loved this place as much as if she'd been born here. And, of course, the last time he'd seen her . . .

He frowned, remembering that he'd have to brief Meg on everything that had occurred while she was gone. There'd been increased Aquila attacks on the far western flocks. *But the bad news can wait,* he decided.

Meg grinned at him, then turned back to the interior of the ship. Reaching in, she gave a hand to the hidden occupant, steadying her as she adjusted to the change in gravity.

The new crew member emerged . . . and kept on emerging. Thom was startled to realize how tall she was.

A vagrant breeze blew her dark, wavy hair around her face; she brushed it away, inhaled a lungful of air, and looked around. "I *do* feel buoyant!" she signed to Meg. Thom was surprised at her ease with the language. He'd been struggling with it for two years, and while he could readily interpret what was said to him, he always felt like a klutz while signing.

Then the newcomer's eyes met his, and suddenly Thom understood Bruce's teasing. She smiled shyly, and he realized that he'd been caught gaping like an adolescent.

"This is our other biologist, Thom," Meg signed to the young woman. "The Grus call him . . ." She made a name-sign that meant "relaxed," and Tesa laughed. Meg turned to Thom. "This is Tesa, from StarBridge."

He signed a greeting in Grus, but it came out, "The fish are happy to see you," and they all laughed. "I always did ha~ a problem with greeting signs. Did Meg show you *her* ~me-sign?"

Tesa shook her head, while Meg made a rude ~ce.

"She's called, 'First-One-There'—'Speedy' for short." He fended off a glancing blow that turned into a warm hug. "I got a call when you left. They told me about the voders."

"I'll bet they did," Meg signed.

"And," Thom continued, "I heard our new partner wants to see the sunset." He suddenly felt a stab of embarrassment.

Tesa was deaf, and he'd signed the word "heard." Would she be insulted?

Tesa noticed his abrupt change of expression. "What's the matter? Did I do something wrong?"

His hands fumbled. "I thought maybe, when I signed 'heard,' I offended you."

Tesa rolled her eyes. "Oh, that. Don't be silly, that's just an expression. I'm not sensitive about my deafness."

"Oh, good. I, uh . . ." He trailed off awkwardly, feeling foolish again. *You've been in the wilderness too damn long,* he thought wryly, *if seeing a strange woman does this to you!*

"Tesa's deafness won't be forever, either," Meg was signing. "Once the First Contact's confirmed, she can have that problem corrected." Meg was looking at Tesa warmly, but the younger woman had turned her attention to the scenery again.

"Well," Thom interjected, pulling her line-of-sight back "I hope you'll be patient. I've never known a deaf person before."

Tesa gave him a knowing glance. "But I thought we were all deaf on Trinity. Meg turned her ears off the moment we landed."

He looked confused, until the older woman showed him the gold orbs on her earlobes.

"My controls," she told him. "They're a lot more reliable than the nullificrs." Meg seemed so much like her old self that Thom felt an immense sense of relief, remembering the way she'd been after Scott's death.

"Well, if we stand around here much longer," Thom signed, "we'll miss sunset." Crooking his arms gallantly for the two women, he led them to the hillock's steep edge.

The hillock was a high, dry land mass, thick with a rust-colored ground cover, shrubs, and a scattering of trees. Behind them to the west was an old-growth forest, the giant trees forming a hazy mass on the horizon.

The marsh stretched clear to the horizon. Brilliant blue sky and white, fleecy clouds were reflected in the stretches of open water. Everywhere it seemed the peak of autumn, with trees in riotous displays of reds, oranges, yellows, and soft browns, making the occasional splash of green startling. Mosses in soft blues and lavenders cushioned their every step.

Meg sat where she and Scott used to, near the edge. Seeing

her love for this place reflected in her eyes, Thom knew she had buried as many ghosts as she could.

He gestured for Tesa to sit between them. Pulling her long legs up to her chest, she gaped at everything, trying to drink it all in with her eyes.

Above the eastern horizon hovered the three celestial bodies the people of Trinity called the Sun Family. The day of Scott's death, they'd been in a tight triangle, an unusual configuration. Since the gas giant planet and the red dwarf sun were at the farthest reaches of this solar system, changes were gradual. While the triangle had been steadily drifting apart, it could still be seen. The sky had already begun to color, and red-gold reeds nodded their heavy heads in the breeze.

Tesa turned to Thom, and he felt himself blush as though she'd caught him at something. He reddened easily, a trait he'd damned his father's genes for on many occasions.

"These sunsets are different from Earth's," he signed to her inanely, feeling embarrassed, "but just as beautiful."

"More so," Meg signed. "No contrails."

That seemed especially to please Tesa. "When I was little," Tesa signed, "I'd watch sunsets with my grandparents. When the stars came out, they'd show me which little light represented my parents' latest work station. They'd sign, 'Tell Mom and Dad you love them.' And I'd sign with my little fingers, convinced my parents were watching me from the stars." She held up her hand in a sign he'd never seen—the thumb, index, and pinky finger extended, the middle and ring fingers folded against the palm.

The colors shifted as the red dwarf—the "Child" star to the Grus—dipped lower. It would be the first to disappear. Bands of scarlet ran across the horizon.

"Last time I was on Earth," Thom signed, "I couldn't even *see* the sunset. I was in New York."

"What does a biologist do in New York?" Tesa asked.

"Surveys songbirds in Central Park," he answered.

"On Shassiszss," Meg told them, "they're more interested in the night sky. I missed this terribly."

Oranges overlaid red.

"Once, when I was eight," Tesa signed, "my dad and I were watching a beautiful sunset, and I asked, 'What kind of sound does the sunset make?' He gave me a funny look. 'It's too beautiful to make noise,' he signed. 'Sunsets are silent.'

That made me so happy! I feel the same way right now.''

Thom realized he and Meg were both giving Tesa that "funny look." In fact, Meg's eyes were a little glittery, he thought.

"Sorry," Tesa apologized, "the hiber drug makes me ramble."

Meg patted her and smiled, then suddenly gripped her arm, pointing. Thom peered, straining to see what she was showing Tesa. He finally saw them, a flock of high-flying birds coming in from the east. They were too far away to see clearly, just a ragged vee formation and wings beating steadily in that distinctive two-beat pattern. It was the Grus.

CHAPTER 5

◆

The Grus

They moved fast, on huge, outstretched wings, long, black wing-fingers spread to aid their maneuvers. After circling the waterway, they pointed their dark legs downward, backwinging slow and easy, parachuting, barely disturbing the water as they landed. In a world of color, their simple black and white feathers and red crowns were striking. When the last one touched down, the flock lifted their heads to the suns and called.

Vibrations ran through Thom's body. He glanced at Tesa and felt inordinately pleased at her wide-eyed amazement.

When their calling ritual was over, Thom cupped his hands and shouted. When the Grus turned and saw Meg waving at them they began flapping and jumping exuberantly, many breaking into dance. Then the flock stretched their wings and ran forward, taking to the air, heading for the hillock.

As the humans backed away from the cliff edge, Thom made a sign over her heart, to show them it was beating wildly. For a moment, it seemed as if the avians might land on the humans; they were buffeted by the wind from those great wings. Then the avians alighted, shuffling and shoving one another to find a good location near Meg, surrounding the humans in a forest of legs, necks, and wings. The Grus' trim, oblong bodies were level with Tesa's shoulders. When they stretched their necks they towered over her. Tesa stared up at them in awe.

Meg became lost in a cloud of black and white feathers, as her Grus friends enveloped her under their wings in a special greeting, reserved for family. When Thom caught a glimpse of Meg's face, he could see it was streaked with happy tears.

He noticed, too, a scattering of birds that stood outside the group, observing everything warily, remaining uninvolved. There'd been a lot of that lately, and it made Thom uneasy.

Tesa pulled at Thom's sleeve as the chaos began to subside. "Is that Taller?" she asked.

Thom glanced at the great bird conversing with Meg, then nodded, startled. "Yes, it is." It'd taken him months to learn to tell one of the avians from another.

Just then, Taller moved gracefully away from the crowd and approached Thom and Tesa. Thom moved to make introductions.

"This is Taller," he signed, formally, "the tallest Grus in this territory." This was the closest the Grus came to a title.

Suddenly the avian pulled himself up until he was standing nearly on tiptoe, his neck rigidly straight, towering over his flock, fixing them with a cold glare. They respectfully lowered their heads, even those who were still hanging back.

For the Grus, height was an important factor in social status, and these days, Taller needed every little help in clinging to his precarious leadership.

"And this," the avian signed, "is the human who will fulfill the plans of my son, Water Dancer, and our human friend, Puff."

Thom saw Tesa's quizzical expression and knew he'd have to explain Scott's name-sign later. Taller had given it to him because Scott's bushy moustache always puffed out when he spoke. The name-sign imitated this with the fingers mimicking the dangling moustache as it blew with the force of Scott's breath.

Slowly the avian approached Tesa, never lowering his height as he circled her slowly, walking stiffly. Tesa was trying hard to hide how rattled she was by his examination. Finally the avian stopped, staring pointedly at her face, his deadly black bill inches from her nose. Thom admired the woman's nerve. She barely flinched, then gazed back unblinking.

Thom had trouble enduring "the look" as the Grus called it, a test that, they believed, would reveal the lies hiding in the back of a dishonest person's eyes. Thom, ever the biologist, had tried to still his nerves by memorizing the unique bill that could pluck out his eye like an hors d'oeuvre, the perfectly round golden eyes, and the black hairlike feathers that sparsely covered the red crown up to where the gleaming white began. It hadn't helped—he would invariably avert his eyes.

Taller continued to peer down his bill, making him seem almost cross-eyed. Then, as familiarly as any Terran bird, he cocked his head to look at Tesa first with one eye, then the other. It was a comical gesture, and for a second, Thom thought Tesa might burst into giggles, but she controlled herself.

"She has good eye color," Taller signed. "Is she named?"

The question was phrased as if Meg and Thom were Tesa's parents. Names were significant, since they were "earned."

Before Meg or Thom could answer, Tesa began signing. "In my homeland, I'm called 'White Spirit Animal.' This name has special meaning for my people."

There was an explosion of activity. With a great flap, Taller leaped into the air, landed with a bounce, then bowed. Several others imitated him, some twirling in the air.

Tesa looked stunned.

"You have a *real* name!" Taller signed when he settled down. "You are the first of your people that has come here with a *real* name. Well, welcome to the World, White Spirit Animal. The White Wind people greet you."

Tesa looked up into Taller's golden eyes. *Damn,* Thom thought, *she's shaking all over. She's in love,* he realized, and was surprised to feel a stirring of jealousy. *She's fallen in love with these big birds just like Scott did.*

"The name given you in your homeland will always be your name there," Taller signed. "But, to make the World your new home, the White Wind people will give you one of our names, as though you had been hatched here." He peered at her. "*Good eyes.* That's what we will call you. Good Eyes."

Then the huge white avian walked away, parting the flock. Stretching his wings and taking long strides, he sailed easily off the cliff edge. The others paraded up to Tesa, one at a time, scrutinized her momentarily, then followed Taller.

Forgetting Thom and Meg, Tesa ran to the cliff edge. Thom

started after her, irrationally worried that she might leap off the edge with them, when Meg snagged his arm.

"And where are you going, Romeo?" she demanded.

He blushed furiously, hating his fair skin.

"You're very young, Thom," she signed, her expression kindly. "Too young, I felt, for this job when you first came here. But you're a good worker, and you believed in Scott. You earned my respect a long time ago." She hesitated, then continued, "I know you've been alone here for months . . . I know you don't fit in well with the *Crane* crew."

Thom sighed. It was just like Meg to talk around unpleasantness. Lauren had become infatuated with him as soon as he'd arrived. But Thom had just endured a bitter divorce and wanted only to bury himself in *his* work, too.

At first he'd accepted Lauren's attentions, but it'd been a mistake. He wasn't ready for any kind of relationship, even the most casual. He'd wound up hurting Lauren with an abrupt rebuff. Thom knew he could've handled the situation more tactfully, as Bruce, Lauren's resident big brother, had been quick to point out. As anguished as Thom had been by Scott's death, it had been a relief to spend all his time on Trinity and not have to face Lauren's cold anger, which only reminded him of his ex-wife.

Was it only yesterday that he'd gotten the news that Jane had remarried? Glancing at Tesa, Thom realized that his sudden interest in the newcomer might be his psyche's way of telling him that he'd finally healed.

"I didn't bring Tesa here," Meg continued, "to fall in love with *you*. She has to fall in love with *them*"—the older woman indicated the Grus—"and she has. Don't interfere."

Tesa was crouched at the edge of the cliff, watching the avians spiral down into the marsh. After landing, they'd separated, some pairs disappearing into nest shelters, or mates relieving their partners from egg incubation duties so they could feed. Younger birds would form small groups and, in secluded areas in the reeds, sleep, balanced one-legged, in the open water. Tesa's body slumped as though she felt empty now that her "first contact" was over.

The tiny "Child Sun" had disappeared, and the large "Father Sun," the solar system's yellow star, was half hidden by the horizon. It seemed huge, red, wavering in the thick atmosphere. The "Mother Sun," the bright gas giant, still hovered in the sky, now rampant with color.

Thom turned to Meg. "You're right. It's just . . . she's got a lot of presence, wouldn't you say?"

"I'd say."

"Meg," Thom signed, "we've got to talk, and Tesa's not paying much attention to us—let's head for the shelter. We'll come get her when supper's ready."

The older woman nodded, and the two walked toward the shelter. Thom tried to decide what to tell her first, what was most important. He'd have to warn her of the Grus' feelings about Taller's decision to take Tesa into his family. Even the leader's most loyal followers thought it was a mistake. There were three suns. There were three moons. There were three members of the Grus family—father, mother, and child. Some of the less loyal flock members blamed the attack that killed Scott and Water Dancer on their plans. How else, they said, could such a disaster strike on a day that historically omened good luck?

Tesa sat at the cliff edge, relieved to be alone. She felt weak from hunger. She hadn't eaten anything since before hibernation, and that, combined with side effects from the hiber drugs, made her feel as if she were on a spirit fast.

Only the Mother Sun still twinkled above the horizon and the sky was turning violet. She took a deep breath, as though the air, with its smells of earth, grass, and water, could wed her to this world . . . and make it hers.

She wanted to belong here, to become part of this beautiful, wild place. Glancing back toward the large Quonset-hut shelter, painted in a camouflage pattern in Trinity's autumn shades, Tesa watched as Meg and Thom went inside.

She pulled the two eagle feathers from her hair. How long had it been since she'd danced? When she lived at home, it had been like *breathing* to her, an integral part of her life.

Tesa had earned her feathers by acts of bravery. Reaching into her pocket, she pulled out the leather wrapping that protected the red stone pipe, the *canunpa*, her grandfather had carved for her. Then she held the feathers and pipe in her open palms and stretched her arms out before her. Turning to the four directions, she offered a prayer to the Wakan Tanka, the Great Spirit, of this world.

"I come with clean hands and an open heart," she signed.

All living places have what the Dakota call *wakanda*, the Iroquois *orenda*, the Athabascan *coen*—the living *power* that pervades a place. For Tesa that had been missing on StarBridge, a lifeless chunk of shattered planet spinning in vacuum. But Trinity was full of life, full of *nagi* as Doctor Blanket had said.

Then, putting the pipe back in her pocket, she took a feather in each hand, stretched her arms like wings, and feeling the drumbeat in her heart, the drumbeat that was the beating heart of this new world, Tesa began to dance the Eagle Dance.

She watched her shadow imitating the great soaring birds of Earth. Her feet and legs took up the rhythm as she turned in circles, moving naturally, compensating for the low gravity with an easy grace she only felt when dancing. And as she moved, she found herself envisioning the bronze wingtip against blue sky. Closing her eyes, she opened herself to the image and followed the dream-bird, heedless of the proximity of the cliff edge. Behind her eyelids she could see the vision that had haunted her hibernation. A lone, soaring bird, looking for . . . what?

Shuddering, she opened her eyes to see a shadow of wings on the ground, crisscrossing her own. Startled enough to think she might be having a true vision, Tesa continued to dance, turning, spinning, watching the new shadow. It was the vision she'd always feared, the vision that would turn her into a *heyoka*, something she didn't want to be.

The winged shadow grew larger, darker, turning circles in time with her silent drum. Tesa tried to regain her calm. Finally, she stopped and looked up, her heart fearful but open to the Eagle Spirit, her palms sticky with sweat. But the shadow wasn't a spirit . . . it was an Aquila.

An *Aquila*! Her mind and her heart went to war. She glanced at the marsh, wondering if the Grus would notice the great predator and erupt in a chorus of warning calls. But she felt no thrilling vibrations and decided the Aquila must not have violated her "boundaries." This single hunter might have been winging westward after ranging in the eastern savannahs.

Was there any way to communicate with it? Had anyone ever tried? Or was it just viewing *her* as nothing more than a potential meal? It was foolish, but she didn't feel frightened now. The Aquila was magnificent!

Scott's notes had warned Tesa that the Aquila was every bit

as big as the long-extinct Teratornis of Earth. The larger female's wingspan spread to sixteen feet, a foot longer than the Grus'. Her body, stretched tall, was about four feet high. The massive bird spiraled down as Tesa stared, riveted. As she watched the Aquila, the bird also watched her. Clutching her prayer feathers, she met the bird's gaze.

The huge avian alighted on an old, dead tree that clung to the edge of the cliff. Tesa could see the ruby-red eyes clearly. A female, then. The males were smaller and had golden eyes.

Meg had given Tesa Scott's notes on the voyage, and the young woman quickly realized that the older biologist had no idea how much work her partner had done on Aquila behavior. Scott wrote that he had wanted to do more, to even try contacting the elusive predators, but the Grus' long-standing enmity with the creatures had made that impossible. Dutifully, Tesa had gone through everything about the Grus, only stealing a few moments here and there to read about the Aquila. She'd never told Meg about the material, and kept those files separate.

As she met the Aquila's red-eyed gaze, Tesa wondered, *What would you do, Scott?* Then, slowly, she walked toward the tree.

Clamping onto the leafless treetop with strong talons, the raptor made a great display of flapping her wings, as though she would pull the old tree out of the ground. She opened her wickedly hooked beak—screaming her own calls, no doubt.

Tesa stopped ten paces from the trunk. As Taller had, the Aquila peered at her with one brilliant red eye, then the other.

Then, without warning, she flattened her feathers and launched herself up, gaining altitude quickly. Tesa looked back at the tree, watching it sway as if that could reassure her the Aquila had actually been there. As her gaze traveled down the trunk, something glistened on a low limb.

She scrambled a few feet up the trunk, reached for the shiny thing, and snagged it. It was a feather from the Aquila, colored gold speckled with bronze. Clutching it, Tesa jumped down, then spun wildly, narrowly missing the edge of the cliff.

Scrambling backward and grinning, she looked to the horizon. The Mother Sun had disappeared, and the twilight was darkening. Opening her palms, Tesa displayed her three prayer feathers, thanking the Great Spirit for this gift—this *sign*—on her first day in this new world.

Then she took the three feathers, and wrapped them in the protective leather, and slipped them into her pocket. A touch on her shoulder startled her.

"Was that an Aquila?" Meg asked, pointing toward the distant speck that was the avian. Her face was drawn, somber, totally unlike the happy person who had helped her off the shuttle. Before Tesa could answer, the older woman shaded her eyes, peering. Tesa felt her exuberance waning.

"Thom says lone ones have been doing flyovers. I'll never feel comfortable if even one of them is around."

The biologist looked at Tesa. "Thom says that last week a group of Aquila attacked a flock of Grus in the west, much closer to this territory than they usually come. They caught the Grus just before they would've returned home. It seemed *calculated*. That's the time of day when the Grus are heavy from food and a little off their guard. They carried off *four* young birds."

Tesa looked stricken, the hidden Aquila feather suddenly becoming a heavy weight in its secret place.

Meg forced a smile. "I'm sorry, I shouldn't overreact. Come on, supper's ready and Thom hates his food to get cold."

As they drew close to the shelter Thom met them, handing Meg and Tesa each a large, red fruit. With a bow, he signed, "This is a class restaurant, mesdames. Your appetizer."

Tesa smiled her thanks and bit into sweet, tart flesh and realized this was the source of the delicious "orange juice" Meg had given her on board the *Crane*. The intense flavor flooded her mouth, making her ravenous.

Thom's cheerful expression faded as Meg pointed out the speck in the sky that might be an Aquila.

"Maybe I'm being paranoid," Meg signed. "I didn't get a good look at it. Tesa was watching it before I got there."

Thom looked at her. "Was it an Aquila?"

The younger woman hesitated. She thought about Taller. How would she feel if anything happened to him? In her mind's eye, Dr. Rob was saying something about taming the Wakinyan. The shadow of a bronze wing crossed behind her eyelids. Everything was all jumbled up, doing battle in her head with the last remnants of hibernation drug. She touched the pocket that held the prayer feathers and the pipe.

How could anyone get into such a complicated situation after being here less than an hour? She remembered the Thunderbird's exclamation, *What a backward-forward way to be.*

"No," she signed, gazing at Thom. "I'm sure it wasn't."

CHAPTER 6

♦

The Taboo

Taller stood in the human beings' shelter, wondering if he'd made a mistake. Just this morning he'd looked at the calendar cloak and realized it had been three fruiting seasons since the Year the Humans Came. Three seasons, and he'd never stepped inside their shelter. It felt wrong to be inside such an alien thing, but then, the humans were alien, and he'd befriended them. If he'd made a mistake, he'd done it long ago.

He gazed about at the cluttered, other-Worldly place. Relaxed had said they'd named it after Puff and had pointed to a slab of wood attached to the entrance. Relaxed had said Puff's *real* name was on it, that this building was now THE SCOTT BEDFORD MEMORIAL SHELTER. The wood was beautiful, yet the lines burned into it showed no awareness of the wood's own pattern. The humans either had no aesthetic sense or the worst eyesight of any diurnal creature Taller had ever communicated with.

Then Relaxed had said this building would last forever and always bring honor to Puff. Taller comforted himself that the wood was of the World and would age and crumble. The time it took to decay would mark the days of his grief for his friend. He would *not* mark his grief by the aging of a shelter that would last forever. He didn't think Puff would want him to do that.

These painful memories only reminded him of Water Dancer and his family. The hatching cloaks of Dancer, his mate Rain, and the unhatched chick now hung outside Taller's nest shelter, marking the days of grief. Rain's cloak and the chick's were already unraveling, but Dancer's cloak with its complex patterns of old legends had been woven by Taller's mate, Weaver, who had earned her name through her skill. His son's cloak would last, but not forever. Not even mountains lasted forever.

Taller swallowed a hard lump of grief. The dark wings of Death had never before flown as they had that terrible day, not in all the seasons of Taller's life. When he was young, it was only the foolish chick of foolish parents that had ever been caught by the hunters—but things were different now.

Taller gazed out the windows at the slanting rays of polarized light that led him to the Sun Family and asked as he had every day since his son's death—*Why does Death take us as though we were nothing more than simple water dwellers?*—but he had stopped getting answers to his prayers long ago.

Once you lost the Sun Family's favor, your people's loyalty would be next. He'd seen their signs. Since Dancer's death, the worst of it was he could no longer deny it in his heart.

Things had changed when the humans came. Some blamed everything on that. *They disturbed the atmosphere and changed the weather, they upset the Moon Family and changed the tides, they angered the Sun Family and changed the sunsets.*

Taller had seen more than seventy seasons of weather, tides, and sunsets, and knew that was nonsense. Except for Death. That he could not deny. How was it the humans had come just as Death decided the White Wind people were easier prey than a spawning?

Some days, Taller wondered if he hadn't lived too long.

Fluffing his feathers, he pulled his crown up tight, dimming its color, and moved on through the shelter.

The floor's unnatural surface was slick; his sharp claws rattled uselessly against it. He was plagued by an itch between his right eye and his bill, but he didn't dare lift a foot to scratch it, for fear his other would slide out from under him. He blinked his third eyelid. He was looking for Good Eyes.

Taller snaked his head around some obstacles—"furniture" Puff named them. He could hear the sound of a muffled waterfall. He listened. Something—or someone—was moving in the water. That would have to be Good Eyes. Relaxed and First-One-There were outside, supervising the food collection.

He moved closer to the water sounds. Could the humans make a waterfall *in* their building? Well, they could fly without wings in a *ship* that could travel so high that one night Taller had watched it become a star.

Puff said the ship took them to a *bigger* building where humans could live even though there was no air outside it. The day Puff told him that, Taller knew he'd done the right thing in befriending these aliens. There would be no way to drive people like this away, people who set up house next door to the Moon Family. To survive, the White Wind people would have to learn to live with them and whatever changes they would bring.

But a waterfall in a building? *That* would be something to see. And if Good Eyes were there, he could talk to her at the same time. Though why the humans need a waterfall in here when all the water of the World was just outside, he could not guess.

This area was crowded, and he walked cautiously around the things the humans collected from the World. Taller sometimes helped them collect objects, but he never understood why they wanted them. Maybe they were like the rousettes, always hoarding things they couldn't eat, and not knowing why.

Here was a row of beautiful stones, there a mound of bright leaves. The humans "preserved" them so they would always look alive, even though they had died. Puff had explained that. On the World, everything had to be "preserved" to ward off famine. It broke Taller's heart to watch the human beings eat "preserved" food, some of it years old, so he had showed them the fresh food his World offered, and watched them grow healthy on it.

Taller turned, nearly upending a pair of blue antlers, shed by a Leaf-Eater. Next to that was a row of bleached skulls—a Leaf-Eater's, a Digger's, and a Tree Ripper's. The humans must need to consume bone-building minerals, Taller thought, or perhaps they needed to gnaw and file back their teeth. People with teeth had different requirements than his own who had the superior edge with their bills. Teeth, after all, fell out.

He'd finally located the source of the water sounds and was trying to remember how to open the "door" when something behind him, something lovely, caught his rear vision, making him forget about the waterfall. Taller focused one eye on it.

Under a row of windows was a platform, its soft surface held up on stilts, and lying on it was something beautiful. It was a "blanket." He'd seen many blankets, but never any like this.

It was rich with all the colors of the World, with an intricate, sharp-angled design set against a white background. The weave was similar to other blankets, but this was not woven in one piece. No, this was many little pieces all put together to make a pattern that contrasted shades of orange, reds, and yellows. Taller eased slowly onto his hocks to examine it, to relish the play of light and color, to enjoy its artistry.

Of all the things Puff had shown him, nothing touched the great bird as did this beautiful blanket. His heart raced.

Oh, there were the wind chimes, and Puff had explained how they made them, but that was craft, turning sand into stone, even as lovely a stone as crystal glass. This was different. This was the ability to turn color and shape into something that transcended color and shape. His eyes devoured the beauty of the old star quilt. He was so distracted that he never heard the water stop or noticed Good Eyes emerging from a room behind him.

Finally, the Sun Family had sent a sign. Had he done the right thing in befriending the humans? *Yes.* He held in his feathered fingers proof that the humans were not just beings who could communicate, but rather fully intelligent people— the humans were capable of *art*.

The best advantage of being planetside was the availability of a natural water source that, for Tesa, translated into a long, luxurious shower. There wasn't anything quite as good as washing away months of sleep debris.

She turned the water off and reached for the purple towel

someone had thoughtfully left out for her. After a brisk rubbing, she wrapped the towel around her hair, changed into a fresh StarBridge jumpsuit, and opened the door.

She was startled to discover Taller, hock-sitting before her bed, meticulously examining her quilt with one eye, then the other, while running a finger along the tiny stitches.

Suddenly he spotted her with his rear vision. Her purple-turbaned head was too much of a surprise and he leaped to his feet, stretched to his full height, and bounced his head against the rigid ceiling. His feet slid out from under him. Spreading enormous wings to counterbalance, he managed to sweep off every object that had the misfortune to be nearby, scattering and smashing dozens of artifacts in a rain of destruction.

When Taller had steadied himself, he folded his wings and fluffed his feathers out as his crown expanded, flaring a brilliant red. Fragments of feather fluff drifted gently to the floor. A final plume-settling shake restored his dignity.

And I thought I was clumsy, Tesa thought, appalled at the devastation the avian had wrought. *He must be so embarrassed.*

"You surprised me, Good Eyes," Taller signed simply.

She nodded and signed back, "We surprised each other."

He fixed her with a large golden eye. "That is a most unusual decoration on your head. Doesn't it hurt your neck?"

She'd forgotten all about the turban, and felt a stab of guilt when she realized it was no doubt the cause of his alarm. She removed it slowly and explained its purpose.

Taller tucked his neck in a tight S curve, gracefully easing onto his hocks so that he appeared to be kneeling, only backward. He touched the quilt. "Is this yours?"

"Yes," Tesa signed. "My grandmother made it for me."

"How did she make it?"

"By piecing together scraps of old cloth," Tesa explained.

"She made this from *old scraps*?" He gave her one of those piercing stares. "Do you value this?"

"It was given to me the day I was born. I'll be buried in it when I die. It's a part of me."

His head and neck shot up straight, but then scrunched back into an S as he turned his head to view the ceiling with one cautious eye. "This is a beautiful thing, Good Eyes. When you come to live with us in the shelter, you'll bring it?"

"If I may," Tesa signed.

"Please. Weaver will love this. I came to ask if you'd see

the egg today. The chick is talking. He'll be out soon."

Tesa feared that her morning ritual of coffee and breakfast was probably disrupted forever, but if she had to don stilts and wade through the marsh without even a snack she would expire. Before she could respond to Taller's cryptic request, the avian turned his head toward the front door. Meg had entered, but Tesa felt a touch of disappointment that Taller would break eye contact with her over a sound, like any hearing Terran.

"So, can you come?" he signed, even though his head was turned completely around.

How weird! Tesa thought, realizing he could still see her.

"I hope you weren't startled by your wake-up caller," Meg signed before Tesa could answer the avian.

"No more than he was," Tesa told her.

Meg glanced at the debris-littered floor as Taller casually rearranged a few feathers. "So I see. We'll pick it up later. Breakfast is ready, and so is the coffee."

Tesa wanted to cheer.

Thom was pouring black, steaming liquid into a mug when the three stepped outside. "Coffee's only decent when it's made outdoors," he signed.

Tesa nodded, trying not to feel self-conscious as Taller peered over her shoulder into the cup Thom handed her. She gazed at the vividly colored sky and the lacy clouds that skittered across it. Three Grus were nearby, probing the ground.

"Take a look at breakfast," Thom suggested.

He ushered her to a mossy spot under an aged tree whose bright yellow leaves overhung the ground the way weeping willows did. Orange and red woven mats were heaped with organic matter laid out on the blue and gray, moss-covered ground.

That's breakfast? Tesa wondered. The fruit the Grus called round-red fruit was there, as were other appetizing-looking things, but some things looked decidedly unappealing. Like the round, wet, dark brown thing the size of a fist, with appendages like an anemone's, that began to slowly roll away.

"Have a seat," Meg signed, casually moving the brown thing back to where it'd been. "The Grus collected this for us, since you needed a crash course in foraging. You'll have to feed yourself *and* the chick when you live in the nest shelter.''

When Tesa folded her legs, Taller did too, hock-sitting near her. The anemone thing began to roll away again. Tesa realized it wasn't just *rolling*, it was moving under its own power—it was *crawling*. Taller grabbed it gently with his bill and returned it to its place.

I've seen that thing before, Tesa thought. *It was in Scott's notes* ... The sticker-ball again attempted its futile escape. ''That's an edible water plant,'' she signed, ''a 'traveling thorn-fruit.' Whenever it's on land, it migrates toward water.''

Taller snatched the rolling plant and swallowed it. With morbid fascination, Tesa watched its outline travel slowly down the length of his throat.

''I'm so hungry,'' she added, ''it almost looked good to me!''

Meg tossed her a long, yellow tuber. ''Try this.''

Tesa pulled out her Swiss Army knife, scraped the tuber clean, and bit into it. Chewing, she signed, ''This must be 'heart-berry root.' It's sweet and crunchy and has edible flowers that produce a red berry with medicinal properties. But the tuber part is best.'' She was grateful that sign language allowed her to talk with her mouth full.

Breakfast continued until Tesa had sampled everything. The others helped her demolish a heaping mound of large, shelled bivalves that were better than oysters.

''I'll never eat again,'' Tesa complained, patting her stomach as she glanced at the pile of shells and plant remnants.

''You said that last night, after dinner,'' Thom reminded her.

''I'm disappointed,'' Meg signed, ''no pearls.''

Tesa sat back, relishing a sense of belonging that had crept over her as she remembered the information she'd studied from Scott's notes. She wanted more than anything to show everyone, especially Taller, that she was right for this job.

The three Grus still wandering around the campsite had found something and were playing toss with it. Tesa decided they must be young birds, since one still had some cinnamon-colored feathers around his head. Bouncing on their toes, they flung the object into the air, then leaped after it, kicking.

Suddenly the battered thing landed in Tesa's lap and she jumped. It was cold and clammy—some kind of dead animal, amphibian maybe. *I've seen this in the notes, too,* Tesa thought.

The young Grus lowered their heads as Taller glared at them.

"It's okay, they didn't mean it," Tesa signed. She turned the animal over gingerly, trying to remember what it was.

"This is a 'circle-swimmer,'" Tesa signed, recognizing it, finally. "They're inedible for Terrans, but the Grus can eat . . ." No, that wasn't it. She glanced at Meg and Thom and suddenly realized something was wrong. They were staring at the thing, shocked. Taller peered pointedly at the dead creature, then turned away to rub his face along his back. Tesa didn't miss the significance of his expanding, glowing crown.

What is it? Tesa thought frantically, glancing at the pitiful corpse. *Why is everyone upset?* Finally, she noticed its wound—a deep puncture wound caused by a curved talon.

Then she remembered. The circle-swimmer was one of the Aquila's favorite foods, and the only way the damned thing could've gotten here was if the Aquila she'd seen yesterday had dropped it. Would Meg realize she'd lied? Tesa glanced at her, but the older woman didn't meet her eyes. Thom, however, did.

"Well, the name's right, Tesa," Thom signed, holding her eyes steadily, "but the circle-swimmer isn't native to this area. He must've been dropped by a passing Night Flyer."

The biologist was trying to bail her out, but Tesa had the uncomfortable feeling that he had caught her in her lie.

"You're probably right about the Night Flyer," Meg agreed. "You said a pair has passed over almost every day . . ."

Taller stopped washing his face and fixed Thom and Meg with a stare, pointedly ignoring Tesa. All of his feathers slowly stood straight out. "The Night Flyers occasionally eat water-dwellers," he agreed, "but they prefer warm-blooded beings like the rousette. Both of you know that." He turned a fierce, one-eyed stare on Tesa. "Only Death prefers the circle-swimmers."

He looked at Tesa full-faced, but she did not yield to the impulse to scoot away from the point of his bill.

"You will learn," Taller signed, "as Puff did, that we never speak of Death. The truth is that Death will eat *anything* that lives. You'd be foolish to think they'd hesitate to taste the flesh of a human being."

Glancing at the submissive posture of the young Grus, Tesa dropped her head, copying them. "I know you're telling me this to teach me how to live in your world, Taller. I won't forget."

Graciously the Grus settled his feathers, pulled in his crown, and cast a covetous eye on the coffee in the bottom of Tesa's cup. "Could I taste that?" he signed.

Tesa dribbled the cold dregs into a saucer, and the avian scooped some liquid into his long bill. Squeezing his eyes shut, he shook his head violently, spraying coffee everywhere. "That's horrible!" Taller signed, "but... better than yesterday."

"Taller has a love/hate relationship with coffee," Meg told Tesa, wiping spatters off. The older woman seemed relieved that the tense moment had passed. Tesa was glad, too, but she found herself avoiding Thom's intent gaze.

A vee of white flashed low overhead. Ten members of Taller's flock were winging through the air, pumping their wings hard, calling. Tesa felt a shiver of vibration. Taller leaped to his feet and threw his head back. The force of his call rocked Tesa, raising the hairs of her body like pathetic vestigial feathers. Wincing, Thom touched his ears, adjusting his nullifiers. The three Grus youngsters took off, winging hard to catch the group climbing into the sky.

Thom gestured at Meg. "They must be after the shuttle."

Tesa shaded her eyes and finally saw the *Patuxent*'s twin, the *Baraboo*, high in the atmosphere, banking with graceful ease. The Grus spiraled higher, until they looked like a handful of snowflakes caught in a whirlwind. Tesa was thrilled with the beauty of their flight, until she realized they would intersect the trajectory of the incoming shuttle. As the *Baraboo* angled in, the Grus veered closer.

Meg and Thom were shading their eyes, watching, and Taller had his head cocked, one eye peering skyward. Tesa wondered uneasily why the flock would get so close. The flyers began weaving dangerously in and out of the ship's path, their aerial acrobatics becoming a risky ballet. The White Wind people were *escorting* the shuttle to their World.

Suddenly one of the avians at the end broke formation and tried to overtake the leader. Tesa squinted as the lone Grus swerved across the *Baraboo*'s path. The ship overcompensated, ran, and... Tesa gasped, but the shuttle quickly recovered and stabilized. The bird swooped away, far from the flight path.

Missed, Tesa thought, releasing her breath in a whoosh.

Then the bird fluttered and fell into a deadly spiral. He flapped desperately, but could not gain control and yielded to gravity even as Taller ran to climb into the sky.

CHAPTER 7

♦

Falling

Behind him, Taller could see the humans standing as if rooted. Ahead of him was a falling body flailing weakened wings. Taller swam through the air, feeling it flow over his body, friendly, malleable. *What would it be like to have it turn against you, your life's ally?*

His flock swerved and dived to get beneath their pinwheeling companion. *They won't make it,* Taller thought.

The injured yearling was Flies-Too-Fast, the same youngster who'd carelessly thrown that filthy carcass at Good Eyes. He'd returned from his flyaway—the adulthood rite every chick took at fledgling—only last month. This was when youngsters became reckless as they struggled to earn a name, impress a lover. That made the old leader think of how Good Eyes had accidently brought the dark shadow of Death among them. But she, too, only a juvenile, new to the World. Like Flies-Too-Fast, whose mistake could shatter him upon the World.

The flock had reached the plummeting bird, and there was a flurry of activity as the strongest flier attempted to maneuver under the stunned and injured yearling. Suddenly they surrounded him, hiding him. Glancing backward, Taller saw the tiny specks of humans, helpless, tied to the ground. The pattern of the World swam beneath him. *Not high enough*, he thought, *these wings, too old* . . . Straining, he pushed on. It had been years since there'd been a free-fall rescue.

The big twenty-year-old, Kills-the-Ripper, and his mate, Moon Dancer, maneuvered beneath the youngster. Beside them was Taller's elder daughter, Shimmering, helping them to stabilize. The three moved closer together, their wingbeats synchronized, their primaries brushing one another. *Directly under!* Taller silently commanded. *You must be directly under the one falling!* But they hesitated, fearing the risk, and the youngster slipped through their net, hurtling past them.

Taller was not ready to let one of his own meet death through something not of the World. Leveling out, the old leader sailed under the plummeting yearling. The youngster's keel hit him hard across the back, where his lungs were, knocking the air out of him, making him wobble—but they slowed. Flies-Too-Fast hit again, and they teetered wildly, but Taller stabilized, his fingers brushing the younger bird's. That touch pulled the yearling out of his panic.

The chick flapped hard, once, twice, then settled, lying heavily across Taller's back, moving his wings synchronously with the older avian who now labored to sail into a long, controlled spiral. *Not enough . . . These wings too old . . .*

Then the powerful Kills-the-Ripper was beneath them, his mate on one side, Shimmering on the other, the three forming a cushion of safety. They slowed until finally Taller felt the weight of the youngster lifting, as he began to glide on his own.

The flock re-formed into a ragged vee, Taller in the lead, Kills-the-Ripper in the place of honor on his right. Flies-Too-Fast would be last, his parents beneath him for assistance.

The humans' ship had already landed when the people lowered their legs and parachuted onto the hillock near Good Eyes and the others. Taller met the newcomer's gaze and started, flaring his wings in surprise. Her large golden eyes seemed all at once like Puff's—they held the same caring, the same concern.

Tesa struggled to slow her breathing, reminding herself th no one had been hurt. The injured Grus had come down to fast, stumbling before finding his legs, but he seemed fine now.

Taller appeared calm as he met her gaze, only his crown and a flaring of his wings indicating his inner turmoil.

Tesa broke their locked gaze only when Thom touched her elbow.

"The *Baraboo*'s down," he signed, "let's see how they are."

Tesa had forgotten that the shuttle had even been involved in the near tragedy. She looked at the ship that was twin to the *Patuxent*, the one they'd arrived in yesterday. *Only* **yesterday**? she thought with a start.

She turned back to see Taller and nearly jumped to find him right beside her. Meg came over quickly. "That was some flying!" she signed to Taller. "Are you all right?"

"Yes, and the yearling will recover," Taller assured her. "And your vehicle?"

"Our ship's fine," Meg signed, "but I think the crew is little shook up."

"Let me speak to the youngster first," Taller signed. "Then I wish to address the crew." He turned to Tesa. "Come with me, Good Eyes." It was a request, not an order.

The "escort" flock was clustering around the ship, except for the two adults hanging back with their injured yearling. As Taller and Tesa approached, they attempted to screen their child.

"The humans are visitors on the World," Taller signed to them. "They are our invited guests. Considering the danger Flies-Too-Fast placed them in, a gift seems appropriate. Flying is not natural to humans, so we must be cautious."

His suggestion seemed to take the edge off the parents' nervousness. After a rapid exchange of signs, they flew off toward the marsh. The youngster remained, head lowered nearly to the ground, elbows flaring so that his wings looked like a cape.

"Why would an adult, fresh from his flyaway, hide behind his parents?" Taller asked him.

Reminded of a Grus chick's ritual of independence, the youngster raised his head, pulling his wings in tight. As significant to them as the Plains Indians' *hanblechia*, the vision quest, the flyaway was a chick's time to discover the World. Only when he'd learned something of importance could the youngster return home. He might be given a new name. There'd be a dance in his honor, and he'd be given his hatching cloak. From that day on he was an adult.

Of course, not all chicks returned. Inevitably, some died. Bad news travels on wings, and when the parents found out, they would attach the cloak to the outside of their nest shelter and abandon the building, as a monument of grief to their lost child.

Some youngsters joined other flocks or formed their own. Once established in a new flock, the yearling would return to collect his cloak and give a dance. For the Grus, as long as there was life, there was a reason to dance.

"You must ask the humans to forgive your recklessness," Taller told Flies-Too-Fast. "Your foolhardy act might have caused your death."

The avian lost his timidity. "But I wasn't close to the ship! Something invisible sucked up the air, making me tumble."

The force-field, Tesa thought, *he must've gotten close enough to trigger the Automatic Protection System.* When the shield snapped on it would create a vortex. "He's telling the truth," she told Taller. "The ship can defend itself."

Taller looked at the bold youngster thoughtfully. "Puff said nothing could hurt the ship, but now we know that in protecting itself, the ship can hurt us. Let Loves-the-Wind look at your wing—she'll know how to help it. But first, we'll all talk to the humans." He moved purposefully toward the shuttle.

The yearling stepped up beside Tesa. "You're the *new* human!" he signed as though his dressing-down was already forgotten. "The one who can't hear." He eyed Tesa's small ears with open curiosity even as she noticed the few cinnamon-colored feathers around the yearling's head.

"Yes," she signed. "I'm called 'Good Eyes.' And you?"

"Flies-Too-Fast." The sign meant more than that—it meant recklessness, fearlessness. The yearling's body language indicated that, at the moment, he was chagrined to tell her, though she suspected at other times he'd sign it with pride. They told us you can dance. Would you dance with me? As he finished asking, he sprang into the air.

Tesa felt awkward. She didn't want to do anything clumsy that might embarrass the youngster, but she was tempted by his high-spirited joy. She tried a few steps. Flies-Too-Fast spun, leaped up, and she followed, startled at how high she could jump in the reduced gravity.

"You can! You can really dance!" He seemed thrilled with Tesa's short performance, and she was flushed with excitement, until she realized that *everyone* had turned to watch.

"You've given him quite an honor," Taller signed.

Is that good or bad? Tesa wondered. Meg's and Thom's faces were equally unreadable.

The *Crane* crew was out of the ship now, and as the Grus moved away, Tesa could see their drawn, anxious faces. Lauren's was pasty-white and she was crying. Bruce had an arm around her. Tesa noted their nullifiers and Terran voders.

Peter's dark face was bobbing in a sea of white bodies in the *Baraboo*'s hatchway, as Grus heads snaked around on long necks, and black, stick-thin legs moved back and forth.

Taller strode forward while Tesa struggled to keep up, Flies-Too-Fast beside her.

Bruce was speaking to Lauren, who, after reading his words, hurriedly wiped her eyes and nodded. Dr. Li stepped out from behind Bruce as she took Lauren's readings with a medi-scanner. The doctor jumped as one of the Grus slid a sleek head over her shoulder and peered at the glittering device. Her brown hand tightened protectively around the instrument before it could find its way down a Grus gullet. The doctor gave Lauren the standard "okay" sign, then said something to Bruce.

Tesa dug in her pouch for her voder and turned it on. *What a nuisance,* she thought, irritated. It was one thing to use it to record the language and customs of the Grus, but another to need it to communicate with her own species.

She suddenly glanced at the cluster of humans. She was used to thinking that hearing people could hear *everything*, but on Trinity they'd *all* be deaf. What was it like for *them*? Did they feel funny using their voices? Could they learn to *see* the way she did? She suddenly felt sorry for them—and then felt instantly confused. Was this how hearing people viewed her?

"Who was the ship's flyer today?" Taller signed to Meg.

"It must've been Lauren," she signed. "She looks shaken."

"I'll talk to her, as would the yearling that caused the accident, if you'll translate for me," Taller signed. Flies-Too-Fast was standing behind him, making himself small.

Lauren hesitantly stepped forward, looking haggard. "What should I say?" she asked Bruce.

"Just listen . . . uh . . . read," Bruce told her.

"Did any of you suffer any injury because of this one's

foolish act?'' Taller indicated Flies-Too-Fast with his bill.

"No," Lauren said, "but I was afraid we'd killed him."

Meg translated impartially.

"It was a terrible moment that ended well," Taller signed. "Please don't feel this incident means we have poor judgment."

Lauren swallowed, as though gearing up her courage. "As the . . . flyer of the ship . . . I *do* question the judgment . . . of allowing your people to escort the shuttle."

Scowling, Meg hesitated, but Taller stared at her, so reluctantly she translated the sentence.

Thom looked startled. After reading his voder, Peter voiced a warning, before remembering Lauren couldn't hear it. The computer tech wasn't paying attention to her voder; she was staring up at Taller. The other Grus began milling, excitedly. Feathers were being fluffed, crowns expanded.

It's too dangerous!'' Lauren insisted.

Bruce put a hand on Lauren's shoulder to say something, but Flies-Too-Fast stepped forward before he could.

"Please, don't," the yearling signed. "I'm at fault here, and I'm sorry. What I did was wrong, so punish me, but don't forbid the others the joy of flying with your ship. It's the only way we can share the sky." He lowered his head and moved behind Taller, who dipped his own head, acknowledging that the youngster had signed well. The yearling's parents had returned, and huddled with him.

"If the humans feel the escort is too dangerous," Taller signed, "I will forbid it."

Oh, no, Tesa thought, catching sight of Meg's drawn face. *This is* **their** *world! We mustn't tell them where or when to fly.*

Lauren was about to say something when Tesa interrupted. "We'd never do anything to make your skies small, Taller, flying with your people honors us." Tesa glanced at Lauren nervously.

"Good Eyes signs for all of us," Meg interjected quickly into the tense pause. Everyone seemed to relax, except Lauren, who gave Tesa a tight smile, then turned away.

Taller had one eye trained on Tesa, but did not respond. His crown, however, returned to its "relaxed" size and color.

Flies-Too-Fast stepped up to Lauren and held something out. His parents were close behind him, peering anxiously. A shock of sparkling white stretched across his long, black hands.

"This is my hatching cloak," he signed, one-handed. "My mother wove it from my father's design. I want you to have it."

The humans looked at one another, surprised. Lauren opened her mouth, but said nothing, just took the cloak as carefully as if she were being handed the Unicorn tapestry. "Thank—thank you," she stammered. "It's beautiful. I'll treasure it."

This seemed to release everyone's pent-up emotions, and the flock burst into a chorus, forcing the humans into a flurry of nullifier adjustments. Goose bumps swept over Tesa.

"Since that's resolved," Dr. Li said abruptly, "can Tesa put her index finger in here, please?"

As Tesa obliged, feeling the cold, stinging sensation that followed the scanner's blood test, she watched Dr. Li struggle to ignore Taller, unabashedly observing the proceedings.

"Well," Dr. Li spoke aloud, "going planetside was the right medicine for her." She pocketed the instrument, flinching away from an avian who was covetously eyeing the shiny tool.

"So," Peter said, "shall we unload the ship, now?"

While the ship was unpacked, Meg brewed fresh coffee, as Bruce and Lauren assembled new equipment. Thom and Peter stayed in the shuttle, moving things around and unpacking. Most of the flock left, becoming bored or hungry, but Taller remained. So did Flies-Too-Fast, hanging in the background.

Meg was showing Dr. Li new food items to be analyzed, when Thom stuck his head out of the ship and motioned to the avian leader. "They've brought it," he signed, standing beside Peter in the doorway. The two men stepped out, Thom holding a small packing case with the StarBridge logo on it. He glanced at Meg, guardedly. Peter looked uncomfortable.

Everyone stopped as Thom placed the case on the ground and unsealed it. A sparkle of whiteness caught Tesa's eye. With a shock, she realized they were unpacking the Grus skin, the one he had shown her back at the school.

Thom stepped back as Taller approached. Slowly the avian spread the tanned skin on the ground. Tesa realized this might be the remains of someone he'd known.

Taller touched the thing with his fingertips and the point of his bill. It was too monstrous to believe. He smoothed the feathers, trying to control his emotions, not wanting to lose himself before these aliens—these beings that were tied directly with this horror. What had he ever done to bring this horror on himself, on his people, on his own children?

He looked up, his eyes following the slanting rays of the suns and called loud and long, heedless of the humans' delicate ears. The Sun Family would *not* ignore him this time.

See this! He sent his prayer-thought on a beam of rage to the implacable gods. *This is my* **son**. *See what has happened to all the training, all the preparation . . . all the love. Is it not enough to allow Death to destroy an entire family? How can you permit this atrocity—my son*, **preserved**?

He could feel it on his hands, his bill, taste it in his nares and on his tongue. That stench was there, as it was on their "clothes," and on the things of the World that they would not permit to decay. And now on Water Dancer's remains. The spirit of his child could never travel to the Sun Family if his wings were here. And what could Taller possibly say to Dancer's mother when he brought this sorrow home?

Facing the Sun Family, Taller called again, a short, bitter call. Then he collapsed, folding his legs, spreading his wings across the ground, gently touching his bill to the skin.

None of the humans moved. Bruce and Peter looked wooden. Lauren kept swallowing as though to keep from crying, and even Dr. Li seemed gray and shrunken. Thom was wiping his own reddened eyes while supporting Meg who was weeping.

Tesa had felt a numb horror as she read Meg's words.

"It's Water Dancer, oh, God . . . it was packed and sealed when they gave it to me . . . I never *looked* at it . . . but he *knows* . . . just look at what it's doing to him . . . he *knows* . . ."

Taller's movements spoke of anger . . . and hopelessness. A fat tear slid down Tesa's nose and hung suspended off the end.

Taller finally stood, seeming smaller, shrunken. He draped the skin over the base of his neck, then turned to T___, trying to appear normal, but his crown had dulled to __ unhealthy plum. "Will you come and see the egg?"

"As soon as I can," she signed to the avian.

Without another word, he started taking long, graceful strides toward the cliff edge, his great wing flaps blowing leaves, dust, and instruction flimsies everywhere.

Flies-Too-Fast stepped up to Tesa. "When the egg hatc

and the son grows, there'll be a dance. You'll dance then?''

She signed, ''Yes, of course.''

''Then everything will be right again. You'll see.'' He ran for the cliff edge, the last of his people to leave.

CHAPTER 8

◆

The Crew

Meg sat heavily in the chair, its unyielding blue plastic hard against her spare frame. It never took long for the *Crane* crew to come inside and that last incident with Taller had been all the excuse they needed. They weren't comfortable outdoors, even as she and Scott had never been comfortable indoors. The older woman shifted. She ought to get up, make tea, do something to break the tension—to erase the vision of Dancer's skin and Taller's grief. Right now she felt anything but buoyant.

Bruce was busy closing the windows and activating the sound shutters. Once they were sealed, everyone could remove their nullifiers. Meg frowned. She and Scott hated the sound shutters. You couldn't get any fresh air when they were down, you had to rely on air conditioners and filters. You might as well be in a city high-rise as on a wilderness world.

Besides, watching Bruce draw the shutters was like getting one of his pre-accident lectures. *The building should be kept shuttered for* **safety**. *You might need it in an emergency*. After the accident, however, he'd said nothing. She could still see his stricken expression as he'd strapped her onto the stretcher.

She closed her eyes. It had been their choice to keep the shutters up, hers and Scott's. They knew the risks.

A hand touched her shoulder. Thom smiled warmly and tapped his ears. Returning the smile feebly, she turned her hearing on.

Tesa entered, glancing at the clear shutters. "What're they for?" she asked Meg.

"Sound," Meg explained. She hesitated awkwardly.

"So you can hear safely?" Tesa asked casually. "I didn't know the shelter had these. They weren't down last night."

"I don't like them, but they make it safer"—she indicated herself and the others—"for us."

Tesa made a motion that seemed to say, "I understand," or maybe it said, "too bad." As though wanting to change the subject, she pointed to a cluster of small holos grouped on a nearby shelf. "Are those people part of your original crew?"

Meg looked at the short scenes that replayed endlessly. "Yes—that's all of us in this scene." She indicated fifteen happy people horsing around, eternally making rabbit ears over one another's heads. *Were we ever really that confident?* Meg wondered. "We took the holo the day after we found Trinity," she told Tesa. She named the people and described their duties.

Meg moved on to another holo. "I'm sure you recognize Scott, and myself, Bruce, and Lauren. These other two people . . ." She looked at the clean-faced, sandy-haired man whose arm hung casually over Bruce's shoulders. Jim Maltese had been Bruce's closest friend, and Deborah, the black woman in the picture, had been like a daughter to Meg. She missed Deborah so much . . . but they hadn't been interested in a First Contact . . . and they had never forgiven Meg and Scott for calling the CLS.

The elderly woman shook her head. "These people were friends of ours, then."

Thom came forward with a cup of hot tea. "Thought you might like this," he said to Meg. Smiling at Tesa, he said aloud, "How about you, can I get you anything?"

Tesa met his eyes, then glanced at the voder on her wrist. Shaking her head, she turned away. *Thom looks stung*, Meg thought. *I've got to be more patient with him.* He'd done everything asked of him all the months Meg had been gone. He might've handled the situation with Lauren a little better, but no one takes rejection well. However, because of that, Meg hadn't anticipated his sudden infatuation with Tesa. Sipping her tea, she felt its welcoming warmth travel through her.

"Well, Lauren," Peter spoke suddenly into the uncomfortable silence, "how does it feel to be a wealthy woman? Almost makes our rodeo ride down here worthwhile."

The technician, who'd been carefully packing the Grus cloak into the same case that had held Water Dancer's skin, gave him a wry look. "Let's see you say that when *you're* piloting and one of them puts the ship into a spin." Lauren ran a gentle hand over the gleaming cloak. "It's beautiful," she said wistfully, "but it isn't mine. It belongs to the people of Earth."

Tesa tapped Meg. "I don't understand," she signed. "Flies-Too-Fast gave it to her."

"It's in our contracts," Meg signed and spoke, so her conversation with Tesa would include the others. "Anything the Grus give us is a *diplomatic* gift, not a personal one."

"That's what happens when you stop being an explorer and start developing a First Contact," Bruce said, looking at Tesa. Meg frowned, knowing his words weren't really for the young interrelator's benefit. "If they allowed people to make a little profit on these endeavors, there might not be so much outside interest in scuttling them."

Bruce can never keep his politics out of any discussion, Meg thought with a scowl.

"At least we can keep this on the *Crane* until the next supply ship comes through, and enjoy it," Lauren said, ignoring Bruce as she usually did when he dragged out one of his many soap-boxes. "It'll probably end up in the Smithsonian."

"When I think of what might've been," Bruce continued, shaking his head. "Tesa, there's a plain about six hours from here. When I first saw it, I thought, that's where I'll put my town—Carpenterville! In a few years it'll be Carpentertown, then eventually—the city of Carpenter! I can still see it. But then, of course, we had no idea what we were going to find. If we *had*, we could've guarded our transmissions better . . ."

"No doubt," said Szu-yi evenly, "they would've been so well guarded that no one would have *ever* known."

"That's not what I meant," Bruce responded with a poisonous smile. "I *meant*, we could've prevented anyone like the privateers from finding out about the Grus. Dr. Li can't help her attitude, Tesa," he added sarcastically, "she's never known any ambition but to be a good government worker."

"A respectable desire," Szu-yi responded emotionlessly. "I certainly never had *your* interest in being a profiteer."

"A *colonizer!*" Bruce snapped. "There's a difference!"

"Enough," Meg held up her hand. "I was hoping by now you both had learned to get along better."

Tesa had kept track of the conversation by quick glances at her voder. Looking squarely at Meg, she signed, "Why isn't anyone talking about what happened with Taller and the skin?"

The others read their voders, then self-consciously exchanged glances among themselves.

"I should've looked at it first," Meg said disgustedly. "I would've recognized—"

Tesa shook her head. "You didn't recognize it when you saw it. Taller did, and you responded to his reaction. But—"

"Am I reading this right?" Bruce interjected. "Tesa, you think *Taller* knew that skin was Dancer's *before* Meg told him?"

Tesa nodded. "It was obvious. He reacted before she did."

"Did it look that way to the rest of you?" Bruce asked the others. No one responded.

Tesa was visibly annoyed. "*None* of you realized that? But this is important! Taller's ability to recognize and grieve for his son can be significant in proving his intelligence."

"Well, I don't know about *that*," Bruce drawled. "The Terran elephant does both those things and I don't think we're ready to submit that species to the CLS for a First Contact."

Meg had been afraid they'd get into this. Neither Bruce nor Lauren believed the Grus to be the intelligent people she and Scott knew they were. However, the two technicians had had enough confidence in Scott to believe he could convince the CLS. They'd given up everything in the hopes they could establish this First Contact—and it had all been shattered by Scott's death.

"I see," Tesa signed simply. "I had thought no one wanted

to discuss Taller's reaction because it was too painful. But that's not it at all. You can't recognize what's happening in front of you, or agree on it, so you won't identify significant cultural responses—and then you won't document them. Don't you want to prove that the Grus are intelligent enough to deserve protection from exploitation?''

Everyone quickly nodded their assents, except Bruce. "I don't know about the exploitation part. My motivation is purely chauvinistic. I want Earth to get our full-membership CLS status before those damned Simiu shut us out, maybe forever."

Tesa physically recoiled. "So we can shut out the Simiu?"

Bruce nodded unabashedly. "We've got to teach 'em to respect Terrans. Half of 'em have been trying to discredit us since the *Désirée* incident. It's no secret that the Simiu will do everything they can to block any Terran membership bid that'll come up, but right now our half memberships make us equals. So, we've got to get *full* membership before them. Then we can try and block them—and we'll have more power to do it. If they stop us this time, we might never get another chance."

"Bruce," Tesa signed, "none of that matters! The *only* thing that's important is whether or not the Grus are intelligent."

The weatherman pointed to Tesa's Mizari voder. "I'm hoping that thing, l'il darling, will solve that problem. Since that's the same device the Mizari use to back up their claims of intelligence for other marginal species, we should do the same."

Tesa looked confused. "What species?"

"Are the Ri intelligent *enough*," Bruce asked, "or have the Mizari *decided* they are so they can control—pardon me, I mean, 'protect'—the shisso seaweed from which they derive that drug that extends the Mizari life span? How can we know, since the Mizari insist the Ri are so shy that the sight of any alien—other than themselves, of course—cause one of those overgrown squid to die of shock. But the Mizari have their magical voders to back them up." He was warming to his subject now, his face animated. "Well, the Grus produce something of great value, too, so let's take the voder and document what we need to so we can protect them."

He moved closer to Tesa to make his point. "The bottom line is this, l'il darlin'. Trinity can get us full membership in the CLS. So, the Grus damned well *better* be intelligent."

Meg rubbed the bridge of her nose wearily. *Welcome to the real World, Tesa,* she thought bitterly.

"I'm afraid I must agree with Dr. Carpenter," Dr. Li said. Every head in the place turned. "Who can *really* judge such a nebulous thing as intelligence? We just have to hope that we can prove this claim and establish Earth's full membership. Tesa must understand the way things really are."

"So," Peter asked Tesa, "*do* you know how things really are?"

She hadn't been looking at him however, and didn't realize he'd spoken to her. Bruce got her attention and pointed to her voder. She read it and faced Peter. "I understand that you would all feel differently if you had bothered to learn to sign Grus. Then, you could've picked up the pieces when you lost Scott, and Meg had to leave. You would've had more documentation for the First Contact claim, and you wouldn't have been so dependent on that faulty voder program. More importantly, if you signed, you would all *know* as Scott did, as Meg does, as I do, that there's no question that the Grus are intelligent *enough*."

She looked at Bruce squarely. "At StarBridge, I knew people who'd had communications with Rigellians, who'd met the Ri. They had no doubt about their intelligence. When you communicate with beings in their own language, you *understand* them—you build bridges. But you just want to rely on *this*"—she pulled the voder off Bruce's wrist—"because it's *easy*."

The meteorologist's eyes followed his voder as Tesa pulled it away. "What's she saying, Meg, damn it? I can't . . ."

Tesa demanded through gestures that he maintain eye contact with her. She signed as Meg translated, "This is how you communicate, Bruce. Talk to *me*, not to this *stupid* machine."

Bruce looked intently into Tesa's golden eyes, then remarked, "There's a lot in those eyes, darlin'."

Without glancing at the voders, Tesa signed, "If you could sign Grus, you'd see a lot more in their eyes, too."

Bruce seemed shocked that Tesa had understood him.

"And if you signed Grus," she continued, "you would *know* that Taller recognized his dead son." Tesa handed him his voder.

"Signing is not my job," Bruce said with a grudging smile.

"It wasn't Scott's job either, was it?" Tesa asked.

He read the voder now with obvious reluctance. "I'll make a deal with you?"

Tesa looked at him, uncertain. He repeated the sentence and she nodded that she understood.

"I'll study Grus signs . . . if Dr. Li will."

Tesa held up a hand and turned to Meg. "Did he say he'd study Grus if the doctor would also?"

"That's right," Meg signed wearily.

Tesa looked at the doctor, who was sitting, wooden-faced.

"I'll have to have *someone* to practice with," Bruce drawled.

"No, thank you," the doctor stated flatly.

"Come on, Uncle Bruce," Lauren interjected quietly. She only used that endearment when she was determined to have her way. "I'll be your practice partner."

Bruce started to argue, but Lauren gave him a look that made him grin and back down. "Okay, honey, I never could refuse you anything. We'll learn to sign Grus. That should be something."

Yes, thought Meg, *that certainly should.*

Through it all Thom had said nothing, Meg noted, but had watched with quiet interest.

"Well, now that intergalactic relations have taken a giant leap forward," Peter said, "can the starving immigrants eat?"

Peter carried a precarious pile of dishes into the kitchen area. "You really *wash* these?" he asked Thom, incredulously.

"Doesn't make any sense to make the recycler sterilize and reformulate dishes for such a small job. Life's simpler here."

"Is that so?" the black man wondered. "I caught that look in your eye over the hearts-of-reed soup. Isn't there something you want to tell me?"

Thom quickly glanced over his shoulder. "And I thought you offered to help out of graciousness."

Peter snorted. "I wanted to keep you from making a fool of yourself when you tried to get Tesa's assistance."

"I can't figure her out. She was a lot warmer yesterday."

"Maybe you're coming on too strong," Peter suggested. "Or maybe she's afraid Lauren might slit her throat."

Both men laughed quietly. "Still, it pisses me off when she puts on that deaf routine," Thom said.

Peter raised his eyebrows. "Routine?"

"You know, I say something and halfway through she looks away and tunes me out. She can follow what I'm saying."

"Why don't you sign to her?"

"Ahh, I feel so uncomfortable doing that. I'd like to be a *Terran* when I talk to Tesa, you know? Use a human language."

Peter nodded. "Yeah, but your language isn't *hers*."

Thom stopped scraping dishes, then reluctantly nodded. "When did you get so smart in matters of the heart?"

"I wasn't aware it was matters of that particular organ we were discussing. Actually, it's just too painful for me to watch you bumble your way through another star-crossed affair. It's bad for business, friend." Peter pushed the pile of plasticware into the basin of thin suds and turned on the sonics. "And speaking of business, something's on your mind, something you couldn't tell me when we were unloading the shuttle."

Thom turned so that he could keep one eye on the dining area. Meg had gone back outside with Dr. Li to load plant samples into the shuttle. Bruce, Lauren, and Tesa were huddled over a new computer work station, correlating some kind of programming using Tesa's Mizari voder. Thom didn't want that particular instrument picking up this conversation, since none of them knew its range or limitations. Finally, deciding that the voder and its operator were well occupied, Thom continued,

"We had a visitor yesterday," he said. "An Aquila. Dropped a calling card, but didn't fly low enough to excite the Grus."

"Well," Peter began, "you've got to expect that now and . . ."

"Tesa saw it," Thom interrupted. "Then, when we asked her, s lied to us." The whole thing with this new "inter-relator" g under his skin. If they could've just maintained the status quo for two more months they might've been able to finish up and get out of here. Who could have expected Meg to come back at all, never mind so soon and with someone else?

"Is that why you're coming on to her, to gain her trust?" Peter gave him a cockeyed, better-try-another-tactic look.

"No," Thom said. "But I'm not happy about her lying to me."

"So, brush up your technique, try to win her over," Peter said, carefully keeping his expression casual. "She worked with raptors, maybe she was just captivated by the big eagle. Things'll go better if she trusts you. We can't afford to have her get in our way, not when things are so close to breaking. I just hope you do better this time than you did with Lauren."

Thom looked annoyed. "Do I have to hear about that forever? It didn't cause *you* any hardship to pick up the pieces."

Peter gave him a toothy grin and glanced at Tesa. "Hey, and I wouldn't mind helping you out again, old pal."

Thom gave him a sour look. "So, what about the Aquila?"

"Bruce is coming," Peter whispered, then smiled warmly at the weatherman. "Well, 'Uncle Bruce,' did you get that program squared away?"

"You can stow that uncle stuff," Bruce said, "only Lauren gets away with that. Yeah, the program's running. That Mizari voder's one clever piece of equipment, but its operator is a little closemouthed about showing it off."

Peter and Thom exchanged a glance. Then, they both looked at Tesa, with Lauren at the work station. Turning the sonics off, Thom let the dish water drain, then activated the quick-dri.

"Meg said something to me about an Aquila leaving its lunch hereabouts," Bruce said to the other men, guardedly.

"We were just talking about that," Peter said. "I don't know that it's anything to worry about."

"You don't think we should reconsider using sonic perimeters?" Bruce asked. "I'm not burying another friend on this poor excuse of an Eden. I won't risk Meg."

"Calm down," Peter said. "One Aquila isn't necessarily the advance guard for an invasion."

"But we're not doing *anything*," Bruce insisted. "If we can't use the sonic perimeters, then how about an early warning system, or some kind of investigative work?"

"You know the problem, Bruce," Thom reminded him, stacking the cleaned, dry dishes. "If we get caught messing around with 'Death,' we're out of here."

"Scott wasn't afraid to violate the taboo," Bruce insisted. "I looked through his paperwork—he'd planted cameras at scattered nest sites, to study their behavior. We could reactivate those cameras through the satellites. We might find out why they're flocking and working cooperatively, when they were only independent predators before.''

"I thought of that," Thom assured him. "I spent weeks trying to reactivate those things when Meg was gone."

"You never mentioned it before," Bruce said warily.

"I was afraid you'd object. I figured if it worked out, fine, and if it didn't, no one needed to know. Well, it didn't." He could see Lauren signing something tentatively to Tesa.

"The cameras were trained on active nests," Thom continued. "There were six of them. Three were destroyed when the trees they were in were felled in electrical storms. One of them developed a hardware problem and burned out. Another one won't function because something's built a nest on top of it, and the last one just plain disappeared. Something may have carried it into a burrow."

"The one under the nest," Bruce said. "Can't we clean it?"

"They don't exactly have a 'self-cleaning' cycle. Bruce, that thing isn't three meters from an active Aquila nest. Scott must've planted it during an inactive period but now it can't be approached safely. All our other cameras are in use for active research projects, so we can't remove any of them without damaging that research. I tried to figure out some way to substitute one, but Dr. Li would raise too many questions."

Bruce looked disgusted. "If she'd ever done any exploration work, she'd know not everything can be done by the book."

"She knows more about the research approval system than anyone on Earth," Peter reminded him "Without her, this project hasn't got a prayer."

"Maybe," Bruce grumbled.

"Maybe, if you were nicer to her, Bruce . . ." Peter trailed off suggestively.

Bruce's venomous look and Peter's cynical grin indicated a joke well worn.

"I'm serious," the meteorologist said. "I'm not burying anybody else—not even Dr. Li. If we can't do approved research on the Aquila, we'll just have to rely on the oldest Terran technique for coping with nuisance wildlife."

Peter and Thom looked puzzled.

"Eradication," he said coolly. "How much do you think someone would pay for one of those damned buzzards' skins?"

Thom and Peter studiously ignored each other.

"Here comes Tesa," Bruce announced, barely moving his lips.

Thom sighed. Things had been a lot simpler when he was down here alone. He glanced at Tesa's wrist and saw that her voder appeared to be off. Its small screen was blank. "*Now* you come to help with the dishes?" he asked, speaking and signing.

Tesa raised an eyebrow and smiled tentatively, handing him two glasses. "No, you forgot these. I thought you'd forgotten how to sign, as well, but now I see you've remembered." Her smile grew warmer.

Thom felt Peter giving him one of those I-told-you-so looks.

CHAPTER 9

◆

The Egg

As she watched the shuttle take off later that afternoon, Tesa felt as though she was seeing off summer guests. It was nice to see them come, but nicer to see them go.

The air was cool, and there was no breeze. Inside the shelter, Thom was opening the sound shutters. *He'll make a good husband someday,* she thought, smiling.

Meg touched her arm and she turned to see the older woman holding the dreaded stilts. "Taller wants you to see the egg. We can't disappoint him."

Tesa's face fell as she gingerly handled the collapsed contraptions. She'd forgotten all about them. Sighing, Tesa stepped into footpads that felt alien and clumsy. Meg had already strapped in and was moving around with such ease and grace, Tesa felt even more self-conscious. Tentatively, she moved her foot, signaling the stilts to rise. They came alive, growing into four-foot-tall leg extenders. Their matte-black color matched her shoes and StarBridge jumpsuit.

"Take a few minutes to reacquaint yourself with those, Tesa," Meg signed. "There's a gentle slope to the marsh."

Slope? Tesa forced herself to be calm.

"I'm ready," Thom signed, striding up on his own stilts.

His approach was so sudden, Tesa lost her balance and accidentally signaled the stilts to collapse—however, because of the lower gravity, the reaction was slow enough for her to recover without falling. Trinity's buoyancy just might save her.

"You okay?" Thom asked, concerned.

"Great recovery," Meg signed, barely smiling. "Let's go."

Meg had told the truth; the beaten pathway that curved down the side of the bluff *was* angled gently. Tesa grew more confident as they descended, Thom first, then Tesa, then Meg. The vast waterway stretched before them, its autumn-hued reeds nodding lazily, creating undulating waves of rich color. Then they were swallowed by the wetland and solid ground turned into thick mud that sucked at the stilts' long-toed feet. Soon, Tesa's legs ached, and her face was coated by a slick sheen of sweat. Before long, the water covered her thighs.

The air was alive with insects from the tiniest gnat-sized to some nearly squirrel-sized. They were repulsed by Terran body chemicals, but that wouldn't last forever. Eventually, the stinging, biting, and poisonous arthropods would adapt themselves to the taste of bitter human, but, Tesa hoped, not too soon.

Small mammalian, reptilian, and amphibian forms darted through the air, splashed in the water, and clung to the tall reeds. And there were avians—so many avians—all paddling, diving, perching, and peeking at the strange travelers.

Eventually, they met Grus. Being on their eye level was as startling for Tesa as it was for the avians. They stared, eyes round, crowns flaring as she waved and forged on.

Just when Tesa was convinced her legs would give out, there was a break in the reeds. In the center of a wide circle of clear water sat a large nest shelter perched high on its platform. A jumble of multicolored woven reed mats made its steep A-framed walls look thrown-together haphazardly, but, yet, it seemed homey and familiar. Many Native Americans had made shelters of tule or reed mats—the Nez Percé, the Thompson Indians, the Yokut, the Umatilla. To someone light-years away from a summer tipi camp, this looked like home.

Tesa realized suddenly that the Grus who had been escorting them had now melted back into the reeds.

Meg drew near. "Thom and I will wait here for you."

The young Indian felt a stab of panic. "You're not coming? How'll I know what to say? Suppose I do something wrong?"

"I thought StarBridge students were trained in diplomacy," Meg signed, her eyes sparkling.

"I never took Nest Entrance 101."

"We didn't want to make a big deal about it, Tesa," Thom signed, "but Scott never got inside the shelter."

Tesa suddenly realized she would be the first human to set foot inside a Grus dwelling, the shelter that was built solely for the rearing of a child, the most important thing in the avians' lives. "I understand," she signed with small motions.

"Just act naturally," Meg signed, then adjusted Tesa's collar and smoothed her hair. She smiled sheepishly. "So, I'm nervous, too."

The striking white form of a mature Grus came out of the structure to stand in the water, eyeing the humans. *Taller,* Tesa thought. Then another stepped through the shelter's entrance and suddenly she wasn't sure. The second one came down to perch one-legged where the water lapped at the base of the platform. Tesa decided that had to be Weaver.

Thom caught her attention. "We'll wait for you here."

"Standing in the water?" she asked, surprised.

"We've got warmers on," he assured her. "We'll be fine."

"Good luck, Tesa," Meg signed. Tesa took a deep breath, then strode across the clearing. The ground gradually sloped up, until the water lapped shallowly at the stilt's ankles while the fabric of her StarBridge clothes drained and dried rapidly.

The Grus Tesa had decided was Weaver faced Taller. "You were right about her eyes, my friend!"

"Friend" was only a loose translation. Like most sign language, meaning was often relayed in spatial terms—how close to or far from the body a sign was performed, how fast or slow. In Weaver's hands that sign became a lovely endearment.

Taller dipped his head, flaring his wings. "It's good you've arrived to see the egg while the light is still strong." He swiveled his head around, peering at Thom and Meg almost suspiciously. "I'm sorry they can't join you. It must've been hard to leave them at the boundary."

Tesa was grateful for his sensitivity to her feelings.

Hurriedly Weaver walked up the almost vertical platform. "The chick has been tapping all day," she signed from a nearly invisible slit in the shelter's wall. "Come speak with him, Good Eyes, so he'll know you."

Tesa had no idea what she was expected to do. How could

she sign to the chick in the egg? She looked back at Meg and Thom, but Taller was already walking up the platform and she couldn't afford to miss the subtle indentations where he was placing his feet. She asked the stilts to collapse, and of course, they refused. When they finally obeyed, they folded so fast she was thrown forward, nearly fell, and barely recovered in time to step off onto the platform.

"Are you all right, Good Eyes?" Taller asked as he and Weaver peered down from the top of the platform.

Tesa glanced over at Meg and Thom, both of them trying to swallow worry and amusement. "I'm fine. Really."

"Puff never did well on those things," Taller signed. "He thought they were alive and had a grudge against him."

Tesa grinned, hugely relieved. "I must've got his pair." She started up, letting her buoyancy steady her, carefully placing each foot before lifting the next. The reeds were slick and one wrong move would send her sliding into the marsh. Finally, Tesa followed Weaver and Taller through the narrow slit that was the shelter's entrance.

The first thing that caught her attention was Terran. Hanging randomly from the steeply angled roof were a dozen different sets of glass wind chimes. Long rays of sunlight slanted through the reed walls and glinted off gleaming crystals, casting dancing rainbows everywhere. When Rob Gable had told her about them, her reaction had been negative, but now her feelings changed. These were artistically created, perfect crystals hand-cut by masters. She imagined they were perfectly tuned as well.

Each one had a legend written on it. The closest was in Gaelic and English, with drawings of Grus signs beneath. It read, "To our friends, the people of Trinity. In gratitude for your magnificent gift, your friends across space, the people of Waterford, Ireland, send a token of appreciation. May the skies rise up to meet you and the wind be ever at your back."

Pulling her attention away, Tesa surveyed the rest of the shelter. The atmosphere was warm and humid, but the air smelled sweet, like cut grass. A partially finished cloak was rolled against one wall, its warp and woof fibers trailing into a rough ball. Flat woven containers and mats were stacked neatly by it. Bundles of long feathers hung from the walls, as did sheafs of colorful grasses, and a mesh bag of woven grass filled with short, fluffy feathers and down.

Tesa was dazzled by crisscrossed shafts of light and bouncing colors. She squinted, focusing on the walls that were almost obscured by the dancing rainbows, realizing that some of the patterns weren't moving. Moving closer to the wall, she suddenly saw that it was alive with vibrantly colored designs, so intricate they incorporated sunbeams and even the wind chimes' rainbows into their imagery. The outside had looked haphazard because it was the wrong side of a woven picture.

I'm the first human who's ever seen this, she thought excitedly, glancing at the forgotten voder on her wrist. It was faithfully recording, cramming everything she was seeing into billions of bits of information she could analyze later. *Wait'll you see **this**, "Uncle Bruce"!*

"Who made this?" she asked Taller, touching the walls.

"It's my design, executed by Weaver. We think it's our best—but at our age, we should have some proficiency."

Tesa stared at the designs avidly. "It's *wonderful*!"

"I'm glad you like our story-walls."

"*Story-walls?*" Tesa asked.

"These images teach the chick about the beauty of the World and its dangers, too." He pointed to something above her head. "For example, here's the story of the Beautiful But Deadly Fish. It's easier to see in the morning, because it relies on the first light to bring out the sparkling water and the gleaming fish."

Tesa peered at the spot. "Show me the fish."

"Here," he pointed. "And this is the sickly chick who hasn't heeded his parents' advice and eaten the deadly fish."

Tesa could barely make out what might be a drooping neck and two legs, but most of the picture eluded her, and she was damned if she could see any fish. Well, the symbolism of a Two Gray Hills rug could be obscure unless you knew what to look for.

"Good Eyes," Taller signed, "come into the nest, please."

She looked where he indicated, at the center of the shelter. The heart of this structure was a large nest, wide and almost flat, with a glittering, woven cloak heaped at the bottom of its gentle bowl shape. The centralized nest reminded her of the Sepapu or Earth Navel, the holy place in Pueblo kivas.

Weaver was hock-sitting on the rim, staring at the cloak.

Taller stepped into the bowl, positioning his huge feet with utmost care on either side of the cloak, then settled carefully onto his hocks. "Puff said that he and Meg were like family," Taller signed. "Humans make families easily?"

"I guess we do," Tesa admitted.

Taller looked at Weaver. "In all the World there's nothing as important as the family, but our families are always the same. Two parents focus all our care and love on a single child until it's grown and gone its way into the World. Then it's no longer our child, but a friend, so we can focus on the next child."

He and Weaver locked eyes, though he signed to Tesa. "In all the histories of the White Wind people, the Gray Wind, or our cousins across the World, there have never been more than two parents to raise one child. Now, all that changes."

Tesa paid rapt attention as the avian turned to her.

"We're too old, Weaver and I, to be having children," Taller signed. "In truth, I'm too old to lead my people . . . however, I do still lead them. Some of them feel this child was sent by the Moon Family, as reparation for losing Water Dancer."

"It's just the kind of reparation the Moon Family would send," Weaver signed bitterly.

"Gifts from the moons," Taller told Tesa, "are mixed blessings. Children make you see the World anew, the way they see it. But, the child of an aging leader with no mature male offspring in his territory is not just any child. I'd devoted the last twenty years of my life to teaching Water Dancer to be the leader I am, a leader as my own father was. Will I have another twenty years to give to the child in this egg?"

The white avian gave Tesa the full force of his stare. "If this child is a gift from the Moons, then it's possible we may not live to see his maturity. If that happens, it will be up to you to see him safely through to adulthood."

ME? Tesa's mind reeled. This was going far beyond anything she'd learned at StarBridge. *Calm down,* she scolded herself. *Scott would agree in a second. Can you let him down?*

"You see, the Moon Family can't affect you," Taller told her conspiratorially, "because you're not of the World."

"I understand," Tesa signed, more confidently than she felt.

"I know that you can't hear," Taller signed, after a brief pause, "but, tell me, can you make sounds?"

Tesa hesitated. "Not like you're used to hearing."

Taller's gesture seemed like a shrug. "All the sounds humans make are unlike those I'm used to hearing. Can you learn new sounds?''

This was her weakest area. ''What kind?''

''The brood sound the parent makes to the chick. You must speak to him now, so that he'll know you when he hatches.''

So, you really do **speak** *to the chick.* ''I'll need your help. I can use this''—Tesa indicated the voder—''to show me how to match the pitch, but I'll still have to 'feel' it in your throat.'' She taped a code into the voder and the screen came to life with flickering patterns. ''That's an image of the wind chimes' noise.'' She tuned them out. ''Okay, I'm ready.''

Taller took her hand in his feathered one. Tesa was fascinated by his incredibly long, flat digits. They looked more like jointed feathers than useful fingers, and the tiny, fine black feathers covering them were like stiff, wiry hairs.

Casually, he drew her hand to his chest, pulling it under his soft, white feathers as he pressed her fingers against his keel. ''Feel the sound here,'' he signed. He placed her other hand where his throat met his bill. ''And here.''

His skin was hot to the touch, and so thin she could feel his rigid, ribbed trachea. On his keel, the feathers beneath the long surface ones were short and fluffy, trapping the incredible heat that radiated through his thin skin. His brood call rumbled against Tesa's fingertips like a combination of Bast's purr and a dog's low growl. It was oddly comforting.

Tesa looked at the sound patterns she'd have to match to imitate that purr. She tried it once, timidly, then stronger.

''Good,'' Taller signed, encouragingly. ''Try again.''

They did it together, while Tesa watched their patterns become more and more alike. *So speech therapy was good for something after all*, she thought with wry amusement.

''That's fine,'' Taller told her.

Weaver manipulated the cloak with her bill. There in the center lay the uncovered egg. Tesa could have held it easily in two hands. It was oblong, its base color a soft grayish green, speckled in brown and red splotches—perfect camouflage against a bare nest. It almost seemed artificial.

Tesa glanced at her voder. Weaver was purring at the egg, and it rocked in answer to her voice. There *really* was something alive in there. The Indian woman felt a flush of excitement.

''Touch the egg,'' Weaver signed to her. ''Speak to him.''

Touch it? Tesa thought nervously. Gently she cradled the egg, feeling its living warmth, the porcelainlike texture of its shell. An irregular tapping tickled her palms. *We're family, now*, hoksila, *little boy*, Tesa thought to the egg. *We're blood, you and I . . .* She became aware of a thin, faint thudding that was the chick's heartbeat. *The heartbeat of the World.* It was a drumbeat that her body wanted to turn into a flash of dancing. *. . . This child . . . is not just any child . . .*

Tesa felt she was the center of a *hunka lowanpi*—a making-of-relatives ceremony. Bringing her face near the egg, she purred. The vibrations against her hand grew stronger. The egg rocked. He was answering her! She prayed, ending it with the traditional phrase, *mitakuye oyasin*—all my relatives—the phrase that tied her people to their world and all beings in it.

Then the egg rocked hard against her hands and suddenly cracked! Tesa pulled her hands away as though she'd been burned. *Oh, God, did I do that?*

Taller and Weaver hovered over the egg. Near its large end was a tiny spiderweb crack, shaped like a star. The two avians leaped up, threw back their heads, and called loud and long.

Taller's golden eyes were round in delight as he finished his call. "He's pipped!" he signed to the human. "What a wonderful sign for our new kind of family."

Weaver moved to cover the egg with her body, but Taller blocked her. Carefully, the avian leader eased himself onto the egg, chest first, adjusting his breast feathers until the egg was warmed by his body. Weaver hovered anxiously over him. This close to the hatching, she would only stop incubating when he insisted. Convincing her to eat was another matter.

"Did you know the chick would pip tonight?" Good Eyes asked. Her startling eyes were as wide as Taller had ever seen them.

"I thought, perhaps—but he's early. Early chicks are strong—eager to see the World, impatient to get on with life." He said that for Weaver's benefit. She needed this chick to recover from Water Dancer's death and the desecration of his body. Though really, she had handled that better than he had.

"The suns have their reasons," she'd said when he'd brought her the skin. "Perhaps Dancer is still needed, and through his skin, he still lives."

Her signs had comforted him in a way he'd not thought

possible when first he'd touched his son's remains.

"The chick will rest now," Weaver told Good Eyes. "It may be an entire day before he begins cutting his way out."

"Return to your own shelter," Taller signed. "Sleep there. Come back in the morning and be part of our family."

"How early should I come?" Good Eyes asked.

"Before the Father Sun," Taller signed.

"I'll be here." She turned to leave, her eyes moving about the shelter. Perhaps the humans weren't as nearsighted as he'd thought. Good Eyes peered again at the story of the Beautiful But Deadly Fish. *I gave her a true name*, Taller realized.

Once outside the shelter, Tesa exhaled in a rush, her legs buckled, and she sat down in a heap. She'd move into the shelter tomorrow, a week ahead of time! She threw up her arms and slid down the slick embankment on her butt, jogged through water toward Meg and Thom until she remembered her stilts. She waded back, strapped them on, then plowed out to her waiting mentors.

Exuberantly, she grabbed Meg's shoulders but the water was too deep and they started to fall. Meg latched onto Thom who floundered wildly trying to steady them. They managed to regain their equilibrium without a dunking.

"The chick's pipped!" Tesa signed as soon as she could.

"You nearly knocked us in the drink, *Good Eyes*!" Thom answered. He was tense, edgy.

"The chick's early?" Meg signed, unsmiling.

Tesa sobered instantly. "Taller said that meant the chick was strong. Was he just saying that?"

Meg shrugged.

"As if we didn't have enough to worry about," Thom signed.

"We thought we'd have more time to teach you Grus ways . . ." Meg explained. "You've only been here a *day*."

"No sense belaboring it, Meg," Thom signed.

Tesa felt deflated, their concerns sweeping away her enthusiasm. She shivered. Her feelings were wrong, backward.

"The first few weeks you can use your voder to study our files," Meg signed, with a tight smile. "The chick will still be sleeping a lot then." She looked at Thom as though trying to make him feel better. "It's the best we can do."

A jagged fork of lightning ripped across the late-afternoon

sky, high in the atmosphere, its bright flash obscuring, for the briefest second, the light of the setting suns.

"Oh, no, don't tell me we're going to have a storm on top of everything else," Meg complained.

"Doubt it," Thom assured her, "it's too high up."

Another bolt seared the heavens as Meg and Thom began wading back to the camp.

Tesa waited for more lightning but none came. *They can't hear the thunder, either*, she thought fearfully.

CHAPTER 10

◆

Scott's Notes

Tesa knelt on the narrow bed, staring at the star-studded night sky. She was wearing her favorite sleep shirt with its faded StarBridge logo. Feeling chilled, she pulled her old quilt up around her.

Trinity's three moons were creeping over the horizon, two full, one the thinnest crescent. Father Moon, Mother Moon, New Hatchling Moon. A good sign, according to the Grus —the Moons of the New Hatchling . . . unless Taller's chick was their gift.

Meg and Thom had regained their optimism during the walk back. Thom had made an elaborate dinner, topping it off with a heart-berry pie. During the meal, Tesa had been able to shake, for a while, the worry she'd felt after leaving the nest shelter.

Tesa told the biologists some of the things she and Taller had discussed, but hesitated telling them about the story-walls. She wanted to see them better herself first.

Now dinner was only a satisfied memory and the long night lay ahead. Her eyes strayed to her jacket, hung on a convenient chair, hiding her feathers.

She thought of the Aquila feather, how it had glittered in

the twilight like metal, its quill rigid, strong, a puff of soft down floating at the base, alive, quivering with power. Tesa rubbed her forehead, trying to erase the chaotic fragments of dreams that kept drifting across her mind.

That lightning this afternoon had been heat lightning—nothing more, she told herself, firmly. She refused to see it as a sign meant for her, a sign to make her wonder whether she'd chosen the right path. If she started believing *that*, she'd then have to wonder exactly what her dreams were telling her to do.

Rob Gable, she knew, had had no idea of the level of responsibility the Grus would expect of her. He'd seen this assignment as an unusual pair project, no doubt—one that would be completed in about a year. But now, Tesa realized, there was more than that involved. And she couldn't help wondering whether she was doing the right thing in parenting this chick.

Already, human contact had changed the avians in subtle ways. Humans had renamed their planet, renamed the Grus themselves. *Why do we keep calling them some old Latin word?* Tesa wondered. *Even I do it, and I* **know** *how it feels to be renamed as though you didn't exist before you were* **discovered***!*

This child Tesa would soon be helping to raise—what would be normal for him? What effect might she have on the avians' culture? Were the privateers really the greatest danger the Grus faced, or could it be that twenty years from now cultural anthropologists would look back and chronicle a sociological disaster aided by a naive woman who had ignored her dreams and the bitter lessons of her heritage? She remembered Sacajawea.

Tesa pulled the quilt tighter, trying to shake off her fears. Some people had space travel and some people didn't; that was an inescapable reality. If the humans couldn't prove the avians' intelligence, Trinity would be thrown open for colonization, and then the Grus would undoubtedly suffer the same grim fate other primal peoples had.

But one thing had changed since the days of Columbus and the Conquistadores. She'd been sent to be the interrelator—to understand *them*, become one of *them*, prove their intelligence. Then, if there were a thousand humans here—and in ten year there might be twice that—it wouldn't matter if *none* of the believed the Grus were people, because the interrelator would.

And *nothing* happened without her say-so. That was her job, to speak for the people, to keep their world *theirs*.

So, Tesa scolded herself, as she headed for the desk terminal, *stop fretting and get to work*. As she skimmed through Scott's brief notes on chick-rearing, she was brought up short by the mention of Aquila. Leaning closer, she read the decision Scott had made two years before.

"I've given up discussing the Aquila with Dancer," Scott wrote. "He insists the Aquila are 'uncivilized,' that they're 'mindless killers.' His proof is that the Aquila nest without shelters, that they have no sign language, and that they are predators that eat the Grus—a potent argument, that last one. However, the Grus are predators themselves, preferring live food to any other. The difference in housing could be cultural. As for language, many Grus find *us* 'uncivilized' since our language is spoken. To them, vocalizing is primitive, used only for declaring territory, or love, or warning off enemies. To them, only signing is language, with its poetry of movement and its rich literature of sign combinations. Opera would have no meaning here—Mozart would be only cacophony."

Tesa smiled at that last sentence.

"I've taken six old cameras that were left by Jamestown Founders," Scott's notes read, "and placed them at three different unoccupied Aquila nests on the fringes of the oldgrowth forest, about two hours' flight from camp. Dr. Li would have my ass if she knew, since we've been 'officially' ordered to discontinue any research on the Aquila. The government is scared senseless that our expressing any interest in that taboo subject will jinx our contact with the Grus—at the same time they're so worried about angering the Founders that they're wrapping this whole venture in tons of red tape.

"Anyway, the cameras aren't official government equipment, so Dr. Li can't forbid something she doesn't know anything about. Even Meg's forgotten about these relics. Then, if I can get enough data, maybe I can find out once and for all if these creatures have even a shred of intelligence."

Tesa read how Scott had set those cameras up with heavy-duty batteries and extensive memory-storage capabilities. *Those things might still be out there*, she realized, *waiting for someone to scan them. So where are they?*

"This is the first secret I've kept from Meg," Scott wrote. "After the cameras are set up, I'll record the coordinates."

Tesa signed in frustration. She'd have to look through all Scott's stuff to find those markers—volumes of material! Reaching for her Mizari voder, Tesa interfaced the two computers so the voder could search for the coordinates hidden in Scott's files. The Mizari voder should only take minutes to find the electronic markers Scott would have used to connect him to the cameras. Once she got those markers, she could remote control the cameras—turn them back on, if they'd been shut down. She was excited, as though she and Scott now shared a secret.

Suddenly feeling the eerie sense of another's presence, she jerked her head up. Thom stood right in front of her, watching her over the back of the small terminal.

"How long have you been there?" she demanded, startled.

"A moment," he signed apologetically, his face coloring. "Not even a minute. I . . . uh, that is Meg and I . . . turn our nullifiers off at night. I called you . . . but I forgot that you . . . uh . . ." He stood with his hands poised clumsily in the air, at a loss for words.

Of course. He'd forgotten she was deaf.

"After that," he went on lamely, "I didn't know how to get your attention without scaring you. Now I feel like an idiot!" He looked bemused and uncomfortable, obviously perplexed by a code of behavior he'd never encountered before.

Casually, Tesa blanked the screens and moved away from the terminal, gathering her quilt around her like a buffalo robe. *Relax,* she thought. *He doesn't have the faintest idea of what you were doing.* She moved beside him, taking his role.

"When you want to get the attention of a Deaf person," she signed, "you can wave, like this." She flapped a hand vigorously at the chair she'd just vacated. "Many Deaf people have some hearing, so you can shout, but that won't work with me. The most effective way to get my attention is to stomp the floor." She thumped her foot against the slick tiles.

Thom glanced guiltily in the direction of Meg's quarters. When Tesa looked at him questioningly he explained, "She's probably sleeping. Wouldn't want to wake her . . ."

Tesa smiled at him tolerantly. *He's so transparent!*

Glancing at the terminal, Thom asked, "Are you studying Scott's stuff?"

Tesa nodded.

"I hope Meg and I didn't make you paranoid about that—really, you should be sleeping . . . like Meg."

"So, why aren't you?"

He shrugged, moving aimlessly around the area, then turned quickly toward the open window. "A rousette's calling! That's a golden red, night-flying mammal that looks like a cross between a fox terrier and bat. It makes a hauntingly lovely sound."

As he signed away in biologist mode, Tesa watched, amused.

"The Grus call them," he made a double hand motion, " 'little ones with a big noise,' or, 'they wake us up.' Scott and Meg were frequently roused at night by that piercing sound . . . so Scott called them 'rousettes.' " He looked out the window again with an expression that indicated he was listening.

"They sound so sad," Thom signed. "Like . . . someone who's lost something, or never had something. No—like someone who wants something he can't have."

Tesa looked at him, smiling. "Why do I get the feeling that you've come to tell me something? Ever since we were introduced, you've been barely holding something back. Just—tell me!"

Thom's eyes moved quickly around the room. "My . . ." His hands fumbled. "She got . . ." His cheeks reddened again. "I can't sign it in Grus."

Tesa handed him some paper and a pencil.

Gratefully, he scrawled across the page, handed it to her. "My wife got married yesterday," it read.

It was Tesa's turn to look befuddled. She could see why he hadn't been able to sign that in Grus.

"To someone else, I mean," Thom signed, not looking at her, then held up his hands as though he wanted to start over. "I took this job to get away from Earth." He scribbled another message. "My wife wanted a divorce," it read. "I didn't," he signed. "I was still in love with her. There was another man . . . it was a mess. I wanted to get as far away as I could."

"This is pretty far," Tesa agreed noncommittally.

"Yes . . . and no. When I first came aboard the *Crane*, Lauren made a play for me . . . and I thought, why not . . . but I wasn't ready. I handled it badly. After Scott died, I took Meg's place and was happy to be alone. It gave me time to recover."

Tesa was surprised at the turn his story was taking, knowing that telling it was costing him something.

"When you're hurt really bad," Thom signed, "sometimes you just want to hurt someone back. Then you only want work—no emotion, no love, no hate. When you hit that stage, you can't even notice when you start to feel better." His eyes met hers for a second. "When you stepped out of that shuttle and turned around to look at me—all of a sudden, I knew I was over it. I felt emotions I didn't think I'd ever enjoy again. A stunning woman smiled at me—and I liked it!"

Tesa blinked at him, standing there in her nightshirt and old quilt. She certainly didn't feel stunning.

"I didn't mean to tell you all this," Thom signed, "but . . . I thought we'd have days to get to know each other. Now, in a few hours you'll be leaving. I couldn't let you go without saying . . . something . . ." His hands fumbled as he stared at the floor. "I just wish . . . we didn't have this language barrier."

"What barrier?" she signed. "You've been quite eloquent."

He shook his head. "I feel clumsy, groping for phrases I know instead of speaking spontaneously. If only you—" He broke off abruptly.

"Could hear?" Tesa felt a coldness steal over her.

Thom's expression softened. "It'd be easier. Meg says you're having corrective surgery done next year."

"Meg's *wrong*!" Tesa flashed the signs, anger taking her so quickly she couldn't think, only react. "And who would it be easier for? For *you*, that's all. You and your damned Mozart. You wish I could hear? Well, I wish *you* were deaf. Then I'd know whether the things I see in your eyes were there on purpose. I'd trust your signs, instead of wondering what you really mean. Hearing people hide behind words and sounds."

"You don't want the surgery?" Thom was startled.

"No! And I'm sick of everyone telling me to get my ears *fixed*! They're not *broken* as far as I'm concerned! I'm tired of being defined as a walking malfunctioning ear. I'm a *person*! No, I *don't* want the surgery! Not in a year, not ten years, not *ever*. I'm Deaf! I'm Indian! I'm damned proud of both those things!" Tesa stopped suddenly, realizing that halfway through her tirade, she'd lapsed into ASL, that Thom couldn't follow her signs. In anguished frustration, she yelled, "OH, SHIT!"

Thom gestured desperately at her to be quiet and then tried futilely to suppress his own shocked laughter. "Okay, okay—

you don't have to have to have it done if you don't want to. They're *your* ears! I sure don't care."

Tesa found her anger evaporating. "You don't?"

"Why should I? You've obviously functioned quite well all these years without hearing. If you feel that strongly about not changing, then I'm on your side. Just stop yelling, *please*!"

Tesa began to smile in spite of herself. "You're just saying that to placate me."

"No, I swear. You've got to do a million things in this life to make other people happy. I lived in New York for two years to please my wife, and look where that got me. Somewhere you've got to draw the line. And I can see where you've drawn yours. I admire that."

"Aren't you going to give me a hard time about Mozart?"

"Who?" Thom asked, obviously confused.

She spelled the name again. "You don't know Mozart? He's a composer of classical music. I thought hearing people couldn't live without that experience."

"The only music I care about is the loon's, or the meadowlark's . . . or the rousette's."

Tesa sighed and relaxed. "It's my own fault Meg thinks I'm having the surgery. I didn't want to argue with her . . . or my parents, either."

"Your parents think you want it?" Thom looked surprised.

"It means so much to them. I said I'd have it done next year . . . but it's just not right for me. You're the first person I've told this to since leaving StarBridge . . . actually, you're the first hearing person who hasn't tried to change my mind."

"I can't believe anyone would try to change *your* mind."

Tesa looked rueful. "Most hearing people can't imagine why anyone would want to be *disabled*."

Thom gave her a penetrating stare. "You're not disabled, and anyone who thinks you are is stupid."

They stood, eyeing each other for a few minutes.

"So, is this what we're going to be?" Thom finally asked, meeting her eyes. "I'm *hearing* and you're *deaf*? I liked it better when I was Thom, and you were . . . a stunning woman who smiled at me." He moved closer to her and ran a finger along the edge seam of her quilt. "I read that in the old days, if an eligible woman was interested in a young man, she'd invite him inside her buffalo robe, and they would stand outside her family's tipi, wrapped up together in plain sight, whispering softly, while everyone pretended not to see them.''

"When did you read about that?'' Tesa asked, smiling wryly.

"Last night,'' he confessed. "I looked it up. I love old traditions, don't you?''

She laughed. *"This* is *not* my family's tipi!''

He nodded. "And . . . I don't know how to whisper to you. Tesa, how do deaf people talk when they're holding each other?''

"By finger-writing on each other's backs,'' she explained.

He moved boldly, surrounding her, quilt and all, with his arms. Pulling her close, he wrote on her back, "Like this?''

He smelled woodsy and clean, like Trinity did, like home did, and his scent raised the hairs on her arms. Even through the blanket, she could feel the strength in his body, his arms. Goose bumps sprouted along Tesa's arms as she realized how attracted she was to him.

His eyes glittered in the half light of the terminal. He spelled, "Kiss you?''

No, she thought regretfully. She was too aware of the lack of privacy, the nearness of her own bed—and the role she'd have to play with the Grus in the morning. Reluctantly she shook her head and stepped back.

Thom looked disappointed, but released her graciously.

Tesa reached for the pad of paper. "In your reading, did you find out about Iktomi?'' she wrote, showing him.

He shook his head.

"He's a trickster,'' she signed, "a spider being, a legend. He must have followed me here . . . to bring us together the night before I join the Grus.''

"Does he always introduce . . . lovers?''

"Only if it will cause trouble,'' she signed ruefully. "Soon, I'll be in Taller's shelter . . . I'll be one of the White Wind people. I think then we might see each other differently.'' That was Iktomi—making people want what they couldn't have. She wondered if he'd given the rousette its voice.

"You must be crazy if you think I'm giving up that easy,'' Thom signed. He moved to take her in his arms again.

She pulled away. "No! You're rushing me, Thom!''

"You really mean that,'' he signed, realizing it himself.

She nodded. "This is happening too fast. We only *met* yesterday! And I'll be here for a long time.''

"Out *there*, not *here*. When will I see you again?''

"We'll make time," she assured him, amused by his urgency. "But, that's not really what we both came here for, is it?"

"It's not against the rules," he signed, looking abashed.

"I have my own rules, Thom."

He sighed, capitulating. "You really think we can find time to get together while you're in the shelter?"

She shrugged. "If I tell Taller I want time alone—"

Thom's head swiveled abruptly, breaking their eye contact, preventing Tesa from finishing her sentence. Her hands hung uselessly, while he scanned the darkness around her room. When Thom turned around, her tight-lipped expression startled him.

"I thought I heard—" he started to sign.

Tesa whipped her head around before he could finish, showing him the effect of breaking eye contact with a signer. Touching her cheek, he turned her head gently.

"I'm sorry," he signed. "I thought I heard Meg . . ."

"Thom," she explained patiently, "you don't want me to be *deaf*, but I am. You don't want to be *hearing*—but you are. Sound is, and always will be, more important to you than anything I might have to say."

"That's not true! I made a mistake. These are new rules for me, but I can learn them. And this is one I won't forget."

"Yes, you will," she signed. "Just like you forgot I was deaf when you first showed up. You're careless with your eye contact. I've watched you with the Grus, and you're the same way, and you know how they feel about 'the look'! It could make them think you're dishonest, that you've got a hidden agenda. And it makes *me* suspect your sincerity. It seems as though the only thing you can remember is that I'm a woman."

"Listen . . ." he began, and then blushed over that sign.

"Stop that. I'm *listening*."

"Meg will be furious if she finds me here with you."

"That's ridiculous," Tesa insisted. "I'm an adult."

Thom shook his head. "She'll be furious with *me*. She warned me to stay away from you. She's afraid I'll distract you, or maybe . . . myself . . . but I had to talk to you."

There was a long, awkward pause. Finally, Tesa signed, We'll meet somehow. We'll start over. Good night, Thom."

He left, moving surely through the shelter.

With mixed emotions, Tesa sat down at the terminal. She

no longer knew how she felt, or what she wanted . . . except, that she wished again that Thom were deaf. She banged a key on the terminal angrily, calling up her previous program.

A sudden synchronized blink from the Mizari voder and the hologramic terminal distracted her, then a series of strange symbols flickered across both computers simultaneously. They began flashing in strobelike beats, like two computers talking back and forth with no human interference.

It was now so late that the *Crane*'s computer was collecting data from the robot probes. The surge of information transfer flooded the terminal and the voder.

Tesa turned them off. Let the machines have their private conversations, she'd check on those markers tomorrow. She glanced out the window, and had to search for the moons. Father Sun got up early. In three hours she'd be starting a new life.

Curling up on the cot, she wrapped up in her quilt as though it were a cocoon, and tried not to think about someone lying not twenty-five feet away, looking at the same stars, trying not to think about her. *Can he still hear the rousette?* Tesa wondered.

Meg stared at the curved ceiling anxiously. At last, the glow from Tesa's computer had turned off; at last, the young woman had crawled into her creaky cot. But was she sleeping? Meg doubted it. And Thom? He was still tossing and turning.

Meg heard a groan from his room, and the complaints of Scott's ancient bed as Thom flopped over one more time. Her face burned. Thom had *heard* her stumble against that new piece of equipment. *You deserved to get caught,* she could hear Scott scold her. *You old busybody.*

Oh, shut up, she argued back. *You wouldn't care if this whole place turned into a* razgul, *a copulating free-for-all.*

What's wrong with that? Scott's memory-voice bantered back.

That's not how work gets done! You wouldn't listen to me when Thom first came aboard and look what happened.

What happened? Two consenting adults . . .

The Crane *was in an uproar. Bruce acted like an overbearing father, and Lauren was hurt, embarrassed, and a* suka, *a bitch to work with for weeks . . .*

Until Peter won her affections. It worked out fine. You always let these things bother you too much. And now you're panicking because Thom's interested in Tesa. Shame on you, tiptoeing around, spying on them, like a wicked stepmother.

Chertovski durak, *you damned fool, we don't have time for that! He promised me . . .* Meg stopped the mental dialogue with herself. She was having more and more of them since she'd come back, as though Scott was always perched on her shoulder whispering in her ear.

Scott would've thrown Thom at Tesa. He would've insisted Meg and he go away so the lovers could have privacy. Scott would be chuckling merrily while forcing Meg to sleep on the ground. It was all part of his humanity, his warm, loving nature. It was why the Grus had taken to him so quickly. It was why Meg loved him so much. Her best friend, the finest person she'd known.

Scott, **golubchik moi,** Meg flung an arm over her eyes, *I miss you so much.*

Taller stood on one leg in the inky water, peering into the darkness. The night sounds of the marsh washed over him, familiar and comforting. Weaver had eaten well, while their chick slept in his egg. When she'd returned to the nest to take over incubation, she'd felt confident, she liked Good Eyes, and she'd seemed happier than she'd been in months. As soon as she'd settled herself, the chick had begun cutting his way out.

Below the marsh sounds came the noisy splashing of the humans as they approached. They were early. That pleased him.

Suddenly First-One-There and Relaxed broke through the reeds and waved a greeting to him. He dipped his head politely to them, finally seeing Good Eyes. First-One and Relaxed were giving Good Eyes last-minute instructions, as parents would. First-One was warning her about the cold and ordering her to eat well. Relaxed signed several times, "Please be careful."

Taller cocked his head to one side.

There was something new in the way the humans interacted, in the way Relaxed looked at Good Eyes, the way he and First-One glanced at each other. Could Relaxed be courting Good Eyes? Humans did not burst into spontaneous dance when they became interested in each other. Puff had told Taller that their courting was different, very physical. Also, some humans, like Puff and First-One, had relationships of companionship that never culminated in sex or child-rearing. That, to Taller, seemed sad.

Taller had a sudden flash of jealousy. No one would interfere with *his* family, of which Good Eyes was now a part.

The three humans shared gestures, which involved embraces and the touching of their soft lips. Finally, Good Eyes looked at Taller, and her eyes held his steadily.

She turned back to the others and signed, "I'll be fine. I'll eat three meals. I'll brush my teeth. I've got to go!"

Suddenly Relaxed held out a hand, palm forward, his short, five fingers making a sign Taller had never seen. The thumb, first finger, and last, tiny finger pointed up, the two middle fingers held down. First-One saw the sign and copied it.

The young woman returned the sign with emphasis, and then spun around and marched resolutely to where Taller waited.

The avian held up his own three-fingered hand, trying to imitate the sign. "What does that mean?" he asked Good Eyes.

Her alien eyes gleamed at him. "It's a sign from my world." She made it for him. "It means 'I love you.'"

Taller looked at Relaxed. With great deliberation, he enveloped the human with his wing and made her a part of his family.

CHAPTER 11

♦

Parenthood

Tesa danced on the air, a little flying thing with shiny wings, following the trail of drifting sweet smoke into the tiny sweat lodge. In the center of the lodge was a shallow circular depression. That was where the hot stones should have been, sending up their purifying steam, but instead, there was only a bundle made of gleaming feathered cloth. Inside the bundle something moved, something alive.

Beside the bundle stood a Grus, just fledged, his long, black primaries at odds with his layered cinnamon and white feathers.

"Come outside," signed the Grus, beckoning to her as he slipped through the slitted opening of the lodge.

Disoriented, she followed. The Grus yearling stood among giant trees, beside a bundle made of feathered cloth. Inside the bundle, something moved, something alive. "This is the answer," he signed, simply. "Look."

She was suddenly filled with fear. An angry Wakinyan emerged from under the cloth like a genie from a bottle. The massive black thunderbird, swathed in mists and clouds, soon towered over them. It opened its beak in what had to be a terrible scream.

I can't hear it, she thought, panicking, *I can't hear it!*

Jagged streaks of lightning rent the sky. She looked back at the sweat lodge and realized, with a sick feeling, that its entrance was facing east, not west as she had originally thought. This was the sweat lodge of a *heyoka*. She felt the Wakinyan's mocking words. "What a backward-forward way to be."

Tesa turned to the Grus but he dissolved, becoming instead a gigantic red and white bear, whose terrible jaws were split in a hideous grin.

She fled back into the sweat lodge, away from the laughing bear, away from the Wakinyan, only to find a white bundle where the hot rocks should be—inside the bundle, something moved.

Something alive.

Tesa felt a soft tickling against her throat. Her sleep-fogged brain tried to respond, but her tired body refused. She snuggled deeper into the soft cocoon but finally realized that there was something *alive* in her bed.

She edged away and peered down. Beneath her chin a ball of sleeping fluff reacted to her withdrawal by snuggling closer.

Forgot about you, thought Tesa to the chick she'd watched hatch a few hours before. He was dry now, his cinnamon fluff highlighted by blond tufts around his beak and behind his wings. His infant trust helped dispel the worry Tesa had felt on waking. The chick was undoubtedly, Tesa felt, the most beautiful thing she'd ever seen, and she loved him unconditionally.

When Tesa had entered the nest shelter in the early morning darkness, the interior had been so black she could barely make out the brilliant whiteness of Weaver's reclining form. Soon, though, a luminous, dusky glow began to penetrate the gloom through thousands of thin slits in the tule mat walls.

The chick had nearly finished cutting out of the egg, and as the Mother Sun followed the Father, he'd pushed out. His wet down had clung to his spindly neck and tiny, fingerless wings. His dark and swollen legs had been full of edema that would be quickly absorbed. He'd lain there, one big blue eye staring at his parents as though wondering what the crowd was for.

Tesa had fallen in love with him, but the hatchling would not see very well for several days. Because of her dark clothes and coloring, he could only focus on her poorly, if at all. For Tesa, that was disappointing.

Weaver had probed deep into the nest with her bill, pulling out small globs of mud from its foundation. Traditionally, the parents fed the chick mud so that he would be forever part of the World. The mud would give him water, the nourishment of minerals, trace elements, and micro-life, along with the digestive aid of fine sand that the small, toothless being needed. Tesa had thought again of the Hopi's Sipapu, the Earth Navel in the kiva symbolizing the birth of all humans from Mother Earth.

The wet hatchling had gobbled the bits of marsh mud greedily from Weaver's and Taller's bills, as Tesa pinched some between her fingers to present to him. Suddenly something tiny and sharp had jabbed her thumb and blood had welled around the mud. Tesa had removed a sliver of shell and, at Taller's insistence, had fed the chick the mud glob, colored with her blood.

"Now," Taller had signed, "you are a part of him, also." Then he'd urged her to rest. The two Grus had already prepared a place for her on the rim of the nest, where she could feel the gentle warmth of the decaying reeds. Taller's and Weaver's own hatching cloaks had made the mattress and blanket.

"I won't disturb you, lying here?" she'd asked Weaver.

"Not once I tuck my head," the female had assured her. "Taller says I could sleep through a marsh fire."

Tiredly, Tesa had slid between the cloaks. The subtle bottom warmth, and the soft, white feathers had lulled her within seconds. The presence of the large avian next to her had seemed like the most normal thing in the World.

How long had she slept? Had she dreamt? Typically, she couldn't remember. Without letting in cool air, Tesa pulled her head out from under the cloak. The light was strong, and dust motes and bits of feather fluff danced on gentle air currents. Beams of light bounced off the wind-chime crystals, fragmenting into thousands of rainbows. The nest was empty, except for the hatching cloak haphazardly heaped in the bowl. Neither avian was inside. However, the structure was not unoccupied.

Some of the rainbows weren't from the crystals at all, but were, instead, a swarm of gossamer-winged, long-bodied insects. They flitted around, capturing the sun on wings and bodies and refracting it. The arc of their perpetually moving translucent wings turned them into flying rainbows.

Those must be the insects that interested the Grus in crystal wind chimes! Tesa realized delightedly.

An adult Grus entered the shelter, slipping gracefully through the entrance. It was Weaver, Tesa decided. Her long avian face seemed by now very different from Taller's. "Is the chick still sleeping?" the Grus asked. "Taller would have warmed him, but you're his parent, too, so we decided you could do that as you slept. It gave us a chance to feed. We collected food for you. Have you seen all the shimmerings?" Weaver was obviously very awake.

Tesa rubbed her eyes, realizing with a pang that there'd be no coffee from her favorite chef today. She felt a sudden squirming, then the chick popped out from under the covers. He opened his mouth, probably cheeping, so Tesa purred at him. This mollified him, and he burrowed back under the cloak.

"That won't keep him quiet for long," Weaver assured her. "He's hungry."

Taller entered. "While you slept, I thanked the Sun Family for our good fortune," he signed to Tesa, "and told the flock that the hatching went well. Now you're awake, and hungry?"

Tesa nodded, and indicated the cloud of iridescent insects.

" 'Shimmerings,' " he signed. He stretched a wing, watching as dozens of the creatures alighted along his feathers, like living jewels. "They hatched shortly after you fell asleep. This is the first hatch in a long while. It's a good sign. The shimmerings predict rain, which means plentiful food. And they're excellent food themselves." Casually, he plucked the insects off his wings, tossing them to the back of his throat like so many grapes. They seemed to take no notice, as more alighted in their place. "Chicks hatched the same day as the shimmerings," he signed, "are blessed."

"But the shimmerings are gifts of the moons," Weaver warned. "The chicks are promised lives of newness and change."

Tesa thought of the Chinese curse, "May you be born in interesting times."

When the chick's head popped out again, he saw his natural parents. He scrambled out, hobbling clumsily, fluttering his wings endearingly, his beak opening and closing. Weaver snapped up a shimmering and, with fingers and bill, quickly dissected out the soft thorax, offering it to the chick, who gobbled it down.

"Puff told us humans don't eat many insects," Weaver commented as she set about preparing another morsel.

"Some humans still do," Tesa signed, crawling out from under the feather cloaks. "Nowadays, though, there's not much insect-eating on Earth." *Especially not before coffee*, she thought.

"Interesting," Weaver signed with the kind of movement that told Tesa she wondered how the human had ever survived childhood. The chick had finished off six segments and now burrowed under Weaver's plumage as she settled herself on the nest.

"Come outside and eat," Taller bid the human, "while the food is still fresh."

As she stepped out of the shelter into the full light of day, Tesa paused. Everything about this morning on this alien world, with these alien people, had seemed as normal as summer tipi camp. Now, she looked at the marsh and felt a rush of vertigo, as if she were on a time machine, hurtling so far back that she could see the Mennominees in birch-bark canoes gathering rice in Wisconsin, or the Athabasca whose name meant "a place of reeds and grass everywhere." Around her there was nothing but distant hills, marshland, tule hutches, and swaying reeds.

Tesa could not see the landing pad, the camp shelter, or the shuttlecraft. She could have been the only human in the World, alone with the White Wind people. Breathing deeply, she drank in the smell of the World, the smell of her new home.

Holding her hands out, she prayed her thanks for the beautiful day and the healthy baby.

"Are you praying?" Taller asked, his head cocked to one side. "We thought only First-One-There prayed, and only in front of the . . ." His sign meant "hard square, talking, sign-ing."

Computer, thought Tesa. He must've seen Meg observing a telecast of a religious service. "The people of my world have many different beliefs. I like to start my day with prayer.''

"Tomorrow, we'll pray together, then.'' Taller was hock-sitting on the platform, removing food from mesh bags that could be carried over a neck and still permit flying. There was round-red fruit, heart-berries, large fern fiddleheads so tender they could be eaten raw, and a pile of bivalves. The shimmerings were everywhere, thousands of them, and in the sunlight they were even more startling. Suddenly she noticed an alien object beside Taller. It was silver, oblong—and not from Trinity.

"What is *that*?'' she asked Taller, indicating the thing.

"This? Well, I don't know. I found it where the reeds begin. I thought you might've dropped it. It was caught on the reeds by this webbed material.'' He indicated the carrying strap as he handed the object to Tesa.

"Oh,'' she signed, feeling both foolish and delighted, as she took it. "It's an insulated container.'' She uncapped it and found a drawing inside the top—the ASL "I love you'' sign. "Relaxed must have brought it this morning.''

At the sight of Thom's name-sign, Taller's crown flared suddenly, and his feathers fluffed. Surprised by his reaction, Tesa explained, "It's fresh, hot coffee. Won't you try some?''

The avian's reaction subsided. "Yes, that would be nice.''

Picking up a long, narrow bivalve shell, Tesa poured him a taste. Taller clacked his bill as he savored the drink. For once, he did not spray it everywhere. "Interesting,'' he decided. "It's better each day.''

"If we leave the empty container where you found it, Relaxed might bring us more tomorrow.'' Tesa carefully watched Taller's reaction to this suggestion.

For a moment the avian seemed to be warring with his own feathers, but finally, he slicked them all down. "Puff told us that humans guard their territory, but not against everyone.''

"Not against friends,'' Tesa agreed.

"I've never understood that,'' he signed bluntly, "but you may find it hard to understand us.'' He indicated the sweep of marsh. "Here, we get plenty of rain and food, but it's not like that everywhere in the World, and it isn't like that here every fruiting season. Because I'm the leader, because I found this place to live, Weaver and I have the best territory. For years, we have had no children.''

He paused, as if remembering. "All those empty eggs were hard on Weaver. We allowed others to share our food, so they wouldn't fight us for it and splinter the people's loyalty. Then the humans came. Since then, we've been pressured more and more for this place. I've allowed others to share it, hoping to keep the people's loyalty. But once we knew our egg was fertile, that we would have a child—then we couldn't share anymore."

His signs slowed. "The egg changes us," he explained carefully. "It makes us jealous. Allowing you to come here was difficult, but now we accept you as our partner. Relaxed is not our partner, and he does not endure 'the look.' I'm not sure how I feel about his presence in our territory, and I'm not sure how I feel about his interest in you." Taller reached over and moved a stone. "Are you in love with Relaxed?"

"I don't think so . . ." Tesa felt confused, "not yet."

"You speak like a youngster being courted for the first time." That familiarity seemed to comfort him. "I'll return the container where I found it. If Relaxed comes, I'll tolerate him." He handed her the stone. "I made this for you."

It was a well-crafted stone knife, made to fit her palm.

"It's beautiful," Tesa signed, and reached for a bivalve. Its tough muscle yielded easily.

Taller looked on indulgently. "By the time the chick grows fingers you'll be an expert," he assured her. The little one's fingers would grow out of his wings as his feathers did.

A flash of white among the reeds caught Tesa's eye. Taller must've seen it also, since he was instantly on his feet, patrolling the platform with long, purposeful strides. Tesa could see several Grus near the boundary of clear water.

Why are they here? she wondered, concerned.

Taller fluffed up, then dropped his head to his feet, arching his body into an extreme bow—threatening the others to keep their distance. He was furious, his crown longer and brighter than she had ever seen it. In spite of this, a large male casually stepped out from the reeds into the clear water.

Taller leaped into flight, landing near the trespasser. The others took to wing, but the lone male stood his ground. The two huge avians squared off, eye to eye, then Taller rushed the stranger, wings outstretched, head extended. It was too much for the interloper, and he flew off, Taller following him a short distance before circling back to the nest platform.

Triumphantly, the aged leader threw his head back and called.

"Who was that?" Tesa signed when Taller finally sat beside her. "What did he want?"

"That was Kills-the-Ripper," Taller signed. "He was in the escort yesterday, when Flies-Too-Fast was hurt."

"I remember," Tesa signed, recalling the avian that had been unable to save the yearling.

"He's always wanted this territory, *and* the leadership of the White Wind people. He hates your people." Taller paused, looking warily over the marsh. "Last year, a Tree Ripper destroyed his nest shelter and tried to eat his egg."

Tesa looked alarmed, but Taller reassured her. "It happens to those who nest too close to the trees. The Ripper is a formidable neighbor, usually tolerant of us, but if he has the urge to eat egg, it's usually safer to let him have it and lay another. But Ripper's egg was talking and he could not bear to see his son devoured. He rushed the huge animal and pierced him through the eye, right into his brain, killing him. And he has been very hard to live with ever since."

I guess so, Tesa thought, amazed.

"The people were swayed by that," Taller signed, "but, yesterday, when he couldn't catch the chick, he lost some of his name's glory. He may try to gain it back some other way."

"As your partner, what should I do?" she asked.

"Protect our son," Taller told her. "Now, enjoy your breakfast while it's still fresh."

The rest of the day seemed, if anything, a lazy vacation filled with food, rest, and the care of a carefree infant. This was the most relaxing time Tesa had had since the day she had been passed over for her tapping.

She learned the stories on the shelter's walls, though she still couldn't see their imagery, and fed the sleepy chick whenever he demanded. Tesa couldn't bring herself to kill the lovely shimmerings, so instead she offered other things. *He needs a balanced diet,* she told herself.

As the suns dipped close to the horizon, Tesa pulled her star quilt out of her backpack to incorporate it into her bed. When Weaver saw it, she became as interested as Taller had been when he'd seen it in the Quonset hut.

"May I have time to study this?" Weaver asked, peering at the quilt, first with one eye, then the other.

"Of course," Tesa agreed.

"This design is giving me ideas . . . ." Weaver signed, "but I'll need time to think about it."

Once darkness crept through the shelter, Taller went to stand one-legged in the marsh, to guard his family through the night. It was too early for Tesa to even think of sleep, so she slipped outside. This would be a good time to look at Scott's electronic markers.

When she stepped onto the platform, Taller was there, rigidly attentive, staring pointedly into the reeds. Tesa followed his gaze, worried, but then she saw the flash of silver that meant Thom had come for the insulated container.

"He's waiting for you," Taller signed, without taking his eyes from Thom. His feathers raised slightly, then settled.

"Perhaps you should tell him it would be better for him not to come anymore," Tesa suggested to mollify the uneasy avian.

Taller stared at her. "Do you wish to speak with him?"

She met his eyes levelly. "Yes, I do."

Suddenly the avian ruffled his feathers and shook himself all over like a dog settling his fur. "Then, by all means, talk with him," he signed, then stepped back inside the shelter.

Taking advantage of her moment of privacy, Tesa slid down the embankment, slapped on her stilts, and quickly strode through the water. However, when she approached the reed line, she found herself strangely reluctant to cross that boundary.

Thom stared at her as the first moon lit the sky.

"The coffee was wonderful," she signed, feeling inane.

"I wasn't sure he'd find it," Thom answered, "*or* if he'd deliver it." He seemed reluctant to sign Taller's name.

"I looked for you on the bluff, but didn't see you."

"I saw you now and again," Thom signed. "You seemed pretty absorbed in what you were doing."

It's happened, already, Tesa thought bitterly. *We're different. He acts like I'm someone's wife, and I feel like one!*

"Does Meg know you're here?" she asked.

Thom smiled slightly. "Oh, yeah. We . . . had a long talk. We understand each other. It's okay." He looked at her as though she were a hologram from another solar system. "I thought about you all day today—I couldn't get anything done. I can't come any closer, but can't you come over here?"

No, Tesa realized with a sudden shock, *I can't*.

Thom stopped smiling. "Is it going to work, Tesa, with you

and the Grus? I've had a lot of second thoughts about it today.''

That startled her. "What are you talking about?"

"I'm just not sure it's right to expect you to live with them, become . . . what? Taller's second mate?"

He's just jealous, she told herself. He couldn't understand what the chick meant to her, what this kind of life meant to her. "Give it time, Thom. Give me a chance to do my job."

His quick smile returned. "You're right. I'm just wishing we could be together." Thom looked over her head suddenly, and she followed his gaze. Taller had emerged from the shelter and was studiously preening. "You'd better go. Coffee'll be here in the morning." He blew her a kiss and strode away.

When Tesa climbed the platform, Taller stopped preening. "Your interest in him might be easier to understand," he signed, "if he were taller." Before she could respond, he flew to the clear water and took up his one-legged watch.

It was not until the third evening that Tesa had time to call up Scott's markers that were patiently waiting for her in the computer. There were six of them, one for each camera. Eagerly, she ordered the system to see if any of the equipment was still functioning. Scott had put two cameras at each nest, just in case one failed. She wouldn't let herself believe there wasn't at least one functioning. She looked at the first nest.

Suddenly the small voder screen went black.

At the bottom of the dark screen she read that the first camera had been destroyed by lightning. Nest One's second camera had no video, but it did have audio. *Now, won't that do me a world of good?* the young woman thought, disappointed.

Fearing the worst, Tesa then asked the voder to tell her how many cameras were nonfunctional. Her heart sank as she read that one camera at each site had been destroyed. *Well, that still leaves me two working cameras, and this "hearing" one,* she told herself optimistically. She asked the voder to connect her with the good camera at Nest Two. She'd carefully muted the voder earlier, so it wouldn't attract Taller's attention.

The small screen abruptly flared into color and Tesa sucked in a sharp breath.

She was looking at the edge of a giant nest built of sticks, twigs, and tree limbs. On it perched a massive female Aquila, ruby-red eyes blazing, beak opened, screaming into the wind.

As Tesa watched, another of the bronze creatures, this one golden-eyed, landed, holding in its talons a stout limb.

They're nesting! Tesa realized excitedly.

The smaller, golden-eyed male fitted the limb carefully into the construct only to have the female rip it out and throw it over the side.

Now, there's intelligence, Tesa thought, amused. *Any fool could see* **that** *wasn't the right color.* She asked the computer how much memory was left, and was surprised to find that it was completely available—that nothing was stored in it.

That can't be right, Tesa thought. She ordered the camera to record from dawn to sunset and then called up the last marker. The last camera at Nest Three was also fully functional, but it was spying on an empty nest. All its memory, too, was available.

They could come back, she thought. *I'll keep checking.*

Tesa realized that she could use the ''hearing'' camera at Nest One to her advantage. If that nest were inhabited, the camera could record the Aquila's vocalizations and Tesa could program her voder to try and translate them. It would take time to limit the voder's other functions, but it might be worth it.

The computer confirmed that it could hear occupants in the nest.

Wanting to give the voder's memory all the space it needed, Tesa scanned her files to erase or download them into external storage chips. She didn't want anything to limit the voder's ability to set up a mapping algorithm.

She'd wiped most of the files when she came upon something she hadn't even known she'd recorded. It was a conversation between Peter and Thom days ago, probably when the two had been washing the dishes. She felt guilty looking at it—it was, after all, nothing more than eavesdropping—but when she saw that Peter had brought her name up, her curiosity overcame her compunctions.

There was banter about Thom's interest in Tesa, and Lauren's feelings about that, and then the sentences became garbled and broken up. *They must've turned on the sonics,* Tesa decided, scanning to see if there was anything else in the conversation she could decipher.

The garbage cleared. Then the voder identified Bruce. His sentence was plain.

"Meg said something to me about an Aquila leaving its lunch hereabouts," he'd said.

Tesa felt a shiver of dread.

Peter remarked that he and Thom had been discussing that, but for Tesa, that conversation had been ruined by the sonic washer. Peter downplayed the significance of the Aquila's visit, but Bruce wasn't so easily put off. He wanted to do something, to be assured that the ground crew was not in danger. The next sentence rocked Tesa.

"Scott wasn't afraid to violate the taboo," Bruce had said. "I looked through his paperwork—he'd planted cameras . . ." The weatherman wanted to find the cameras, reactivate them. Tesa realized with a stab of dismay that the *Crane* crew could've already downloaded those camera memories to study them, which would explain why they were empty.

Thom said he knew about the cameras, and had looked for them. The next thing he said only confused Tesa. He insisted that *all* of the cameras were nonfunctional.

Tesa sat back, staring at the display. It might've taken Thom longer to find Scott's markers than it had Tesa, but she did not doubt that he'd found them. If he'd found them, then he'd probably been the one who'd downloaded those memories. But why would he lie about it?

Tesa didn't like finding out that Thom was capable of lying. Whatever his motives were, she would have trouble viewing him the same way now. *Remember, he can't endure "the look,"* she thought.

She tried to shake off her hasty suspicions. After all, *she* had no intention of telling anyone about the cameras, either. The Aquila *were* taboo. Maybe Thom felt compelled, as she did, to continue Scott's work. Still, his lying unnerved her.

You hypocrite, she scolded herself, **you** *lied to* **him** *barely an hour after you'd arrived.* She squeezed her eyes shut, confused. *What a backward-forward way to be.*

Tesa opened her eyes to reread Bruce's bitter words.

"If we can't do approved research on the Aquila," he'd said, "we'll just have to rely on the oldest Terran technique for coping with nuisance wildlife."

Tesa felt like ice. She purged the memory without reading the last sentences. She knew that Terran technique all too well.

Eradication. Extermination. Extinction. Genocide.

Gazing at the lone Grus standing in the inky water, guarding his family, guarding her, she thought bitterly, *Taller . . . if you only knew who really was the* **Death**.

CHAPTER 12

◆

The Coup

The shimmerings predicted rain, and rain came. Two days of it, a gentle, steady soaking that effectively canceled Tesa's visits with Thom. But the coffee still arrived every morning.

Tesa was busy recording Grus legends and filming the story-walls. Even though the chick's eyesight had improved, he still had trouble focusing on Tesa and she worried that she might be too alien for him to accept.

She was also tired of referring to him in third person. The Grus explained that the right name would eventually "show up," that it was no one's special task, as it was among Tesa's people.

But on the chick's fifth day in the World, the sky was bright and cloudless and no one could go near the slitted opening without finding him under their feet. As the Father Sun edged over the horizon, Taller stuck his head through the slit, while his son stood comically between his legs, peering out onto the World, his blue eyes enormous. Stretching tall, the chick flared his stubby wings out straight, scared to death.

"He can wait," Weaver told Tesa. The avian was on the

nest, working on a cloak. "I want to finish this, first." She unfolded the material and stood in one smooth motion. "I've never attempted anything like this . . . It might not work. If it hadn't been for your blanket, the idea would never have occurred to me."

Tesa stared at Weaver, confused. The avian asked the human to stand, and when she obliged, the Grus female draped the feathered material over her.

"Taller helped with the design." Weaver drew the luxurious folds over the human's shoulders, "but I'm not sure it's right, yet." She laced grass thongs together and the material began to form sides, then sleeves.

Tesa slid her hands into the three black "fingers" at the end of each arm as Weaver fitted them to her, making them smaller. The woman stood like an obedient dressmaker's dummy, and soon was wearing a white, thigh-length, feathered garment that laced up the front and had a cowl to cover her head. With black pants, the shirt made her, in coloring at least, a Grus.

While Weaver was busy knotting up the other sleeve seam, Tesa examined the workmanship, but as she fingered the material, she received a shock when she recognized the tanned skin that had once belonged to Taller's son. The garment was pieced together, like a quilt, from weavings and Water Dancer's skin. Under other circumstances, it would have been a perfect dancer's costume.

Taller, watching from the doorway, must've seen the change in her expression and realized she was upset. "We couldn't use it for mourning," he signed, "because it won't decay. Then, Weaver saw your blanket and decided that by wearing it, you might help Dancer's spirit reach the suns."

Weaver had stopped working and looked at Tesa with concern.

"I'll wear this with respect for Dancer's honor," Tesa signed, "and in the hope his spirit will lend me his heart."

The two Grus bobbed their heads and said nothing more.

Tesa ran her hands over the shirt and thought about Water Dancer . . . and his death. Where was his *nagi*, his soul, now?

The chick was oblivious to the adults' discussion and continued beseeching them through body gestures to be allowed outside. His comical insistence on doing something he was plainly frightened to do broke the somber mood.

As Weaver finished the last seam of Tesa's costume, Taller

slipped outside, pretending to take little notice of his son's alarm. Weaver went next, bending down for a moment to purr some confidence to the little one. When Tesa followed them the chick could do nothing but scramble along behind or be left alone.

The shimmerings had multiplied fantastically after the rains and the shadow shapes of animals slipped in and out of the reeds. Flocks of jewel-colored birds swooped around.

The chick watched his parents walking away and finally jutted his wings out and jogged after them down the embankment, running right into the back of Tesa's legs. Picking himself up, he shook himself and marched resolutely between his two mothers. But when they stepped into the water, he stood hesitant.

Tesa waded out without stilts until she was thigh deep while the Grus adults stayed near, probing for delicacies underwater. Within seconds, the chick launched himself after them and was paddling around their legs.

"I had no idea he'd be able to swim so well," Tesa signed.

"We're born to water," Taller told her. "It's not something we *learn,* we just know. But chicks can drown, or large fish and hardshells can pull them under to eat them."

Tesa's eyes widened, and she stared at the water until her eyes burned.

"Do human children swim?" Weaver asked.

"Yes, but we have to be taught." Tesa had been a water baby, something the therapists thought would help her coordination. She'd never feared water—an advantage during her training for the Ashu, hours that now weren't going to be wasted after all.

Soon the two Grus moved away, hunting. The youngster followed them, then sailed back to Tesa, swimming around her, making her laugh. He *could* see her better now that she wore the costume.

"He sails along the water like the shuttle sails the air," she signed to the Grus, casually. They gave each other a significant look and Tesa thought, horrified, *I think I just named him* **Shuttlecraft***!*

Taller made a sign. *Sailor*, Tesa thought, pleased. *I can live with that.*

She uprooted a grass plant to feed him the soft pith. "Hello, Sailor," she signed, but he was distracted by a shimmering that landed on his back. Spinning in the water like a puppy after his tail, he struggled to catch an insect almost a quarter his size. Tesa watched, smiling. She had given him his name, and he could see her as clearly as Taller or Weaver. How could things on Trinity get any better?

As Taller and Weaver ranged farther away, she fed the chick water plants and halfheartedly tried to catch him a fingerling fish. Sailor was watching her attempts with childish fascination when he was distracted by something behind her. Before Tesa could pull her attention from the fish that had just slipped through her fingers, Sailor's eyes widened in panic, his beak opened, and he reared back in the water, flaring his little wings. Terrified, he spun and paddled furiously toward Weaver, who was back at the platform. Tesa felt a burst of vibrations from the female's call that sent shivers down her back. This felt different from the other calls, it felt frightening.

Oh, shit, she thought. *What's behind me*? Slowly, fearing what she might see, Tesa turned her head.

Kills-the-Ripper was bearing down on her, wings spread, yellow eyes filled with murder. *How could you let this happen?* she chastised herself. Then her brain screamed, *MOVE!*

The avian's lethal black bill came down like a knife as Tesa dived into deeper water, kicking off hard. She *was* too slow and the rapier point punctured her calf, but she kept on kicking in spite of the fiery pain, striking out for clear water, drawing Ripper away from the nest shelter, away from Sailor, using speed she'd developed when training to live with the Ashu.

The water churned violently as the Ripper landed almost on top of her. She jackknifed right, knowing she couldn't get far enough fast enough to save herself. Then another pair of thin, black legs splashed beside her, blocking her attacker. Gasping for air, blinking, Tesa strained to see what was happening.

Taller had come down in front of his enemy and the two avians were battling. There were no social preliminaries, no dancelike moves. They'd thrashed to the shallows for their deadly kick-fighting. As if their bills weren't weapon enough, their small, innocuous-looking claws were sharp as quick-silver scalpels, inflicting deadly, bloody wounds.

Ripper's after the leadership, Tesa realized. *He'll have to kill us all.*

Suddenly the male combatants drew apart. Taller was bleeding, dark red blood streaming down his white neck and spattering one wing. They circled, looking for an opening. Then, to Tesa's amazement, Taller began to preen his back.

He's stalling, Tesa thought.

"You've destroyed our way of life!" Ripper's signs were devoid of respect. One of Taller's eyes was fastened on the challenger, even while he adjusted plumes. "You allow this monster"—Ripper pointed to Tesa—"to pollute your child as their alien bodies pollute the World. I will kill you!" But instead of attacking Taller, the challenger flew at Tesa.

Before she could react, Taller took to the air. At the same time, three other Grus, a male and two females, exploded from the reeds, winging down on Weaver. Weaver stood her ground on the platform, shielding Sailor with her body.

Save our son, Taller had said.

Tesa dived underwater, heading for the platform, trusting Taller to stop Kills-the-Ripper. She struck shallows and staggered to her feet yards from the platform, where Weaver struggled to keep herself between her enemies and her chick. Tesa gulped air and wondered what to do, when, through the forest of legs, Sailor spied his alien parent. As Tesa stared, horrified, the tiny chick dodged through the gauntlet of limbs and hit the water, swimming. The two attacking females pivoted and came after him.

Weaver used the distraction to go after the male with a fury. As Sailor swam straight to her, Tesa splashed toward him, then snatched him, one-handed, out of the water. Then she turned and ran. Frightened, Sailor flailed, scratching her hands with his small, sharp claws. Tesa raced through ankle-deep water, refusing to think about the pain shooting up her leg with every stride. If she could only reach the reeds, she and Sailor might be able to hide.

How futile it was to try to outrun someone who could *fly.*

Tesa's lungs were screaming when one female landed easily before her. The human spun, but the other, a much shorter avian with a stumpy bill, was behind her, neck stretched to attack.

Tesa dodged to one side, then feinted to the other, all the while cradling the chick against her. For a moment she was able to evade the females' outstretched wings and slide past them, only to be quickly blocked again. She managed to shield Sailor from one of the attackers, only to feel a stab of searing pain knife through her shoulder from the other's bill. Tesa sagged to her knees in the mud.

The taller female aimed for Sailor, still gripped tight in Tesa's hands. Dimly, Tesa was aware of Weaver winging her way to them, her own opponent floating dead in the water, but another, new female was behind her. Desperately Tesa tried to get to her feet, but skidded in the slick mud and fell. Curling her body around the chick, she fought to keep both their heads above water. A powerful kick struck her kidneys. She inhaled mud.

Gagging, Tesa saw a stubby-bill bearing down on her. She couldn't endure another stab, so she rolled, taking it in the side. She was lucky. This time the Grus hit only feathers.

Thinking she had a piece of the human, the avian worried the garment, pulling at it fiercely. Latching onto the alien's bill as it tugged at her shirt, Tesa held Sailor out of the water and rolled, using her body weight to overbalance the avian.

With a wrenching yank that made her painfully aware of every wound, Tesa pulled the female off her feet. She fell across the human like a tree, spreading her wings to counter-balance, accidentally creating a shield against the taller Grus. The tangled avian, her head held partly underwater, struggled wildly, slamming her bony wrists and elbows against Tesa's head, knees, and ribs. Glimpsing the second bird through thrashing feathers, Tesa saw her dancing around, eager to aid her friend.

Then there was a shadow of wings and Weaver attacked. The Grus behind her landed and went after the short-billed female lying across Tesa. That was too much for the one still standing, and she lost heart and fled, Weaver right behind her.

Tesa was kicked again and again as her prostrate opponent tried to free herself by using the woman's body to gain her footing in the mud. Finally, she heaved herself upright by pushing Tesa and Sailor completely underwater.

When Tesa broke free, she quickly checked Sailor, who was shaking his head and sneezing. Tesa's bedraggled, mud-spattered opponent was being set upon by two avians, the female that had helped Weaver and—she squinted—Flies-Too-Fast! They attacked fiercely, their dark legs leaping, kicking, slashing.

Cradling the chick—incredibly uninjured, if muddy and terrified—Tesa scuttled out of reach. Glancing around, fearfully, for Taller, she saw that he was blood-spattered but seemingly tireless as he fought Kills-the-Ripper—and which was his blood and which his opponent's, she couldn't tell.

Suddenly another shadow hovered, and Tesa leaped to her feet, only to curse in pain. Two black and white diamond-shaped flying sleds hung over her. Meg's and Thom's anxious faces peered over the sides. *No,* thought Tesa, frantically, *Taller's got to settle this without our help or he'll never hold his leadership.*

The bedraggled, stubby-billed female broke at the sight of the alien contraptions and fled, Flies-Too-Fast giving chase. The remaining female approached Tesa slowly.

"I'm Shimmering," she signed, "Taller's daughter. Are you all right? Is the chick . . . ."

Tesa showed the female the muddy, protesting baby huddled in her hand. The sight of the sleds was too much for Sailor and Tesa could feel the vibrations in her palm from his panic-stricken cries. She looked at Taller. He must've heard his son's call over everything else, Tesa realized, because his crown suddenly flared anew, and recklessly he rushed his adversary.

Almost immediately, Ripper's crown became dull and shrank. Then Taller felled him with a powerful kick. As the avian collapsed, Taller hammered his enemy's skull with his bill, pounding the life out of him. Finally, when Kills-the-Ripper floated dead at Taller's feet, his limp feathers waving on the current, the blood-streaked leader stood tall, threw back his head, and trumpeted his victory. The water around his legs was streaked with red.

Suddenly Weaver was at Taller's side, matching his call. Shimmering answered them with her own, and then Flies-Too-Fast landed near and joined the chorus. Tesa was buffeted by sound waves so powerful they rippled the water. That victory call would be carried through the marsh from territory to territory. To kill the one who'd killed the Ripper—there'd be no challenges to Taller's leadership now.

Wearily, Tesa waded to the platform and plopped down, tucking the terrified, shivering chick safely under her damp costume, against her warm skin. Thom and Meg hovered their sleds low, peering worriedly at her.

Then Thom moved to step off into the marsh, ignoring Meg's stern head shake. As soon as his feet hit the water, Taller was there, blocking Tesa, staring wild-eyed at the human male.

Weaver put herself between them. "There have been enough challenges," she told her mate in calm, measured signs.

Thom stared at Taller thin-lipped, his face drawn and nearly as red as Taller's crown. Slowly the male Grus lowered his stature. Moving his head closer to Thom's face, he gazed at him unblinking. Thom returned the stare levelly, never moving. As though that solved everything, Taller signed a greeting of fishing and friendship. The human returned it cautiously.

Meg parked her sled a few feet above the water and approached Tesa. "Are you all right?" she signed brusquely. "What in the world happened? Thom was watching the shelter, trying to see the chick, and the next thing I knew, he was grabbing sleds and signing like crazy." Meg produced a medi-scanner and turned it on, forcing her to stop signing.

"Tell *me* what happened," Thom signed to Tesa as he joined Meg. Tesa had seen his expression before—on her father whenever she'd ignored her own safety and done something risky. *You can't earn eagle feathers by covering your ass,* she thought.

"It was an attempted coup," she signed. "But . . . we won."

Meg and Thom shared a look, then glanced at the floating bodies. They were probably ready to send her back to Star-Bridge. No, not StarBridge. Go past StarBridge, do not pass Go, do not collect 200 credits, go straight to Earth. Just because she was a little banged up.

Actually, Tesa had to admit that she looked terrible. She was plastered with mud, blood, and broken feathers, and her leg and shoulder bled sluggishly. Her once-beautiful Grus costume had a ragged hole, which alone made her want to cry. *The rest is just a flesh wound,* she thought inanely. That cliché, from one of Dr. Rob's tacky, racist westerns, seemed crazily appropriate.

"'An attempted coup,'" Thom repeated. "How many of those can we expect now that you're part of the royal family?"

Before Tesa could respond, Meg began to itemize her injuries. "Tesa, this is serious. Your leg is punctured, and infection is setting in. Your shoulder's not much better, and there's joint involvement there. Your nose and cheek have hairline fractures and there's swelling building up around your eyes. You've got two cracked ribs, and we'll have to do a body scan to make sure your kidneys aren't compromised." She stopped, as though to compose herself, her blue eyes glistening.

"We saw the beating you took, Tesa. We thought you would be killed."

Tiredly, Taller peered at Ripper's dead body, feeling an empty revulsion. Later, others would carry the bodies away and leave them somewhere where no others had ever been left. Kills-the-Ripper would be ostracized in death, even as his mate and the others that had sided with him would depart in shame and travel the world in solitude, never again lifting their voices to the suns. He pitied them, and himself, for being unable to prevent this wasteful tragedy.

"Say something to Flies-Too-Fast," Weaver signed, "and to our daughter. They risked themselves and their status."

Had Taller been killed, it would have been his allies that flew the skies alone. It was always safer to hang back and declare loyalty to the victor.

His daughter was the last of his children still in this flock. Her mate had been dead a year, yet she'd found no other to replace him. If she didn't soon, he knew, she never would. Today, Flies-Too-Fast's reckless courage made him seem older than his years. Taller narrowed his eyes as he watched the two. Weaver could make the arrangements. She was an excellent matchmaker, and who would deny her after today?

Yes, he decided, it would be a good pairing. He would let them stay here and feed Sailor. The presence of the chick was bound to stir up their romantic feelings. He felt better. Something good would come of this, after all.

Then he looked for Good Eyes and felt uneasy all over again. Relaxed and First-One-There were hovering over her with things not-of-the-World. The humans still felt responsible for Good Eyes, but they had to realize that that was no longer true. Especially Relaxed. Why *had* he given the human that name?

Taller and Weaver moved to stand on either side of Good Eyes. "What kind of customs do your people have," Taller asked, "that you worry over survivors instead of calling to the gods your gladness that she saved herself and our child?"

The two humans glanced at each other.

"Forgive us," First-One finally signed, "but our friend's taken a terrible beating. We're worried about her."

Taller supposed it was one of their un-Worldly *things* that had told them about her injuries since poor Good Eyes was so muddy it was hard to see what had happened to her.

Suddenly Sailor popped his head out through the laced-up shirt, plainly startling Meg and Thom. Almost as a reflex, Tesa snagged a shimmering off her arm and pulled it apart. The chick gobbled the soft parts greedily. Taller felt a grim amusement as his human partner stolidly grabbed another insect, creatures she had seemed loathe to injure barely an hour ago.

Timidly, Flies-Too-Fast stepped forward, head lowered, offering a silver-blue fingerling fish to the chick. Taller indicated his approval, and Sailor grabbed the fish. The yearling glanced nervously at the two Grus adults, maintaining his deferential posture. Shimmering also seemed unsure whether to stay, but the chick was too much for her to resist. She peered curiously around Flies-Too-Fast, and then they suddenly shared eye contact. Embarrassed, the two slowly backed away to leave, but Weaver indicated they could feed the chick. After all their years together, Taller and Weaver rarely had to speak to share the same plan. The two young avians began searching the area, striding the water side by side.

Taller looked at his son, exposed to war and death and aliens at the tender age of five days. Well, it was what the shimmerings had promised, wasn't it?

"Taller," First-One asked solicitously, "are your wounds serious?"

The bloodied avian eyed her for a moment. "My people will support me now in what I wish to do. Are the wounds serious? Dissension among the people is always serious." He turned to his human partner with a piercing stare. "But it will all make for a glorious dance, won't it, Good Eyes?"

"But, Taller," First-One signed, "you're bleeding so much."

Suddenly she looked old to Taller, really old. She had changed since Puff had died, and he realized that she was too old to make a new partnership, that she would forever be alone. He felt an incredible sadness for his human friend. "Weaver will help me," he signed, to comfort her. "The wounds are minor."

"Taller," Relaxed interjected, "we've got to take Good Eyes with us to our sky shelter."

Good Eyes let out a sound, which startled Taller and Weaver so much, Taller had no chance to react to Relaxed's outrageous statement. The human male was ignoring Good Eyes' angry expression and protesting signs. First-One was chewing her lip, seeming torn between agreeing with Relaxed and fearing the intrusion into the avian family.

Taller wondered, not for the first time, what made humans think they could speak for someone they weren't partnered with?

"I know you have your own special medicines there," Taller signed slowly, "however . . ."

"I'm all right," Good Eyes protested. "I just need a few days rest. It's really just a . . ."

"You're *not* all right!" First-One-There argued. "You need treatment!"

"Can't you bring your medicines here?" Taller asked.

"She needs to be examined with special equipment that can't be moved," Relaxed explained.

Taller held Relaxed's gaze with his own. For the second time today, the human didn't flinch or look downward. He was telling the truth, at least about the medical care, but there was something else behind his eyes, something Taller didn't understand. "Take her then, if you must," the leader signed.

Good Eyes seemed stunned, and the other humans gave each other a look that Taller didn't find the least comforting.

"Return her to us by nightfall," Taller added. "No later."

Their expressions did not change. Once they had her aboard their shelter they could find excuses to keep her there.

"They have no intention of letting me return," Good Eyes signed to Taller, angrily. "They're afraid, because of Puff."

"What kind of people would we be if we weren't afraid for you?" First-One signed, her temper flaring. "You don't have the sense to be afraid for yourself. I swear, you're just like him. Rushing in where *fools* fear to tread . . ." She wound down suddenly and hung her arms limply.

Relaxed turned to Taller. "We can't promise she'll be back by nightfall. We don't know how badly she's been hurt."

Weaver stepped between the arguing sides. "Friends! There's been enough combat for one day. If Good Eyes can't go to the sky shelter and return the same day, she must stay here. This infant has seen enough to scar the soul of an adult, and now you'll take away his parent? He'll think she *died*."

Taller turned to First-One-There. "You're right, she is like Puff, and like Water Dancer, too. They were like two eggs from the same parents. They were fearless and rash, and far seeing. They had great heart. And they were willing to sacrifice themselves for the good of others.''

He addressed them all. ''Don't you think the White Wind people will tell the story of this day so that all the people of the World will know it? Dances will spread from one marsh to the other, telling about Good Eyes, a land-bound being not-of-the-World who became bound to us with her blood and pain. Isn't that why she came here, to become one of us, so your people and ours could be allies? This is an important memory for Sailor, for all of us. Good Eyes is a part of this family, forever.'' He turned the full force of his gaze on the humans who wanted to take his partner away, who might be reluctant to bring her back.

''Return her to us by nightfall, healed,'' he told them, ''or I will fly to the sky shelter to get her myself.''

CHAPTER 13

♦

The Stories

"If you weren't so beat up, I'd be really pissed at you," Thom signed as he checked the readings on the null-grav couch that would protect Tesa from the worst of the shuttle's thrust.

"You *are* pissed at me," she signed. The numbing cold from the ice wraps covering her wounds only compounded her discomfort.

"Do you have any idea what I was going through watching you get the shit kicked out of you down there?" the biologist asked, then gently molded an ice wrap around her face.

"Not half what I was going through getting it done!" She yanked it away, smacking his hand. "Am I going to have to console you because I got hurt? And I am *not* your helpless lover, so just stop acting like a nursemaid." She slapped the ice wrap back on her face too hard, and saw spangles.

He lifted the wrap, to be sure she could see his signs. "You're not *my* lover," he reminded her, bitterly. "You're the *partner* of a feathered *alien*."

Her hands moved tiredly, "You can't build a relationship on jealousy, Thom."

"Relationship!" he signed. "*What* relationship? I've let you know how I feel, but you tell me nothing. I'm not even sure if we're *friends*!'' He sat on the couch, turning away from her.

With an effort, she sat up and touched his shoulder. He gazed at her solemnly. ''Of course we're friends,'' she signed. ''If I've been cool to you, Thom . . . it's not that I don't care about you . . . but I'm not sure *how much* I want to care.''

She stopped then, hesitant to say more. What was the point in worrying about her feelings toward someone when she'd be returning to Earth in a year? How soon before she'd resent him, resent that he'd be able to stay and work on Trinity? She thought of Mahree Burroughs and Rob Gable—thought of how much longer their separations were than their times together. Could any relationship be worth that?

Without answering, he touched her face gently and kissed her mouth—one of her few unswollen places. Her eyes closed as she accepted the kiss. There was no pressure in it, no demands—just a pleasant, caring touch, with a hint of passion behind it. When Thom pulled back, Tesa surprised herself by following him, sliding an arm around his neck and kissing him back.

They separated and Tesa sank back down, exhausted—and more confused than before. She couldn't help but smile. ''Will you try to deal with my situation with the Grus any better?''

He smiled weakly, looking chagrined. ''I'll work on it. But Meg was worried, too, you know.''

''Meg has an excuse. She's already had one friend die.''

''And now I know we are, at least, friends.'' He laughed good naturedly. ''Okay. But I won't be your biggest problem aboard the *Crane*. Just wait till *Bruce* sees you.'' He strode toward the front of the ship to his copilot's seat.

Tesa groaned inwardly, anticipating *that* reception.

When they'd docked with the *Singing Crane*, Meg watched Thom pull off his sound nullifiers. ''How're you doing?'' she asked.

He shrugged. ''Trying to decide if I want to kiss her or kill her. Incredibly relieved that she's here, out of danger.''

Not good, Meg thought. Thom could see his own place at Trinity, but he still didn't understand how critical Tesa's role was. Having gotten over the shock of the battle, Meg knew Tesa had done what she'd had to.

''Bring that couch through here,'' Dr. Li's crisp, businesslike voice came through the open airlock. The small woman marched into the ship and leaned over Tesa's prostrate form. "We got your transmissions, Meg. Looks like you've done everything for her that's in the protocol. Let's get her to the infirmary."

Meg sighed. Would Szu-yi ever address Tesa personally? Thom had moved over to the couch and was translating what the doctor had said, since Tesa's Mizari voder was covered with mud.

Bruce grinned at Tesa while unlocking the floor bolts so the couch could float. "Forget Sacajawea, hello Chief Joseph!"

Tesa nodded, lip-reading the name of the Nez Percé chief who'd known when to fight and when to retreat. "I hope," she signed as Meg translated, "that I, too, 'will fight no more, forever'!"

Bruce made a clumsy sign to her, a Grus compliment that meant "you are one with the World."

Thom's surprised expression was almost comic. He clearly had not expected this reaction from the meteorologist.

Peter came around the other side, his dark face drawn with concern. He and Bruce floated the couch onto the station and down the long corridor to the infirmary.

"I saw you counting coup on that big female," Bruce said to Tesa. "That was quick thinking, girl."

"I can't believe this," Thom complained. "I thought you'd be *furious*."

"Who, me?" said Bruce.

"Yeah, you. You were the one who was dead set against having 'a human woman living with a bunch of primitive . . .'"

Bruce shot Thom a look that silenced him on the spot. "*I* can recognize when the right person's been selected for the job."

Peter coughed theatrically at the sparring males as they pulled up beside the infirmary's diagnostic bed. Dr. Li scooted around them, reaching for equipment.

Lauren was already there, setting up the scanner. When she saw Tesa, she paled. "Honey, you look *terrible*! Are you okay?"

Tesa was signing, "It's only a flesh wound, only a flesh wound," over and over. Meg wondered if she was delirious.

"Lauren, set up for full body imaging," Dr. Li said. "I want a good look at those kidneys."

Bruce and Peter moved out of Szu-yi's way as she gently removed the ice wrap from Tesa's face. The swelling around the Indian woman's eyes and nose looked even more shocking with Tesa's light eyes squinting through.

Szu-yi's face softened. "You really did take a beating, Tesa. You must feel terrible."

Tesa shook her head, not understanding what Dr. Li had said.

Szu-yi simply said, "Never mind. We'll fix it." She patted Tesa's knee consolingly.

The doctor's sudden change reminded Meg of Szu-yi's gentle touch while she'd examined her ears, and the doctor's grief when she'd realized she couldn't save Meg's hearing.

The doctor scissored Tesa's pant leg away, uncovering the bloodied, dirty stab wound on Tesa's calf.

"What a beauty," Bruce said quietly.

Thom's frayed nerves unraveled. "Dammit, Bruce, there's nothing beautiful about it! She nearly got *killed* down there."

Peter shot Thom a warning look, but Bruce only seemed amused. "My, aren't we protective all of a sudden?"

Lauren's face clouded over as she stared at Thom.

"You're both right," Dr. Li said quietly. "Tesa could've gotten killed," she told Bruce, "*but*," she turned to Thom, "she doesn't need coddling. She needs rest and medical care. That's me, Lauren, and Meg. The rest of you get out. Now."

"What is this?" Bruce complained. "Suddenly only women are capable of nursing care? Sexism rears its ugly head?"

"Uncle Bruce, we have to get her undressed," Lauren warned. She seemed in control of her feelings, but, Meg noted, she avoided eye contact with Thom. "I think Tesa would be more comfortable with just 'us girls.'"

"Let me get these two hotheads out of here," Peter offered agreeably, moving in between Bruce and Thom, "so I can remind them about the benefits of peaceful working relationships."

"Let's get her out of those clothes," the doctor said, once the door closed behind the men. She held up a cutting tool.

Tesa gestured for them to stop, indicating her shapeless top. For the first time since the battle, she looked upset. "Don't cut this," she signed feebly, fumbling with lacings crusted with dried marsh sludge and blood. Meg realized suddenly that what she was wearing was made of feathers, matted now, and broken. Where had she gotten it?

"Weaver made it," Tesa explained.

"What's she saying?" Dr. Li asked. Lauren showed her the translation on her voder.

Tesa's eyes brimmed with tears. "It helps Sailor focus on me . . . it honors Water Dancer's spirit . . ." Overwhelmed, she began sobbing.

Lauren gently patted the younger woman's arm and stroked her matted hair. Meg was alarmed by Tesa's breakdown, but Dr. Li was unperturbed. "She's okay. Her body's just realized all the excitement's over," she said matter-of-factly.

Moments later, Tesa pulled herself together. "I'm sorry, I don't know why . . ."

Dr. Li nodded reassurance. "Don't apologize, Tesa, it's just chemistry. Let's get you out of this shirt."

"Weaver *made* that?" Meg asked, fingering the garment. The young woman nodded while awkwardly wiggling out of it.

"It must've been beautiful once," Lauren remarked, "but it's a wreck now."

"They've never done anything like this before," Meg said.

"Taller helped design it," Tesa added, still sniffling.

"Peter's mother was a textile curator at that big Senegalese museum," Meg remembered. "I bet he can do something with this. Take it to him, Lauren. This represents something important. We need to document it. And, Lauren . . . make sure Bruce sees it."

The technician looked amused. "Sure thing, Meg."

Later, as Meg and Szu-yi studied the readout of Tesa's body scan, Meg told Szu-yi what they had had to promise Taller.

"How *could* you?" The doctor was incredulous. "Tesa needs two days in the regen and time to rest!"

Meg shook her head. "She goes tonight. We wanted her to become one of them, well, she has. I can't go back on my word."

The doctor's thin lips drew tight. "This is totally irregular. There are protocols about medical care. You're asking me to okay her release when I don't think she's ready."

"Release her on my say-so and register your own protest. You'll be clear, and any consequences'll be on me."

Szu-yi shot Meg an angry look. "You think that's all I'm worried about, accountability? I'm worried about *her*, her infection, her pain. You think I demand things be done by the book so I can cover my ass? I do things by the book because that's the *smart* way to do it. Protocols are written by people who've found the best way, the safest way, not necessarily the *easiest* way." The doctor shut her mouth with a sudden snap. It was the most Meg had ever heard her say on the subject.

Scott and I never did anything by the book, Meg realized. *Szu-yi thinks that if we had, Scott might still be alive.*

Scott's ghost whispered irreverently, *You call that living?*

Hours later, Tesa emerged from the regen unit stiff and sore. Her face still had some swelling, and there were dark crescents under her eyes. The doctor had implanted her puncture wounds with a powerful antibiotic, antiviral regen drug that would stimulate rapid healing. The regen unit had repaired the worst of her organ and bone damage, but had not had the time to do much with the body bruising.

Tesa didn't care. The Earth-normal gravity was depressing, the air smelled canned, and she was feeling claustrophobic. Except for a moment, Dr. Li reminded her too much of the doctors that had treated her as a child—doctors who would never speak to her, only to her parents. She missed her avian family.

"It's good you still have pain," Dr. Li said to Tesa. "Your aches will slow you down, prevent you from reinjuring yourself."

Tesa knew Dr. Li was angry about her having to leave, so she showed the doctor something she'd filmed on her voder. "That's Sailor," Tesa explained, showing the doctor footage of "her" baby. "That's why I have to go back."

Dr. Li only nodded, still frowning. The young woman felt disappointed that she didn't warm to her blue-eyed, downy baby.

"I've seen them before," the doctor said, her expression tight. "At my home in China, in Zhalong. But there, the Zhalong cranes are only shoulder high."

"Szu-yi grew up in a farming community near a famous crane nesting ground," Meg explained. "In the late nineteen hundreds, when cranes were endangered, a captive breeding facility was established there to save them."

"Hand-raised cranes hatched at the facility were released into the surrounding wetlands," Szu-yi said. "And the tame cranes began to fight the farmers for control of the marsh. The farmers harvested reeds, grass, and fish and disturbed the nesting birds. Wild birds would have abandoned their nests, but not the Zhalong cranes. They fought the farmers—and trained their chicks to do the same. Now, there are thousands of pairs at Zhalong. They nest in your yard and attack you if you want to hang your wash. As a child I was terrified."

Her expression grew distant. "My father wanted me to overcome my fear, so he stole an egg from a nearby nest. We hatched it, raising the chick like a pet. I loved that little thing. Then he grew up and joined the flock. A few years later, he brought a mate to our yard. When I went out to see him, how mature he'd become, how beautiful—he attacked me viciously, nearly blinding me. It was *his* yard now, not mine. I was his enemy. So you see, there's great irony in my working here." She tried to smile, but a dark fear haunted her eyes. "Don't expect that baby to love you as long as you'll love him. When he matures there'll be no place for you in his heart, only for his new family."

Tesa wanted to remind the doctor that the Grus were not the cranes of Earth, but the doctor had planted a seed of fear. When Sailor matured could he still love her the way she'd love him? *Why worry?* said her inner demon. *You won't be here that long. You'll be back on Earth, getting* **fixed***!*

Tesa limped through Peter's door into a room rich with vivid colors splashed across Senegalese blankets and rugs. The computer specialist sat cross-legged on his bed, surrounded by Grus mesh bags packed with short, downy feathers and skeins of colorful grass. Across his knees was the cloak Flies-Too-Fast had given Lauren. He was comparing its weave with Tesa's shirt.

A great window dominated the room, and through it a semicircle of Trinity reflected the suns still on her face. Tesa looked at it longingly and had to force herself to bring her attention back to the people in the room.

Bruce was also on the bed, leaning against the wall, legs stretched out and crossed at the ankles. Between the two men sat Lauren, winding up remnants of grass. Tesa was disappointed that Thom was not there.

Her feathered costume was balled up in Peter's lap while he finished tying a knot, his handsome hands moving expertly. He turned the repaired garment right-side out, shook it, and said something. Tesa glanced at her voder.

"Nothing comes loose," he'd said. "How does it look?"

Tesa held back grateful tears as she looked at her shirt, clean and beautiful again, then she grabbed Peter in a warm hug.

"I used to help my mother restore Pima feathered baskets," Peter said, his words marching across Tesa's voder. "There's some similarity in technique. That battle was quite a lot to put a valuable artifact through!" He looked at Tesa with a wry expression. "Not to mention a pretty good interrelator."

"Tesa," Bruce asked, "when did you have time to make this?"

Tesa looked up from the voder, startled. "I didn't make . . . "

Meg gave Bruce a disapproving frown.

"You're a native dancer," the lanky weatherman insisted. "You're used to making costumes."

"*Weaver* made this!" Tesa signed sharply, trusting Meg to translate. "I never even *saw* it until it was almost finished. You're just selling the Grus short again, Bruce!"

Bruce turned the edge of her garment over. "Come on, Tesa, this thing's pieced together like a quilt top," he said, plainly disbelieving. "You *had* to show them how to do that."

"Weaver figured out the technique herself," Tesa insisted, "after seeing my old star quilt. She created new techniques to join the skin to the weavings. To make clothing for an alien species—especially when the maker has never worn any herself—is pretty sophisticated. Surely, even *you* can see that!"

Bruce shook his head. "Forgive my skepticism, but old beliefs die hard, l'il darlin'. I can still remember the first day I saw this pretty marble." Bruce indicated Trinity hovering over them. "That day I thought—I'll bring my family here, build a city, make the kind of money I'd always known I'd make by going into space. Then Scott and Meg found the Grus, and that dream ended. But that was okay, because we'd get something better out of it. We'd help get Earth full CLS membership."

He scratched his thinning gray hair. "If, as you say, Weaver made this for you—and, of course, I'm not doubting your word . . . well, that could be the proof Earth needs. I *should* be thrilled . . . but there must still be a part of me that kept on hoping that I was right in the first place . . . that someday there'd be cities on Trinity that I'd helped build.''

The Indian woman looked at the others, confused, wondering how many of them shared Bruce's feelings.

"Tesa," Meg tried to explain, "when we found Trinity, none of us had any First Contact experience. We were colonizers.''

"I'd never stepped off a space station!" Lauren told her. "I collected and organized data, and kept the robot probes running. It was two years before I set foot on the planet.''

"And you?" Tesa asked Peter.

"Thom and I had no extraterrestrial experience," Peter admitted. "We had to have special training before we came. Szu-yi had worked with the Simiu, but they were so sensitive and unpredictable, she asked for an assignment with minimal contact''—Peter laughed dryly—''and ended up with her favorite phobia.''

"Remember, Bruce," Lauren said, "when Scott first told us that he thought they'd found an intelligent species?"

He nodded. "I told Scott he was crazy. I said they looked more like a food source then Earth's best shot at CLS membership.''

Tesa tried to mask her shock when she read those words.

"Scott was furious," Meg reminisced. "You two fought over making contact with the Grus.''

"I respected his opinion," Bruce insisted, "but when I watched the Grus playing catch with a stick, or spending hours fixing their feathers . . . their intelligence was hard to accept." He gently touched the feathers on Tesa's shirt. "But when Scott said he wanted to call the CLS, whose side was I on?"

Meg smiled and nodded, obviously remembering.

"I backed you and Scott all the way," Bruce said, "and when the Falcon and Deborah tried to stop you—"

Tesa frowned at the strange reference on her voder, but Meg quickly explained. "That was Bruce's nickname for Jim Maltese, because of a holo-vid show they'd seen—*The Maltese Falcon.*"

"—I was the *only* one on your side," Bruce continued. "I even convinced Lauren. But that's the past." He indicated the Grus shirt with a grim smile. "This . . . will change things. This will shut up all that Simiu chatter. Once the Grus' intelligence is confirmed, Jamestown Founders will lose its claim to Trinity, forever.''

Tesa shook her head, frowning. Having accepted the shirt, Bruce was now really making too much of this simple thing. Her garment wasn't a patch on the story-walls, on the complex legends of the White Wind people. There was a secret in those beautiful walls, and in the cloaks, a secret Tesa hadn't been able to ferret out. Maybe someone on the *Crane* could.

Tesa lifted her hand to get their attention, and when they turned to watch, she began to sign about the world inside the nest shelter. She told them about the stories she could almost see, about the fracturing of light through a shimmering's wings, about how Weaver searched through piles of feathers or strands of grass to find just the right one for her project, when, to Tesa, they all seemed identical. She realized that she was moving her hands in the same artful way her grandmother did when she was telling a good story, and that the others were watching her with the rapt look a good storyteller always gets. It pleased her that they stopped looking at Meg, who was translating aloud, and watched her, and the picture images she was creating.

Finally, Tesa patched her voder into one of Peter's computer links and called up the story-walls. The group looked and glanced at one another, curiously. They couldn't see it, either.

"The stories are there," Tesa insisted. "Taller and Weaver tell them, and the chick follows it on the wall—but to me it's invisible. They keep a calendar on a cloak. They show me things, and they feel *sorry* for me that I can't see it." She keyed in the Lakota words *sintkala waksu*. "This is what we call the stones we use to heat the sweat lodge. It means 'bird stones.' They have designs on them that our ancestors said were drawn by birds. The designs disappear after a while and then, it's said, only the birds can see them.''

Lauren looked confused. "What do birds see that we can't?" No one seemed to know.

"Szu-yi's taken some simple medical scans of the Grus," Meg told Tesa, "but nothing as specific as opthalmology studies.''

"She'd never get that close to their faces," Lauren agreed.

"They act pretty silly when you start waving scanners around them," Bruce agreed, "even when they're *not* trying to eat them.''

"Of course, they want to eat it," Meg chided him, annoyed. "One way they recognize food is by how it reflects sunlight. Shiny things are delicacies." That made everyone look at one another as though they'd just discovered another key to the puzzle.

"It's not just shiny things," Tesa signed. "And what's the connection between their food and their art?" She picked up the woven cloak and stared at it.

"Specialized vision helps animals find food . . ." Peter mused, "see enemies, recognize one another . . . but there's a big jump between that and"—he picked up the cloak—"creating art."

"When the Simiu met the *Désirée*," Tesa signed, "they showed the crew a film they'd prepared in all available light spectrums, many of which were invisible to humans."

"But," Bruce argued, "that was one technologically advanced race meeting another. The Simiu and the Mizari both see in a slightly different light spectrum than we do, yet we can see most of their art, even if some colors are a little bright. Why would the Grus create art *only* in a spectrum we can't see? You said you *thought* you could see some of the image, but not well enough to be sure."

Tesa's brows furrowed—she felt stumped.

"If there's something there," Meg said, fingering the cloak, "then it's got to be in their feathers. We could analyze the feathers, ask the computer."

Bruce looked doubtful. "*Lots* of chemicals in feathers."

"So, let's get started," Lauren said impatiently, and taking a feather from one of the bags, she pulled a scanner from Peter's pocket and asked the computer for a chemical breakdown. A list of complex, impossibly long words rolled across the screen.

"Now, ask it how those chemicals show up under different light spectrums," Meg said.

Lauren talked to the computer. "There are a couple," Lauren said, "but this one stands out. Porphyrin. It's visible under ultraviolet light." The computer diagrammed the feather, with the porphyrin highlights lit up in a distinctive pattern.

Lauren asked the computer how many avian species throughout the Known Worlds could see in ultraviolet.

"Sixty-five point six two percent of all known avian species can see ultraviolet markers," the computer replied.

"Like insects," Peter said, smiling.

Lauren asked what else avians could see in comparison to human beings. "Ninety-four point eight three percent of all avian species can see polarized light."

"Well, ultraviolet markers would help them find food," Bruce said, "and polarized light probably helps them navigate. But what has that got to do with artistic expression?"

Tesa grew excited at the information about ultraviolet light, remembering how Doctor Blanket had looked draped over her shoulders. "Is there a light damper on board?" she asked.

"No," Meg told her, "but Szu-yi has a hand-held ultraviolet lamp. She uses it to check for certain fungi on the native food, like aphlotoxins. Lauren, call her and ask her to bring it."

Tesa considered asking Lauren to page Thom as well, but thought better of it. He'd just have to find out later.

"What's going on?" Szu-yi asked when she entered.

"Have a seat," Meg said, taking the instrument. "You might get to see something interesting."

Meg handed Bruce the light, then gestured at Lauren to darken the room. As soon as the lights dimmed, Tesa felt cut off, since she could no longer see if anyone was speaking. Suddenly Bruce pushed the lamp into her hand, indicating she should be the one to shine it on the cloak. She took the small device and thumbed its switch, flooding the cloak with a dark, purple light. She could just make out the surrounding crew's interested expressions.

"Oh, shit," Tesa breathed, making the others laugh.

The cloak lit up with bright orange markings that formed stylized, pictographic designs, formed by weaving feathers so that the chemical markers made specific patterns. *How many cloaks are on Earth?* Tesa wondered. *What secret literature has been back there all along, under their noses?*

Tesa turned the light onto her shirt. The feathers of Water Dancer's skin had their own colorful pattern, while the patch-work weaving showed family images—a nest shelter, an egg, a chick, each different, yet with a definite theme. The shirt was more like a quilt than Tesa had ever realized.

Peter's repairs showed up garishly, the UV markers placed every which way, totally haphazard. They had seemed almost invisible under white light.

Lauren lit the room again, dimly enough so the designs could be seen. Everyone was talking, but Tesa ignored her voder. She wanted to fly down to Trinity, to splash through the marsh and tell Taller that she could see now, she could *really* see.

She felt someone staring at her and looked up to meet Bruce's eyes. There'd be no cities on Trinity now, his eyes said. *I want to be glad,* his eyes said, *I want to be . . .*

Somewhere inside him, Bruce was still arguing with the spirit of Scott Hedford. Tesa found that comforting. Where she came from, spirits usually won.

Meg touched her shoulder. "We need to document all this, Tesa, but if we don't start for Trinity soon, Taller will be banging on the airlock door. Thom's downloading data in the control room. Go tell him what we've learned—I'm sure he'd rather hear it from you—then ask him to get the shuttle ready. You can keep that lamp, Szu-yi has others."

Tesa nodded numbly and limped out of the room.

By the time Tesa reached the computer room, she wanted to run. Excitedly, she imagined the look on Thom's face. *We've done it, Thom!* she told him in her mind. *This'll prove the Grus are intelligent beyond a shadow of a doubt!* She saw herself hugging him . . . she imagined them kissing. She limped faster.

The computer-room door opened at her touch. Thom was at a console by a terminal, his back to her, looking down at a hand-held screen, while the large holo-display flashed, strobe-like. Tesa glanced down at her voder. It was flashing as it had that night in the shelter with classic downloading images. She touched the voder to turn it off when a message line abruptly trailed across the bottom of its screen.

"We'll go over it again later, Peter. In the meantime, check sectors twelve and fourteen along Black Feather's flock's migratory route. Both areas are extremely isolated, and favorite roosting grounds for that flock. Next to Taller, his eldest son carries the most diplomatic weight. If we're careful, we might get lucky. It'll be harder from now on, with Tesa around, but the right plan could really pay off."

Something twisted inside Tesa when she read that, something sick and frightening. It was one thing for Thom to lie about cameras and Aquila but this sounded like a conspiracy.

Thom started, suddenly aware of her presence. She hit the "save, off" sequence on her voder, so he'd see only a blank screen if he looked. Casually he shut the computer down as though he were done with his work.

"How long have you been there?" he asked, obviously surprised. He was so rattled that he'd forgotten to sign.

"Does it matter?" she asked.

"No," he said, "of course not . . ." Clumsily he began to sign. "You're a pretty quiet person."

"Did I scare you?"

He shook his head, amiably—hiding his real feelings.

"I always think hearing people can hear *everything*—I never expect to surprise them."

"Did Meg send you after me?" He glanced at the time on one of the computers. "I guess we've got to get back . . ." His eyes stole a quick glance at her voder. "I was just leaving some notes for Peter on a program he's working on. Taller's eldest son is the leader of a nearby migratory flock and we're trying to keep track of his travels, you know, just for insurance. If anything happens to Taller, he might be another contact for us."

Tesa nodded, struggling not to let her suspicions show.

Thom suddenly took a long look at her. "Peter did some job on that garment . . . and by the looks of things, Doc did a good job on you. Those small shiners won't take long to fade."

Tesa modeled the tunic and her relatively wound-free body. "Almost good as new—both of us." Her heart wasn't in the light banter, though. Thom seemed to be studying her as though he were trying to see through her brain. *No wonder he has trouble with "the look,"* she thought bitterly.

Tesa smoothed the feathers of her shirt, as a nearby ventilator draft made them wave gently. The repairs, garish under the UV light, had disappeared again. *Just like some people,* she thought, *who appear to be one thing in your presence, and something different when alone.*

Thom gestured to get her attention. "You're upset with me. Is it about . . . what happened before? I mean between me and Bruce? I can tell something's wrong, Tesa."

She shook her head. To distract him, she pulled the small UV lamp off her belt and shined it onto her shirt, explaining briefly how they'd made the discovery.

He seemed genuinely stunned. "This will change everything!"

"Once the documentation is done," Tesa answered, "the First Contact confirmation will just be a technicality. My place in Taller's family is established, so our diplomatic mission looks pretty successful. I can't see what could go wrong after this.''

His brow furrowed pensively.

Why isn't he happy? she thought. *Unless he didn't want their intelligence confirmed.* "You don't seem pleased," she signed.

Thom regarded her thoughtfully. "When this First Contact is confirmed, they might decide your work is finished as soon as Sailor goes on his flyaway. They could send you home, then." He smiled wistfully. "That might break my heart, Good Eyes."

He was looking at her so appealingly that it almost broke *her* heart—but not her resolve. She'd study that message again. What *could* she do if Thom—and *Peter*?—were involved with the murders of the Grus?

"Let's not talk about my being sent to Earth," Tesa signed. "We've got to get the ship ready, and I want to go home."

Instead of bristling at the reminder that Tesa wanted to be with the Grus, Thom seemed to relax. Acting like his old self, he offered his arm and she made herself take it. As they strolled to the docking bay, the weight of the small Mizari voder seemed to increase with every step.

CHAPTER 14

◆

The Death

Tesa watched Trinity through the shuttle's small viewport and tried to think only of Sailor. But somewhere there were killers on Trinity, killers who would strip the skin off his back. Was there a connection between those murderers and a man she found so desirable? She didn't want to believe that.

Trinity wouldn't be the first planet where privateers had come in before contact was firmly established. Those planets and their native peoples bore the brunt of suffering, victims of bureaucracies that were too far away to give adequate protection. Someday, StarBridge graduates might be able to end such senseless exploitation—but that was years away yet.

It still took time to properly establish First Contacts. Even with the new information about the cloaks, Sailor would, no doubt, be fully grown before the CLS board would finalize the Grus' First Contact. How many skins could the killers collect in that time . . . especially if they had allies on the *Singing Crane*?

Tesa shoved those thoughts away. She didn't want to think about that . . . or about Thom, sitting with Meg in the pilot's section, his back to the passenger seats. She chewed her lip, remembering his last remark—would they send her back to Earth as soon as Sailor left on his flyaway? That was only six months away! She'd have to find some reason to stay.

They hit atmosphere, and Tesa's heart quickened, eager to be home again, eager to see Sailor. But her eyes kept returning to the Mizari voder on her wrist, and its secret information. Assuring herself that Thom and Meg were absorbed in flying the *Patuxent*, Tesa tapped into the voder, and it began strobing.

She suddenly felt cold all over as she added another code and the strobing slowed, showing a collection of biological data, notes, and maps. Thom hadn't lied about one thing— this information was about Taller's son Black Feather and his flock. There were satellite maps of the various routes this elder Grus took in his wanderings. They knew *a lot* about this flock.

Thom's message to Peter began to trail across the bottom of the screen. Tesa froze it. There were older notes written above the trailing message that had gone by too fast to read before.

"These are two of Black Feather's favorite stopping points on the return trip," the note read. "It's also a good spot for Aquila to pick off sub-adults separated from their families." That reference only worried Tesa more. The earliest skins had all had Aquila marks on them. "When Taller's chick matures," the note continued, "he may start his flyaway journey with Black Feather's flock at this location."

The mention of Sailor's future disturbed Tesa, and she looked away, trying to sort through conflicting emotions. Then, suddenly, a flash of white outside the window caught her by surprise. She strained to see what it was she'd glimpsed.

The escort flock spiraled about the *Patuxent* as it descended, now thousands of feet above Trinity's surface. Tesa happily recognized Taller in the lead. There was a long, dark line down his neck, but his wounds didn't slow him.

Elated, Tesa recognized Flies-Too-Fast, fourth in line from the leader. His partner on the other side of the vee was Taller's daughter, Shimmering. Tesa felt her heart lifting.

Movement at the edge of Tesa's vision drew her eyes from the disappearing Grus. There was something on the western horizon, like a strange, dark cloud. She squinted, leaning against the window. Then her forgotten voder began flashing, pulling her attention back.

"EMERGENCY! EMERGENCY! SECURE SAFETY HARNESS!" the voder blinked rapidly, in red. She sat back immediately and strapped in, peering around the seats at Thom and Meg, who were moving their hands rapidly over their control panels. They must've sent the warning to her voder. She looked at it again and saw a message trailing across the bottom as the voder overheard the two pilots. "Can we outmaneuver them?" Meg was asking.

"We're going to get caught up here with the escort like sitting ducks!" Thom complained.

"Don't you think I know that?" Meg retorted. "We can only go down so fast . . ."

Oh, no, Tesa thought, her confusion clearing. She pressed her face to the viewport. The dark cloud was now a score of red- and gold-eyed Aquila.

The Grus were coming into sight again. Glancing at the voder, Tesa read Meg's words. "I'm broadcasting an alarm call."

"Level out," Thom was saying, "we can use the ship to block them!" Then the voder addressed her, quoting Thom. "Are you strapped in, Tesa? Wave, if you're reading your voder." She stuck up her hand, and rechecked her safety harness.

Tesa felt an agony of helplessness as the dark forms drew closer to the escort. The ship leveled, and the Grus evened off with it. The avians were calling, answering Meg's recording.

The flock dipped under the belly of the ship as the Aquila surrounded them, the wind ruffling the feathers on their massive wings, the suns glinting off their bodies, their gold, curved beaks, their lethal talons. They flew brazenly, as if they owned the skies. Could any of these predators be the ones she'd watched innocently building their nest?

Thom and Meg must have shut off the ship's Automatic Protection System, because the Aquila came so close, the APS should have been triggered. Remembering that the shuttle was built for research scanning, Tesa pulled up a screen from a table in front of her seat for a more complete view.

The Grus clustered closely beneath the shuttle, temporarily

protected, as the Aquila negotiated around the ship. Then, without warning, the Grus dropped into a sharp spiral, losing altitude fast. As they did, the letters "APS ENGAGED" flashed on the screen, and suddenly the Aquila were hurled from the ship in a tumble of wings and loose feathers, as they were struck by the invisible force shield.

That blow bought the Grus valuable time as they continued their descent, but several predators had already pulled out of their tumble and were rocketing after their prey.

Without warning, the ship turned on a wing and fell, leaving Tesa's stomach a hundred feet up. Meg and Thom were coming right up the tail feathers of a large female Aquila who was zeroing in on Taller. Tesa stopped looking out the window where the world insisted on turning upside down around her, and stared instead at the instrument readings on the screen.

Using the APS in a focused beam, Meg aimed it like a repulsor ray and hit the big raptor square, knocking her away. The avian fell, but grabbed enough air to parachute into water.

Taller veered out of the spiral, the escort leveling out behind him, and again the shuttle swooped to follow. This time Tesa couldn't ignore her nausea. She threw up all over the seat beside her, the bitter acid biting at her throat.

Taller was heading toward a young forest, drawing the Aquila far from his territory. The predators closed in again.

A male reached for Flies-Too-Fast, but before the curved talons could grab the young Grus, a brilliant blue and red wave flowed between them, disorienting the killer. Like an airborne tide, the mass of color engulfed the Aquila.

The escort swerved away from the woods as the air around the ship colored with thousands of small jewellike birds. Taller had lured the Aquila to a communal nesting site where predators would not be tolerated and the Aquila were swarmed, pecked, and pursued for encroaching on the small birds' territory.

The bronze predators struggled for altitude and began splitting up haphazardly, fleeing the army of tiny but tenacious attackers. The shuttle was also under attack and the viewport was alternately covered, then cleared of the valiant little birds. The two pilots had turned the APS off to prevent damaging the avians while the *Patuxent* maneuvered through the flock.

By the time the ship settled onto the landing pad, Tesa felt as though she'd come through a combat mission. The viewport was streaked with bird droppings and the odor from the seat beside her was terrible. She unstrapped her safety harness and rubbed her aching stomach. Meg came back and looked sympathetic.

"Poor kid," she signed, consolingly. "You got airsick?" Besides some tension in her face and shoulders, she revealed little of the turmoil she'd just been through.

Tesa nodded. "That first drop was a religious experience."

"I'll bet. Well, the robot sterilizer will take care of it. Taller's here to take you home . . . I got the feeling he doesn't quite trust us to let you go. You can take your sled if you think you're ready for another flight." She smiled tiredly.

Tesa eased out of the seat. Meg adjusted her nullifiers, reminding Tesa that she didn't need her voder now. Moving to turn it off, she remembered her file. The pilots had turned off the red alert once they were out of danger, but Tesa hadn't been paying attention to the voder then. Now her screen was blank, as though waiting for a new command. She tried to bring up the file she'd captured on the *Crane* but it wasn't there.

Meg must've noticed her startled expression. "Were you working on anything when we engaged the red alert?" she asked.

Tesa nodded, noncommittally.

"The emergency override's pretty strong. If your file was open, it probably overwrote it. Hope it wasn't important."

Tesa shrugged. "No, it wasn't important." She checked the directory to be sure. It was gone. Turning the voder off, she masked her annoyance.

"Bumpy ride, huh?" Thom asked, coming alongside them.

She nodded again. "None of the Grus were hurt, were they?"

"Everyone made it home safe," Meg assured her.

Thom cracked open the *Patuxent*'s door and the light of Trinity's setting suns flooded the ship. Stiffly Tesa eased down the ramp. Once she had her feet back on Trinity's soil, the delightful buoyancy eased her aches and lightened her heart.

The escort flock surrounded them as soon as the three humans moved clear of the ship. Flies-Too-Fast stood proudly beside Shimmering, his head scant inches above the tall female's.

Taller moved forward, looking tired, one wing drooping.

"It's been a long day, hasn't it, Good Eyes?" he signed.

In spite of everything, Tesa grinned as he came over and enveloped her under his wing. Thom moved away, but this time with no outward show of resentment.

Taller directed an adult to escort the flock to the marsh, and after they bounded off the cliff, he addressed Meg and Thom. "Thank you for returning our friend to our family."

The sign he used for "friend," Tesa noticed, was similar to the one she'd seen Weaver use, which delighted her.

"I thank you also," Taller continued, "for your help against Death. It was courageous flying. We'll never forget it."

"It's what any friend would do, Taller," Meg assured him.

"Let me get your sled, Tesa," Thom signed, and headed for the camp shelter.

"Tomorrow," Taller signed, as he, Tesa, and Meg strolled easily after the man, "we will thank the Blue Cloud people. It's been a long time since we've needed their help."

"You mean the small blue and red avians?" Meg asked.

"Yes. My father negotiated a compromise with them before I was an egg, and occasionally, it comes in handy."

Tesa and Meg gave each other a look. "How does someone of your stature," Tesa asked diplomatically, "negotiate with such a tiny creature?"

"I wasn't there," Taller admitted, "but the Blue Cloud people are so numerous, and so inclined to overpopulation, my father got them to agree not to overrun our feeding grounds. In exchange, we stopped eating them." With that, the avian casually drew up one foot to delicately scratch an itch behind his eye.

"I see," signed Meg, though her expression was so dismayed, Tesa nearly burst out with nervous laughter.

Taller turned to Tesa. "Sailor has been difficult to feed all day, and keeps watching for your return. I suspect he won't sleep until he sees you safely settled in your bed."

Thom arrived with the sled, setting it to hover, so Tesa could comfortably pull herself up on the diamond-shaped flier.

The Indian woman exchanged good-bye hugs with Meg and Thom, then eased herself onto the sled, adjusting the controls. It was usually better to lie flat on your stomach for long trips, but for short, easy flight she preferred to sit. The hand grips that permitted manual maneuvers were still easy to reach, and the restraining field held you snugly on, either way. It was possible to lower the force-field, so your upper body was free, but Tesa didn't need to have the wind in her hair right now.

Taller waited until she signaled she was ready, then moved toward the cliff edge. She signed to the sled to follow.

As they lifted away from the cliff, Tesa was thrilled to realize that she was really *flying* with Taller. Her heart raced.

Taller kept a careful eye on her, she noted, as they spiraled slowly over the marsh. They passed over groups of yearlings, and pairs near nesting shelters who lifted their heads and called. Tesa felt Taller's answering cry tingle over her arms. Finally, they circled their own nest shelter, and she was surprised by how calm and peaceful everything seemed. Nothing remained of the deadly battle that had been fought hours ago.

But then she saw strange hatching cloaks attached to the nest shelter. They must belong to Kills-the-Ripper, and the male that Weaver had beaten. Not trophies, they were hung to mark the days of grief that Taller's family would have to mourn for the members of their flock that they'd been forced to kill.

Taller set down in the water without a splash, as Tesa cautiously hovered the sled beside the platform and stepped onto the slick reeds. She intended to carry the lightweight sled up to the platform, but then a small, cinnamon-colored head popped out from the slitted doorway. Tesa dropped the sled in the mud, stretching out her arms.

Wings outstretched, Sailor hurled himself down the ramp with such abandon that he tumbled right into Tesa's shins. He picked himself up to flutter against her legs, imploring her to feed him, brood him, and never leave again.

Tesa plopped down, cross-legged, letting the happy tears flow, as Sailor clambered into her lap. When she looked up, Weaver and Taller were standing near, their angular faces close to her and Sailor. It was wonderful to be home.

When she finally stood to follow them into the nest shelter, she remembered to pull the sled out of the mud. As she propped it against the shelter's tule mat walls, she glanced back at the cliff. There, sitting at its edge, watching the last shreds of the sunset, were Meg and Thom, yet even at this distance Tesa could tell that Thom wasn't looking toward the horizon. He was watching her. Hesitantly, she held out her hand, as she'd once done as a child, and made the ASL I-love-you sign. Then she stepped into the nest shelter, leaving the humans behind.

CHAPTER 15

Sailor

Why do children grow so fast? Tesa wondered, watching Sailor preen the long, black primaries of his fully grown wings. *He's almost as tall as his father,* she marveled, recalling the tiny cinnamon chick that cuddled in her lap only six months ago.

His color was more golden now, with white feathers peeking through. His eyes were a stunning aquamarine, as they changed from blue to golden yellow and the long, dark rapierlike bill seemed outsized for his face.

Every day his movements were becoming more graceful, his flying more powerful. Tesa watched him with both admiration and dread, knowing that soon it would be time for him to leave on his "flyaway," his rite of passage into adulthood.

When he comes back—will I even be here? she wondered. The human crew expected to receive confirmation of the Grus' status any day now. By the time Sailor took his flyaway, the first of his people to have a close relationship with a human, Earth would have a successful First Contact and would have been voted full membership in the Cooperative League of Systems.

Tesa wanted to be happy, but she couldn't.

She felt guilty, but her departure from Trinity was looming too close for her to celebrate any victories. She found herself understanding Bruce's feelings.

She noticed Sailor laying his head along his back, looking at her like the child he still was despite his incongruously adult body, and her concerns slid off like so many dream shadows.

"Let's go flying," he signed, plaintively.

"Without Taller and Weaver?" she asked. "We should wait."

"We'll go by ourselves."

A month ago he wouldn't step into the reeds unless he could see one of them, but now he only wanted to be with Tesa. Soon, he'd go without her, as well. He treated her sometimes as a parent, sometimes as a cohort, because of her smaller size. Some nights, as they slept side by side, and he rested his long neck across her, she'd remember Szu-yi's warning. She couldn't imagine him leaving her behind, and not loving her when he returned. Or her not being there at all.

Sailor was distracted by something swimming around his legs. There was a flash of blue and silver, and the sudden jab of his sleek head, and then a moment of wrestling with a fish that seemed much too big for him to swallow. In a moment it was gobbled down, headfirst. "I'll go alone," he threatened, while the bulge in his throat slid downward.

"You'd better not," she warned.

He gave her a one-eyed look, then started running, stretching his wings, finally his legs lifted up, trailing water.

He's bluffing, thought Tesa. No, this time he was really going, just because he could. She turned her sled on so fast it almost left without her, and flopping onto her stomach across the flat flyer, she quickly pulled up beside him. "Your father will kill us," she signed, but he couldn't answer in the air. All she could do was follow him—and enjoy herself.

Tesa activated the shields that protected her from the wind, set up the passive restraint field, and called up her mapping grid, set flush on the sled. She knew where they were headed.

Just as Thom had predicted, Sailor's flights usually ended up in Black Feather's territory, to see if his brother's group had returned from their annual southern migration. Today was no different as they banked over Black Feather's river.

"They're not back yet," Sailor signed as soon as they'd alighted on the bank of the wide river. The meandering waterway, edged on its opposite bank by a dense forest, played host to many avians, but, at the moment, no Grus. Sailor's whole body spoke of his disappointment.

"Well, it was a nice flight," Tesa signed consolingly.

"Look!" Sailor pointed to a group of squat-legged birds, who carried comical, flapping pouches on their long lower bills. They were "Travellers," ungainly avians who were adventurous explorers—the Johnny Appleseeds of Trinity. They carried genetic material in their pouches to seed barren waters.

"Black Feather," Sailor signed admiringly, "follows the Travellers. They know the best routes to *everywhere*. If they're here, it won't be long before he will be, too."

As Sailor grew, Tesa had learned that the Grus could converse with many of the World's beings. Signs were involved, some body movements or gestures, and occasionally vocalizations. She recorded it all on her voder, but this cluttered up her files and slowed its ability to translate the Aquila vocalizations she'd collected from her "study nests."

Weaver felt that Sailor's aptitude for the World's languages was greater than her other children's had been, because of Tesa's influence. The young woman taught Sailor some American Sign Language and Plains Indian Sign—a language more adaptable for him since it required no facial expressions. Sailor eagerly learned those "un-Worldly signs."

"Well," Sailor signed cheerfully, determined to make the best of their trip, "we may as well get something to eat."

Tesa grinned. "Anything special in mind?"

"How about black nuts?" he signed. "They grow at the edge of that forest." He pointed farther west with his bill.

Tesa was familiar with that forest. The trees there dwarfed Earth's Sequoias and were so wide that it took minutes to walk around them. One of her Aquila study nests was located there.

Over the months she'd watched the Aquila pair finish their nest and lay a single egg. As Sailor's adult feathers began to come in, that egg had finally hatched. Unlike the Grus, this chick was helpless, its legs too soft to even support its own weight, and its black-tipped predator's bill was constantly open in endless screams whenever it was awake. Its only activities seemed to be eating and sleeping in a boring, repetitive cycle.

Even her translation program seemed redundant. Everything the voder repeated was either untranslatable or involved hunting or flying. It was all becoming a sad letdown.

The only interesting thing that had happened regarding Aquila while Sailor was growing—or actually, *hadn't* happened—was that ever since the escort flock had been attacked, the Aquila had not been seen again.

"This is the best season for black nuts." Sailor's signs snapped Tesa out of her musings. "We could take some home."

Even though the big raptors nested in that forest, Tesa and Sailor would be in less danger there. The Aquila preferred to attack in open areas near water, since it was hard to maneuver those tremendous wings around huge trees.

Tesa hopped up onto her sled. "Let's go. I'm starved!"

Miles from Black Feather's roost site, Sailor and Tesa found the heavily laden trees. Greedily Sailor wolfed down small, dark nuts, as Tesa easily cracked the papery shells and enjoyed the rich, sweet kernels. They collected four mesh bags of nuts while stuffing themselves on the delicious nutmeats.

While they were eating, several large animal shapes slipped in and out of the shadows, sharing the trees' bounty with them. There were blue-antlered Leaf-Eaters, some small canis-form predators, and the ever-present avians. Once, a flock of small, gold avians erupted from the ground, startling the two friends, and they looked up quickly. Deep within the copse of trees, ambling along the nut-strewn ground, was the ominous red and white roan Tree Ripper.

"Rippers aren't much for conversation," Tesa remembered Taller saying as the two stood silently still while the ferocious, temperamental killer lumbered by, sampling the nuts as she went. The great bearlike omnivore would've dwarfed the great Kodiak bear, and Tesa had stared at it in awe and terror, wondering if even the monstrous cave bears of Earth's past had ever been that big, with claws that long, or teeth that sharp. The huge predator ate her fill, then shambled on.

"Aren't you full yet?" Tesa finally complained, reclining on a mossy spot free of nuts. She was watching the suns' rays slant through the tops of the impossibly high trees, wondering which one held her study nest. She had a sudden, sharp memory of Dr. Rob saying "maybe you could tame one, like the old falconers did." She laughed. Wouldn't Taller love *that*?

Sailor daintily wiped his face on his back. "I'm full now. Maybe we can come back in a few days and have some more."

"Maybe," Tesa agreed. "Maybe Black Feather will be back

then.'' *Maybe next time you'll come by yourself,* she thought with a pang. She stood in one smooth motion and hoisted the bags onto the sled, securing them with a restraining shield.

"I could carry one," Sailor assured her.

"Why bother? The sled can hold them."

"Are these all for us?"

"They're for Relaxed, First-One-There, and our friends in the sky shelter." Sailor had stiffened in response to Thom's name-sign, jerking his head up, since he still didn't have an unfeathered crown to display his emotions. Like Taller, he was jealous of Thom.

"Besides," she told him, ignoring his reaction, "if you ate them all, you'd just get sick." She climbed onto the sled and sat cross-legged, knowing the flight back with a chick stuffed full of food would be a slow, easy one.

As they lifted off, Tesa thought of Thom—things had never been the same between them since that last shuttle trip. Whenever he visited her, Sailor always seemed to be there between them. Tesa had almost been glad of that, since she was so torn about her suspicions. However, except for that one vague computer message, Thom had done nothing to arouse suspicion.

But the damage had been done. Tesa couldn't trust Thom. Even if there was no connection between him and the privateers—a concept too horrible for her to accept—there was still a side to him he kept carefully guarded.

She dismissed her troublesome thoughts. It wasn't smart to get distracted while flying.

As they leveled off, she looked back at the forest, hoping she might glimpse her study nest. A dark blot in the north sky caught her attention. She stared, but the objects were too far away to be clearly seen. Tesa punched up the long-distance scanner.

The readout chilled her. Six Aquila were steadily closing in on them. She looked at the screen, sickened. Even if they increased their speed, they'd be overtaken in minutes.

What the hell are **they** *doing here?* Thom wondered as he peered through the high-powered binoculars across the wide expanse of river that separated him from Tesa and Sailor. The two had just landed—probably looking for Black Feather's flock. Bruce had said that the southern spawning had been especially rich this year, but even so, Thom thought the flock should've been back by now.

The touch of a human hand on his shoulder startled him so much that he rolled and came up on his feet poised defensively.

"Easy there, old friend," Peter said amiably.

"You scared the shit out of me," Thom grumbled.

"I've been watching you, peeping Thom," the dark man said teasingly. "When are you going to stop spying on that woman? You'd have to grow feathers to get her attention. Give me those." He focused the field glasses across the river. "Well, they're taking off. Let's take cover, just to be safe. They're heading west, so they'll be out of sight soon."

The two men moved away from the river's edge until they were hidden within a copse of dense shrubbery.

"So tell me what's so important," Thom asked, watching the two leave, "that I had to leave camp at a moment's notice?"

Peter looked at him knowingly. "Couple of things. We just got the word—the Grus have their official status."

Thom was surprised. "Well, that's great, but won't that be announced to everyone?"

Peter nodded. "But I wanted to discuss something with you, privately. Earth's First Contact claim is jeopardized."

Thom's eyes widened in alarm. "How? Why?"

"The Simiu claim they have proof that *all* the privateers and *all* the purchasers of the skins are Terran," Peter explained. "They say Earth has murdered the Grus for profit, and thus should not get *any* credit for First Contact. They also presented evidence that there's been a link between the crew of the *Singing Crane* and the privateers since the beginning."

"What kind of evidence?" Thom asked quietly.

"Computer dumps, transmissions, stuff like that."

Thom paused, his mind racing. "But how could they get them? Those things are coded . . . classified!"

"You know how. Someone passed them on, to make sure that we'd look as bad as possible."

Thom looked at Peter. "So, who's the Judas?" They had been arguing about this since before Scott had been killed. "You've been working on this for months, don't you have any answers?"

"Me?" Peter flared angrily. "Who almost blew everything a few months ago on the *Crane*, right in front of Tesa? Suppose that had been Bruce peering over your shoulder?" Peter shook his head and held up a hand. "Hey, we can't afford this, Thom. We've got to work together, figure out what we can do."

The blond man nodded. It was just the two of them, after all.

Thom had been the special wildlife investigator who had first spotted an illegal Grus skin during an unusually thorough customs check at the Luna importing base. Peter, his partner for several years, had broken the code on its counterfeit data-card erroneously identifying the skin as a genetic reconstruction. Thom was a well-trained biologist and experienced investigator who recognized that even the best reconstructions didn't have the look, the feel, of that skin. It had been a satisfying case, but neither of them had expected it to lead to this job.

While they were being recruited, the two officers had asked why the entire founding party, Meg, Scott, Lauren, and Bruce, couldn't be replaced, since there were fears even then that there was a hidden connection between the original exploration team and the Grus skins. There was no tangible evidence, they were told, and Jamestown Founders would scream that the crew's removal would endanger their claim if the First Contact were denied.

Thom gazed at their unspoiled surroundings. "When we got here we said, 'Hey, we're up against amateurs. We've got superior technology. We've got training. We'll clean this up in two months and be home for Christmas.' That was two years ago, and we haven't even ID'd the conspirator."

"Hey, we've had a pronounced effect on Grus survival," Peter said defensively. "The attacks had been escalating when we arrived, but things slowed to a crawl by the time Tesa got here, and no skins have been taken since then."

"And the attack on the escort flock?" Thom asked.

Peter shook his head. "I can't find any link between those sorry buzzards and whoever's skinning the Grus."

Thom had been screening transmissions, the strobing, condensed computer talk the orbiting robots traded with the *Singing Crane*, trying to find a correlation between those, missing Grus, and Aquila attacks. There was only the vaguest of patterns. Someone was being very careful.

Peter let out his breath. "And I still can't prove any connection between the *Crane* crew and the privateers."

Thom shook his head. He was convinced there was a traitor, and that it had to be Bruce. The weatherman's bitterness over the potential fortune he'd lost was common knowledge. Thom knew he was prejudiced. He didn't like Bruce, and he couldn't imagine Lauren being clever enough to maintain a relationship with Peter while hiding something so monstrous. Dr. Li was too bureaucratic—or was that the perfect cover?

"If there is a Judas," Peter continued, "they've put codes so deep inside the system that their partners can bleed off all our communications without leaving a trace."

"Well," Thom asked, irritated, "what *do* you know? You didn't call me over here just to hash over old news."

"The privateers are holding on to the Grus skins—I think they're stockpiling them on Trinity. Nothing's passed into or out of Sorrow Sector in months. Of course, that's just driving up the price. I do know the privateers here have only got one ship, which makes it easy for them to stay out of range. Right now they could be doing anything from hiding on the dark side of a moon to camping out in a rain forest. But my big news is this—these privateers, who *are* all Terran, have been totally financed and outfitted by the Simiu—the Harkk'ett clan."

Thom recognized the name of that old and politically well-placed Simiu family—it was the clan that had been shamed fifteen years before by the suicide of a youngster named Khrekk' during the First Contact between the Simiu and the humans. It was hard for Thom to understand how, so many years later, that perceived shame could still be so raw to that clan, but the bitterness of dishonor was, for the Simiu, strong motivation.

"When I found out about the Simiu involvement," Peter said, concerned, "it gave me a really bad feeling. That family doesn't care about those skins, or even about the Grus. They're trying to satisfy some twisted notion of honor, so they'll do whatever it takes to foul Earth up."

"Like what?"

"If humans kill Taller and Sailor, it's all over for us here. The Grus won't allow us to stay."

"Which will leave them totally unprotected," Thom said. "And by the time the CLS can send help—"

"There wouldn't be anything left to protect." Peter's face was drawn. "Besides, the privateers don't give a damn about Simiu honor, they're just in it for the money. They could see this as their last chance to take every skin they can get their hands on." He stopped, collecting his thoughts. "I've sent all this information to Earth. I've told them we're still working on it, but...I've recommended...that the CLS intervene now, before it's too late. Of course, it'll have to go through channels first, and then there's travel time. They can't possibly get here before two months, at the earliest. That's probably going to be too late."

"So what do we do in the meantime?" Thom asked.

"I still have a few tricks up my sleeve," Peter said. "Have you got your Mizari voder?"

Thom pulled it out of his pocket. The advanced instruments had only arrived two months ago, and by then they were no longer needed to establish the Grus' intelligence. Thom and Meg were using them now to document differences in the translation programs between the Terran and the Mizari voders. But Thom and Peter had spent enough time working with the simple-seeming devices to appreciate their capabilities. Peter said he was sure someone had deliberately sabotaged the previous delivery, to keep these sophisticated computers out of the crew's hands.

"I've spent a lot of time working on these babies," Peter told Thom, staring at his with unconcealed admiration. "Talk about *power*! You can even communicate with *satellites* using them. Pull in transmissions from ships in the outer atmosphere and get their coordinates."

Thom looked suitably impressed. "You think we can locate the privateers' ship with it? Just from their transmissions?"

"I can't find any way to effectively block it," Peter told him, "however, when you ask it to trace a transmission to its source, you'll tip your hat to whoever's transmitting."

"Oh, that's a real advantage." Thom rolled his eyes. "That's like a telecommunication tap that beeps!"

Peter pulled a tiny memory card from his pocket and waved it at Thom. "That's why I created this little work of art. This program allows you to trace a transmission without tipping your hand." He gave Thom the card. "It can be tricky to install, but I can talk you through it. With me listening on the *Crane*, and you down here, we might be able to pick up dialogue between the privateers and their contact on the *Crane*."

Thom pocketed the program. "Then maybe I can go calling on those bastards when they aren't expecting me."

Peter shook his head. "Yeah, well, I wouldn't be too eager about that if I were you. They're not hampered by First Contact restrictions the way we are. No doubt they're armed.''

Ever since the *Désirée* incident, when the presence of a single weapon ruined the delicate political ballet of that First Contact, Terrans were forbidden, by Earth, to bring weapons onto new planets. They could only protect themselves with sonar repelling devices and other defensive equipment.

Peter glanced around the river. ''The reason I wanted to talk to you here was that I thought Black Feather might be back. He moves around so much, I wanted to try talking to him, see if he's seen anything unusual in his travels.''

''I'll check tomorrow,'' Thom said. ''He should be back within the next few days.'' Sailor would probably take off by then, Thom realized. Meg felt Tesa should go home for her surgery soon after the young avian left. If Peter was right, Thom wanted her back on Earth. Then he could stop worrying about her.

Sailor saw Death behind them and gave an alarm call, but he still had a child's voice, which wouldn't carry. He was terrified—more terrified even than that time Good Eyes had lifted his small body to save him. Only predators lifted you up—and never to save you.

He was heavy with food, but even if he'd been empty, he couldn't outfly Death. Good Eyes was clinging to her flying device, her eyes wide with fear. Could she fly ahead, warn his father, save herself? Maybe, but there wouldn't be time to save Sailor, so she wouldn't leave him, he knew that.

He couldn't think about Death killing Good Eyes right in front of him, in the air. All they had to do was damage her device, and she'd fall, unable to save herself, and with no flock nearby to catch her. And what could he do, to save the one who'd saved him? He felt his heart breaking from fear and guilt.

Glancing behind him, he saw the terrible red and gold eyes that could terrorize a victim into making a last, fatal error. Then Good Eyes was signing, ''Head for the forest.''

Some of the ancient timbers had suffered from fires over the centuries, and were hollow inside, though still alive. Those were her favorite trees, and she loved climbing around inside them. Could one of those save them from Death?

They'd been following the river, but the forest had traveled with them. He followed Good Eyes' lead as Death gained on them.

"Whatever happens, keep going," Good Eyes signed. "Get inside a hollow tree. They can't fly easily in the forest."

Well, neither could he, but Sailor couldn't point that out to her now. And what did she mean, "whatever happens"?

Without warning, Good Eyes dropped behind, placing herself between him and Death. He was terrified for her, but angry, too. He should be protecting *her* since he was the one who could *fly!*

Death drew closer and the group began splitting up. Suddenly an enormous female was on Sailor's left, a male on his right, pulling up as easily as if the young Grus were standing still. He concentrated on the forest.

With a scream that cut through him like ice, the female reached for his unprotected back. And then a shadow passed over him, there was a thud, and the female tumbled, loose feathers fluttering past him. Good Eyes had actually slammed her device into Death and knocked her away! Tesa hovered over Sailor and then veered after the male, who folded his wings and dropped out of sight, wary now of the alien contraption.

The youngster felt a wild surge of hope as the forest came closer. Two more avians flanked him now, while two others moved aggressively against Good Eyes.

One female screamed and grabbed for the human. At the last second, Good Eyes flipped her sled upside down and the deadly talons clanged harmlessly against its hard surface. The female jerked a foot up as if in pain and clenched it into a fist. She dropped back. The male flipped upside down himself and tried to impale Good Eyes, but she righted the little vessel and he, too, struck the underside. The pair drew back, confused.

Good Eyes had freed a mesh bag from its invisible bonds and was swinging it over her head. The four remaining avians called to one another, unsure how to respond. What had ever fought Death in the air, or had somersaulted as they did in the attack?

The human rushed them, then flung the bag. It smashed into a male, exploding into a rain of black nuts. This startled the avian so much he just folded his wings and dropped out of sight. She reached for another bag, swung and let it go, but the others knew what to expect and moved out of range. But some of the fight seemed to have gone out of Death.

And then the forest was there, and Sailor had to worry about trees that could shatter a wing, as they rushed past him. He weaved and dodged through the heavy stand, brushing a trunk and bruising a finger, but nothing worse. Then he spied a towering tree that had had its core burnt through. At its base was a small opening—but it was big enough.

He parachuted to a jarring landing, collapsed his wings and scurried inside, his slim form slipping through the narrow opening that led into the wide center. He peered up through the chimney of the tree at thin streaks of sunlight. There was a sudden crashing, then something warm rushed in against him, scaring him so bad he jumped, hitting his head on a narrow place.

It was Good Eyes, alive and safe! His relief was so overwhelming, he became a child again, purring and trembling his wings, wrapping his long neck around her for comfort.

She slid her arms around his body, purring back at him with her funny off-key rumble that he loved so much. Both their hearts were pounding, and she was sticky with the sweat she released when she was hot. He glanced up quickly. Something was not right. On her arm was not sweat, but blood. Her blood.

Her feather shirt was ripped, her flesh showing through, and a slash across her arm seeped blood. He stared at it, eyes wide.

"It's nothing," she signed. "It doesn't even hurt."

He peered in amazement. She'd been touched by Death and lived. She said it didn't hurt. This parent of his was more strange—and more powerful—than he could have ever imagined.

Tesa looked around, confused, as her hand grazed the rough, carbonized interior of the old tree. Had she dreamt of eagles, or flown with Aquila? She rubbed her eyes to rid them of their gritty feeling, the sense of unreality she couldn't shake.

She looked up the chimney of the tree—the light was waning. She and Sailor had lapsed into an exhausted sleep after their narrow escape, their bodies demanding immediate relief after pumping out enough adrenaline to fuel an army. She reached for him folded up beside her, his head tucked.

As he lifted his head, Tesa pushed herself to her feet. She ached. Except for the talon scratch on her arm, she would've gotten out of this unscathed if she hadn't leaped off the sled and misjudged her footing. She'd gone sprawling ass-over-teakettle over a huge root, skinning her knees and palms.

"Come on, Sailor," she signed, "we've got to go."

"Is it safe?"

"I can't believe they'd wait for us this long," she assured him with more confidence than she really felt.

Poking her head out of the tree, she gazed around. Afternoon light slanted through the multicolored leaves, throwing shadows of orange, green, and red, like sunshine through a cathedral window. The angled shafts were like the polarized light Sailor could see. She stepped out cautiously and moved to her sled. It had some new dings and small dents, but it was still functional. She couldn't shake the feeling that they were being watched. Tesa turned her sled on, setting it to hover.

She turned back toward the entrance, where the tip of Sailor's bill was peeking out. She waved at him to emerge, and he stepped out slowly, nervously, peering everywhere, his feathers standing straight out.

Tesa wanted to console him, but she couldn't. They weren't alone, they just hadn't found their observer yet. She inched around the tree and soon found their watcher. A female Aquila clung with one foot to a limb, about fifty feet off the ground. The other foot was injured and she held it in a fist, resting on the wood. This was the same female that had attacked her, Tesa realized, the one who'd struck the underside of the sled so hard. There seemed to be something else eerily familiar about her.

The Aquila eyed her, first with one ruby eye, then the other, but made no move to attack. Sailor touched Tesa with his bill, then slid his head over her shoulder, staring in wide-eyed fear at his mortal enemy. They could get to the tree's entrance before the Aquila could reach them, Tesa decided, and that injured foot made her seem less threatening.

Then Tesa realized why this Aquila seemed familiar. This was the same female that had scolded her the day she arrived on Trinity. *And she's the same female I've been observing in the study nests*, Tesa decided with a cool certainty. The cynical part of her brain tried to deny the coincidence, but the instinctive part of her knew she was right.

She wants to communicate, Tesa felt. *She was trying to tell me something that first day, and she's come back to try again*.

Was it just luck that made Scott pick *that* nest for his camera, or had he interacted with this same female? If he had, that might've been what made him plant those cameras against everyone else's edict. But wouldn't he have written about it?

Not if everyone would've thought he was crazy, she realized. She suddenly felt Scott's presence very strongly—his memory and his spirit—and a shiver washed over her.

Help me do the right thing, Puff. Mitakuye oyasin. Ignoring Sailor's startled expression, Tesa stepped forward and signed a greeting to the avian.

The female leaned forward, clutching her precarious perch, and spread her wings threateningly, opening her beak. Tesa turned her voder on, calling up her weak translation program.

". . . safe hunting before . . . (untranslatable) . . . the skies . . ." The incoherent fragments trailed across the small screen.

Sailor touched her shoulder. "What are you doing?"

She hesitated. She was afraid to tell him she wanted to communicate with a creature his people so despised. "Can you understand what she's saying?" she asked the youngster.

He looked shocked. "Saying? She's screaming, that's all." His signing set the Aquila off on another chorus of shrieks.

". . . Our nests . . . the World . . . (untranslatable) . . ."

Tesa wanted to shake the voder, make it translate.

She stared at the bird. If *you're intelligent, you could change your behavior, the way the Grus did with the Blue Cloud people*. The avian threw her head back, as though laughing. Tesa signed again, asking the predator why she wished to kill people who never hurt her, people who were not her true food.

The avian became more agitated. Tesa looked at the voder.

". . . to kill the trees . . . (untranslatable) . . . come from (English word) Earth . . . to kill the trees . . ."

Tesa froze the translation and stared at it, incredulously. Sailor was also amazed. He had heard the Aquila say an English word, a word he'd heard other humans say. Earth. The planet.

Tesa swallowed and decided to use her voice. "I come from Earth," she said in English.

The voder repeated the sentence about coming from Earth, then, ". . . you kill the trees . . . now, (untranslatable) the others kill them . . . (untranslatable) burn nests . . . the children . . . until the White Winds die . . . (untranslatable) . . . go back to (English word) Earth . . ." The rest trailed off into gibberish.

Then, without warning, the Aquila launched herself off the limb and threaded her way through the forest. Tesa eased herself onto an upthrust root and stared at the voder, frustrated.

This is just like all my damned dreams. Snatches and fragments—but that beast said an English word—a word she had to learn from another human being. She realized that Sailor was staring at her in stunned surprise.

"What's the matter?" she signed, wanting to ease his fears.

"You spoke to Death, Good Eyes," he signed timidly.

"Well, I might as well have spoken to this tree."

Sailor looked in the direction the Aquila flew. "Yes, but when you speak to trees . . . they don't kill and eat you."

"Well, neither did she. We'd better get out of here." She realized the youngster was thoroughly shaken by this new experience. "Sailor?" she signed.

"Yes?"

"I don't think we should mention this to your parents."

He gazed at her for a long, telling moment, giving her "the look." "Yes," he finally signed, "I think you're right."

They lifted off for home together.

Peter parked the little solo shuttle they called the *Demoiselle* behind a mass of shrubs. According to Thom's maps, this brackish marshland was usually the final staging area for Black Feather's flock on their return to their river home. Thom would check the river tomorrow, but since Peter had told the *Crane* crew he'd be planetside for a few days, the Senegalese man decided he might as well catch up with the flock himself.

If Black Feather's flock hadn't reached this marsh, then they'd be too far away to find today. In that case, he'd just finish his mapping survey—his excuse to be on Trinity.

As he walked through the soggy marsh, he touched the sound nullifiers in his ears, adjusting them for the onslaught of noise that usually surrounded a roosting Grus flock.

He was almost through a stand of small, wiry trees eking out a living in the saturated ground when he became aware of the change in the air. Brackish marsh always smelled to him like a charnel house because of all the decaying vegetation. *This stink could gag a crow,* he thought, just as a flock of green, pigeon-sized carrion-eaters burst from the ground in an agitated cloud.

Peter pushed through the trees, finally seeing the feeding ground, but it was a long moment before he *truly* saw it.

Bodies, one after the other, were stretched out, raw, bleeding—skinned. Black Feather's entire flock—dead. Over a hundred avians—living, breathing, intelligent beings—had been slaughtered. Their exposed muscles lay red, nude in the bright sunlight as scores of carrion-eaters converged on the feast. They were only the beginning, Peter knew. Soon there would be armies of insects, rodents, carnivores descending on the grisly scene until not one morsel, not one bleached white bone, was left. On Trinity, everything was food to someone.

Struck with horror, he took a cautious step back, even as his brain registered the other details he had yet to notice.

There were Aquila everywhere, like bald eagles converging on the Chilkat River in Alaska. They were perched in the scrubby trees, in the water, and on the bodies. Dozens of Aquila, more than he had thought lived on the World, were feasting in this open cemetery. He swallowed bitter bile, trying not to notice how they were all staring at him as he took another step back.

Slowly he removed his nullifiers, then took another cautious step. Then he heard it, the soft snick of a modern weapon—

And the strange, quiet voice that said, "That's far enough."

CHAPTER 16

♦

The Sweat Bath

Weaver pulled her head out from under her wing, listening. She heard it again, a soft noise, like a rousette's whimper. She snaked her head over to Good Eyes' bed.

The human tossed fitfully, her face contorted, reflecting the nightmares she conjured up. These last two nights had been the worst, since Sailor had begun sleeping outside with his father. Perhaps, Weaver thought, she should've expected that.

She'd seen many children pull away, and remembered every one—especially those who never came back. It was hard on a parent's heart, but it was part of life's cycle.

But to Good Eyes, this was all new. *When the first one leaves,* Weaver thought, *every parent's heart breaks.* Sailor might go this morning. Things had changed with her son since he and Good Eyes had had an adventure they would not discuss. That was typical. The first big adventure, the thrill of independence, and then the wish—the need—for new places.

A soft moan escaped Good Eyes. Weaver touched her gently, trying to comfort the sleeping woman. Some nights she could ease her out of the dream, but tonight, the human sat bolt upright.

"Has he left?" Good Eyes signed. "Is there lightning?"

"He's here," Weaver assured her. "There's no storm."

The human blinked, rubbed her face, then looked around.

"It's morning," Weaver signed. "He may . . . leave soon."

The Grus saw the human's soft lips tremble, heard her sharp intake of breath. Good Eyes covered her face with her hands. Her shoulders shook, and she made hard, choking sounds. Her sorrow was so vivid, Weaver also felt a flood of pain, pain she thought she'd learned to accept.

When Good Eyes looked up, her face was wet. "Does it always hurt like this, to see them go?" she asked.

Weaver wanted to say something that would lessen the ache, but she could only sign, "It always hurts. Every time."

The human took a deep breath and rubbed her face hard. "Okay, I'm all right now. Can I . . . is it okay to go outside?"

"Of course. The parents should be together on this day."

When they stepped onto the platform, they could see Sailor on one leg, not far from his father, his body poised with anticipation. Father Sun touched the western sky, coloring it with reds and blues. The Mother Sun was now so close, she came up beside him, but the Child Sun would not be seen for hours.

Sailor looked at Taller. "I'll remember who I am," he signed the traditional parting phrase. He turned to Weaver. "I'll remember where I live," he told her as she had told her own mother. Then he faced Good Eyes. There was no traditional saying for his parting from her. "I'll remember what you taught me," he promised. He ran across the clear water, lifting effortlessly, as Taller threw back his head and called, announcing to the World that his son was grown, his son was leaving. Weaver answered his call with her own ringing voice.

Good Eyes signed the words every parent felt on this day. "Come home safely. Come home soon." Then she held up her hand in the human sign that meant "I love you."

Meg walked through the shelter, toweling her freshly washed hair, and found the note Thom had left on her terminal.

"There's fresh coffee for you and a thermos for Tesa. I'll

be in late, so don't wait dinner. Any emergencies, just tap into my voder, I'll respond. See you, Thom.''

"This place is worse than a hotel," Meg grumbled. She and Scott used to do everything together, they were a team. Well, those days were over. Perhaps she could spend her time working with Scott's stuff now that things were slowing down around here. She could probably get a bunch of papers out of it—coauthored posthumously by old Hedford. She didn't want anyone to forget who it was who'd made the big breakthrough around here.

There are breakthroughs yet to be made, she felt him say.

"Hmph," she grunted, ambling into the kitchen and pouring herself some coffee. The front door opened, and Meg was startled to see Tesa. "Well, good morning!" she signed, surprised. "Is your coffee that late?" she asked, smiling.

Tesa's sad expression wiped her grin off. "Sailor's gone," the young woman signed. "He left a few hours ago."

Ya durak! the older woman chided herself. *You should've been able to tell that as soon as you saw her face.* "Oh, honey, I'm sorry. Are you okay? Come on, sit down, talk to me."

Tesa let herself be led to the small dining table. "I'm okay," she insisted as Meg poured her a hot cup. "I know he had to go, but . . . he never looked back. *That* was hard." She wrapped her hands around the steaming coffee cup. "Did you know that the Grus abandon the nest shelter after the chick leaves?"

"I knew something happened to it, but I wasn't sure what."

"It's too painful to go back there anymore, so they sleep outside," Tesa signed. "When the chick returns, they give him his hatching cloak, and they move back in until the yearling gets established in a cohort group his own age. But if the chick dies on the flyaway, they hang his hatching cloak outside and let the whole thing decay."

"Well, we have plenty of room for you here, Tesa."

Tesa gave her a small, tired smile. "I didn't think you'd leave me sleeping in the water on one leg. I came to ask for a different kind of favor."

"What is it?"

"First, what will happen to me now that Sailor has left?"

Meg sat back. "Well, we didn't know when that might happen, so we couldn't make definite plans, but . . ." She smiled, wanting Tesa to know she was looking out for her best interests. "We thought you might be ready to go home. You deserve a break and you've put your surgery off for so long. Once you have that done, well, you could go to the Ashu Mizari as you had originally planned, or . . . perhaps come back here as a diplomatic liaison."

The young woman nodded, but seemed to draw away.

"Tesa," Meg asked, "what do *you* want to do?"

Tesa looked at her with that long gaze she'd picked up from the Grus. "I don't know what I want. I feel overwhelmed. Right now, the thing I want most is to go off by myself, have a sweat bath, and pray for answers."

Meg knew little about Tesa's spiritual beliefs; however, as a religious person herself, she had to respect Tesa's needs. She wasn't sure how she felt, though, about her going off alone. "Can't you build a sweat bath here on the knoll? There's plenty of room, and Thom and I would respect your privacy."

Tesa shook her head. "I need to be away, to find my answers, to build my lodge—maybe to even ask for a vision."

Meg felt a twinge of alarm. Didn't Indian visions sometimes require fasting and hallucinogenic drugs or self-mutilation? "Well, I don't know, Tesa . . ."

The young woman fixed her with an intent gaze. "I haven't been able to practice my religion since I left StarBridge."

Meg felt more comfortable knowing she'd practiced her religion at StarBridge. Rob Gable wouldn't have tolerated anything harmful. "How much time are we talking about?"

"Four days," Tesa signed. "Four is an important number to my people."

"How far will you be going?"

"To a forest I visited the other day with Sailor."

That couldn't be too bad, Meg thought. They'd been able to go and come back in the same day. "Will you take your voder with you and pay attention to it, even when you're praying?"

Tesa looked surprised. "Oh, sure. That's a reasonable request. And I'm not foolhardy, Meg. I'll keep the sled hovering, just in case." She smiled confidently.

Meg still felt a little uneasy. "I'd feel better about this if Thom were here . . ."

Tesa reacted strongly. "My religious practices are none of Thom's business! He's an agnostic, what respect could he have for my spiritual needs? Besides, you're *his* supervisor, why—"

Meg held up a hand to interrupt. "We were never much for rank around here, Tesa. I like to get everyone's opinions on things of importance."

Tesa seemed concerned. "Are you going to ask everyone on the *Crane* if I can do this?" Her signs were subdued, not angry.

"Well, no. It's really none of their business, either. Or Thom's." Frankly, it worried her to have Tesa go off alone— but she'd already done that many times with Sailor and had taken small jaunts on her own, alone. She knew the young woman was experienced and levelheaded. "All right, Tesa, it's all right with me. But don't forget about the voder, or the sled."

The young woman seemed to deflate with relief. "Thank you, Meg. When I come back, I'll know what path I've got to take."

Meg watched her leave and noticed an added lightness in her step. *Thom will probably be furious when he gets back, but that's too bad. She deserves this small request.*

And when she gets back, Scott's ghost teased, *she'll have* **all** *the answers.*

It was hard for Tesa to leave Taller and Weaver. After Sailor's departure, the flock came to offer good wishes and assurances that Sailor's flyaway would teach him the things an adult had to know. The avians told funny stories of gentle mishaps, and narrow escapes that were never really dangerous. Their concern was touching, especially since they treated Tesa no differently from Sailor's biological parents. After they left, Tesa packed and tried to explain why she needed time alone.

Taller and Weaver accepted her news with good grace, but it was clear they had hoped she would stay with them.

"I'll be back in four days," she promised.

"Perhaps we'll take a trip then," Taller suggested.

"I'd like that," Tesa signed. She wanted to see a lot more of Trinity before she'd have to leave. The Grus seemed as reluctant as Meg had to bid her farewell when she signed good-bye and headed toward the dark forest where, only two days ago, she and Sailor had had their strange interaction with the Aquila.

• • •

Thom wondered if his own good sense hadn't been distorted by Peter's dire predictions. He sat at the river's edge where Black Feather's flock should have been, and wasn't, and wondered why these avians were so late returning, and where the hell his partner was.

Bruce had told him that Peter wasn't expected back on the *Crane* until tomorrow, that he was mapping ground coordinates for satellite surveys. That was one of the easier things about working with scientists. Research required large amounts of uninterrupted time, so investigations weren't as difficult as they had been on other jobs. But this job had its own problems.

It wasn't anything like tracking down illegal imports of protected wildlife on Earth, or setting up elaborate stings to stop the poaching of rare creatures, though it had seemed similar enough when they'd been recruited.

Well, if Peter wouldn't answer a signal, and he hadn't since the day before yesterday, Thom could go *looking* for him, but that was a very time-consuming prospect. It would probably be more efficient to go looking for Black Feather. Thom could check out the two nearest roosting sites, and that would only take a day or so. Peter had probably gone looking for the tardy flock himself.

If Thom found the flock, he could talk to the avian leader, ask if he'd found anything unusual in his travels. Thom had spoken to Black Feather before, with Taller present. Taller's son was tolerant of humans and trusted his father's judgment. Then, if Peter had gone looking for the avians himself, Thom would find him and give him hell for ignoring his signal.

Thom recalled Peter's warning with an uneasy dread. He'd felt a terrible foreboding since then. *It's Trinity*, he thought, looking at the clear-running river. *It wakes up that ancient part of you that can instinctively save your life if you'd only listen to it*. He shivered suddenly in the still, warm air.

Actually, that hadn't been *his* thought at all. That had been something Scott had said to him a long time ago.

He piloted his sled along Black Feather's migratory trail.

Tesa inhaled air that felt like fire, as the steam from the hot rocks filled her up and poured out of her as rivulets of sweat streaked her nude body. It had taken her hours to construct her small beehive-shaped hut, to find twelve flexible saplings to take the place of Earth's white willow trees, and plant them securely in the forest soil. The saplings were joined to make a square at the top that represented the universe—north, south, east, and west. She couldn't cover the exterior with blankets, so she'd used autumn-colored conifer boughs.

In the center of the tiny lodge she'd brushed away the forest flooring and scooped out a hollow for the rocks, just the way grandfather Bigbee had taught her. The shallow depression represented *wakicagapi*—all the dead loved ones. The scooped-out soil was patted into a path leading to the sweat lodge, a path for spirits, and as she shaped the little ridge, Tesa had hoped that Scott and Water Dancer would join her in the *inipi*, the sweat bath.

She'd found the stones all over Trinity during her trips with the Grus. They were different from the stones on Earth, but they had one thing in common—they had designs on them only avians could see. She'd built her fire in the old way, the pattern of the sticks and logs representing the universe and her part in it. When the rocks were hot, she'd carried them into the lodge with a forked stick and placed them into the hollow, first the grandmother rock for the earth, then four rocks for the universe, then the grandfather stone on top for the sky.

She'd burned her sweet grass and lit her pipe filled with red willow bark from Earth as she watched the smoke rise. Taking a dipper she'd made, Tesa had filled it with cold water from the soft-sided, woven pail Weaver had made her and thrown the water on the rocks. Now the steam filled her every cell.

Everything she was doing had been done for thousands of years—but not here. On Trinity, this oldest of ceremonies was new. Splashing more water on the rocks, Tesa endured the purifying steam, waiting before she would lift the flap the first of four times, and sign *mitakuye oyasin*—all my relatives.

Even as she signed the prayers, following the ancient rites, everything she was doing was tying her to Trinity. The rocks, the soil, the saplings, everything in the lodge was from the World. As she inhaled the breath of the rocks that cured ills and eased pain, she prayed for answers. The heat surrounded her, and as she bent over the dipper, she saw her face in the water. Thinking of her dreams, she felt uneasy.

The dreams had not cared where she slept. They were always just behind her eyelids, waiting for her consciousness to slip away. The part of her as old as mountains—her instinct, her *nagi*—was trying to guide her. Tesa breathed deep, clutching her pipe and closing her eyes, and bid the dreams come.

By the time Thom approached Black Feather's nearest roosting site, it was nearly dusk. He came in high over the staging area and felt a stab of disappointment when he didn't see any bright flashes of white. He circled and pulled up his binoculars, trying to identify a huge flock of small, greenish avians.

He recognized the carrion birds, a species not often seen in Taller's territory. In fact, he'd never seen more than twenty of them, but the marsh was crawling with them, so many they appeared like a swarm of iridescent beetles.

Finally they noticed him and, startled, lifted off the ground in a great green cloud. He passed through them cautiously as they examined him. They circled in mass, then prepared to settle down again.

But not before Thom saw what their bodies had been hiding.

Thom grabbed hold of a handgrip in stunned horror. The picked remains of Black Feather's flock lay in clusters of bones and drying sinew. Even as the carrion birds settled down, Thom recognized what made this very wrong picture even more wrong.

There were *no feathers*. If the flock had been felled by a sudden disease, or a natural toxin, or even if they'd been wiped out by Aquila, there would be feathers, like snow, littering the grass, blowing around. But there were so few you could count them. The entire flock had been killed and skinned, quickly and professionally, then left for the elements to clean up.

Thom felt naked sitting out in the open, an easy target for some smug killer who could, with a modern weapon, stop the electrical current that kept his body running—giving the carrion birds yet another meal.

As he filmed the grisly scene, his biologist's mind wondered a little hysterically if there would be a population surge of carrion birds because of the sudden wealth of food. Thom descended and skimmed the ground, his mind careening wildly.

He aimed for a tight group of stunted trees, wanting to get

under cover. He hovered the sled, yanked off his nullifiers, and listened for a long time. The only sounds were the soft-throated cooing of the carrion birds and the endless whispering of the wind. He slid cautiously off the sled.

This was a good vantage point. He couldn't be seen from above or from the site of the attack.

As he walked toward a natural opening in the trees, something tripped him. Thom caught himself, spinning to make sure nothing could take advantage of his accidental misstep. He glanced at the thing that had snagged his foot, seeing something half-submerged in the brackish water, covered by a blanket of tall grass. He leaned toward it, and something primal in his mind screamed at him to run, get the hell out of there.

He pulled the grass away and stepped back in shock as he looked into Peter Woedrango's face. The rich, dark skin was gray now, the black, laughing eyes, sightless. After a moment of stunned anguish, Thom ripped more grass away, wanting to know what or who had killed his friend, his partner.

It had been a modern weapon, he was sure, even though whoever had done it had tried to make it look like an animal attack. The surprise on Peter's face was typical of the short blast that shut a body off without bursting a capillary. The weapon could've been Terran, but that didn't matter to him at this moment. What mattered was that Peter was dead, and Black Feather's flock was dead.

He was cold and sick inside, looking at his friend, wanting to gather him up and take him back. But he needed time to think. He'd find the *Demoiselle* and pack Peter into its emergency vacuum suit, then chill the body to stop the decomposition. Then he'd come back tomorrow, maybe with Bruce, to bring Peter and the *Demoiselle* back to camp. And he would watch Bruce's face when he saw the body. Peter had been his friend, too, especially after Scott died. What kind of a man could let his best friends be killed just to make money?

Thom stared long and hard at Peter's body, as though remembering how it looked would motivate him to go on. He stared at the gaping wound where Peter's heart and lungs had been, where his soft organs had been torn out and consumed in a way only the great raptors could do. *Like Prometheus*, he thought bitterly, *only yours won't regenerate, old buddy*. But

Thom wasn't fooled. He knew the Aquila had come only after Peter was already dead. There was no spilled blood anywhere, only some that had seeped out of his torn organs and mixed with the marsh water in the cavity left behind.

The Aquila weren't Death here. That title belonged to another species.

CHAPTER 17

◆

The Flyaway

Sailor stood hock-deep in the river's swirling water, feeling, for the first time in his life, lonely. He dipped his head for a drink, then tilted it up, feeling the cool water slide down his long throat. Well, he wouldn't be lonely, he thought, once he found Black Feather—or at least, not as much.

What is it about this river, he wondered, *that only the wrong people show up?* The last time he'd been here, Relaxed had been hiding on the far shore, watching Good Eyes. He was always spying on her, but whenever Sailor told her, she merely waved at Relaxed, then ignored him. To Sailor, Relaxed seemed like a predator, always watching, waiting for you to be careless.

Two days ago, when Relaxed had been at the river, Sailor had said nothing. If he'd told Good Eyes, she might have wanted to speak to the human male. Sailor was already feeling the pull to leave, and the time he'd had left to spend with Good Eyes was short enough. He'd had no desire to share it.

So, he'd suggested they go eat black nuts. Thinking of what had happened then made his feathers stand up, so he shook himself, wagging his tail so that everything fell into place. He was acting like a baby, letting these memories clutter up his mind and make him lonely and depressed. He was on his flyaway now, learning things that would make a difference to him, to his people. But where *was* Black Feather?

Lifting out of the water, he flew to the opposite shore, near Relaxed's hiding place, landing near some Travellers who were squatting on the dark soil of the bank, preening. Maybe they had seen Black Feather. Sailor edged nearer, hoping to speak to them.

Finally, two of the avians, elders by the look of them, stopped grooming and addressed the young Grus. They knew who he was, they said. They told him, in their truncated language of bill-clapping, that they had wanted to speak to him the other day, but were afraid to while those not-of-the-World were nearby.

Respectfully, Sailor explained that they did not have to fear his companion, since she had earned her place on the World before he had fledged.

They knew that, they said. They'd been referring to the two who had been on this shore.

Two? Sailor turned one eye on the Travellers, using the other to examine the ground and the impressions of Relaxed's footwear. Each of the humans wore a different pattern, and they were easy to recognize. Finally, Sailor saw a fragment of pattern from the dark-skinned human called the Collector, because of his interest in salvaging feathers.

Why had he been here? Sailor wondered.

The two had hidden here, the Travellers told him, talking to each other in their strange spoken language. They must have been angry, since their voices rang with feeling. Even when they parted there was much unresolved between them. You could see it in their bodies and their faces.

Sailor felt uneasy, but he needed to find Black Feather. Behind him, in the reeds, he was surprised by a flash of blue. The Blue Cloud people were busily building, weaving their fragile, baglike nests to sturdy reed stalks. But their people had agreed long ago not to nest where the White Wind people lived. Too many things seemed suddenly out of place.

The Travellers clattered, pulling Sailor's attention back. They'd wanted to speak to him the other day, they told him. They had wanted to give their condolences to him and his father.

Sailor blinked in confusion but did not reply.

Black Feather had been a good companion, they said, clacking and snapping. A companion and a protector, who had watched over the nests of the Travellers as though they had been his own. Never again, they said, would they travel the pathways of his migration because of the evil that had been done to him and his people by those not-of-the-World. Then the stout-bodied avians returned to their preening.

Sailor felt cold all over, as though his feathers had been saturated. He'd been foolish to think he could interpret the Travellers' chattering talk. He'd thought they'd said *condolences*—but they must've said *congratulations*.

Hesitantly Sailor asked if the Travellers knew where Black Feather was, and why he had not yet returned to the river?

Several of the squat-legged birds glanced at one another, then exploded into flight. The elder pair waddled into the river. With his longer legs, Sailor easily kept up with them. Frightened now, he implored them for information.

Finally, the old male stared at the youngster with one eye. He would never have said anything, he told Sailor, if he hadn't thought that the massacre was common knowledge. It wasn't the Travellers' duty to bring messages of sorrow and pain.

What had happened? Sailor asked. He didn't understand.

As Sailor stood rooted in shock, the elder explained how his group had been accompanying Black Feather's people on their migration, and were resting with them at a staging ground not a day's flight from here. Then the aliens had appeared, hovering over the flock in their large, silver ship. The Travellers had been terrified.

But Black Feather had not been afraid. His father knew them, he'd said. They meant no harm. And then he'd fallen dead, still reassuring his people. They had all fallen, right where they stood. Some of the Travellers had been caught by the invisible force and they, too, fell dead. Anyone who could, had fled, but not one of the White Wind people had been spared.

That had been days ago, and his people could still barely speak of it among themselves. The Blue Cloud people had told them that the aliens came out of the ship on big, flat flying things that hovered over the dead. The aliens then walked through the marsh, cutting the skins off the White Wind people. They had even made a fire while they worked, and threw one of the dead females on it, then ate her after she was burned up.

Later, the Blue Cloud people said, the aliens were so insane, they even killed each other. The World had changed forever, the Traveller observed mournfully.

Sailor asked whether the Old Male thought his father's people were in danger.

Weren't all the people of the World in danger, wondered the weary elder, since those not-of-the-World had dropped out of the sky? They killed indiscriminately, taking only the skins of the dead and leaving them where they lay to pollute the marshes.

The World itself had to fear beings that killed without touching and had no respect for their victims' remains. Even Death feared them, so capricious was their power.

Then the pair of Travellers swam away, leaving Sailor alone with his grief. The cooling touch of the river flowing around his legs was the only thing anchoring the young avian to reality. Overwhelmed with sorrow and confusion, he ducked his head underwater, as though that would take the heat from his blood. Then he turned and strode toward the nests of the Blue Cloud people.

They panicked, flying wildly around him. They had the right to build here, they insisted. This territory was open now.

Sailor assured them he knew that. This calmed the small creatures, and they halted their manic flight.

But *how* had they known the territory was open? Sailor asked.

Oh, everyone knew now, they said, but they had not taken just anyone's word, oh, no. They had sent scouts to be sure, oh, yes. Wasn't it terrible? So sad, and such a waste. The whole flock, dead. And *skinned*. Sickening. Had he seen it?

No, Sailor told them, numbly, he had not seen it.

Terrible, terrible. Don't go, they warned. They'll get you like they got the others. Did Sailor know why the aliens were so crazy, why they would kill people just for their skins? He had lived with them, wasn't he afraid they would kill him?

Sailor assured the Blue Cloud people that the humans he knew were not like that.

The Blue Cloud people said nothing for a moment, and that in itself was startling. Then they politely informed Sailor that perhaps he did not know the aliens as well as he thought. Their scouts had been at the massacre sight. They had seen the dark alien there, the same alien that had been here arguing with the pale one, the same pale one that had been inside the silver ship that had flown near their old nesting site.

A feeling of numb detachment flowed through Sailor.

Yes, said the Blue Cloud people, more to one another than to the young avian. The two aliens had argued here, then the dark one had gone to the massacre site and looked on the dead with his teeth showing, as if it made him hungry.

Sailor tried to imagine the Collector, a human he'd always considered funny and kind, grinning as he viewed the corpses of his kin. How many feathers could be collected from a flock?

The other human must have followed him, the Blue Cloud people said. That one with yellow hair. Then, when he'd found him, he killed him, just by pointing at him.

Killed him? Relaxed had killed the Collector? Sailor pressed the small avians, knowing they could spread rumors like wild-fire, but knowing also that they were the best informed people on the World.

Oh, yes, they said. And after the light one had pointed the dark one dead, he then opened up the dark human's soft organs to tempt Death, who had tasted the organs, but couldn't finish them. Even Death could not eat those not-of-the-World, and nothing else would either. Finally, the pale alien had covered the body with grass and left it there. So wasteful. So crazy. Why did they do those things?

How could you explain insanity? Sailor responded. How could you understand what was not-of-the-World? Perhaps that was what he was supposed to learn on his flyaway.

Sickened and despondent, the youngster wondered what to do. It was taboo to return home until the flyaway was finished. The Blue Cloud people would take this information to his father, and Sailor would have to go on.

Then he thought of Good Eyes. She had wanted to visit the dark forest again. At the time he wasn't concerned, but now he thought of Relaxed, who could kill his own friend, then prepare his body to be consumed by Death. He remembered how Relaxed looked at Good Eyes. She would not understand the Blue Cloud people's warnings. Sailor knew where he had to go.

* * *

Tesa eased herself into the clear, cold water, its icy touch feeling like an electric shock as it flooded her open pores. The water had collected in a cavernous wound in the earth, created by the torn roots of a massive tree that had toppled over. The bottom of the dead giant towered over her like a hinged lid, its broken roots reaching out like a halo of frozen tentacles. She felt as though the cold water were shrinking her skin.

The day she and Sailor had escaped the Aquila, she'd known she had to come back, to touch trees older than the human race and watch the light change colors. Even at that tense moment, she'd known this would be a good place for a sweat bath.

She had wanted, also, to find the nest she'd been studying. It hadn't been hard. Tesa gazed up at the tree nearest the sweat lodge, her eyes following the outthrust limb that held the nest, suspended hundreds of feet over her tiny hut.

Finally, feeling more invigorated than she had in years, she hoisted herself out of the hole and scrubbed her skin dry with soft-needled red conifer boughs she'd cut earlier. She dressed, enjoying the warmth of her jumpsuit and feathered shirt. Shaking open her quilt, she wrapped up in it.

Pushing wet hair out of her eyes, she looked fondly at the small, beehive-shaped sweat lodge, as the rays of the setting suns bathed it in colored light. It was a good sweat lodge, one that would stand for a long time before returning to the elements, one she could use again and again.

But that comforting thought lasted only a moment. Something about the lodge bothered her. As the suns' rays angled obliquely through the sheltering trees, she realized the entrance to her lodge faced west. That's where it was supposed to face. But if it faced west, it should be bathed in the light of the setting suns. Instead, the suns' light touched the back of the lodge.

Tesa frowned. On Trinity, the suns set in the east because of its retrograde rotation. She knew that. But did that mean she should have built the entrance facing them? Tesa felt disoriented. Only a *heyoka* placed his entrance facing east—facing the *rising* sun. But that was on Earth. This was a different world, with different rules. A backward world. She clutched her blanket tighter as she realized what had happened.

She'd been disappointed when, during her sweat bath ceremony, she could still only recall fragments of dreams. Now, a flash of dream came to her, a sense of déjà vu. In it, the entrance to the sweat lodge had been mistakenly placed toward the rising sun. She had looked into the water and seen the face of a laughing bear . . . or had she seen Laughing Bear, her grandfather? Had she seen the face of a *heyoka*?

As if that were the key, memories flooded her mind, dreams of Aquila and Wakinyan, of lightning and silent thunder. She understood everything now, and that comprehension settled over her like a cold mantle. She *was* a *heyoka*, on a *heyoka* planet.

Thoroughly shaken, Tesa started to walk back to the hollow tree where she'd hidden with Sailor. Her belongings were there, except for the sled, hovering at a discreet distance like a patient dog. Picking up the voder she'd left on the sled, she strapped it to her wrist.

But what task could a *heyoka*, a backward-forward contrary, be fated to perform on Trinity?

A stiff breeze blew up suddenly, and she squinted through the treetops, wondering if it meant rain. She thought she saw a flash of white, but it disappeared behind a massive trunk. When she found it again, moving toward her, her heart felt lighter.

It was Sailor; the white had been his underwings. By the time he backwinged to a landing, Tesa felt a premonition of trouble. A sudden gust scattered the leaves.

"The weather is changing," Sailor signed abruptly. "There could be lightning."

How appropriate, Tesa thought bitterly. "We can stay out of the rain in my lodge," she signed, pointing.

Fat drops splatted onto Tesa's shoulders as the two friends crawled into the tiny shelter. Though the rocks were no longer steaming, the lodge was warm—too warm to stay fully dressed. She dropped her blanket and pulled off her feather shirt, leaving on the dark jumpsuit she typically wore beneath it.

Sailor folded up as small as he could manage, and still almost filled up the lodge. His overlapping cinnamon and white feathers almost made him disappear against the oranges and reds of the lodge walls. It began raining heavily; even through the dense canopy of the trees, tiny rivulets trickled into the shelter. Suddenly Sailor's head jerked up, one eye cast toward the domed ceiling.

Tesa felt cold with fear. "What is it?" she demanded. "Lightning?"

"Not lightning," he signed cryptically. "Something else."
Eerily he snaked his head out the entrance, then whipped it
back inside. "Good Eyes, look!"

Tesa scrambled past him to stick her head out. She could
barely make out the edges of dark, swollen clouds through the
onslaught of rain. The huge outthrust branch overhead was
swaying as it sheltered the sweat lodge from pelting water.
Sailor slid his head out beside hers, pointing.

At first, she could only discern a flash of silver-gray, but
then the sharp edge of something not-of-the-World came into
focus.

What's the Baraboo *doing here?* she wondered, recognizing
the familiar shape. *Are they looking for me?* She glanced at
her voder. It was flashing, strobelike.

Sailor's eyes were wide with fear. Tesa was tempted to call
the ship using her voder, but something held her back. Everything about this felt wrong.

Suddenly a flash ripped across the sky, a bolt of power that
blew the top off a distant tree, as though someone had dropped
a bomb into its center. Ribbons of wood flew in all directions
as the top slowly toppled in the reduced gravity. The explosion
startled Tesa, making her flinch back into the lodge, nearly
landing on the hot rocks. She crept cautiously toward the entrance again. *That* was no lightning.

With the massive treetop blown away, she could see the ship
much better. When the next bolt erupted from its side and
decapitated another giant, Tesa tried to figure out what was
happening.

The shuttles aren't **armed**! she thought blankly. Unless . . .
the *Baraboo* carried mining equipment, the kind Jamestown
Founders might use to excavate large ore deposits. Some of
those machines were only modified military weapons that used
concentrated energy beams. Could Bruce have convinced the
others to eradicate the Aquila? The first step would be to disrupt
their habitat.

All at once Sailor jerked his head back, staring at the close
ceiling. "Run!" he signed, then leaped to his feet in one strong
move, pushing against the top of the lodge with his back. He
flipped the dome over like a turtle shell before the human could
even get to her feet.

With a powerful grip that belied his thin fingers, the avian
latched onto her wrist and hauled her up. Confused and fright-

ened, Tesa scrambled for footing as Sailor began dragging her away. She glanced up, following his gaze.

A tree was falling on them. No, not a tree, a limb—a limb bigger than the biggest tree on Earth. It had been sheared from the parent tree and was falling slowly toward them.

My nest! The Aquila chick! her mind screamed, but Sailor yanked her hard, nearly pulling her down. Regaining her feet, she reached for the sled, still gliding steadily beside her. She leaped upon it as Sailor took the lead as they flew through the dark, rain-soaked forest.

Tesa stole quick glances back, watching the limb fall. Above it, the *Baraboo* hovered, gray and threatening. The Aquila parents careened around the ship, as helpless against the metal monster as the Blue Cloud people had been. Suddenly the male struck the ship with his talons, slamming his wings against its forward viewport. As he pulled away, a blast of energy caught him, vaporizing him in one shocking second.

The violence of it made Tesa want to vomit, but she was still too frightened for herself to do anything but flee.

Another blast reached out for the female, but she had learned her lesson. Veering off erratically, she flew away. The shuttle did not pursue her.

Tesa and Sailor slowed to a stop and watched the giant limb finally crash, smashing the overturned sweat lodge, obliterating it. The chick cradled in the massive nest had to have been killed. Tesa's angry tears were invisible on her rain-soaked face. She turned away.

Tesa glanced at her voder, still strobing. She would order them to stop the attack. *She* was the interrelator. They had no right to damage Trinity's environment or kill its inhabitants, no matter what the Aquila had done.

She was about to tap an order into the voder when a line of dialogue trailed across the bottom of her small screen. The *Baraboo* was communicating with someone.

"Destroy the camera," the message read. "It might have filmed you. I'll get Albaugh to pick it up later."

That was not coming from the ship. Tesa asked the voder to locate the coordinates of the speaker. The voder confirmed the transmission site. It was coming from the *Singing Crane*.

"We're being monitored." This speaker was aboard the ship. Tesa realized, too late, that her probe had alerted the shuttle's crew to her presence. "Who is it?"

"It's not Albaugh," the *Crane* said, "but it could be anyone else. Get out of there."

"Negative," replied the ship. "We'll take out the camera. *And* the witness."

"Negative, yourself!" ordered the *Crane*. "Do you read? Negative on that last."

"You're overruled," said the ship. "No witnesses."

They're going to kill us, Tesa thought with surprising calm. Realizing she was being pinpointed through the voder, Tesa gestured to Sailor as she sped away. A blast of power slammed the ground where the two had been, starting a fire that was quickly snuffed out by the rain. As soon as the bolt struck, she slapped the voder off and shut down the scanning equipment on the sled, praying the ship would think she'd been hit.

The Grus youngster paced her through the woods as she dodged and weaved, heading for their hollow tree. They had to get inside . . . and hide until the ship left.

"Father Sun is up," Tesa signed. Sailor uncoiled his neck.

The human had crept out a few times in the night, peering through the trees, searching for the shuttle's colored lights. She'd never seen any, but she was still too frightened to risk turning on her voder. She had even shut the sled down, for fear the ship's crew might trace her through its power cell.

It had been a long night as the two friends huddled together in the belly of the hollow tree. It had been hours before they had mustered enough courage to even sign to each other, but finally, Tesa had turned on a small lamp, and they began to talk.

Sailor told her of the massacre, and of Peter's death at Thom's hand. This news was more than Tesa could handle, and she cried, hugging her knees, while Sailor, grief-stricken himself, tried futilely to console her.

When she thought of Thom, the pain was sharp, but after what she'd read on her voder she could no longer deny his involvement. His and how many others? Even so, Tesa believed it was the privateers that had masterminded and committed the massacre, though it seemed *someone* had loaned them the *Baraboo* to do it.

She laughed bitterly. There would be no First Contact now. Not on Trinity. There was nothing she could do about it, either.

Sailor wondered if the *Baraboo* had followed him. He

couldn't imagine any other reason for its appearance, until the ship attacked the Aquila. He confessed that part of him had rejoiced when the male had been killed, but then another part of him was repelled. It wasn't right, he decided, for outsiders to kill the creatures of the World, even creatures as despised as Death. The whole thing had him thoroughly confused.

Tesa also wondered why the ship had appeared. Scott had speculated that there might be some connection between the criminals and the Aquila. But what kind of a relationship could it be, if the humans slaughtered the Aquila and their chicks?

Tesa and Sailor had discussed these questions long into the night, but still had no answers. Now, in the pale light of morning, they cautiously left their hiding place.

Searching the sky, Tesa could not see the shuttle and Sailor couldn't hear it, either. Hesitantly, Tesa turned on her sled, leaving the scanners off. She did not dare activate the voder. Besides, who could she call, who could she trust? She refused to believe Meg was involved, but if she risked contacting her she might be putting the older woman in danger.

Sailor helped her remove her things from the hollow tree and secure them on the sled. "Let's go back to the sweat lodge," Tesa signed. "I want to salvage my blanket and feather shirt."

The young Grus looked at her skeptically with one eye.

She didn't tell him she wanted to search for the Aquila chick, though she held little hope that it was still alive.

When they reached the attack site, Tesa ran her hand over the blackened end of the giant limb. They walked the length of it, one on either side, until they found the sweat lodge remains.

The lodge was completely obliterated, with only a few saplings sticking out from under the limb to mark the place. A little farther away, Tesa found a corner of her grandmother's quilt and a piece of her feathered shirt poking out. She pushed against the limb, but they were too far under to dig out without help. She fought back tears, not wanting the loss of these two things to become her breaking point. *They're not lost forever,* she told herself. *I'll get them out someday.* Taking a deep breath, Tesa walked on.

Sailor hesitated when he recognized the remnants of an Aquila nest, but finally followed. Tesa pushed on, wanting to know the worst. For some reason, she felt that someone other than the chick's mother should know of his death and mourn him.

The end of the limb fanned out into many smaller branches, cupping the nest. Tesa could not see the chick. Had a predator carried off his body already?

Scrambling through the flexible branches, she pushed aside the flaming red leaves.

"What are you doing?" Sailor signed.

By now Tesa was searching frantically, and his question triggered the flood of tears she'd been barely holding back. She shook her head, unable to answer, and kept searching. Finally, seeing how upset she was, he began timidly poking through the leaves. Tesa stifled a surge of manic laughter as Sailor dutifully explored even though he didn't know why.

"The baby," she explained, "I've got to find the baby."

His willingness to help visibly fading, Sailor explored with less interest. Suddenly he jumped back so violently, he had to fan his wings to land. Tesa scrambled to the spot, heedless of branches that slapped her knees and shins. His reaction had to mean he'd found the chick, alive!

When she pushed back the cushiony curtain of leaves, the chick lunged at her, nearly grabbing her thumb. Tesa fought for control. Out of the nightmare and bloodshed, *something* had survived! She began pulling off her boot, planning to use her sock to hood the chick.

She glanced at Sailor. He was keeping his distance, standing as still as one of the trees behind him. He must think she'd gone crazy. Well, perhaps she had, but she was *damned* if anything else would die today!

Yanking off her sock, Tesa rolled it up, then pushed back the leaves with the hand holding the sock and grabbed the chick's head with the other. Holding the thrashing avian's head, she pulled the toe of the sock over his beak until the anklet was down around his hunched shoulders. She could feel the vibrations of the Aquila baby's terrified screams.

Wrapping her arms around his plump body, Tesa lifted the chick carefully out of the cushiony leaves that had no doubt saved his life. Unable to see, the avian now offered little resistance. He was big enough to fill her arms. She set the creature carefully on the forest floor.

He had a few bruises, a couple of cuts, but nothing was broken. His legs, a pale yellow, jutted out from his pelvis uselessly, both feet curled around small pieces of wood, but even so, the young talons were sharp. His down was a soft gray-white, but dark feathers were starting to push their way out.

Cautiously Tesa removed the sock hood. The avian's eyes were still brown, as they'd been when the creature hatched, but now flecks of red showed through, like slivers of rubies.

A female, Tesa thought, pleased. The females were the dominant sex among the Aquila and were larger than the males.

Then Sailor asked the question that jarred Tesa out of her private reverie: "Are you going to kill it now?"

Tesa looked at him darkly, trying unsuccessfully to bank her anger. If she loved the Grus, if she considered herself one of them, killing the Aquila was only logical. Every one that lived to adulthood would someday take a Grus' life in order to sustain its own. But she was a *heyoka* now. She would never again do what was expected of her.

"No," she signed, "I'm *not* going to kill her!"

Sailor seemed to deflate a little then, and signed, "Oh, good. I've had my fill of pain and death. What *will* you do?"

Good question. She'd never find the mother, and Tesa was afraid to return to the humans' base. She didn't know who she could trust. The privateers or their *Crane* conspirators might kill her before she could tell what she knew. Her quilt and her shirt pinned under the tree would convince the others she'd been crushed in her sweat lodge when the limb fell. They'd think the sled had been destroyed with her, since she'd promised to keep it nearby. Pretending to be dead, she thought with grim irony, had to be one of the greatest contrary acts of all time.

She looked at the cumbersome, half-grown Aquila chick sitting awkwardly on the ground, staring apprehensively at her two strange captors. Tesa clearly remembered her dream where Sailor had shown her a bundle of feathered cloth and signed, "This is the answer." Inside the bundle had been an angry Wakinyan—a thunderbird.

Are you the answer? she asked the chick in her mind.

"You've got experience with raptors," Dr. Rob had said. "You could tame one, like the old falconers did."

She turned to Sailor, a being she had sworn to love and protect. Then she looked at the Aquila she could not bear to see die. She wondered if, when the chick opened her beak, she was crying for her parents.

I still can't hear you, little thunderbird, Tesa thought, *. . . but I could if you used sign language*.

A great calm suddenly settled over her. "We're leaving here," she told Sailor matter-of-factly.

"Will you put that garment back on its head before we leave?" he asked curiously.

"*We're* leaving," she repeated. "Thunder is coming with us."

Sailor's feathers stood straight out. "Thunder? Death's child? Are you joking?"

"I'm not. You're on your flyaway. You have to learn things to help yourself and your people. You and I are going to learn to communicate with your old enemy. If we can talk with her, we can negotiate a compromise, just as your grandfather did with the Blue Cloud people. What would your people think, if you could convince Death to stop eating them?"

Sailor said nothing, so Tesa began loading sticks from the nest onto the sled. The chick needed to cling to them to help shape her feet until her soft bones stopped growing. The Travellers would tell them a route west, where a good hiding place lay—far from here, where they could raise Thunder.

After hooding the chick again, Tesa carefully lifted the avian onto the sled, placing her in the miniature nest. The chick was shivering, so she took a feather cloak from the back of the sled and covered her with it. Her dream image came back strongly. This was right.

Finally, when she was ready to go, Sailor signed, "What will you do if we fail?"

"You mean, if we can't teach her sign language?"

"Yes. If my people are right, and Death is nothing but a conscienceless predator, what will you do?"

Tesa looked at him steadily, so he could test her if he wanted. "If we fail, I promise you, I'll kill her myself."

"Fair enough," the Grus youngster agreed.

Tesa settled herself on the sled, and the strange trio lifted off the ground, flying through the dark cover of forest to find refuge somewhere on the World.

CHAPTER 18

◆

Thunder

It'll be just like a pair project, Tesa told herself, thinking of the team-work exercise developed at StarBridge. *Except there'll be three of us.*

They were four days into their journey, and a thousand miles from home when they found the old volcano the Travellers had told them about. It had blown its top ten thousand years before and collapsed, creating a bowl-shaped caldera. They crested its rim, stopping to catch their breath in the high altitude, and looked into the enclosed ecosystem that was about to become their home.

The walls of the volcano towered thousands of feet over the shores of its crystalline blue lake. The Travellers assured them they had stocked it well. Stands of stately autumn-colored conifers formed dense patches of aged forest that climbed the inner walls. Old woodland was bordered by shrubby areas that opened into lush meadowland.

Near the lake, the walls were pockmarked with old Tree Ripper dwellings, caves they'd carved in the hardened lava, but hardly any of the great beasts wintered here now. If a cave had no smell, they were told, it was safe to use.

207

In the center of the beautiful lake was a small, conical island whose plume of steam attested to the volcano's lingering life. There'd be plenty of hot water there.

When Tesa had first seen the volcano in the distance, it had looked to her like a giant tipi with an open smoke hole. Now, with a surge of happiness, she descended into the caldera.

Taller stood outside the door of the humans' shelter and noted that slab of wood bearing Puff's human name was beginning to split. The pain of his human friend's loss had just begun to lessen, and now there were new deaths to suffer through.

First-One-There appeared at the door and seemed startled to find him. Her fleshy face was drawn, gray. She did not look well, but then, wasn't his own crown shrunken and pale these days?

"Taller," she signed, "I didn't know you were here."

"I need to speak with you alone," he signed.

The human woman stepped outside. "We are alone. Relaxed is out working with the others."

The two old friends strolled toward the cliff edge. "How is Relaxed?" the Grus leader asked.

"These last two weeks have been hard on him," First-One signed. "He still blames himself, probably because he found both of them. He thinks that if he had been here, he could've stopped Good Eyes from going away. He feels responsible for the Collector's death as well, but I don't know why."

"Relaxed is no more to blame for that than I am for Black Feather's death. If I hadn't introduced him to humans, he might've been more cautious . . . Yet, the pain is raw."

"I think it's . . . Good Eyes' death that is causing him the most trouble. She was so young . . . " First-One's chin trembled.

"We all loved her," Taller signed comfortingly. When the human could not respond, he draped his wing over her momentarily. "That's why I wanted to speak with you. I've heard things lately. Some things I ignored, some I paid attention to. I'd like to tell you what I know, but I must ask you not to share it with the others."

"Why?" First-One asked.

"Because this information may lift hopes needlessly."

"Lift hopes? What do you know? What have you heard?"

"I have heard that Good Eyes is alive," Taller signed. "I have heard she is with Sailor on his flyaway."

First-One's shoulders sagged. "I can't believe that. If she were alive, she would contact us. We had to tell her *parents* that she was dead. We had to tell them we couldn't retrieve her body until we got better equipment. It just about killed them. Good Eyes' friends and her adviser on StarBridge took her death very hard. And what about the pain it caused us? She would never have let us suffer like that if she were alive."

"Perhaps she felt she had no choice."

First-One stared at him. "You know something else."

"I've also *heard* that Relaxed killed the Collector."

"That's crazy! That makes less sense than . . . "

"I agree," Taller signed. "Relaxed came to me himself with that bitter news. His feelings about the Collector and Black Feather seemed too genuine to doubt."

"It's more horrible than that, Taller," First-One added. "It implicates Relaxed in the slaughter of your son's flock. It would mean he was working with the Terran privateers who want to disrupt our alliance with your people."

"You have worked with this man for years. Could Relaxed be responsible for that?" Taller could see that this was a new thought for her. "The Blue Cloud people who gave me this news gave it to Sailor as well. If he told Good Eyes, we can't know what decisions she may have made because of it."

"Do *you* believe Good Eyes is alive?" First-One asked. There was a sudden light of hope in her eyes.

"I believe she's alive," he assured her, "and with Sailor."

First-One—There looked at him with her watery blue eyes. "I dreamed of Puff last night, Taller. He kept telling me everything would be all right, as soon as Good Eyes comes back."

"As long as the skin of Water Dancer is on the World," Taller signed, "his spirit keeps her safe. That's what Weaver believes, and I agree with her. But I don't believe Relaxed killed his friend. That's the way it is with news from the World. Some of it's accurate, and some of it isn't. Please, don't share this information, for your safety and for Good Eyes'. They'll return from their flyaway when they've learned something special. I believe that."

The older woman paused, then added, "Good Eyes' parents are coming to Trinity to retrieve her remains. The company they work for is donating a-grav units powerful enough to levitate the tree. I only found this out today, or I would've asked your permission earlier . . . ''

"Who could deny a parent's right to grieve?" Taller signed graciously. "I only wish that I could welcome these people to the World for a joyous reason."

Meg watched Taller step off the cliff edge, her mind full of turmoil and guilt. *He confided in you*, she castigated herself *you could've done the same*. But what should she have said? *Since we've failed in our diplomatic mission, Taller strangers will be taking our place. I know you weren' asked . . .*

She could see him growing taller, his crown flaming red Taller had been very cooperative with the humans, even friendly. But he believed it was *his* choice as to who and how many humans visited the World. He would not like this, no one bit.

All Meg's work, and Scott's, would be for nothing if the First Contact were denied, but now that decision seemed inevitable. The massacre of Black Feather's flock, and Peter's death—both obviously the work of humans—had insured it Meg ran a hand over the name of her partner burned into the hardwood slab. Perhaps she had not told Taller because she could not let herself believe that Scott's death could be so pointless. With a sigh, she let herself back into the shelter.

It's just like a pair project, Tesa reminded herself, swallowing her frustration, as Sailor dropped a huge, flopping fish at her feet, then stalked out of the cave. *Except that the pair hates each other*. She dispatched the fish quickly with her stone knife. then sliced meaty strips from it.

The small group had been at this for two weeks, with little progress. Thunder shrieked, Sailor sulked, and Tesa worked. Sailor had willingly accompanied her here, but soon after they'd arrived he'd begun having second thoughts. To his people the Aquila were Death, pure and simple. He was, as he constantly reminded Tesa, too *young* to be a parent. He'd finally agreed to stay to "protect" Tesa, so that the monster would not kill her, but he reminded her frequently of her promise to slay the creature when the "experiment" failed.

Tesa endured this, since she was convinced that once Thunder started signing fluently, everything would change. She kept telling herself this as the long days stretched on, and the cold nights grew lonely. Since he was being a father, Sailor insisted, he would behave as one. He slept on one leg in the cold waters of the lake every night, leaving Tesa alone with Thunder.

As for the Aquila, she was anything but cooperative. Her sharp predator's bill was forever open in endless screams. She was either starving or full, there was no middle ground. And in spite of all Tesa's efforts, Thunder seemed capable of learning only the most rudimentary signs. If the voder hadn't shored up Tesa's belief in the Aquila's intelligence, she would've given up long ago.

When Tesa discovered pink and brown streaks in the cave's wall that indicated raw iron ore, she wondered if there were enough to block transmissions. Nervously turning her voder on, she found she could not transmit anything from inside the cave.

If I can't transmit, she knew, *they can't read me*. It was safe to use the voder in the cave.

She wanted Sailor to learn Thunder's language, but he balked. "Spoken language has no value," he informed her matter-of-factly. "Besides, if your device can understand *it*"— he pointed to Thunder—"why should *I* bother?"

"Not it, *her*!" Tesa insisted. "This device makes mistakes. Only *people* can really understand languages. I can't hear her, so I'm depending on you. You've got to try."

He had simply turned away and preened.

That was a week ago, Tesa thought, *and what have I accomplished since then? Maybe my parents are right. If I could hear, I could learn the language, maybe even speak it . . .*

She showed a strip of raw fish to the Aquila chick who was glaring from her makeshift nest at the back of the cave. "This is fish," Tesa signed. "Fish is food. Are you hungry?" *Total language immersion*, she thought with wry amusement. Best way to learn a language was to have to depend completely on it. Too bad her student didn't appreciate that. "Tell me what this is," Tesa bargained, "and you can have it." *If you don't, you royal pain in the ass*, she thought, *you can damn well starve.*

The chick lunged for the fish, but Tesa pulled it out of reach. *I won't get away with this much longer. Soon she'll be chasing me for it. I'll have to bring in a perch for her soon*, she thought absently.

"Thunder, what is this food? Is it fish? You tell me." Tesa glanced at her voder.

"I'm starving!" the chick was screaming. "The hunted are killing me! Mother! Mother, save me!"

Tesa's attempts to get Thunder to use name-signs was another effort in futility. To the Aquila you were either "the people,"—themselves—or "the hunted"—everyone else. *Hell of a philosophy*, Tesa decided.

"*You* are *food*!" the Aquila chick insisted, staring at Tesa. "You and that other! *MY* food! Mine and my mother's! Mine and my father's! The hunted are food! The hunted are . . ."

How can she continue to punctuate everything with exclamation points? Tesa wondered tiredly. *Do these people ever use declarative sentences?* Sailor said the cave walls muffled most of the chick's sounds. The last thing they needed was a curious Aquila coming to investigate Thunder's cries for help.

"Your father is dead," she signed patiently. "I'm sorry about that. I don't know about your mother. I'm your mother now, me, Good Eyes. Sailor is your father. We feed you. We keep you warm. Here's some fish." It was red with its own blood, something the Aquila could not resist.

"I'M STARVING! I'M STARVING! I'M STARVING—" The monotonous litany trailed across the screen.

Now we're making progress, Tesa thought with an almost sadistic pleasure. "Tell me what this is." She waved the fish.

"Fish," signed the chick with a short, begrudging motion.

"What do we do with fish?" Tesa asked.

The chick pulled her short neck deep into her hunched shoulders. "Eat," she signed to the walls.

"Good," Tesa signed with false cheerfulness. She had signed with primates that had showed more finesse than this irritable baby. She held out the chick's reward.

Thunder's head flashed forward, the black-tipped beak burying itself in Tesa's palm. In spite of the pain, Tesa grabbed the chick's head, immobilizing it before Thunder could pull out a chunk of her flesh. The piercing sensation shot up Tesa's arm, but she bit her lip, not wanting to cry out and alert Sailor. She removed the sharp bill tip and stepped back, releasing the chick's head at the same time.

Contemptuously the young Aquila signed, "You. Food. You. Food. You."

Yielding to her anger, Tesa threw the entire fish into the

nest, and it slapped the chick hard. Thunder pounced on it, tearing it apart, swallowing it scales, fins, bones, and all.

Choking back angry tears, the human wrapped her bloody hand. Wanting to distance herself from the chick before she yielded to the temptation to wring the fledgling's neck, Tesa ignored her throbbing palm and picked up the leister she'd made. The three-pronged spear of the Northwest Coast Indians enabled Tesa to fish almost as efficiently as Sailor did. She'd catch something for dinner, poaching it over one of the steam vents with grain she'd stolen from the gleaners' storehouses.

The rabbit-sized mammals, which looked like overgrown voles, were compulsive gatherers. When she raided their burrows, Tesa always left something else so that it seemed more like trading. But even though she could make snares and traps, she couldn't bring herself to regard the gleaners as prey. Suppose they could communicate? Suppose they were intelligent? She tried not to think about the water-dwellers they were consuming. If she stayed on Trinity, she'd have to become a vegetarian just to be safe. What could she say to Dr. Rob if a creature that had once been one of her food staples eventually received CLS status?

Tesa looked back at the cave. You're either the people, or the hunted. *Yeah.* **Just** *like a pair project.*

Thom wasn't sure what else could go wrong on a project that had already hit big-time disaster, but he knew he was watching a problem in the making now. He stood by with Meg as Bruce and Lauren unloaded the shuttle, while Dr. Li kept inventory.

This is a big mistake, Thom thought, but kept it to himself. He and Bruce were locked into a quick-draw situation, waiting for each other to blink. Bruce did not believe Thom's story of how he'd discovered Peter and Tesa. Thom believed Bruce's attitude was just a smoke screen for the meteorologist's own involvement.

Lauren had been grief-stricken after Peter's and Tesa's deaths, almost incoherent. Now she seemed numb, unnaturally calm. Thom worried about post-traumatic stress syndrome, but then, weren't they all suffering from the same pain? Even Dr. Li's cool, detached manner had crumbled in the wake of the double tragedy. Meg had told him that the doctor couldn't sleep at night, and that Bruce was keeping tabs on her use of self-prescribed mood changers.

"This is a big mistake," Meg surreptitiously signed to Thom. Her choice of signs jarred him.

"What do you mean?" he asked.

"All of us living down here, no one manning the *Crane*. It's a mistake, I can feel it." Her jaw was set in an expression of disapproval he knew too well.

"The *Crane* is fully automated, it doesn't . . ."

"I *know* that!" her signs were sharp with annoyance. "I'm worried about us. We've all changed. It started with Scott's death, and it's just kept going wrong since then."

"Have you talked this over with Bruce? Maybe . . ."

The older woman's eyes flashed in anger. "Talk with Bruce? *He* never *asked* me how I felt about this, he just *told* me he was doing it. He even bullied Szu-yi into going along with him. He says you and I aren't safe here. And no more of your lone exploratory trips, in case you haven't heard. Two of us have to be together at all times." Meg let out an exasperated breath.

Is that so? thought Thom.

"And I'll tell you something else," Meg signed. "Taller's angry. Bruce didn't ask *him*, either. Then, when I said something to Bruce about that, he just snorted at me! I apologized to Taller, but that doesn't solve anything."

Thom felt a headache coming on, one he suspected would be around for quite some time. If Bruce had no respect for Taller's feelings, Thom could be sure the meteorologist would have even less for his. But the biologist *had* to have time to go out alone. Peter's program could trace the transmissions emanating from the privateers' ship, but Thom needed harder evidence, he needed to *find* them, *see* their ship.

The last time Thom had followed the privateers' trail, the coordinates of their transmissions had . . . led him to the forest that held Tesa's massive tomb. A ship had been there, transmitting during the storm, but most of the transmission was garbled because of weather interference. Thom didn't know why they'd been there, and the ship had left long before he'd arrived. But he had found the limb, and Tesa's quilt.

Any thought of her brought that moment back so clearly, that instant when he'd realized what that fragment of quilt signified. He could still feel the rough bark of the killer limb

. . . and the scream of rage and sorrow ripping out of his throat. He swallowed. And whenever he thought of her, he sensed a thought—or was it a feeling?—*She can't die, Thom. Not on Trinity.* He knew that was just because he hadn't seen her, the way he'd seen Peter.

Bruce or no, he'd have to go out and take his chances, just as Peter had. He *had* to find them. Part of him said, find them and kill them, and lately he hadn't argued with that side. Now, with Bruce's restrictions, it would be harder to get away from the shelter. Thom was confident he could slip out without being caught, but he'd only be able to do it once, so it would have to be the right time. If he tried to return, Bruce would make sure Thom would never get to tell anyone what he'd learned.

It had been a long time since Sailor had watched Good Eyes try to compare what they were going through to some exercise taught in the place called "StarBridge." As the human stood beside him in the frigid water of the caldera's blue lake, he wondered whatever had made him agree, even for a moment, that teaching Death's child to sign might be a good thing to do.

An entire moon phase had passed while they had worked like hive insects to keep her fed, to keep her well, and for what?

Only seven days ago, she had caught some food herself, some venomous, slow-moving reptile, but eating it had made her ill. Good Eyes had tested plants and molds from the meadows with a device—a cell analyzer—on her red knife, then steeped a collection of them in hot water. She'd forced massive amounts of this water into the weakening chick. Later, she had pounded the organs of fish with crystallized nectar she'd dug up out of a ground hive and forced that into the beast. Sailor still wondered how she'd managed to extract the nectar without getting stung. Even more amazing, Good Eyes then built a fire—what creature on the World would *want* a fire?—and heated rocks in it, then brought them into the cave to warm the air.

Poor Good Eyes had worked so hard that when she'd collapsed that night, dozing fitfully, Sailor had had to come in and cover her with a cloak.

He'd taken a long look at Death's child, then. At that moment, while the raggedy chick slept beneath his mother's cloak, Sailor had felt a touch of concern for the creature he'd resented so much these last weeks.

Suppose she dies tonight? Sailor had thought, watching her breath. The place on his head where his crown would one day be shrank with alarm. *It'll break Good Eyes' heart,* he'd thought. He had felt something then for the life he was nurturing that he did not want to examine too closely. He was too young to be a parent. It was ridiculous to think he could develop a parent's heart, a parent's jealous love of a child.

Good Eyes had cared for the chick for three days and nights, and when the creature recovered, was she grateful?

Not likely. She'd just sat there, sullen and reproachful, befouling the walls of the cave, now plastered white with her disgusting body wastes that she ejected like venom in a stream. It was more than any decent person should have to tolerate.

And her "language"? It was such simple gibberish he'd come to understand more of it than he wanted to admit. Unlike his own language, with its graceful compound phrases and elegant poetry of handshapes and motion, the raucous sounds that erupted from Death's throat did little but threaten and demand. And Sailor was very tired of being referred to as a walking meal.

Now, the evil fledgling stood at the shoreline, her fully feathered wings stretched out, her legs strong enough to bear her weight. She marched up and down, demanding food.

It was said that as the child of Death attained its full size, its parents grew to fear it, dropping food into the nest from great heights. The appetite of the child, as it turned food into feathers, was so voracious that it would devour its own parents if they were foolish enough to come too close.

Even Good Eyes believed that now, and spent most of her time in the water with him, where Death's child would not follow. He noticed Good Eyes suddenly shifting her weight in the water.

"What is it?" Sailor asked, as she moved her fish-catcher from one hand to the other.

"The warmers in my pants," she signed one-handed. "I think the left side's failing. That leg's getting pretty cold."

"Can't you stop the blood in that leg?"

"What?" She looked confused. That was the first thing that

happened to people when they became too cold—they would act disoriented. "When we're in the water," he explained, "we stop the blood from flowing into our legs, so we don't get cold."

She smiled feebly. "Pretty efficient. I can't do that." She spied something in the water and drove the fish-catcher down, once, twice, but the big swimmer got away. Sailor impaled it, hauling it up into the air where it couldn't breathe. Good Eyes should've caught this one, it was big and slow.

The human took the crimson swimmer from him and started wading toward the demanding chick.

"Be cautious, Good Eyes," Sailor warned.

The chick was ravenous, but Good Eyes seemed unconcerned. The human stood knee deep in the lake and held the fish up by its gills, tantalizing the maniacal chick. Sailor wondered about her judgment sometimes.

Death's child flared her wings, thrust her head forward, and waded into the cold water. The human waited just out of reach.

The beast rushed Good Eyes, but the human easily held her off with the blunt end of her fish-catcher. Death's child grabbed the shaft in her powerful bill and snapped the end off, then rushed the human again. Good Eyes spun the fish-catcher and threatened the fledgling with the business end. Faced with its three sharp points, Death's child hunkered dismally on the shore.

After an interminable moment, the fledgling signed, "That is fish. It's good to eat and I'm hungry. Please, feed me the fish . . ." The fledgling hesitated, then finished with "my parent."

Sailor could see the disappointment plainly on Good Eyes' face as she tossed the fish to the chick. She still could not get Death's child to use her name-sign. Gingerly the chick took the food, walked up on the shore, and, without so much as a backward glance, began ripping it to pieces. Sailor hated watching that and started to move back into deep water, but Good Eyes didn't join him. Instead, the tired human waded out of the lake and sat heavily some distance from the feeding chick.

Only Father Sun colored the day sky now, but He was the warmest, and Good Eyes sat basking in His glow, rubbing her legs. Putting the fish-catcher on her lap, the human started to sign to the chick. Suddenly Death's child knocked her to

the ground, straddling the human's body, grabbing an arm
in her deadly talons until blood poured from the flesh. Sailor
flew toward them, landing roughly on the heavy chick, kicking
her, beating her with his wings. Finally, the fledgling released
the human as Sailor struck her with his wrists and elbows.

Sailor drove the chick back to her fish. Then he saw the
gouge near Good Eyes' throat and his anger overwhelmed
him. He went after Thunder, intending to fight her to the
death.

Suddenly Good Eyes was between them, brandishing her
fish-catcher at the Aquila, keeping Sailor away with her body.
"Stop!" Good Eyes demanded. "Both of you, stop it this
minute!"

Sailor blinked at her, startled. Was she angry at him?

"I'm sick of all this fighting!" Good Eyes' signs were sharp,
hard. She addressed Sailor. "Were you trying to save me, or
just looking for an excuse to kill Thunder?" She didn't give
him a chance to answer, but spun around to Death's child.
"Don't you understand, if you kill or injure us you'll never
leave here? You'll starve to death?"

The chick hunched her shoulders and looked sullen.

"And you can just stop hurting me!" Good Eyes repri-
manded the chick. "All I've ever done is feed you, nurse you,
save your life, and all you ever do is bite me! What's wrong
with you?"

"Liar!" hissed the chick, and surprised them both by signing
it as well. "Liar. You stole me from my nest to hide me in
the ground. You'll eat me as soon as I'm big enough to feed
you. What's wrong with *you*, who would steal a child and
torture her, instead of killing her quickly without shaming her
memory?"

Good Eyes looked strangely at the chick. "We're not going
to eat you, Thunder. We saved you from starvation, or from
being killed. Your father had been killed. Your mother fled
for her life. You would've died if we hadn't saved you."

Thunder turned a baleful near-red eye on the human. "*You*
killed my father," she signed. "You destroy the trees and bring
fire to the nests to burn the children so you can eat us. My
mother told me. She wouldn't do as you ordered, so you came
in that giant flyer and destroyed our trees."

"That was not me, or my people who did that," Good Eyes
explained. "I mean . . . it was my people, that is . . . they were

humans, but . . ." Good Eyes ran a hand through her tangled hair. "Thunder, those humans shouldn't be here, on the World. They're my enemy, *because* they're your enemy. They're Sailor's enemy, too. And we'll rid the World of them . . . I don't know how, but . . . we will. I'm so sorry about what they've done, so terribly sorry. If I could speak to your mother, I'd tell her, too . . ."

The chick seemed to shrink. "My mother . . . never to see her . . . How will I learn to hunt? How will I know the thermals, or follow the suns? How will I know what's the hunted, and what's not? How will I live without my mother's knowledge?"

Those simple signs struck Sailor hard, for they were questions he might have had to ask, if Taller and Weaver had been killed, and Good Eyes had had to raise him alone. Sailor felt sorry for Death's child, who might never see her parents again.

Good Eyes eased onto her knees, coming alarmingly close to the fledgling. "I wouldn't keep you from your mother, Thunder. When you can fly, we'll return to your forest, we'll find her, and she'll teach you what you need to know."

Sailor's head lifted in surprise. Did she mean that?

"All I ask," Good Eyes signed, "is that you help us communicate with your people. That's all I've ever wanted. Your mother wants it, too. She's tried to talk to me, but I couldn't understand her. Now, you can translate for us. If you will."

The chick seemed to consider this for a moment, then turned her back and consumed the fish.

"Thunder will take to the air any day now," Sailor signed as the fledgling stood on the lake's shore, beating her wings.

"I know," Tesa replied wearily. "I know." She sat at the mouth of the cave, observing the young avian's powerful wings, wings that would carry the raptor away either today or tomorrow.

"What have you decided?" Sailor asked.

Mostly, I've decided that this was no summer tipi camp. It's been the toughest six weeks I can ever remember, Tesa thought. Her clothes were in tatters. Being in the water now meant bone-chilling cold. She'd lost so much weight on their wild, low-fat diet that she was never warm enough. Thunder took so much effort to feed, there just wasn't time to take better care of herself, or the things she needed.

It was getting colder every day and there'd been a light dusting of snow this morning. They'd have to leave soon, one way or another, or risk getting caught by blizzards.

"Will you kill her?" Sailor asked bluntly.

Tesa winced. Once Thunder took to the air, they could very well be her first hot-blooded meal. *Would she do that, now?* Tesa wondered. *And why not?*

That was no obedient falconer's bird flexing her muscles, but a massive killing machine with a mind of her own. *But what kind of mind?* Tesa asked herself. Sure, the avian could communicate. She could even sign when she wanted to. More and more, Tesa found herself wondering if things would've gone differently if only she could hear, if she could communicate with Thunder in her own speech. She'd begun to doubt herself, and all the decisions she'd made that had brought her to this moment.

Of course, since Tesa had promised to return Thunder to her avian mother, the chick had seemed less angry. Yet there was still no love among them, just a sullen tolerance that had done little to give Tesa hope for their unorthodox "pair project."

Should she kill Thunder? How could she, believing as she did that Thunder was a fully intelligent creature? How could she not, knowing Thunder might kill and devour Sailor and her? She felt hot tears building up in her eyes and blinked furiously to drive them back. She couldn't risk Sailor. She cared little about herself, but felt a bitter amusement at the sentiment that could only be a true mother's.

"Well, will you?" Sailor prodded her again.

At times the young Grus seemed to fear the Aquila, yet at others, he almost seemed to care for her. Tesa squeezed her eyes shut. This was getting her nowhere.

"Yes," she signed abruptly, and walked to the cave.

Their little home was no example of good housekeeping. Remnants of past meals were scattered on the floor, which Tesa found disturbing. Of all things she'd let slide, this was the most dangerous. Food scraps drew predators, and the last thing they needed was to call down more trouble on themselves.

Tesa reached for her Clovis-point spear.

She'd made the point in an early tool-making class back

home, and had taken it to StarBridge as a link to her ancient heritage on that all-too-modern campus. After they'd arrived here, Tesa had taken the tough, rubbery skin of a circle-swimmer and used it to lash the Clovis point to a well-balanced wooden shaft. She'd taken her eagle and Aquila feathers and tied them to the shaft. The spear had a good feel in her hands. This was the kind of work it was designed to do, to kill large animals quickly, efficiently. The Clovis people had been expert hunters.

She swallowed hard. Thunder had seen her handling this and the leister as well. She had no fear of these things, so Tesa would be able to surprise the avian with it. Kill her before she knew what was happening. Mercifully. Quickly. A hot tear coursed down the woman's dirty cheek and she brushed it away.

She held the spear by her side, and the eagle feathers brushed her fingers. It wasn't fair that it should come to this, it wasn't right. Her grandfather had told her she'd been touched by the Great Mystery. She had followed her dreams, her *heyoka* dreams, and for what? To raise a child that hated her, so she could kill her or be killed by her? How contrary could her life become on this crazy, backward-spinning planet?

Another tear betrayed her. She swallowed and watched loose pumice roll in front of the cave's entrance from the steep outside walls. The gleaners were always starting mini-rock slides with their constant burrowing.

More pumice rolled and bounced in front of the cave mouth as Tesa started to leave, straightening her shoulders resolutely. Then a dark shadow filled the entrance, and startled, she stepped back, raising the spear.

The looming bulk of an adult, male Tree Ripper filled the cave's mouth. He entered as confidently as a landlord, his nose working to decipher the strange new odors. His beady green eyes blinked as his great body blocked the light.

Oh, shit, thought Tesa, barely daring to breathe as she pressed herself against the darkest nook of the back wall, her skin erupting in cold sweat. *Maybe he won't see me?* Her grip on the spear shaft tightened until her knuckles were white.

Then the huge predator's nose wrinkled, and his tiny eyes focused on the human. His thick red and white coat glistened with its lush winter's growth as he slowly pulled himself up on his hind limbs. Tesa felt her legs go weak as the predator opened his mouth in what had to be a tremendous roar, then faced her with an incongruous grin.

It was the grin of a laughing bear, full of long, white teeth and saliva. The Ripper moved toward Tesa, his arms out as though he wanted nothing more than a friendly embrace.

CHAPTER 19

◆

Homecoming

Tesa's voice welled up and rushed from her throat in a full-blown scream. She was trapped—pinned against the back of the cave, with only Thunder's perch and her Clovis-point spear between her and the Ripper. She'd only get one chance with her weapon; she didn't dare risk a careless jab. Wounded, he'd be more dangerous. The thought made her giddy. *More* dangerous?

Suddenly something landed on the Ripper's back, knocking him forward. Almost grazing Tesa with his claws, he fell across the log perch. She blinked as the sunlight hit her eyes—and realized Thunder had buried her talons in the predator's thick shoulders. The Ripper shook and spun around in the cave, crashing into Tesa and sending her sprawling, but he could not free himself of the raptor clinging to his back like a crazed bronco rider. Dazedly Tesa saw Sailor also attacking the pain-stricken animal, kicking and jabbing at the huge creature's rear as Thunder worried the front. The Ripper wheeled and swiped at Sailor, but Thunder bit into his short, rounded ear.

The beast reared up, crashing back against a white-coated

wall, smashing the Aquila against it. Tesa cried out, scrambling to her feet. The Ripper spun on the raptor, who now lay dazed and helpless on the cave floor. Then Sailor was between Thunder and the Ripper, his rapid-fire kicks and slapping wings startling the predator so much that he stepped back.

Dazed, Tesa felt for a wild moment that she had done this before, back on Earth, thousands of years ago. Gripping her spear, she lunged between her child and the massive predator and slid the point smoothly between the flat ribs, deep into the beast's chest.

His great, shaggy head lifted in a roar that Tesa could feel along the wood, then he swung his paw, shattering the shaft. But the Clovis point stayed where she'd planted it, and the creature's red blood mingled with the roan patches on his coat. He sagged, then reared back and charged. Tesa gasped, helpless.

But, somehow, Sailor was there. The young avian leaped, driving his long bill deep into the Ripper's right eye, impaling his brain. The monster shuddered, then collapsed so quickly that his body nearly pinned Tesa to the ground.

Tesa's legs suddenly shook, then all her muscles went limp and she fell. Stunned and frightened, she looked for Sailor.

The young Grus was bending solicitously over Thunder.

Tesa crawled over to them on her hands and knees. "Is she okay?" she asked Sailor.

"I don't know," he answered, obviously worried. "Are you?"

"I think so," Tesa signed. "You saved my life . . . Sailor . . . you killed a Tree Ripper."

"Only because you weakened him," he insisted.

"Well, neither of us could've done a damned thing if Thunder hadn't pulled him off me. Do Aquila often attack Rippers?"

"No, never," he told her. "Rippers are not the hunted. In fact, they are the only person on the World that Death fears."

Thunder, dazed and shaken, began cautiously stretching her wings. Then she gazed, first with one eye, then the other, at the huge, dead animal filling the cave. She tottered around the corpse. Finally, she signed haltingly, "We—killed him?"

"Yes," Tesa signed.

The Aquila peered at the ragged eye socket, then at Sailor's bloody bill. "You kept him away from me, though he could've easily maimed you."

"Not so easily," Sailor signed testily.

"He could have just as easily maimed you," Tesa told Thunder. "Why did you attack him?"

The Aquila hunched her head into her shoulders. "When I heard your scream . . . I couldn't let you come to harm. Not after what you said about my mother."

The Aquila stared at Tesa full-faced. "I knew you'd fight for each other, but I was surprised when you kept the Ripper from killing me. You could've taken that time to escape. That's something I'd like to tell my mother."

Then Thunder climbed onto the Ripper's shoulders and threw her head back in what was, no doubt, the high-pitched call of her people. *So,* Tesa thought with a spark of grim satisfaction, *we're no longer merely "the hunted." Well, that's fine.*

Thunder looked at her from her furry perch and signed, "Do you think we can eat him, Good Eyes?"

Thom hovered over the terminal screen, using one of Peter's computer pens to manipulate the data. This was like playing one of those old computer games—only in this game there were no points, and you could actually win. *Or lose,* he thought grimly. He'd already lost, hadn't he? A good researcher in Scott, a good friend in Peter, and . . .

Don't get mad, he reminded himself, *get even.* Peter's program had been damned hard to install—especially since Thom kept hearing his friend's voice saying, "Don't worry, I'll talk you through it." But it was working fine, now.

Thom had been able to pick up numerous communications from the ship since he'd installed the program. He'd traced the privateers to their favorite stopping places; he knew their travel routes. Since the *Crane* crew had come down to Trinity, they had moved in ever-tightening circles toward the camp. *That's fine,* Thom thought, *step into my parlor.*

The privateers liked the old-growth forests, especially the area near where Tesa had been killed. Thom was interested in that place himself, and didn't believe it was only coincidence that had drawn all of them to that one spot.

He'd been watching an Aquila nest there months ago, when his computer had told him that Tesa's Mizari voder had also found Scott's old camera and that she was watching the nest, too—observing it almost daily. That had stopped Thom from dumping the camera's memories into his files to study at his leisure. He couldn't risk having Tesa discover his real mission on Trinity; it would only hamper him and put her in needless danger.

That was what he'd believed *then*. Now, he could only curse himself for that decision. *If* he'd confided in her, he could've told her about the privateers' activity in that area, he could've warned her to stay away from there . . .

Thom sighed, and ran a hand through his hair, unable to force his mind away from those events. When the nest he'd been observing had been destroyed by lightning in a storm, Scott's last good camera had been blasted also. When Thom went to investigate, he'd collected the fragments so they wouldn't foul Trinity. He'd felt bad about the nest, and had wondered what had happened to the chick, but he never did find any connection between the Aquila and the privateers. He was wondering what Tesa might have learned when he'd found her quilt . . .

A data-line flashed on the screen. *Well, look at that,* Thom thought. *They are getting overconfident. That's the fourth time they've settled for the night at those coordinates.* Since the *Crane* crew had moved into the shelter, communications between the privateers and their contact were brief, with frequent disagreements.

They sure like that spot, Thom thought. *Maybe it's time for me to invite myself for dinner.* They had to be doing something important there, the way they kept going back. He had to be sure before he left camp, though. Bruce was watching him like a hawk.

Hearing a soft footfall, he glanced up to see the meteorologist watching him. Without changing his expression, Thom saved his file and blanked his screen.

"Why do you do that every time I show up?" Bruce asked, by way of greeting.

"Do you like people reading your mail over your shoulder?"

Bruce's mouth twisted into his mocking, lopsided smile. "You write a lot of letters, but you never send any of them out."

Thom blushed. "That's none of your damned business."

Bruce shrugged. "Where'd you go today, and why didn't you take Lauren, as you were supposed to?"

"She didn't feel well," Thom said.

"The rules," Bruce said tersely, "are, two go out or no one goes out. I could get the idea you're trying to defy me."

"You could also kiss my ass," Thom said quietly, his face flaming. He rose slowly. He was tired of this whole setup. He and Meg were practically prisoners in their own workplace. "I don't work for you, *Uncle Brucie*. Stay away from me."

"You're playing something funny here," Bruce said with a taunting grin, "and I'm going to find out what it is. You *use* people. You used Lauren, then dumped her." He stepped forward so that he and Thom were standing toe to toe. "Then, somehow, you suckered Peter into doing your dirty work— which got him killed. And I'm going to get you for that . . ."

Thom drew his fist back and unleashed it fast, closing Bruce's mouth with a snap. The weatherman hit the floor, but was up in a second, swinging. Thom was ready and blocked the punch. But Bruce caught him with the next one smartly across the chin, and Thom fell over his computer bench, sending equipment flying.

Reaching down, Bruce grabbed Thom roughly by the shirt, hauling him erect. The blond biologist brought his knee up into Bruce's stomach. The older man exhaled in a whoosh, but he still did not release Thom's shirt. He chopped Bruce hard on the neck where he knew it would hurt.

Bruce lashed out wildly, hitting Thom in the ear with a cupped palm, making the shorter man's ears ring. The meteorologist's next blow caught Thom full in the chest. The biologist slugged back, and they caromed across the computer furniture, fighting wildly, swinging, punching, kicking. They crashed over chairs, fell across a table.

Suddenly hands were on them, pulling them apart. Thom heard shouts. Then Lauren was screaming at them as Dr. Li hung on to Bruce and Meg clung to Thom's arm.

"What are doing?" she shrieked. "Have you gone nuts?"

Embarrassed, Thom looked down. He hated losing his temper.

"You two make me *sick*," Lauren whispered in a low, dangerous voice. "We're the only ones left, and you want to *kill* each other! *I'll* call your families. I'm getting good at it."

She stared at Thom, wild-eyed. " 'Mrs. Albaugh, your son died proving a point today. No, we don't know what point, and we probably wouldn't get it if we did.' " She turned around to Bruce. " 'Mrs. Carpenter, Bruce died protecting someone's honor. No, it wasn't necessary, she really didn't have any . . .' "

The computer tech dissolved into wrenching sobs. Bruce tried to console her with a hug, but she slapped at him wildly. "Get *away* from me, just get *away!*"

"I'm sorry, li'l darlin'," the weatherman murmured softly. "Come on, don't cry." He took her in his arms and they walked away, Bruce speaking softly and Lauren weeping.

"I'll check him over in the morning," Dr. Li mumbled. "You didn't hit him over the head, did you?"

"No," Thom said.

"Like I always say," Szu-yi told Meg. "Two men in one work station is one man too many."

Meg looked as though she couldn't agree more.

Thom looked at the older woman apologetically. "You were right. This was a bad idea." He walked over to his bed and fell into it. Dr. Li could check him in the morning as well.

Tesa packed the last of the pemmican into the bags she'd made from the bladder and stomach of the Tree Ripper. There'd been a wealth of blue winter berries along the shrubs, and she'd spent days drying the Ripper's meat, or pounding it with fat and berries into energy-packed pemmican.

Thunder had taken her first flight the day after they'd killed the Ripper. She began hunting, sharing her catches with Tesa and Sailor, and these contributions freed Tesa to prepare for their return.

At first, Tesa had considered leaving the Ripper where he lay, because she had no way of knowing whether the creature was intelligent. As far as Sailor knew, no one spoke to the solitary predators. But it pained Tesa to see the magnificent being deteriorate wastefully. So, finally, she offered prayers to his spirit, thanking him for his meat and his pelt, and asked to share his courage and strength. She made a fire and offered some liver, kidney, and heart to the Wakan Tanka of Trinity, and fed the rest to Thunder.

Laboriously she skinned the animal and tanned the pelt, leaving the head intact and placing two shiny green stones in the eye sockets. She also left the forepaws, but the pelt was so huge, she halved it across the width and turned the bottom half into leggings and a leather dress. It had taken two weeks of hard work, but while she'd scraped the massive hide, then rubbed it soft with brains and fat, Tesa was also planning.

It's nice to be warm again, she thought as she wrapped the red and white furred robe around her, settling the massive skull on top of her head. She'd smoked the dress to make it glove soft, and the leggings, with the hair left on, were snug and cozy. Only her StarBridge shoes had survived these eight weeks—but they were nearly indestructible.

She studied Thunder, who was perched at the edge of the shore. It would be years before the avian would get the distinctive color of her people, but already, the spines of her feathers were glistening bronze. Thunder was busy picking at the Ripper claw that Tesa had strung on a thong of skin and hung around her neck. The avian had needed a talisman to prove to her people that she had indeed helped kill a Ripper. Until she'd made a significant kill, she'd told them, nothing she said would be taken seriously.

In spite of the uncertainty she faced on their return, Tesa felt good about the future. She had followed her dreams.

Tesa glanced at the packed sled and wondered if it could still get off the ground loaded as it was. Sailor and Thunder were both watching her expectantly. She leaned back against the outside wall of the cave, taking one last look at the beautiful caldera. Suddenly she jumped as something sharp and burning pierced the flesh of her arm. She slapped at herself and shook her arm until something small fell out of the folds of her robe. It was an insect from the ground hive she'd raided weeks ago. Moving slowly in the cold, it must've crawled up the wall and under the skin, stinging her on the upper arm.

Tesa stared at it, incredulous. No human had ever been stung on Trinity. When she'd invaded the hive, the hapless creatures had swarmed her, but were unwilling to deal with such alien chemistry. Had this one been elected to give its life to deliver a final chastisement to the un-Worldly thief? Her arm burned furiously. Tesa shrugged off the robe and grabbed a handful of powdery snow, then packed it around the red welt that marked the sensitive spot. What did this mean? That she belonged to Trinity, or that she'd stayed too long?

Her optimism dimmed.

Sailor and Thunder peered at her. She rubbed off the snow as the pain ebbed and redonned her robe. Time to go.

Tesa hovered on the sled as Sailor took his running start, and Thunder launched herself up. Circling the crystalline lake, they cleared the rim of the caldera, heading east.

Tesa chewed on a piece of jerky and worried about Sailor. What was taking him so long? Looking straight up, she checked on Thunder, who was still perched on a high limb overhead.

They'd stopped on the shore of Black Feather's river, by the edge of the forest. They were tired, and they needed information. It was harder now to talk to the Travellers since none of them would get within capture distance of the Aquila. Tesa and Thunder had to camp while Sailor followed the river, information gathering. Today was taking longer than usual, but Tesa supposed she should expect that. The closer they got to home, the more they needed to know.

Tesa fidgeted, wondering where her gold and white child could be, when suddenly she spotted him weaving his way along the river, looking rushed. Thunder dropped down beside her.

"Things aren't right here, Good Eyes," Sailor signed. "I've followed the water for miles and there were no Travellers and the Blue Cloud people who'd been here are gone. So I went into the forest, but it's deserted, food ripe and uneaten, small nests and burrows abandoned. I found no one who could tell me anything.

"Trees have been destroyed," Sailor continued, "recently."

"By lightning?" Tesa asked.

"Or something else," he answered grimly. He turned to Thunder. "I couldn't find any of the high nests of your people."

"How far does this 'empty' area extend?" Tesa asked.

"I couldn't find the end of it," he signed. "I don't like it here, Good Eyes."

Sailor's edginess was quickly transmitted to Thunder, who began glancing around nervously. "I can circle the area from high," she suggested. "Perhaps I can see where it ends."

"No," Tesa signed, "you'd be too easy to spot." The privateers could have been terrorizing the Aquila, but she'd have thought the other animals would return in a day or two—unless, the privateers were now using this area as a base of operations. She couldn't risk stumbling onto the criminals if they were camped somewhere in this wood, but neither did she feel safe taking to the air.

Tesa pulled out her voder. She'd been afraid to turn it on since they'd left the caldera. Perhaps she could watch for transmissions, without asking for a coordinates check. They hadn't noticed her until she'd done that. It was a risk. She bit her lip, turned the voder on, and began scanning.

When she didn't pick up anything, she couldn't decide whether to be relieved or not. Tesa wanted to go, but knew they should stay. They were too tired to travel anymore tonight.

"The humans who killed your father might be in this area, Thunder," Tesa signed. "We'll have to keep watch for them. This device might hear them communicating with others, so we'll have to take turns watching it through the night. If the pattern changes in any way, wake me immediately. We'll have to leave here quickly, in the dark."

The two youngsters looked at her gravely. None of them wanted to run into that terrible killing machine. Sailor said he'd watch the voder first, so she tied it to his back where he could keep an eye on it. Finding a spot in the river, he pulled up one leg and rested. Thunder selected a high perch.

Tesa decided the rust-colored ground cover made a perfect resting place for someone covered by a red and white Ripper skin. Pulling her robe over her, she determined to get as much sleep as she could until it was her watch.

Thom's earpiece beeped, and he was instantly awake and alert. He couldn't afford grogginess these days, living alone in the wilderness. He peered at his Mizari voder, realizing that someone was transmitting now in the late afternoon. He'd taken to dozing during the day, since he had to move around so much at night. That's when the privateers pulled off information from the robot probes. That's when he could trace them.

Of course, Bruce hadn't stopped looking for him either. The meteorologist had to have been furious when Thom had slipped out at night over a week ago. Since then, the blond biologist was forever being roused by Bruce's attempts to communicate with him, his endless demands that Thom return, confess his complicity in the crimes against Trinity and Earth, blah, blah, blah. He had wondered whether Bruce would come after him, but the weatherman's messages insisted it wouldn't be safe to leave "the women" alone.

Thom could just imagine Meg's and Szu-yi's response to *that*.

The biologist figured that Bruce was hoping his partners, the privateers, would find Thom and kill him. Then Bruce could claim they were just eliminating one more competitor for their wealth. After all, as soon as he'd left camp, someone had transmitted a warning to the criminals. Since then, the privateers had been cautious.

All the more reason why he needed to move quickly now. Thom scanned the data, brow furrowed. Someone had opened a telecommunications line, but wasn't sending any messages, as though they were just waiting for something to come in. Could their contact person be late?

Keeping an eye on his voder, he rolled up his sleeping bag and packed it on his sled. The receiver was by Black Feather's river, an area the privateers preferred. Maybe one of them was reconnoitering. It was damned peculiar.

He checked the coordinates. According to his readout, the receiver was actually located *in* the river. Did that mean another glitch in the program? Well, he wouldn't know unless he checked it out. Thom hopped on his sled and took off.

It was dark by the time Thom traced down the transmitter. The red dwarf star the Grus called the Mother Sun was high in the sky, an incredibly bright star. Of the three moons, only the Child was full, and it didn't throw much light.

Thom piloted the sled manually, keeping it as low to the ground as he could. He stayed in the shadows of the trees, overlooking the river, but he couldn't see anything yet. Suddenly the coordinates on his voder began to change. The receiver was leaving the river; it was being carried onto the shore. It came toward the forest, then stopped. When it stayed in the same place for several minutes, Thom cautiously advanced.

Without warning, something huge dropped on him from above, pinning the hand that held his small repulsor gun with a viselike, scaly grip. He felt knives stabbing into his left shoulder as he was pelted with blows. A high-pitched keening made him realize he was being attacked by an animal, but he was helpless to fight back. Involuntarily his left hand yanked on the manual control, making the sled turn upside down, dumping him and the animal roughly onto the ground. Something stabbed his right hand painfully, and the repulsor went flying.

Thom scuttled along on his back, scrabbling to get free, but the creature just shifted its hold, puncturing him in new places. A shaft of moonlight splashed across his attacker, and in that horrifying moment Thom realized that he was about to be killed by an Aquila. He'd known there had to be some connection between the huge raptors and the privateers, but now he would never know what it was. He bucked wildly, desperately trying to free himself before that hooked bill tore open his throat. He had a sickening memory of Peter's body, his organs ripped out, and in real terror he moaned.

The incongruous sound of a young Grus' high-pitched peep rattled Thom's ears, sending tremors down his spine. The Aquila looked up and, to Thom's dismay, answered the Grus' call. But even more confusing was the appearance of a tall humanoid figure, clad in skins, and the unmistakable threat of a sharp stone-tipped spear it pressed none too lightly against Thom's throat. Beside the figure towered a young Grus, his half-white plumage glistening in the dim moonlight.

The Grus signed something Thom couldn't make out, then the Aquila reluctantly clambered off him. Slowly, respecting the spearpoint resting against his Adam's apple, Thom took in a shuddering breath. It was possible he'd struck his head; he could have a concussion. *I'm probably hallucinating*, he thought.

The humanoid pulled the spear back, gesturing at him to get up. Thom couldn't take his eyes off it. Its legs were covered in red and white fur, the same fur as its full-body cloak. Its head was topped by the furred skull of the skin's former owner, which shadowed the humanoid's face so much he couldn't determine sex, race, or planet of origin. Besides, it was hard to concentrate while the Aquila continued to stare at him hungrily, and the humanoid appeared eager to run him through.

He glanced, confused, at the Grus. What the hell was *he* doing here? There was something familiar about the avian. *"Sailor?"* he signed, amazed. The spear point jabbed him cruelly in the chest. He glared at the humanoid angrily. Had the privateers captured Sailor alive? "Who are you?" he demanded. "Show me who you are!"

"Who am I?" the figure signed. Stepping into the light, it pushed back the massive Ripper head.

Thom's legs gave out and he sagged to his knees with a groan as Tesa's yellow eyes stared at him in the moonlight. Thom covered his face. *I'm dead, too. That has to be it.*

The spear point touched his arm lightly. He looked up into the face he'd thought he'd never see again. How it had changed! She was gaunt, her eyes shadowed. The effect only enhanced her prominent nose. It was the most beautiful face Thom had ever seen. Struggling to his feet, he held out his arms. "Tesa, oh, God, Tesa, you're *alive*! I can't believe it, baby, come here."

The Aquila was between them before he'd realized it had moved; furiously it screamed at him. The human took a hasty step back as Tesa signed something to it. It pulled in its wings and closed its beak, but never took its baleful eyes off Thom. He'd never felt so confused.

"What are you doing here?" Tesa asked bluntly.

Thom glanced at his voder and showed her the data on its screen. "Tracing you, apparently. I *thought* I was hot on the trail of the privateers."

"You'd think they'd make themselves more accessible," she signed sarcastically. "How'd you find us?"

"I'm telling the truth! You turned on your voder at dusk, and my tracer program alerted me. I followed the coordinates, but what I expected to find was a Simiu ship and a nest of privateers—not a woman I've been needlessly mourning." He hardly cared about her skepticism. It was just more proof that this was really her, not some phantom illusion.

"Sounds like you had pretty urgent business with these people," Tesa signed.

That's one way of putting it, Thom thought. Calmly he related the chain of events that had brought him to this place. His assignment from Earth, his successes and failures, and Peter's involvement and death.

But as he related these events, especially as he talked of Peter, Tesa's expression grew even grimmer, her eyes narrowing nearly to slits. Even Sailor seemed to be reacting, his feathers fluffing out until the avian seemed to be puffed up with air.

"You've got some damned nerve bringing Peter up," Tesa signed. "The people of the World have named you his murderer!"

"Wait a minute! Look, I just got the crap beat out of me, and then I had to cope with facing someone . . . important to me . . . who I'd thought was dead. *Now* you're accusing me of *murder*?"

Sailor stepped in, relating the information the Travellers had given him weeks ago in Black Feather's territory.

"Sure, Peter and I were there," Thom admitted. "And we were upset, but not at each other. That's when he gave me this program. It was the last time I saw him alive."

"But the Blue Cloud people saw you kill the Collector," Sailor insisted. "They described your skin and hair and beard."

"Sailor," Thom signed patiently, "do you know how many humans have skin and hair like mine? Did they say whether or not that human was taller than Peter or shorter?"

Sailor pulled his head up, with a look that told Thom that hadn't been part of the conversation.

"Don't try to confuse him," Tesa warned.

"I'm not!" Thom protested. "I'm telling the truth!"

"Besides," Tesa signed, "someone on the *Baraboo* destroyed trees with a powerful weapon. They killed Thunder's father, and nearly killed her. *They* named you as their conspirator." She pulled up her voder and tapped in a sequence. "Deny this."

Thom looked at her voder. He noted the date and time of the recording. It read, "Destroy the camera. I'll get Albaugh to pick it up later." His face grew grim.

"Cute. They wanted to be very sure *I* was the one who'd find your . . . remains. I admit I knew that camera was there. *You* knew about it, too. But, someone else did, also." He regarded her squarely. "The day after I found Peter's body, Bruce told me there was a damaged camera in the forest. He caught me flat-footed, since I'd told him months before that none of those cameras was functional. He practically *insisted* that I go get it. So I agreed to go, to see if anything had happened to the Aquila nest. I found the camera, and . . . your quilt."

"Sailor pulled me out of the lodge before the limb hit," she explained. "But your story's a little elaborate. Peter and Scott were Bruce's close friends."

"They were *my* friends, too," Thom reminded her. "Listen, I can *prove* my story! I've got credentials, for crying out loud!"

Tesa lifted an eyebrow. "Going to show us your badge?"

"It's in my collar," Thom assured her. "It's a program card with my credentials, my assignment responsibilities, and other classified information. You can plug it right into your voder." She still had that disbelieving expression. "It's factory sealed! Read-only! I *couldn't* have manufactured it here." He fumbled with a seam in his collar, acutely aware of the sudden tension in the Aquila's body. Finally, he held out the tiny card.

Sailor took it, eyeing it curiously before handing it to Tesa. "I must say, Good Eyes, I see no lie in his eyes."

Tesa only plugged the card into her voder.

"See." Thom showed her his translator. Both their voders displayed Thom's credentials as his machine "read" hers. "Peter's program tells me what you're doing, but *without* notifying you. This is one of the best programs he . . ." Thom glanced at both voders, then looked again. A terse message trailed along the bottom of the two screens, followed by an answer. Thom's voder highlighted coordinates above the dialogue. The sender was at the scientists' camp. The receiver—the privateers' ship—was dangerously close.

Tesa was staring at her voder, reading the brief conversation passing between the privateers' ship and someone at the camp shelter. She looked at him, her eyes softening.

"Apologize later," he told her. "I've got to find that ship, it's near." He moved to leave and the Aquila followed. He froze. "Come on, Tesa, call off your dog. This is serious."

"You're not going without us," she signed flatly.

He was too outraged to respond.

"If you're killed, then no one will have learned anything," she signed coolly. "We've got to exonerate Earth. We'll stay out of your way, but we're coming."

Thom sighed. How did you argue with someone who'd just come back from the dead? "Okay, you can come, but you've got to do as I say. If you give us away, we could all be killed."

Tesa responded stiffly. "I know how to be quiet!"

"Obviously. I never heard you until you stuck that thing in my face. You've got your sled?"

"It's parked over there." She turned to the Aquila and signed something. The predator's body relaxed, but its cold eyes continued to appraise Thom as if he were a walking sirloin.

"Is that thing trustworthy?" he asked Tesa nervously. "I mean, how well trained is it?"

For the first time, Tesa gave him a real smile. "She's not *trained*, Thom," she signed casually. "She's *intelligent*."

CHAPTER 20

◆

The Privateers

Tesa crouched low in a deep, dry steambed that was bridged by a crosshatched stack of trees blown over years before. They had crept through the dry bed to reach this vantage point where they could peer through the untidy logs at the privateers' vessel. Thom explained that it was really a Simiu ship, even though it had been designed to look just like the *Baraboo*. Now that Tesa was close to it, she could see it was much larger than the *Singing Crane*'s shuttle.

It was barely dawn, but the ship's lights made it seem brighter. They'd been spying for hours, eyeing the well-armed guards who kept watch as the rest of the ship's crew slept.

At first, Tesa and Thom had peppered each other with questions about the past weeks, but as the suns rose, they concentrated on watching the increased activity around the ship. The crew was up and working; Thom had counted eight of them. They departed in shifts, taking large a-grav sleds into the woods, always along the same path. The sleds were nothing like Tesa's sleek flyer, but were heavy-duty machines for moving freight. They were slow, but efficient, with strong shields to protect precious cargo.

The crew returned with their sleds piled high with space-proof containers, which they then loaded onto the ship.

Tesa glanced at Sailor, making himself small, his head up like a periscope on a stalk, as he peered at the ship. She knew the avian was thoroughly confused. His people competed for mates, leadership, and territory, but no one tried to keep more territory than he could defend, or wished to have two mates. And no one wanted to lead too big a flock, because things would only get out of hand.

Tesa had explained that some humans felt driven to have so much territory that even their own planet couldn't contain them. Sailor couldn't imagine such a drive, but he'd believed what Tesa had told him.

Thunder, exhausted, was dozing, as though sleeping *under* trees were the most natural thing in the World.

Tesa turned back to the ship. A tall man strode around the side of the vessel, scanning the treetops with binoculars. He was a tall Caucasian—Tesa's height, at least—with a blond beard and hair. Tesa's eyes widened. "Thom! That's Jim Maltese! I recognize him from that holo Meg has . . . only he didn't have a beard then . . ."

The biologist smiled grimly. "I guess to the Blue Cloud people, Terrans all look alike." Then his face darkened as he regarded the most likely suspect for Peter's murder. "*Very* interesting. We've kept tabs on the whole crew who originally found Trinity, and according to Jamestown Founders, Mr. Maltese is currently aboard an exploratory ship in deep space. He's still on their payroll."

"That means . . ." Tesa's eyes widened.

". . . that the Founders have to be involved. I doubt if we'll be able to prove it, but the negative publicity alone will discredit them"—he grinned boyishly—"if we ever get to tell anyone." He peered at Maltese again. "Bruce used to call him 'the Falcon.' They were best friends once."

Tesa stared at Thom. "You think Bruce . . . ?"

"I've thought it for a long time. A lot of things fit."

That depressed Tesa—but would she feel any better if their betrayer was anyone else? A slim, elegant black woman approached Maltese. Tesa recognized the woman Meg had called Deborah, another Founder employee. When Meg had spoken of her she'd gotten misty-eyed, but Tesa couldn't believe that Meg was any part of this.

"Peter *said* they were stockpiling skins," Thom signed. "They must have cached them near here."

Tesa shifted, trying to recognize anyone else from Jamestown Founders, but the rest of the crew were strangers. Suddenly Maltese waved his arms at the others, and they all turned. He was giving orders by the look of his gestures. Tesa knew they were too far away for either Thom or their voders to be able to hear their conversation.

"Looks like they're getting ready to leave," Thom decided. His eyes gleamed excitedly. "I might be able to take out *two* guards . . . I've *got* to get into that ship, disable it. If they get into metaspace, their next stop will be Sorrow Sector, and we'll never catch them."

Tesa was suddenly distracted as Thunder began swiveling her head, staring at the sky.

"What's the matter with her?" Thom asked, alarmed.

"My people!" the raptor signed, looking into the air. "I can hear them. They're coming!"

Then Tesa could see them, in singles and in pairs, massing like starlings before migration. Worried that the Aquilas' powerful eyesight might reveal their location, Tesa ordered Thunder to hunch down. The avian was upset, but she obeyed. Sailor did not have to be told.

Tesa searched for Thunder's mother, wondering if she could recognize the avian—or if she was even alive. The big raptors settled in the trees surrounding the ship. Two Aquila actually landed on the vessel, and walked its length, wings outspread for balance. All the avians seemed angry, upset.

Thom's voder began picking up the privateers' translation program. Tesa glanced at the ship and saw the crew pulling out small devices, then donning the familiar earcuffs of Mizari voders. They'd have to have speakers to project their translated words in the Aquila tongue, Tesa knew. She was disgusted to think how long it had taken her to design her program when these murderers had had a better one all along.

Thom saw the expression on her face. "You okay?"

"Just . . . angry. They can communicate with adult Aquila, and my program can barely translate Thunder's baby talk!"

"Our intelligence thinks a crew was hired from Sorrow Sector to come here undetected and work up that program. That's *all* they had to do, and with the best technology. But I still can't figure out how they got the Aquila to cooperate . . ."

"Technology!" Tesa signed, disgusted. "They can *hear* the Aquila language. *That's* how they translated it!"

Thom stared at her. "Is that what you think?"

She shrugged, confused and depressed.

"Do you think that if you could hear, we might not be in this situation?" Thom asked. She didn't answer. "Have, uh, you changed your mind about having that surgery?" he guessed.

She shrugged, then reluctantly nodded.

The biologist shook his head, smiling. "Tesa, Tesa . . . they can't hear the Aquila's language, at least not all of it."

She turned to him questioningly.

"A large part of Aquila vocalizations are far out of the range of normal human hearing," he explained patiently. "If you had *perfect* hearing and *perfect* speech, you couldn't hear or talk to the Aquila without a voder. I thought you knew that."

She shook her head, surprised by what he'd told her.

"Have the surgery if you want, but *only* if you want it for *Tesa*—not for any other reason."

Tesa blinked, then nodded, smiling. "Thanks, Thom, thanks for telling me," she signed, simply.

He gave her a quick hug, then, glancing at his voder, gestured for her to read the information displayed there. As the privateers called up their own translating programs to communicate with the Aquila, Peter's program was picking up both sides of the interpreted dialogue from the privateers' voders. This would, in effect, allow Tesa and Thom to "overhear" whatever the two parties had to say to each other. Thom nudged Tesa as Maltese moved toward the Aquila perched on the ship.

His words were relayed clearly to Thom's voder screen. "You're late!" Maltese said to the avians.

"Where's our child?" cried the Aquila female. "You promised us the child if we brought the people. Where is he?"

The blond man gestured and Deborah went into the ship. "You'll see him. What have you decided to do? Will you help?"

"It's against our nature to hunt this way," the female insisted. "We don't kill wastefully or consume carrion. We've killed for you too many times. The people won't help anymore."

The dark woman came out with a closed shipping box.

"Are you sure that's your answer?" the man asked the Aquila.

"This is senseless," the female said. "We've changed our whole way of life because of you, and you're not of the World."

Maltese gestured to Deborah and she lifted the container's lid. Tesa could see the hooded head of a very young Aquila chick. The sight of him threw all the avians into a frenzy.

"Are you *sure* you won't do this one last thing for us?" the privateer asked, approaching the box. Tesa's stomach twisted. Casually Maltese wrapped a big hand around the chick's small neck. The baby's beak gaped as he struggled for air.

The parents went wild and flew at the human, but two other men pulled out weapons and hit the nearest trees with powerful blasting rays. They shattered, and all the Aquila took to the air, circling frantically. Terrified, the two parents landed back on the ship, screaming for their suffering child.

Tesa glared at Maltese, infuriated to see how these criminals had discovered the Aquila's intelligence—only to use it for their own advantage.

"Stop!" begged the Aquila. "Stop! We yield for the child!"

Maltese released the chick's neck and slammed the lid closed. Deborah carried the container back into the ship. "I knew you'd see things my way. We'll meet at the scientists' camp when the sun is there." He pointed to a place in the sky.

Three hours from now, Tesa thought.

"Remember," Maltese said, "all the Grus must be killed, and *all* the humans, as well. If anyone survives, I'll wring that chick's neck right in front of you."

The avians thrust their heads out, screaming their hatred.

Suddenly another female Aquila landed roughly on the slick surface of the ship. "Haven't you taken enough from us already?" the newcomer demanded. "You've killed so many males that the trees hold only empty nests. Our children no longer know what is the hunted, and what isn't. Who needs courage to eat the dead? We were Hunters, but because of you we've become what the White Winds have always called us— now, we're only Death."

This avian favored one leg, placing it down gingerly when she stepped. "You have *never* kept even *one* promise. Why should we think you will keep this one, and return this child?"

"We're leaving after this," the human assured them. "Once the other humans are dead, the World will be yours again."

"There's no truth in you," announced the female. "You'll return again and again, until the White Winds are gone, killing our mates and terrorizing our children to get your way. And when the White Winds are finished, whose skins will you want next?"

Maltese gazed at her coldly. "I'd have thought, Rain, that after losing your chick *and* your mate, you'd have learned to keep silent. If the others listen to you, they'll end up just like you—alone and childless."

Tesa grabbed Thom's sleeve and signed, "That's Thunder's mother! I know it!" She glanced at the Aquila chick, who was quivering with excitement at the sound of this avian's voice.

Rain bobbed her head. "We'll obey. What choice have we? At least *this* task will be a pleasure!" She turned one searing red eye on Maltese. "Since you came to the World, I have *waited* for the day I could kill humans and taste their living flesh." She launched herself into the air and the others followed.

The crew of privateers glanced around nervously as they removed their earcuffs, but Maltese only laughed. They grouped the now-empty a-grav sleds and began moving them through the forest. This time, however, every crew member went.

"They were only posting guards to watch for Aquila!" Thom signed excitedly. "Talk about an uneasy alliance. No wonder they're not worried about little old me. Good thing I avoided Aquila territory this last week, or I'd've been lunch!"

"He'll kill that baby, won't he?" Sailor asked Tesa.

"Not if I can help it," she promised grimly.

"This may be my best shot," Thom signed. "They won't be gone long since there are more of them to move the goods." He looked at Tesa. "You stay here. It'll only take me . . ."

"I'm not leaving that chick behind for those murderers!" Tesa informed him. She rummaged hastily through her packs, pulling out an empty mesh bag. "We can waste time arguing, if you insist." She stripped off her bulky clothing down to the remnants of her StarBridge jumpsuit, now cut down to a camisole.

"You are *not* going!" Thom's face turned beet-red. "You'll freeze, dressed like that!"

Tesa began climbing through the log pile. "You coming?"

Thom's jaw clenched. "You are the most infuriating woman!

Why must you do the exact opposite of everything you're told?''

She grinned at him. "I can't help it. It's my way."

She crept on hands and knees over the tangled mass of logs. Thom crawled behind her. When they reached solid ground, they scurried to the ship. Every airlock was open, inviting.

When Thom stepped inside the vessel he winced. "Now I know why all the doors are open," he signed. "This place reeks."

The interior of the ship smelled like a slaughterhouse. Tesa could smell blood, fat, flesh, and strong chemicals. White feathers were everywhere, broken and dirty.

"This ship is too big to search," Thom signed. "How will you find that chick? I can't hear it." He rummaged quickly through the nearest closets. Sealed boxes were everywhere. He snapped one open, only to find glimmering skins inside.

Tesa was moving quickly, frantically, jerking open doors and floor holds. She yanked open a drawer and waved to Thom. "Well, I found *something* useful." There was a neat row of sound nullifiers and a group of small hand weapons.

"Grab those nullifiers," Thom told her.

"Better yet." Tesa snapped open the battery compartment of the nearest one and turned the tiny, powerful cell upside down. "It'll discharge in an hour. But *they* won't know that."

Thom looked at her appraisingly as he grabbed the weapons and stuffed them into his pack. "You know, you have a really nasty streak." He grinned. "I like that."

"If you're going to disable this ship, you'd better do it," Tesa suggested. "I'll find the chick."

As Thom raced to the control area, Tesa pulled out her Swiss Army knife and unfolded the bioscanner. Activating it, she canceled her own and Thom's life readings. Hurriedly she strode through the vessel, scanning cabinets, closets, and floor holds. Finally, the scanner blinked. Tesa pulled open a cramped closet and found the chick huddled in the closed box, shivering with cold. Seeing a pile of clothing, she grabbed a shirt and wrapped the chick, placing him in the mesh bag she'd slung across her chest. She ran back to the control room.

Thom was removing computer boards neatly and stuffing them in his pack. "What are you doing?" she demanded. "Take one of those blasters and melt this stuff to slag!"

"We want them to be surprised," he explained, opening

another console and unsnapping the boards. "We want them to waste time figuring out what's wrong. It'll give us a head start. Besides, if we cause too much damage, they'll *hear* us."

"Oh," signed Tesa. She'd forgotten about that.

"I'm done," he signed, fastening the pack. "These boards are all Simiu, right down to the designer's number. Let's go." They wasted no time getting back to the streambed.

"Let's take this baby home," Tesa told Sailor and Thunder.

"What?" Thom looked alarmed. "Didn't you read what that female *said*! It's way too dangerous, I can't let you—"

"It'll be okay," she reassured him. "Her daughter, Thunder, is with me, and this chick will give us a big bargaining wedge. It's time for me to do *my* job, Thom. Then Sailor and I will talk to Taller, convince him to evacuate the flock."

"*If* you live!" Thom signed, exasperated. "I don't like it, but"—he smiled slightly—"if you could pull it off . . . Look, without the ship, Maltese only has the sleds, and the weapons they're carrying now . . . and the Aquila. They'll be depending on them to make the difference. You really think you can . . ."

"I don't know," she signed, honestly. "I can only try."

Impulsively Thom hugged her, then gave her a brief, hard kiss on the mouth. "Be careful!" he demanded.

Deep in the forest, beside the giant fallen limb, Tesa knelt, fingering the corner of her grandmother's quilt, grateful for modern fabric preservatives that would keep the fibers from being damaged. Thunder clung to the limb that had once housed her nest and called to the skies.

Sailor was apprehensive. Tesa knew he questioned the wisdom of *deliberately* calling down Death. "Good Eyes," he signed, "we must agree on something, before we suggest this compromise."

She looked at him, surprised. "Yes?"

"Let *me* suggest the compromise *after* we return the chick. If I don't speak for my own people, Death—the Hunters, that is—will have no respect for us." He peered at the bundle huddled against Tesa's chest. "This chick can't be part of the compromise. We'll return him simply because my people value children. That's the only trait their people and mine share. I don't know if that's enough to build a compromise on."

"If that's what you want," Tesa agreed.

A shadow passed, then Rain backwinged onto the log.

I KNEW she had to be near here! Tesa thought, anxiety knotting her stomach. *But will she recognize her daughter?*

The Aquila stared warily at the grown chick as Tesa checked the voder on her wrist.

"I'm Thunder, daughter of Rain and Wind," the youngster said, "and I've brought this from my first kill." She plucked out the thong from under her mantle of feathers, the long Ripper claw dangling from it. The older female just stared, clearly disturbed. Tesa tensed. They had no Plan B.

Rain moved her head. "You—you weren't killed when the nest fell, and Wind died?" She seemed stunned.

Thunder told her mother of how she'd sat under leaves, cold and hungry, waiting to die. She told of being found by an alien and one of the White Winds' children. She told about their journey, and how the two fed her, cured her illness, and taught her their language. Then she spoke of how they'd fought together and killed the people's most-feared enemy . . . how two beings who had not hatched her had risked their own lives for her.

Rain eyed Sailor, Tesa, and the conspicuous Ripper robe warily. She thrust her head at Tesa. "I know you! I spoke to you when you first came, but you wouldn't answer me."

"I'm deaf to your language," Tesa explained as Thunder translated. "The day you attacked us, you talked to me again, but I still couldn't understand. I'm sorry."

"You were brave that day," the Aquila remarked grudgingly. "Your courage saved you *and* the White Winds' child. That's why I spoke to you again. I wanted to know why one human could cherish one child's life while another human saw our children only as vermin. You protected that child like a parent."

"I *am* his parent." Tesa indicated Thunder. "And hers, too."

Rain seemed to ponder this, then turned to Thunder. "To kill a Ripper . . . is unknown! The volcano is far from here— you've flown that distance?"

"It took many days, but yes," Thunder said.

Rain turned to Tesa. "It's hard to accept, but you've raised her well—I only wish that you had kept her there. There's nothing for us here now, since your people have made us scavengers. Take Thunder back to the volcano, where she can live freely ... if you stay here, human, it won't be safe for you.''

Tesa and Sailor exchanged a nervous glance. "There may be something we can do about that problem," Tesa suggested, reaching into the mesh bag.

Taller peered at the midafternoon sky. The weather was good, but he sensed something troubling, like the touch of a spirit that couldn't find its way to the suns. He shuddered, then glanced at Shimmering and Flies-Too-Fast to take his mind off it. The two were playing at catching fish, but were paying much more attention to each other than the swimmers weaving safely around their legs. Perhaps there'd be an egg next year ...

"Taller, look!" Weaver was pointing to the west. A young Grus came winging home and beside him flew ... one of the humans' flying sleds! Taller dropped his wings, threw his head back to call triumphantly. His son was *home*! His son and Good Eyes!

When he turned, Shimmering and Flies-Too-Fast had melted into the reeds, to give the parents privacy with their child.

Sailor backwinged into the clear water while Good Eyes hovered her sled next to the platform. Taller and Weaver both were shocked to see what she wore, but before they could wonder much about it, Taller really *looked* at his son. His eyes widened. Weaver saw it, too. Sailor had grown. He stood taller than his father now.

The male Grus swelled with pride.

The adults enveloped the returning wanderers with joy and rapid-fire greetings. Taller could see plainly how weary they both were. "Come into the nest shelter," he urged. "I can see you have stories to tell."

They'd barely settled comfortably before Good Eyes began signing. "Taller, there's something we must tell you, right now."

The avian was surprised at the anxiety the two displayed. Youngsters returning from a flyaway were usually happy to rest and draw out the storytelling of their experiences.

"You must evacuate the flock, *immediately*!" Good Eyes signed bluntly. "Danger's coming, very soon."

Taller felt his crown shrink. "Is it flood?"

"Worse," Good Eyes signed. "It's human." Quickly she

explained about the evil beings who'd killed so many and wanted to kill still more. The avian's feathers stood straight out as she told him that these humans could speak to Death. She said they had even forced those hated murderers to help them. This was a horrifying concept for Taller, that humans could produce individuals so malignant they could bend even Death to their will. The Grus leader felt a wave of helplessness wash over him.

"What can we do in the face of such a threat," Taller asked, bitterly, "but flee? And how long can we hide on our own World?"

"We'll *fight* them, Taller," Good Eyes signed angrily. "My people won't lie down before these murderers, I promise you!"

"You said Death flocked to them like seed-eaters."

"Father," Sailor moved forward to speak. "There's one chance. Let me tell you what happened on my flyaway." Taller's son began to relate a story unlike *any* Taller had ever heard.

"You compare your talk with . . . *Death* . . . to the compromise your grandfather built with the Blue Cloud people?" Taller asked, amazed, when his son had finished his tale.

"The Hunters are people of the World, just as we are," Sailor insisted. "However, the Blue Cloud people all think alike, while the Hunters are individuals. I don't know if . . ."

"Hunters?" Taller stormed. "Killers, you mean!"

"Father, *we* ate the Blue Cloud people," Sailor reminded him. "Until Grandfather changed that."

Taller stood rigidly straight, and Sailor matched his posture. The two stayed locked in position, each unbending.

"My friend," Weaver signed to Taller, "try to understand. We made a new kind of family to solve a problem, and our son and our partner have tried to make a new compromise to end an old conflict. Whether it works or not, they've done this to *help* us. We can't deny their goodness of heart, their strength of spirit."

Taller gazed at her, seeing the wisdom in her words even though he felt torn—and afraid. He stared at the clothing the human had made from such a formidable creature, a creature his son had helped kill. He could not deny their strength of spirit.

"You named this child of Death, Thunder?" he asked Sailor.

"Yes, Good Eyes named her," the youngster replied stiffly.

Taller fixed his son with a cool stare. "Then your name must now be Lightning—the parent of Thunder." He reached into the bowl of the nest where Sailor's hatching clock lay folded; lifted it, and handed it to his son. "Welcome home, Lightning."

Sailor seemed stunned for a moment, then fluffed his feathers and took the cloak as his avian parents enveloped him under their wings. Taller could see Good Eyes wiping water off her face. "I have no new name for you," he told her. Taller thought he could see disappointment etched on her features.

"It seems," he continued, "that all unknowing, I've already given you the best name. Good Eyes, you see what others can't, you see the truth, even when it's upside down, even when it's backward." He enveloped her under his wing, and Weaver and Sailor—*Lightning!* he reminded himself—joined him in the special greeting. Whatever happened, they were a family again.

Meg poured a cup of coffee, trying to shrug off her depression. It had settled on her like a cloud, since the day Thom abandoned camp. It was hard to accept the things Bruce said about him—but it was harder to deny them, now.

She felt as if her sense of purpose had left with Thom. Or maybe it had been trickling away since Scott's death, and she just hadn't realized it. *You're an old babushka,* she told herself. *You can't take the pressure. When the CLS reps come, put in for your retirement. It's time.* In the back of her mind she heard Scott trying to tell her something, but she ignored it. She'd become good at that lately. It was time to get over his death.

She leaned against the kitchen counter. Bruce and Lauren were huddled at the table, as usual, as Bruce worked at cheering the despondent woman. Meg would be glad when the CLS ship arrived—Szu-yi wanted Lauren to have long-term psychological care, perhaps even drug therapy. The doctor didn't think the tech would ever work in space again . . . or maybe anywhere else.

With a sigh, Meg moved to join Bruce and Lauren at the table—when, without warning, the front door crashed open! Thom crouched before them, brandishing a weapon, as though her thinking about him had somehow conjured him up. Startled, Meg dropped her cup and it bounced wildly, splashing hot coffee on her ankles.

Lauren screamed and leaped away from the table as Bruce feinted toward Thom, but then the meteorologist saw the weapon and froze.

"That's right!" Thom said to him. "Don't move. Stay very still. One twitch is all the excuse I need."

Meg could see that the young biologist was strung wire tight. She caught Szu-yi's eye across the room. The doctor had somehow kept her seat through Thom's entrance, and now sat rigid.

"Lauren!" Thom barked. "I want Bruce tied. Get some cable."

The tech just blinked dazedly.

"I knew you'd be back," Bruce said quietly.

Meg groaned inwardly. This was not time for one of Bruce's moments in machoism. "Thom," she said softly. "Let's talk . . ."

"No time, Meg. Lauren! Oh, forget it. Szu-yi, *you* tie him, or I'll stun him." He glared at Bruce. "Stunning a man *your* age could be dangerous. Your heart might not take it."

"Is that the gun you used on Peter?" Bruce drawled.

The expression on Thom's face turned deadly. Suddenly Lauren lurched in front of Bruce, but the weatherman only pushed her away. "Don't, darlin'. He's capable of . . ."

"Tell her the truth!" Thom roared. "You were too damned smart to kill Peter yourself, but 'Uncle Brucie' fixed it so Peter would never bother his little girl again. After I found Peter, you hoped I was close to cracking, so you sent me out to pick up that camera. You wanted me to find Tesa, too."

Lauren collapsed against Bruce, moaning. Bruce stared over her bowed head at Thom, his brows furrowed.

"What camera?" Dr. Li asked quietly.

Meg couldn't believe Szu-yi was going to worry about inventory *now*! She tried to signal the doctor to drop it.

"Scott's camera," Thom barked. "I don't have time for this! Meg! Szu-yi!"

The doctor hurried to the supply cabinet and rummaged for cable. Meg spoke softly, "Take it easy, Thom. We'll tie him." Meg glanced nervously at Bruce, who was trying to comfort Lauren, mumbling to her, stroking her hair.

"Hurry!" Thom demanded. "Your buddy the Falcon's coming for a visit," he told Bruce. "Deborah, too."

"What?" Meg reacted as though she'd been jolted. "Deborah?"

"Yeah, they're coming with a flock of Aquila to turn us all into raptor food." He glared at Bruce. "*You* included, you traitor. Damn it, Szu-yi!"

The doctor waved the cable and approached Bruce.

Lauren had managed to control her sobs. "Szu-yi, stop," she gasped brokenly. "What did you say?" she asked Thom.

Suddenly the front door opened. Thom dropped, swinging his arm toward it. Lauren lunged at him, pulling Bruce with her.

"NO!" Szu-yi screamed as Meg hurled herself across the distance, tackling Bruce and Lauren both, knocking them down. Thom swung back and fired. The shot went over their heads, hitting a sound barrier, blasting a hole in it. Lauren was struggling with Bruce, screaming to be let go. Meg was trying to untangle herself and grab Lauren. Szu-yi was scrambling for cover. Then, as quickly as it had begun, everything stopped.

A tall figure entered the shelter, clad in a red and white Ripper skin, bearing a Clovis-point spear decorated with feathers. The shaggy animal head shadowed the figure's face.

Meg knew immediately that it was Tesa, and was tremendously grateful to Taller for his earlier warning.

Tesa pushed back the animal head.

Lauren let out a moan and sagged against Bruce. "I'm sorry," she whimpered, "so sorry. I told them, begged them not to kill you. But they'd already killed Peter . . . Peter . . ." She looked at Meg wildly. "What happened to Scott and you was an accident! I swear! The Falcon promised . . . no one would be hurt."

Everyone in the shelter stared, immobile, while Lauren sobbed.

She looked into Bruce's face. "It was our big chance, Uncle Bruce, our big strike. They were going to take it all away from us over a bunch of damned *birds*. The Falcon, and Deb . . . they . . . said if we worked it right, we'd all benefit . . . I just had to put in some equipment, transmit some data, be his contact . . . no big deal . . ."

She touched Bruce's cheek. "I knew if I didn't, there'd be no cities named after you . . . we'd never get another chance like Trinity. We couldn't let them take it away." She looked back at Tesa. "But they said no one would get hurt. The Falcon promised. Just a bunch of damned birds. I'm so sorry, Tesa, really, so, so sorry you died . . . and Peter, God, oh, Peter . . ."

She dissolved into sobs and hiccups and incoherent babbling.

Bruce patted her hair. He glanced dazedly at Tesa, but then turned to Thom. "I didn't know about that camera, Thom. Lauren told me about it. I remembered we'd discussed them, that you'd said they didn't work . . . Lauren suggested I ask you to retrieve the camera, so I could try and catch you in that lie. You were pretty glib about it. I just knew that you"—he paused—"you were responsible for everything that had happened. Lauren . . . agreed with me, encouraged me to believe that." He stared at Thom, as though he couldn't think of anything else to say.

Thom's weapon hung by his side. He gazed at Lauren, shock and disgust mingling on his face.

Szu-yi was still kneeling under her computer table, her eyes nervously darting from Lauren to the apparition that was Tesa.

Meg grappled with the multiple revelations that had been flung out in these last few minutes. The pain she'd felt when Deborah had fought her decision to call the CLS on behalf of the Grus was nothing to the anger and betrayal she felt toward that woman now. But that failed relationship was the least of it.

She glared at Lauren as Bruce helped her to her feet, her heart feeling as though it would explode in fury. Before she realized what she was doing, Meg stalked over to the computer tech and yanked her from the safety of Bruce's arms. "*You* killed Scott!" she growled at the limp woman, shaking her violently. "*You!* You did it. You *killed* him, you killed Dancer, and Black Feather and the one hundred forty-three intelligent beings that made up his flock. And you killed *Peter. Suka!* Why didn't you just *stab* him when he lay sleeping next to you!"

Lauren struggled to cover her ears, then Bruce and Thom pulled the two women apart. Meg sagged as she released Lauren, and nearly fell against Thom. He gave her a rough hug.

"You all right?" he asked.

The old woman took a shuddery breath. "Yeah. Fine." She glanced at Lauren sobbing in Bruce's arms and felt nothing, just an aching tiredness. *Oh, Scott, what a mess!* she thought.

"Can I trust you to handle this?" Thom handed her a weapon.

She managed to focus on it. "Where'd you *get* this?"

He smiled grimly. "It's 'borrowed.' Can you handle it?"

Meg took it and checked its settings, range, and power pak. She hadn't handled anything like this in years, but it felt comfortable in her palm. "Sure, I can handle it."

Thom walked over to Szu-yi, handing her one of the palm-sized devices as she continued to huddle under the table. "This is a weapon!" the doctor protested. She touched the small device as though it were a dead skunk. "This is completely against . . ." She lifted her eyes to see everyone staring at her in exasperation.

"These people are coming to *kill* us," Meg said calmly. "We can't let them destroy everything we've worked for! Scott would never forgive us."

The doctor nodded numbly.

Thom approached Tesa. "Did you make your deal?" Meg looked at them questioningly.

"I don't know," Tesa signed. "Rain said she'd talk to her people, but she couldn't make any promises. I can't predict what they'll do. We have to assume we're on our own. Taller, Weaver, and Sailor are getting the flock to go to the woods to hide. Only the escort will remain."

"You did the best you could," Thom consoled her. "Better than I thought possible . . . you're *here*!"

He handed Tesa a weapon, but she waved it away, lifting her spear. "I'll be all right."

Thom looked at her wearily. "You are the most . . . *contrary* woman!" She just grinned weakly.

He held one out to Bruce, but the weatherman shook his head. "I've . . . got to take care of Lauren," he said.

The biologist nodded curtly. "Just don't let her get you killed," Thom warned.

"*I'll* take care of Lauren," Dr. Li said forcefully, taking charge of the woman, who was now snuffling and mumbling her regrets. The doctor handed Bruce her weapon. "*You* can—what's the term—'cover' us." She peered at Lauren. "Maybe I'll give her something to calm her."

"The Falcon's running this show," Thom said to Bruce. "He's not coming to talk over old times. Be careful."

"Look, Thom," Bruce began, ". . . I'm sorry . . ."

"Yeah," Thom said, "me, too. We'll talk about it later."

Tesa waved to get everyone's attention. She tapped her voder to make sure theirs were on and working before she signed.

"Everyone needs to understand something. Under no circumstances is *anyone* to fire on the Aquila!"

Blank expressions greeted her. Dr. Li paled. "Aquila?"

"They are native citizens of Trinity," Tesa signed, "fully intelligent beings. As the interrelator, I'm telling you, the Aquila are *not* to be fired on."

"Tesa, what are we supposed to do," Thom argued. "Let them pick us off like rabbits?"

She fixed him with a determined stare. "It's *their* World. Defend yourself, but do *not* harm them."

Bruce smiled wanly. "Why is it that people who come back from the dead always want their own way?"

A low humming suddenly rippled through Meg's body. "Oh, *chort*! The sound barrier's breeched! Get your nullifiers . . ."

Everyone began scrambling. Meg only had to turn her ears off, and Thom's nullifiers were slung around his neck. Bruce had a pair in his pocket and struggled to get them on Lauren, but she slapped his hands away wildly. Tesa took them and gestured for him to get a set on. She put the protectors on Lauren, holding the woman so the distraught technician couldn't remove them.

Then the sound rocked Meg's body, shaking her spine.

"That's the warning," Tesa told Thom. "They're coming."

Tesa saw the big sleds, eight of them, flying high. She and Thom were crouched low on their own flyers, hiding in the reeds, the bellies of the machines kissing the marsh water.

"Those freight sleds," Thom signed, "aren't as fast as ours, but the shields are stronger. They can repel an energy beam, but as long as the shield's on, they can't fire out. And they can't lower their force-fields halfway like we can."

I suppose that's the good news, Tesa thought nervously.

Aquila flew clustered around the big sleds in a ragged formation. The young woman stared at them, wondering what they were thinking, what they would do. Rain had just stared at them when they'd made their offer—a compromise, for only a day, and if it worked, if they all benefited, then, maybe—

"The Hunters are individuals," she'd said.

Tesa blinked tiredly. Somewhere in that mob was Thunder. If anything happened to her . . .

The reeds nearest them parted, and both humans jumped. Sailor—*Lightning!* Tesa reminded herself—stepped out.

"What are you doing here?" Tesa demanded. "I thought . . ."

"That I'd stay in the forest with the new parents and children?" He looked injured. "I'm part of the escort flock!"

Tesa didn't know whether to be proud or panicky. "Keep your head down, got that? No heroics." If anything happened to him . . .

"Taller will keep us in the reeds until the right time," Lightning told them. He looked at Tesa. "Be careful, my friend." He turned to Thom. "You, too—friend." The avian slipped back into the reeds before the humans could react.

Thom smiled at Tesa. "I guess that means we can date?"

Tesa grinned weakly, turning her attention to the sky. The privateers were expecting the Aquila to hunt the Grus down, one by one. Tesa gnawed her lip. What would the big predators do?

The sky grew dark with Aquila, until Tesa had to search for the eight sleds lurking among the dark wings.

They came closer, until Tesa could read the numbers on one of the sleds. A privateer fired on a nest shelter and it burst into flames. Suddenly the call rang out across the marsh, and Tesa grabbed Thom's arm, pointing.

Three of the privateers clutched at their ears, grabbing at their controls. The calling went on and on and the affected humans finally fell across their machines, unconscious. Their sleds began flying in circles, as the automatic safety controls engaged.

Without warning, the Aquila converged on the unconscious privateers, knocking futilely against the protective force-fields, finally forcing the sleds into the water. One sled's power system failed before it hit, and the field dissolved. The Aquila pulled the unconscious human off the sled, tearing and ripping his body until he was almost shredded. Finally, they dropped him. He'd been dead long before he hit the water.

Tesa's eyes widened at the avians' rage, and she lost any small hope she'd had that the Aquila might ally with them during the conflict.

The five remaining privateers suddenly realized things were very wrong. Two of them were gesturing at the parked shuttles. Thom had assured her he'd disabled both vehicles for their own protection. If the privateers got control of them, they could take over the *Singing Crane* and manufacture new boards for

their own ship. Bruce, Meg, and Szu-yi were stationed near
the shuttles, to protect them.

Suddenly Thom grabbed Tesa's arm. "Is that Rain?"

The big Aquila female was flying low when Jim Maltese
loomed over her in his sled, bent on punishing the dissident
avian. He took aim on the raptor, but a pair attacked him and
he was forced to put up his shields. Deborah came up beside
him and fired on the pair harrying him, killing the male. He
dropped into the water near Tesa, his body sizzling as it struck.

Maltese signaled to his cohorts, and they sped toward the
landing pad and the shuttles. As the five privateers grouped
above the *Crane* crew, Taller burst from cover, the escort rising
with him.

Tesa hit her controls and surged forward before Thom could
stop her. She'd come back from a flyaway, too. She glanced
back and saw the biologist following her closely, wearing *that*
look on his face.

The privateers hovered near the shuttles, trying to land, but
Bruce and Meg kept up a steady barrage with their stolen
weapons, forcing the invaders to keep their shields up and stay
in the air.

The escort flock began spiraling around the big sleds, taunting them.

Suddenly Lauren broke away from Szu-yi. The distraught
woman raced into the open, waving her arms wildly at Maltese.
The doctor ran after her, but missed her first grab and was
forced to chase the tech down as Maltese slid under the escort,
his weapon ready. He was plainly aiming for Lauren.

"YOU BASTARD!" Tesa screamed at the top of her lungs
and pushed her own sled to its top speed. Suddenly Rain appeared and swooped toward Maltese, but Tesa's view became
obscured by white wings as the escort surrounded the sled and
the Aquila. There was a flash of energy as Maltese fired, then
Rain flew away unharmed.

As Tesa watched helplessly, a glistening white body dropped
away from the escort and plummeted limply to the knoll. Furious, Tesa waved her spear and slipped her sled into the now-
vacant slot in the escort flock's vee.

Disorganized, the Aquila assault began breaking up as the
avians became frustrated at being unable to penetrate the energy
shields of the heavy sleds. But the escort flock only became
more cohesive, spiraling around the sleds, forcing them to fly

closer together, forcing them higher into the sky. The Aquila who crowded inside that ascending spiral struck against the sleds randomly, sometimes attacking the privateers, sometimes attacking Thom and Tesa.

Thom had worked his way inside the spiral and fired on Maltese, but his weapon's ray only bounced off the freight sled's powerful energy field, endangering the avians. He pulled back.

The air grew thinner as they rose. The mesh bags Tesa had hurriedly filled with stones were still restrained on the back of her sled. She knelt, her own field holding her lower body snugly, as she pulled a bag free. She swung, then let it fly. It struck Deborah's shields hard and bounced off harmlessly, but the woman reacted instinctively to having rocks hurled at her face and jerked away.

Tesa battered the privateers with rocks, and her assault rattled some of the sled riders so much they stopped paying attention to their location. One well-timed stone caused two sleds to slam into each other, shorting out their fields. The other three got away from them quickly as the Aquila pounced on the now-defenseless sleds. Several of the raptors were killed as the privateers fired wildly to save themselves. But, finally, the sled riders were overwhelmed by the number of avians bent on their deaths, and were ripped apart, then pulled off their sleds and dropped.

The Grus escort kept pushing the big sleds higher. The deaths of the last two privateers seemed to take the fight out of Deborah and another woman. They ostentatiously placed their weapons on the surface of their sleds, indicating to Thom and Tesa their willingness to surrender. *As though* we *have any control over this!* Tesa thought wildly.

Only Maltese kept his nerve. Taking advantage of the confusion, he tried to push through the escort, brushing against Flies-Too-Fast in his effort to break free, but the yearling recovered quickly and kept his place. The human's attempted escape only enraged the Aquila, who mobbed him, blocking his view. The blond criminal's sled wobbled wildly but he managed to control it, though he could do nothing but hover impotently in place. When the tangle of Aquila bodies cleared, Tesa buzzed him, hitting his field hard with her last stone.

He faced her, his face contorted with rage. She hovered her

own sled, her knuckles white as she clung to her spear. A Ripper was one thing. Could she kill a *man*?

Suddenly Thom soared up behind Maltese, flying as close to the bigger sled as he dared. The sky cleared of avians for a moment, and Thom fired on the renegade. Tesa could see the Falcon's protective field shiver where it was struck. Maltese spun, dropped his shield, fired on Thom, then snapped his field up again. Thom's shield didn't shiver—it blinked off, then rose again in a second.

It must've been hit too many times, Tesa realized, her heart sinking. *These shields aren't as strong. If he's hit again . . .*

The cruel grin on Maltese's face told her the same thing had occurred to him. And he had to know Tesa had no energy weapon.

Thom kept firing at Maltese, forcing him to keep his shield up. But then the Aquila and the escort crowded in again, and the biologist was forced to stop. Maltese dropped his shield and fired at the biologist, but Thom's sled was too fast, and he was under the big sled before the shot went off. Maltese's shield snapped up for the second it took him to locate Thom.

Tesa pulled up her spear and rushed the man, knowing he'd dismissed her when he'd determined that she was weaponless. His shield dropped as he prepared to fire again, then she was on him, but at the last second, Tesa could not thrust her spear into the man's back.

Instead, she hit him hard with the shaft, sending the Falcon sprawling across his sled, grabbing for its hand grips. She smacked him again, and he rolled onto his back, leveling his weapon at point-blank range. Then Rain dropped onto him, spearing his shoulder with her good foot. Maltese fired.

The shot went wild, hitting the power cell of Tesa's sled with sufficient force to short it out. Before Tesa understood what had happened, her sled was gone and she was falling. And falling.

Skydiving, she thought dazedly. *Without a power pak. Without a-gravs. I'm* **falling***!*

Then she screamed, and kept on screaming until she realized that wasn't going to help.

Spread your wings, my friend, something said to her. *Didn't I tell you to watch for lightning?*

Tesa spread her arms and legs, feeling the wind tug at her. It felt like sound. Her body steadied and stopped its sickening tumbling. It hardly seemed like she was even moving now. When had she dropped her spear? When had she learned to fly?

Thom watched Tesa plunge toward Trinity, knowing he could not save her. His small sled wasn't designed for that kind of acrobatics, to catch such a large object in free-fall. One part of him was aware that the Aquila had pounced on Maltese before he'd even fired at Tesa's sled, that he was being torn, literally, limb from limb, but that didn't even affect him.

How many times do I have to lose you? his mind cried out as he sent his sled diving after her, vainly trying to close the distance between them. Tesa would land on the camp's knoll, and even in the lessened gravity she would hit like a meteor. Thom pushed his sled.

Suddenly a dark body rocketed past him. The young Aquila Tesa had raised was falling, her wings folded tight for speed.

Then, beneath Tesa was a mass of white wings. Somehow, the escort had gotten under her, and Thom could see Taller and Sailor jockeying into position to cushion her, to slow her fall. He felt no hope for their brave attempt. Tesa's weight, even in Trinity's gravity, would be too much for the Grus. They would only injure themselves trying to save her.

Thunder flew over Tesa. The raptor stretched her wings, her taloned foot slashed out, grabbing Tesa by the wrist. She backwinged desperately, and Thom could see her calling. Above Thom a mass of Aquila were still harrying the two privateers who were trying to descend and surrender. Then suddenly bronze bodies were dropping past him, converging on Tesa with the same ferocity they had their hated enemies.

Tesa saw Sailor's feathered back come up beneath her, but it only added to her terror. She knew they'd keep struggling to break her fall, in spite of the danger to themselves. Taller was beside Sailor, ready to take over when Sailor tired. But it was all so useless Tesa began to weep.

Then she felt a scaly foot grasp her wrist and yank upward, pulling her arm so hard it felt as though it would separate from her shoulder. She looked up to see Thunder straining to slow her fall. Blood ran from Tesa's wrist where Thunder's talons pierced it. Desperately Tesa wrapped her hand around the Aquila's leg.

Then Rain was beside Thunder, and Tesa almost panicked. The Aquila could kill her so easily and be rid of the hated human's influence on her child. But Rain reached and grasped Tesa's other wrist, without scratching Tesa's skin.

Then another female clasped an ankle. Yet another reached for her other leg, but missed. But that was okay, because Taller was under her now, his strength slowing her still more as the Aquila held her tight, all the avians fighting the pull of the World together.

They were moving her over deeper water, she realized, away from land. When the Aquila finally released her, Taller slid out from under her. Tesa twisted, trying to get her body into a diving position, but she didn't have time. She belly flopped painfully into the water. She was stunned, but conscious enough to kick up, and broke the surface gasping. Thom was there, his expression full of fear and concern. But she was unhurt. She had flown with the Grus and heard the voice of the Thunderbird.

Thom was signing frantically. "Are you okay? You okay?"

Tesa nodded at him, treading water. He leaned over his sled, hauling her onto it. He wrapped his arms around her soaking body, clutching her in a frantic hug. Tesa could feel his jaw moving as he babbled at her.

Finally, she took his face in her hands and kissed him, happily.

Huge wings passed over, startling them. It was Sailor— *Lightning!* she reminded herself—making sure Tesa was all right. "I should've known it would be him," Thom signed resignedly.

Lightning beckoned urgently with his head for them to follow as he sped toward the landing pad. Thom held Tesa tightly as he launched the sled in that direction, but when they arrived at the pad it seemed, at first, that everything was over.

The two surviving privateers were restrained with Szu-yi's cable and locked in one of the shuttles to protect them from the Aquila. Tesa noted Lauren sitting on the ground, alone, staring vacantly into space.

A crowd of Grus stood near the back end of a shuttle, so they headed there. Tesa spotted Taller and Weaver, and Lightning's golden feathers. Thom hovered the sled, and they jumped off, weaving their way through the tall, feathered bodies.

Tesa spied Meg and Bruce, then followed their gaze and saw Szu-yi huddled on the ground. She shuddered as she realized what the doctor was doing. The Grus that had been shot out of the escort flock was lying crumpled on the ground, her elegant head in the doctor's lap. It was Shimmering.

The human worked frantically to save the avian's life; she'd already stopped the blood pouring out of the avian's torn neck. Red mottled the glistening white feathers and Szu-yi's arms and hands, but the doctor's hands continued to move expertly.

Dr. Li was packing a small hole in the avian's breast, but Tesa could tell it was useless. The avian's keel had to be shattered, her lungs burned, her air sacs ruptured.

Szu-yi's mouth was moving steadily. Tesa glanced at her voder through blurring vision. The doctor was saying over and over, "Don't die. Please, don't die."

Suddenly Shimmering's legs paddled weakly. The avian's dulling eyes looked up into the doctor's as Shimmering brushed her feathered fingers against the human's tearstained face.

"You're so kind," the Grus signed feebly, "so very kind." Szu-yi rubbed her blood-streaked voder screen clear to read the avian's dying words. Then Shimmering's hand dropped bonelessly and the nictitating membrane slowly eased up over the golden eye.

Szu-yi stroked the silken feathers. "I should've drugged Lauren," she said to no one. Tesa read the words automatically, translating them for the surrounding Grus. "But—the psychotherapeutics aren't always predictable . . . and she seemed better. Then she ran away from me. She wanted them to kill her. This one flew between them, taking the blast they aimed at Lauren."

Tesa suddenly realized that Flies-Too-Fast stood beside the doctor. The young Grus leaned over to lay a black-feathered hand on Szu-yi's shoulder. "It wasn't your fault," he signed to her. He took her hand and tugged it, indicating she should stand. "Those of us that loved her . . . have to lift her to the suns."

Then the young avian stood up rigidly, threw his head back, and called to the skies. Taller, Weaver, Lightning, all joined him until the entire escort flock was calling, calling, lifting Shimmering's spirit up, pushing her on her way to the suns.

Tesa threw her own head back and whooped till her throat was sore, until she began to feel that the body at her feet was empty of everything that Shimmering had filled it with.

Now it was over. Really over.

Epilogue

Tesa dashed out of the shower, her towel draped carelessly over her dripping hair, and banged her shin on a dresser. She wasn't used to such a cluttered environment anymore. She dried herself hastily, then pulled on a fresh StarBridge jumpsuit. There was so much to *do* today, but she couldn't afford to be late for the first human/Grus intercultural dance and powwow. Especially since the whole thing had been *her* idea.

She glanced over at the Ripper robe and clothing. Tesa's mother had worked on them after she'd arrived, improving Tesa's hasty tanning. They looked great, but she wouldn't wear them today. Tesa lifted her feather shirt and appraised it. It had taken quite a beating, but Weaver had labored days over its repairs and it was beautiful again. Tesa had proudly shown her parents its subtle designs with the UV lamp.

Tesa's parents and grandparents had arrived two weeks ago, only a week after the battle with the privateers. Two days later, the CLS representatives had docked with the *Crane*, and suddenly the tiny space station began to look like an intergalactic port. When Tesa had explained to Taller the political importance of the new visitors, he'd graciously invited *all* parties to camp on the knoll and get to know his people and his World. It was good for leaders to know one another, he'd said. That's how compromises were forged.

Rain, however, had been highly suspicious of this new human invasion, but Tesa had finally convinced her it was only temporary, so grudgingly, she'd finally agreed.

Tesa slid the glistening shirt over her jumpsuit and shrugged into it. Pulling damp hair out of her eyes, she turned and was startled to find her entire Grus family standing behind her. Taller was cautiously watching his step, while Weaver peered about the alien structure nervously. Lightning, however, only glanced at the strange setting casually.

"How do I look?" Tesa asked, modeling her feather shirt.

Taller and Weaver exchanged a look. "Different," Weaver finally decided, looking at her with one eye.

"*Adult*," Taller signed.

Tesa grinned at the compliment.

"We wanted to speak to you alone for a moment," Lightning told Tesa. Tesa smiled wryly. These days getting a private moment was seldom easy. "There were some things"—the Grus youngster made the slinky sign for the Mizari Liaison, the Esteemed Shirazz—"told us that we wanted to ask you about."

Tesa knew what they really wanted. The many-tentacled, serpentlike Mizari had lidless eyes. The Grus had found, to their discomfort, that the Mizari could withstand "the look" without even trying. Whenever they spoke to the Liaison, they felt the need to confirm with Tesa whatever it was the Mizari had said.

"Shirazz tells us," Taller began, "that the two murderers you captured will be punished. We understand that they and their cohort"—he was referring to Lauren, Tesa knew—"will be sent away, ostracized by all decent people, possibly forever?"

"That's most likely what will happen," Tesa assured him. Dr. Li doubted that Lauren would ever be able to function normally again, and after the disastrous ending of the privateers' schemes, Deborah and her surviving crew member had seemed almost relieved to be taken away for a long imprisonment.

"My concern," Taller signed, "is this. How will we know that humans like these will never come to the World again?

How can we be sure that we'll never again be victimized by beings with such power? Shirazz tried to explain to us, but First-One-There had trouble with the translation. I thought you might be able to explain better, since you are one of us.''

Tesa sighed. The Grus had a tendency to glaze over whenever she tried to explain economics, and with humans that was often their strongest motivation.

Choosing her signs carefully, the young woman assured her avian family that they shouldn't have to worry about evil Terrans coming to the World in the future and skinning their children. It was only because the Simiu had been willing to finance these privateers that there had been any profit for them in marketing the illegal skins. Trinity was simply too far off the established space lanes to be economically attractive for such limited—and risky—exploitation. Colonizing the planet was one thing, stealing from it was another.

Tesa could tell that the Grus family still wasn't sure they understood the fine points, but they had complete trust in her word. ''You can trust Shirazz, too,'' Tesa promised. ''Even if she doesn't blink.''

The three avians merely exchanged a questioning glance.

''There's one more thing, Good Eyes,'' Weaver signed. ''Something your mother said to us today.''

''Yes?'' Tesa had been pleased and surprised to discover that her family had diligently studied Grus sign language as they traveled to Trinity. They had wanted to be able to talk directly to the people who had treated their daughter like family, the people who had seen her last. Fortunately, they'd been able to get the good news of Tesa's ''resurrection'' a few days before they'd docked. It had been a thrill for Tesa to have her human family step off the shuttle and greet her avian family in their own language. And Lightning had proudly welcomed them— in Plains Indian Sign Language.

''Your mother seems to feel that you'll be leaving the World,'' Taller signed solemnly. ''She tells us that you want to be hearing, as they are. Is this true, Good Eyes?''

So, this was the *real* reason for the visit.

''If you were hearing, Good Eyes,'' Taller signed, ''it would be difficult for you to live with the people. We would always worry about you, and be afraid there could be another accident, that we could harm you, as we did Puff.''

Weaver and Taller glanced at each other almost shyly. ''We

think,'' Weaver signed tentatively, "that there may be another egg next year. We thought you would raise that child with us.''

"Don't worry about what my mother thinks," Tesa reassured them. "I . . . haven't yet talked to her about this. I'll explain it later. Could you do me a favor now? Could you take the quilt to my grandmother? Some of the seams are split and she wants to repair them before the dance.''

Weaver took the autumn-colored quilt from the human, and the three avians cautiously left the shelter. Tesa grabbed a brush and pulled it through her tangled, damp hair. She'd *never* have time to get everything done now!

She noticed the distinctive spicy-musky scent of the Simiu Ambassador before she felt his dry, leathery touch on her arm. "Ambassador Dhurrrkk'," she signed, "you're positively gleaming!''

The handsome Simiu male's sorrel-colored crest stood straight up at her compliment. "Thank you for noticing, Honored Tesa,'' he signed, his violet eyes twinkling. It was odd for Tesa to watch the alien attempt the elaborate Grus signs, but Dhurrrkk' worked hard to be precise and graceful. His aptitude for languages was well known. "I had to look my best for the celebration! But, first . . .''

I wanted a minute to speak with you alone, Tesa filled in mentally.

". . . I felt I had to speak with you alone. It is about"—his crest drooped—"my people, and their involvement in the events that happened on this world.''

"Oh, please, Ambassador, you must know that no one blames your entire race for the actions of one family . . .''

"We must all share the dishonor," Dhurrrkk' insisted. "Not enough has been done in the past to reconcile this bitter issue between our two peoples. I fear now that it has festered so long that many of my people will never change their thinking.''

"I'm afraid you're right,'' Tesa agreed. "And it's no different among the humans.'' She thought of Bruce. She had to admit that the meteorologist was unfailingly polite to Dhurrrkk', but he always gave Tesa the feeling that he was mentally smirking over the "Terran victory'' whenever he addressed the Ambassador.

"However, my people can make sure nothing like this ever happens again," Dhurrrkk' promised. "Regarding the members of Khrekk's family who were involved—many of them have fled to Sorrow Sector. Those that have remained were not party to this crime, but their dishonor is great. I am working on a plan, now, for reparation to the people of Trinity.''

"I have complete trust that your people will do the honorable thing," Tesa signed, graciously.

Dhurrrkk's crest rose again until he was once again his ebullient self. "Enough of this solemn talk!" he declared. "Honored FriendMahree sent me after you. She has finally reached Honored FriendRob. They are talking now on the holo-vid. You must come speak to him.''

Tesa nodded, reaching for her Clovis-point spear. Thunder had found it in the marsh, and as Tesa detached the feathers from its staff, she remembered Bruce calling it her coup stick, after she'd battered Jim Maltese with it, saving Thom's life.

Dhurrrkk' watched as Tesa carefully tied four feathers in her hair—two Terran eagle, one Aquila—and one of Shimmering's pure white ones. They left the sleeping area together.

In the shelter's common room, Tesa saw Mahree Burroughs standing before the holo transmitter, talking animatedly to the man with whom she'd shared one of the universe's best-known adventures. A cool wind blew through the open windows, sending bits of down gusting through Rob Gable's holo-vid apparition. The short, slender CLS Ambassador-at-Large was wearing her sound nullifiers and Tesa could read the captioning of Rob's words.

"A *month*?" Rob was saying with a broad grin. "That's great! How'd we get so lucky? Hey, is that Tesa behind you?"

Mahree turned, her long, brown braid swinging. "There she is, in the flesh!" Tesa still hadn't gotten used to Mahree's proficiency in Grus sign language. The former Secretary-General to the CLS slung a companionable arm around the taller woman. "You have Tesa to thank for our time together, Rob. Since I dropped everything to get here to solve a problem that doesn't exist anymore, I've found myself with time for a decent vacation." She winked conspiratorially. "You didn't know that StarBridge Academy was a part-time resort, did you, Tesa?"

Rob was shaking his head. "You really know how to get people's attention, Tesa. You've got the entire CLS Council in an uproar."

"I'm sure," Tesa signed. "I'm really sorry the way things worked out. To get so close to achieving Earth's official First Contact . . ."

Rob looked puzzled, then glanced at Mahree. "I haven't told her yet," the older woman admitted. "I wanted to be positive, first."

Tesa turned to the CLS representative. "Sure about *what*?"

"Tesa," Rob explained, "not many people have ever found *two* different intelligent species on one planet before. The CLS Council has voted to discount the effect the privateers had on your relationships with the Grus. It didn't hurt that Thom Albaugh had irrefutable proof that Khrekk's clan was so heavily involved, and that Jamestown Founders was also working to undermine the Contact.

"But the fact is that you found *another* intelligent species! And then to get the Grus and the Aquila, whose enmity was steeped in so much tradition, to cooperate for a common goal—I'd say that was a pretty good day's work!"

"And so do the First Councillors, Tesa," Mahree added. "I've just finished speaking to them. Earth is being given credit for a successful First Contact. Terra will have full membership in the Cooperative League of Systems, and"—Mahree's face lit up in a wide grin—"all its inherent perks and responsibilities."

"We *did* it?" Tesa asked incredulously. "We're in? We got it?" She flung her arms around Mahree. The smaller woman returned the hug enthusiastically.

When they broke the embrace, Rob was looking at them wistfully. "Damn, I always miss the best parties. Well, it's great that you've worked out the hookup so I can watch the dance. I understand your family will be joining in? This is turning into a wonderful cultural exchange! The media's picking up the broadcast to give Terrans back home their first look at their First Contact. Not to mention that the whole Academy's going to be watching. Oh, I almost forgot—Jib sent his love. Hell, I practically had to physically restrain him from sneaking into my office during this call."

"Tell him a long letter's coming," Tesa signed. "I miss him so much! I was thinking, Rob, a good pair project on a wilderness planet might be just the thing to really mature that youngster!"

Rob looked at Tesa suspiciously. "You know, Mahree, when those two were together here, it was a miracle I got anything done! But, Tesa, one more question before I let you go. Did you ever get square with your parents about that surgery?"

Tesa shifted uncomfortably. "Not yet. But I'll talk to them today." At least she'd discussed it with Meg. The older woman wasn't sure she understood, but she respected Tesa's decision and was thrilled when she realized that meant Tesa would be staying on Trinity.

Mahree looked up at Tesa. "I need to discuss a few things with Rob, do you mind, Tesa? I don't want you to feel like I'm giving you the rush."

"Which she is," said Rob with a teasing grin.

"No, I've got to get going." She waved farewell as she left Mahree bathed in the glow of Rob's reflection.

Tesa almost made it to the door when Thom stepped inside. Before she could protest, he insisted, "*Two* minutes! I get two minutes of your precious time!" He pulled her toward a more private area. "I've made all the arrangements."

"What?"

"For our getaway. Now don't argue with me. Of course, I had hoped we could go to your caldera, but Bruce says it's hipdeep in snow. Instead, we'll spend four days in Rain's territory—you know, where you took your sweat bath. Strictly business! The privateers spent a lot of time in that area. We need to assess the environmental impact in case they dumped anything toxic, and I'll still have time to write the report . . . before I leave." He watched her, waiting for her reaction.

"Leave . . ." Tesa signed blankly, feeling her chest tighten. "But I thought . . . You said you might stay . . ."

He looked down, nodding. "I thought . . . hoped I could. I wouldn't mind being *just* a biologist again. This special investigator stuff isn't all it's cracked up to be. But . . . I'm going with Dhurrrkk' and Mahree on the *Twilight Blossom*. They'll take me to Hurrreeah, the Simiu homeworld. There, Dhurrrkk' can introduce me to the right families, so I can continue my investigation. There were a lot of people involved. I owe it to Peter and Scott to pursue this as far as I can."

Tesa frowned worriedly. "You're not going to Sorrow Sector, are you?"

"Not if I can help it," he promised. "Anyway, I've got two more weeks here. How about it? Can Ms. Very Important Diplomat find four days to spend with a poor foot soldier about to go into the trenches?"

"What happens after you come out of the trenches?"

He shrugged. "I hear there'll be a few biologists' positions opening up around here . . . maybe I'll apply."

She smiled. "Okay. Four days. We'll see how it goes."

Meg suddenly stuck her head around the wall. "I *hate* to break you two up . . ."

"*Sure* you do," Thom agreed sarcastically. He gave Tesa a quick kiss. "Later."

"*Everyone* is looking for you," Meg signed needlessly as she escorted Tesa to the door.

The young woman looked at the old biologist, enjoying the renewed sparkle in her eyes. It had taken a few days, but Meg's spirits had lifted after their ordeal. Last night, she'd begun telling funny stories of some of the scrapes she and Scott had gotten into over the years. Even the Grus had enjoyed her tales, but Tesa realized it was the first time since she'd met Meg that she'd seen her speak of her dear friend without sorrow.

At the door of the shelter, Tesa stopped Meg. "Will you do me a favor? I need . . . a few minutes to talk to my parents alone. Can you ask them to come in here?"

Meg looked at her suspiciously. "A few minutes? Is this what I think it's about?"

"Please, Meg. I don't want to put it off any longer."

"Okay, I'll send them in. But *only* for a few minutes!"

Tesa's mother came in first, squinting as her eyes adjusted to the dimmer light. AnadaAki was dressed in her best dance costume, and as Dan entered behind her, Tesa could see he was still trying to get his fancy Oklahoma bustle tied just right.

"Tesa," her mother signed, regarding her Grus shirt, "what a wonderful outfit!"

Tesa smiled. "I knew you'd love it," she hesitated, dreading what she had to say. "We need to discuss something."

"Yes . . ." her father signed, smiling as he reached over to gently touch the two alien feathers Tesa wore in her hair.

"You have been through hell these last few weeks," Tesa began, trying not to show her nervousness. "I hate to add anything else to that . . . but I'm afraid I've got to."

Her parents turned to each other, concerned.

"A lot's happened to me, here," Tesa signed, remembering the moment in the forest when she'd realized her lodge faced the wrong direction—when she'd first understood what lay in her life's path. "I've changed. I *know* now, who I am, and the way . . . I want to be. Mom, Dad—I don't want my ears

. . . 'repaired.' To me, they aren't broken! It wouldn't be right for me. I know I might never convince you of that . . .''

AnadaAki's face changed subtly, but she recovered quickly. She started to sign something, but Dan placed a hand on her shoulder. She looked up at him, questioningly.

"Don't apologize to us for your decision," her father signed to Tesa. He looked at Ana. "I had a feeling this was coming. I didn't say anything to you, because I wasn't sure." He turned back to Tesa. "Remember, we spent two months in space . . . with your grandparents!" Both adults smiled, remembering, no doubt, how that sorrowful voyage had started out. "Your grandfather refused to believe you were dead. He insisted he was coming here for a dance, not a funeral! He was being so . . . contrary! Then, when the message arrived that you were safe . . ."

"He must've been impossible!" Tesa signed, grinning.

Her mother nodded. "And then all your father and I talked about was bringing you home with us . . . to have that surgery." Her lip trembled, and she hastily wiped away a stray tear.

"The grandparents never said much about it," Dan signed. "They just . . . disapproved quietly."

Ana nodded. "I ignored them. I still don't understand . . ."

"Maybe you never will, Mom," Tesa signed. "I think there are a lot of things children do that their parents never fully accept. I know you want what's best for me. You want me to be just like you—it's what every parent wants! I understand that better than I did six months ago. But you're looking for the reflection of your own desires in me. I don't want the surgery. I can't do it for *you,* and I don't want it for me."

"Will you be staying on Trinity, then?" her mother asked. Tesa nodded. Ana touched the nullifiers in her ears. "Well, being hearing here is certainly a disadvantage . . ." She started to sob then, so Tesa pulled her into a hug, feeling her father wrapping his strong arms around the two of them. Her mother drew away after a moment, hastily wiping her face. "You'll ruin those beautiful feathers!" she scolded, and gave a good-natured laugh. "I love you, Tesa."

"I know, Mom." The three linked arms and began to stroll toward the door.

"I think you should know, Tesa," her father signed. "There's a good chance that your grandparents may ask if they can stay here." Tesa looked at him, startled.

"The trip took a lot out of them," Ana told Tesa. "I think my mother was frightened of the deep-sleep . . . and when she first saw Trinity, she got this expression on her face."

"I know that look," Tesa agreed.

"And frankly," Dan admitted, "I think my father's interested in Meg!" The three burst out laughing as they stepped outside.

Tesa looked for her grandparents. Her grandmother was sitting beneath the weeping tree, stitching up Tesa's quilt and chatting away, via voder, with the Mizari Liaison. Tesa watched the elderly woman stealing glances at Esteemed Shirazz's beautiful colors and wondered if Grandma was thinking of a new quilt, perhaps in the Liaison's stunning diamond pattern?

Grandfather was clutching a coffee cup, and chatting up Meg. His eyes had that mischievous gleam Tesa was very familiar with, but Meg had one eyebrow cocked—she was on to him already. Thom asked Grandfather something, and the old man laughed. Then he signed to Thom in his rough Grus, "Before I leave here I'll teach you how to make a *really* good cup of coffee!"

Thom just grinned.

Tesa looked over at the dead tree on the cliff edge. Rain and Thunder perched there, watching the newcomers apprehensively. The very sight of the Mizari was usually enough to set the older avian screaming. Tesa would be busy negotiating tenuous compromises between Taller and Rain for a long time to come. The two species would have to work hard to strengthen their new, uneasy peace. The young woman glanced up at the suns. It was definitely time to get started!

Tesa felt as though she'd been dancing for hours . . . but her body seemed ready to dance for days. The Grus had watched her human family present some of their finest traditional dances, and Tesa had rejoiced to feel the pounding drumbeat through her feet again. When it was the Grus' turn, Taller and Weaver had danced of their courtship. Taller had danced of his first meeting with Scott. The entire family had danced the story of the attempted coup. Flies-Too-Fast had danced the story of Shimmering's life.

Now Tesa and Lightning were going to dance the story of their flyaway. Tesa started alone, her eagle feathers in hand,

he feathers of Water Dancer's wings stretched out along her
arms. When Mahree left Trinity, she'd promised to take the
feather shirt and the other remnants of Water Dancer's skin
with her. That and all the other Grus skins would be placed in
a robot probe and released on a course that would bring them
into the yellow sun's gravitational pull. In a year they'd be
swallowed by the Father Sun, and finally, the spirits of their
owners would have arrived to live with the Sun Family.

But for now, Water Dancer was still with her. Imitating an
eagle, Tesa began her Eagle Dance. Soon the shadow of Thunder's wings crisscrossed her own, as the huge raptor flew over
the dancing woman. Then Lightning joined her, too, and as
she felt the silent heartbeat of Trinity thrumming through her,
she threw herself into the dance, into the story of the flyaway.

She glanced up and saw Szu-yi. The doctor was staying on
Trinity, she'd told Tesa. No big explanation. Just that she was
staying. But she'd told Tesa of her decision in Grus sign language.

Closing her eyes, Tesa remembered the crash of the limb,
remembered their flight to the volcano. She tried to match
Lightning's leaps, his spins, but following him exactly wasn't
important—they were telling different sides of the same story.

Tesa saw the people watching and joining in the dance—all
the people—human, Grus, Aquila—and felt her spirit soaring
up and up, right into the suns.

Afterword

A brief note about how this novel came to be written:

Astute readers of my books will have noticed that one name crops up repeatedly in the acknowledgments—Kathleen O'Malley. Kathy has been my literary conscience since mid-1977, when I blushingly and hesitantly confessed to her that I had written a first draft of a *Star Trek* novel. "Really?" she responded casually. "I write, too. Mostly articles, so far, but some fiction, too. I enjoy reading other people's stuff. Maybe you could show me your book sometime."

I smiled evilly, cleared my throat modestly, reached into my briefcase and hefted several pounds of manuscript into her lap. "It's so kind of you to offer! I just happen to have a copy with me. . . ."

Thus began an association that has proved mutually beneficial . . . a kind of symbiosis, I suppose. Kathy's review of *Yesterday's Son* demonstrated that she's a dynamite editor and critic. When she takes her red pen to one of my manuscripts, the story always emerges far better for her (far from gentle) ministrations. When Kathy produces her own fiction, I return the favor. Through the years, we've both improved as writers.

274

When I began envisioning the *StarBridge* series, asking Kathy to collaborate with me on one of the books seemed the most natural thing in the world. As soon as I told her about the universe I was creating, her mind was off and running. Tesa and Trinity began to take shape. Kathy's unique gifts and knowledge—her work with endangered whooping cranes and eagles, her knowledge of ASL and Deaf culture, and her admiration for Native Americans and their culture, wove together like a tapestry. She created a truly unique protagonist and an original, arresting world with multiple cultures.

Then we worked together to integrate Tesa and Trinity into the StarBridge universe. It was a helluva lot of work and great fun.

Reader reaction to Book One of the series has been most gratifying. Many people wrote to say they had enjoyed the first book and were looking forward to Book Two. For those of you who also enjoyed Tesa and Trinity and hate to say goodbye, I have some good news. Another book about Trinity, *Silent Song*, is currently in the works.

Until next time . . .

—A. C. Crispin,
December 1989